The Apothecary's House

Also by Adrian Mathews

The Hat of Victor Noir

Vienna Blood

ADRIAN MATHEWS

The Apothecary's House

MACMILLAN

First published 2005 by Macmillan
an imprint of Pan Macmillan Ltd
Pan Macmillan, 20 New Wharf Road, London N1 9RR
Basingstoke and Oxford
Associated companies throughout the world
www.panmacmillan.com

ISBN 1 4050 4657 0 (HB)
ISBN 1 4050 5095 0 (TPB)

The illustration on p.v 'Ora, lege, relege', comes from the *Mutus Liber*,
in Mangetus, *Bibliotheca chemica curiosa* (Geneva, 1702). 'If it wasn't for bad
luck' on p.204 is taken from 'Born Under a Bad Sign', words and music by
Booker T. Jones and William Bell, copyright © 1967 Cotillion Music Inc and
East Memphis Music Corp, USA (25%) Warner/Chappell Music Ltd,
London W6 8BS, lyrics reproduced by permission of IMP Ltd.
All rights reserved.

1 3 5 7 9 8 6 4 2

A CIP catalogue record for this book is available from
the British Library.

Typeset SX Composing DTP, Rayleigh, Essex
Printed and bound in Great Britain by
Mackays of Chatham plc, Chatham, Kent

To Marie-Laure and Liz

Ora
Lege Lege Lege Relege labora
et Invenies.

Pray, read, re-read, work, and you shall find.

Acknowledgements

For their help with this book, at different stages, I am particularly grateful to Béatrice Roudet, Sebastian Groes, José Lapré, Joan da Sola Pinto and her late husband Oliver, Vernia Landell-Mathews, Graham Woodroffe, Dunstan Ward, Marie-Catherine de Bodinat, Bill Hamilton, Maria Rejt and all at A. M. Heath and Macmillan. My thanks also to the staff at St Benedict's School, Ealing, London W5, for their assistance with the Latin: Dom Alban Nunn OSB, Andy Hardman, Pat Daly and Vaughan Irons. 'Captain' Bob Mohl, Parvin Oet and Michel Flor-Henry helped with houseboat information. The following authors and books, among many others, also came in useful: Lynn H. Nicholas, *The Rape of Europa: The Fate of Europe's Art Treasures in the Third Reich and the Second World War* (Macmillan, 1994); Richard Z. Chesnoff, *Pack of Thieves* (Doubleday, 1999); Jonathan Petropoulos, *The Faustian Bargain: The Art World in Nazi Germany* (Oxford University Press, 2000); Gareth Roberts, *The Mirror of Alchemy* (British Library, 1994); Andrew Aromatico, *Alchemy: The Great Secret*, trans. Jack Hawkes (Harry N. Abrams, 2000); Geert Mak, *Amsterdam: A Brief Life of the City*, trans. Philipp Blom (Harvill, 1999); and Lydia Flem, *Casanova, or the Art of Happiness*, trans. Catherine Temerson (Farrar, Straus & Giroux, 1997).

The Apothecary's House

Part One

One

The old woman, laden with bags, crossed the Stadhouderskade as if her life depended on it, forcing a van driver to swear and slam on the brakes. In the blur of snow along the Singelgracht canal, she held her head low like a battering ram. It was a wonder she could see where she was going. A sense stronger than sight was guiding her with a singularity of purpose that made people stop and stare.

As she made it to the opposite pavement, the early January sunlight peeped through. It fell on the great Gothic frigate of the Rijksmuseum with its cargo of Rembrandts, Breughels and Vermeers. It seeped through a plate-glass light well on which a wood pigeon had died in a corner of the museum's research library, ran its fingers over calfskin spines, slid down the brass banister of the spiral staircase and flamed upwards from the burnished oak table, a stack of post-war auction catalogues, a rotary card-index file, the foxed daybook of a local haulage firm, a magnifying glass and Ruth Braams's goose-pimpled forearms as she raked her fingers back through short, messy, tow-blonde hair.

She folded her arms against her mariner's cable-knit sweater and let her head drop to one side till it almost touched her shoulder. Her skin was pale and cold. The sun was up to its old tricks. Not warmth but the promise of warmth, no sooner given than snatched away. She made no effort to hide her tiredness.

Myles Palmer, the big, ponytailed Englishman – on secondment from Sotheby's offices in a southern suburb of the city –

Adrian Mathews

was working through a box of correspondence marked *June 1943* and typing information into a laptop. Nazi expropriations were his specialist historical field.

'Don't abandon us,' he whispered in English, 'the Cultural Revolution needs you.'

'You know what this job's like?' she said. 'I've just figured it out.'

'Like watching paint dry?'

'No – too passive. It's like picking fly shit out of pepper, wearing boxing gloves, that's what it's like.'

Ruth yawned a fist-sized yawn.

She was thirty-two and had finished her doctoral thesis on domestic typology in the work of Jan Steen, the seventeenth-century Dutch painter, five years previously. Since then she'd helped a friend run a hairdresser's that doubled as an art gallery, manned a bike-rental concession and been a guide at the Van Gogh Museum in the summer for English-speaking tourists and scant gratuities.

A year ago the call had come.

It was from the Amsterdam bureau of the Netherland's Office for Fine Art's restitution project, which was working in tandem with the bureau at the General State Archives in The Hague. Suddenly art historians were in fashion, especially those with built-in crap detectors. Claims were being reviewed and a computerized database and information system set up. Everyone was getting their act together, helped along by a big kick up the rump from the World Jewish Congress's Commission for Art Recovery and the Art Loss Register.

At the start of the Second World War, a quarter of the artworks in Europe had changed hands. Since then they'd been making their way home from that mass exodus in dribs and drabs. Now the last obstacles to the return of looted art, the last conspiracies of silence, were being broken down. This was called 'coming clean' and art historians were the spring-cleaning detectives. A lot of looted art had been repatriated over the decades and held in custody by the Dutch state. Recently it had been put on show and when claimants came forward their claims were investigated. Sales records, letters, snapshots, catalogues, even a scrap of paper with a one-line description of a picture – everything was grist to the mill.

Some museum grandees were in no great hurry. Time was on their side. They'd shake their heads in commiseration. Sound bureaucratic methods are notoriously long and intensive, my friend. If the investigation outlives the claimants or their heirs, what can we do? The work of art remains state property by default. There's nowhere else for it to go. A token payment's sometimes made to funds for Holocaust survivors. But, above all, museums and governments have responsibilities. They don't want to create precedents. They don't want to give away hundreds of paintings without seriously evaluating the validity of each and every claim.

Then again, all too often, the basic title investigation was a dead end. War kills and what remains when the dust and smoke clear? Ownerless property, goods without heirs ... The voice that might have spoken up is silent. The documentation that might have proved a claim is long since gone. And so a painting hangs in a famous art gallery for all to admire, caught in a shaft of gold, white and blue winter sunshine suddenly breaking through the clouds. It brings smiles of pleasure to the visitors' chapped lips and rheumy eyes. A portrait by Nicolaes Maes, a river landscape by Salomon van Ruysdael, Jan Steen's *The Sacrifice of Iphigenia*. Take a long look at it. Who bothers to question its provenance? Who either knows or cares? It's just itself – a canvas sail on the river of time, indifferent to human motives and the upheavals of history. By diligence, miracle or pot luck, it has survived.

Somewhere, the pitch change of a lift motor and the flip-flap of rubber draught excluder on a swing door.

Ruth looked around at the other research rats, blinking. Pieter Timmermans had pegged out in front of the microform reader.

He snored a light rodent snore, head cushioned on folded arms. Myles was trying to decipher a smudged postmark on an envelope with the magnifying glass. Just to distract him, the sunlight had lasered into a white mobile pinprick that danced around like an imp, threatening to singe a postage stamp of the brown-shirted Reichsführer.

Up above on the second tier of gangways, which gave access to a cliff face of books and nondescript ledgers, Bernard Cabrol, the lean French coordinator in his green silk cravat, rested one arm and his flat behind against the wooden book rest on the balustrade. He looked, as ever, like a man kebabbed on the horns of an insuperable dilemma. He bit hard into the gold eraser ring on the end of his pencil and flattened it to an oval.

At an elevated desk in one corner the ill-tempered librarian, who had a cold sore on her lip, peered into the pixels of her VDU then glanced round sharply, as if trying to catch potential fine dodgers or book thieves unawares.

Footsteps . . .

The elderly woman who had battled along the Stadhouderskade now clumped into the reading room. She wore a woollen rapper's cap with an embroidered NYC monogram, glasses with frames like Bakelite post-war TV screens and a black astrakhan coat which, if it had seen more glamorous days, had sworn an oath of eternal silence. The snow was still white and flaky on her cap and shoulders. A wet umbrella poked out of one of several carrier bags from the De Bijenkorf department store that she had wedged under her elbow as she burrowed deep in a handbag. 'Bags,' thought Ruth: a Lower East Side bag lady – took a wrong turn at Lafayette, no doubt, wandering Mr Magoo-like up the gangplank of an ocean-going liner. But there was a shabby nobility about this rag-picker that held her attention.

The librarian half-rose to her feet and froze. Along with everyone else, now, she was listening to a wet clicking sound that had entered the room with the woman. At first it seemed to have something to do with the bag lady's shoes, since it synchronized with her steps, but when she dropped down like a sack of charity cast-offs on the chair opposite Ruth the sound continued, with its own separate life.

The woman plugged an inhaler into her mouth, shut her eyes and pushed down the button. A low, pressurized hiss. The click disappeared. Her breathing eased.

The librarian – who had run her fingernail down to Emergency: Paramedics on the museum phone list – now cursed, broke her irresolute pose, stepped down from her pedestal and drew up alongside at battle stations. 'Yes?'

'I would like a glass of water.'

'You can't just walk in here,' the girl sneered. 'They should've stopped you. This is a restricted zone.'

The old woman was disoriented.

Ruth raised a hand. 'Please – get her a glass of water.'

The girl strode off in a huff.

The visitor noticed Ruth and Myles for the first time. She smiled at Ruth – smiled at the scruffy hair, smiled at the street-urchin manner, smiled at the water-blue eyes, dark eyebrows, schoolgirl complexion, nice lips and that fetching way of leaning forward on folded arms, shoulders hunched slightly, suggesting a lazy agreeableness, a desire to help.

'Where am I?' she asked. 'Why did I come here? Can *you* remember? Do *you* know?'

She didn't bother to wait for a reply.

She poked her glasses up on her thin blue nose and tipped the contents of her handbag across the library table. Keys. Plastic cards and till receipts strapped together with elastic bands. Hair grips. A bundle of letters. Lipstick and peppermints. A silver pillbox. A glass flask of Caron perfume. Among the more unusual items a minute ceramic doll's house teapot, a pair of ivory dice and a packet of geranium seeds. Ruth looked down at the odds and ends. For a moment, she thought they were being taken for a ride. It was some kind of vocational performance test, dreamt up by the Pelman Institute – that, or *Candid*

Camera. The old girl was slumming it from the Felix Meritis theatre, a local luvvie in drag.

Ruth's unworthy thoughts vanished whence they came.

The woman was getting organized. She picked up the bundle of mail, cast her eye over a couple of letterheads – TPG Post, the Dierenopvangcentrum animal hospital – and found the one she wanted, 'Here we are,' she said, teasing it out from the pack. 'I do remember now.' She held her head back to get the right focal length, braced her neck muscles and read the letter to herself. The glasses gave her a studious respectability which had not been in evidence before.

'You wrote this to me,' she said. 'It says you have my picture. So kind! Of course, I saw it at the viewing. That's when I knew. I thought it had been lost forever.'

She folded the letter and smiled at Ruth and Myles.

Ruth glanced behind her. Cabrol had turned round and was watching the show. He was tapping the point of his pencil against his teeth.

'May I see that?' She took the letter and read it. 'Lydia van der Heyden?'

'Yes.'

'You filed a claim.'

'Did I?'

'A year ago. For a painting in the NK-Collection.' She glanced at the name of the painter and the brief description of the work. 'How did you know you could find us here?'

'Where, my dear?'

'Never mind. This letter' – Ruth held it up between finger and thumb – 'is nearly a year old. It's an acknowledgement of one that you wrote to us. It asks you to produce evidence to support your claim. Did you answer it?'

Bags pursed her lips. Her eyes clouded as her thoughts turned inwards. 'I sent a photocopy. A copy of the photograph. I had it done at the post office. The old photograph was all I had.'

'Well, in that case, your claim must be under review.'

'It takes time,' said Myles in his hesitant Dutch, with a sad smile. 'There's a backlog, specially after Christmas. We were off for a week, you see.'

Bags latched a hand onto his shirt sleeve and brought her grey head close to his. He winced. Her breath smelled like old dinners.

'I don't do anything much for Christmas,' she said. 'Since Sander died, that is. There's nothing to celebrate any more. Not at my age, anyway.'

She released him, wrung her hands and looked away, anguished. Then back she came with greater intensity.

'I like the lights on the bridges. I like the little lights, glowing in the dark night, oh yes! Especially when it snows. But I don't go to the Westerkerk for the carols. Too many people, my dear. I go to De Krijtberg on the Singel. It's like the old days. They do the mass in Latin there on Sunday mornings. Sander and I used to go. I love the paintings and the statues. There's one statue in particular, our Holy Mary, Mother of Jesus. Her face is so pure. There are little changes in her expressions depending on the light. Of course, I know it's only a graven image, but I swear she listens to me. She understands. She knows what I've been through.'

Myles nodded, an unconvincing play of fellow-feeling. Ruth heard steps behind. Cabrol was descending the spiral iron staircase – the bureaucrat, the officiant – listening in as he came. She felt his approach like a cool draught of unease.

'At my age,' Bags went on, with the same fixed inward focus, 'there's nothing left. Only your memories. And they go too. You'll find out for yourself one day, believe me. So I try to keep them alive. I think about Asha and Elfried and Sander. That was another world. I remember the good times though. I watch the telly, for the quizzes. I do crosswords. I'm seventy-nine, you know. My doctor says he's seen a lot worse. I had the hip replacement, and there's the cataract and a spot of rheumatism,

Adrian Mathews

but one mustn't complain. I keep going. I make sure I get out every day. Keep on keeping on. That's my motto. You have to, don't you?'

'I suppose you do,' said Myles.

The woman stood up and started rummaging in her carrier bags. 'I brought some brown wrapping paper, and some string. It's not a very large painting. I should be able to carry it, don't you think?'

Ruth and Myles exchanged a glance.

'Um, listen, you don't seem to understand,' Myles began with an awkward laugh. 'Your claim has to be looked into. It goes before a committee. If there's no problem, if it's accepted, they'll deliver the painting to you. In the meantime, you'll just have to be patient.'

Bags stopped her rummaging and glared at him. 'I think it is *you* who does not understand, young man. That painting is mine. It belonged to my father and to his father's father. I do not find walking easy these days. I do not find anything easy these days, for that matter. Nevertheless, I have come here expressly today, through wind and snow, to pick up my painting.'

Myles reddened. 'Well, you can't. What I mean is, it hasn't been established as yet that it is yours. There's an official thingummy to follow – Ruth, what's *procedure* in Dutch?'

'*Procedure*', said Ruth with the right accent and stress. 'I lent you that book called *De Procedure*, remember? Same spelling as in English.'

Bags's brolly fell with a clatter to the floor. She bent down and picked it up, dropping her carrier bags in the process.

'There's a procedure,' said Ruth, as much for Cabrol's benefit as the old lady's, 'that is followed in our front office. We're just researchers. We don't make the final decisions. In fact, strictly speaking, we shouldn't have any contact with claimants at all.'

'Strictly speaking's dead right,' Cabrol chipped in as he drew up behind them.

The librarian returned with a glass of water and accompanied by a security guard. She banged the glass onto the table. 'Still want this, do you?'

'It's true that this part of the library's off limits, if you don't have a card,' said Myles. 'I'll give you the office number and you can get in touch. They'll let you know how things stand.'

Bags lumbered to her feet. 'Oh, I know how things stand. I know exactly how things stand. You have been looking after my personal property and now I want it back. So you will please be so kind as to fetch it immediately.' She had switched to the harsh but exalted dowager tone that elderly women of a certain class adopt when insisting on their rights. Timmermans had woken up and was enjoying the spectacle. Even Ruth's cheek muscles moved in to beat down a reflex smile. It was like something out of an old movie. Amsterdam was a youngster's town. Methuselahs were minority fare, a good deal further out on the margins of acceptability than the thriving fringe theatre of hookers and pot-heads.

Bags launched into her family history again.

The guard had one hand on his hip. His fingers played lightly, like a daydreaming pianist's, on the holster of his automatic pistol. Cabrol wagged a hand to draw the man to one side.

'How did she get through?'

'I was called away for thirty seconds. Had to help a woman fold a pushchair for the cloakroom. She must've just slipped by. I never saw her.' The guard bit his lower lip and shrugged.

Myles handed Bags a card with the front-office number, but she scuffed it to the floor. She was about to go on about her entitlements when the asthma got the better of her. She doubled up, throat clicking, one hand clutched to her ribs. Ruth passed her the inhaler and she cleared her tubes once again.

Cabrol made a little circling gesture to the librarian, indicating the table top, and the librarian began scooping the old woman's belongings together.

'Take your hands off those things!' Bags cried.

She swept round and the handle of her umbrella knocked over the flask of perfume and unstoppered it. A sudden fragrance of old damask roses – drooping Victorian blooms, velvet petals, airless rooms and the ghosts of yesteryear – invaded their corner of the library.

'Great!' said the librarian, dabbing at the spillage with a paper handkerchief. 'That's just what we needed. Now we'll have to live with this pong for the rest of the week!' She continued shovelling the knick-knacks into the handbag.

Cabrol signalled again and the guard grabbed up the carriers and took Bags by the elbow, assisting her towards the door with one hand in the small of her back. He was too strong, too determined for her. She twisted her head round in indignation. 'I will not be treated like this! I will not! If Sander were alive today, he wouldn't stand for it. He'd stick up for me. I want to see the authorities! Who is in charge here?'

Exeunt.

There was the remote thud of a door and the flickety-flack of draught excluder. For a few seconds the woman's complaints continued before the lift doors closed with a sigh and she was borne away.

Two

*R*uth lost track of time.

She was poring over the haulage records and accounts of Abraham Puls & Zonen, the Amsterdam removal firm which – under Nazi instruction – had pillaged the homes of the Netherlands' Jews. Myles was ploughing through correspondence between the Liro Bank and the five commissioner-generals who worked for Arthur Seyss-Inquart, the Netherlands' Reichskommissar. When she next looked at her watch it was five p.m. Four hours had passed since Bags's unceremonious expulsion. Ruth and Myles were alone in the reading room.

Myles looked up.

'All right?' she asked.

He rubbed his eyes with the heels of his palms. 'It wouldn't be so bad if there was a little light at the end of the tunnel. There isn't. There's only a cave. You should read this stuff. It's unbelievable.'

'What is it?'

'IVB4 – Adolf Eichmann's section in the Reich's security headquarters. OK, my German's pretty good but you need a degree in higher euphemisms to decipher their letters and internal memos. You've got these words that mean *requisition*, *safe-keeping*, *custody* – like *sichergestellt* for *secured* – but basically they're all saying the same thing. *Steal. Steal* then *kill.* It's weird how the whole thing's done in this bland office language, as if they were ordering paper clips from the stationer's. You'd think they'd want it to be off the record, but it's just the opposite. The record's a way of legitimizing it. *Alles in ordnung*, you know.' He raised his eyebrows despairingly. 'How about you, dearie?'

'Ever come across a painter by the name of van der Heyden – Dutch, eighteenth century?'

Myles reflected, shook his head. Suddenly he wised up. 'That was the old girl's name.'

'What old girl?'

'Yeah, yeah. There was no old girl. I nearly forgot to forget. So the daub's by some ancestor of hers, is that it?'

'That's what I figured. The names match – hers and the name in the letter. And that's what the claim's all about.'

He slid a CD-ROM into the computer drive and launched a quick search. 'Valckenborch, Valckert, and whaddayaknow – van der Heyden. A single item in general museum stores. A sketchbook or folder of sketches, by the looks of things. One oil piccy in NK-Collection stores. *Recumbent Woman with Mimosa.* That the one?'

'Guess so.'

'According to this, she's not alone.'

'Sorry?'

'There's a rival claim. Name of Scheele – Emmerick Scheele. Cabrol dealt with the filing and docketing.'

'You don't say. Fancy taking a look?'

'At the claim?'

'At the picture, Myles.'

He rested his chin in the cupping Y of his hands. 'What's up? Forget to close down your sympathetic nervous system this morning? That's a big mistake.'

'Shut up, bonehead. It's just mild curiosity. I need an excuse for a walk. I planned on checking out early, anyway. How about you?'

*

They flashed ID at the guard tinkering with the battery on his walkie-talkie and headed down the service stairs to stores.

A head taller than Ruth, Myles rocked from side to side when he walked, as if advancing by an elaborate system of weights and counterweights. His slobby, wide-girthed build went with Harleys, tattoos, leather trousers and Rip Van Winkle beards, though none of these accessories formed part of his style repertoire. With his ginger ponytail, he was more of the hillbilly fatso: dungarees, brushed-cotton lumberjack shirt, fawn suede hiking boots and single Romany earring. Neat Southern Comfort, all the way from Fulham and the Royal College of Art. Some twenty-eight springs had passed him by. Ruth had a soft spot for his spry, camp wit – the motherly, tea and sympathy side to XXL gays – but she preferred him sitting down. On his feet, he was like bad weather, a pall looming over her entire field of vision. He murdered the pure light of day.

'How's Sweekieboude?' she asked, glancing up at him.

'Bad. She's off her food. Just laps up the soya milk, then rips the furniture to shreds with her claws for an encore. She can't get out and about.'

'Out and about?'

'She can't sit on the window sill in this fucking weather is what I mean. Plus, Rex has been pissy with her – *and* me, I should add. It's outrageous.'

'Hmmm. You two heading for a bust-up?'

'I should be so lucky. Rex is the human equivalent of a limpet mine. He does it to annoy me, of course. In the morning, when he's shaving, he sings that Velvet Underground glue song – "I'm Sticking with You." The bloody man knows I can hear him. Plus we've had problems with the guy in the flat upstairs.'

'Oh?'

'He plays the bongos at odd hours of the night.'

'What does he do at even hours of the night?'

'Transylvanian folk dancing, I think. That's what it sounds like.'

'I know the type.'

'What about you, anyway?' said Myles.

'Me? I bought a new bell for my bicycle.'

'Won't be long before that's nicked.'

'Thanks. Oh, and just for the record, some of the smarter thieves take the bike with the bell.'

'Actually,' he said, 'that's not quite what I meant when I said, "What about you?"'

'Ah! Well, you know me. As per usual. I'm somewhere in between.'

'Between men?'

'Between everything.'

'No-man's-land! My dream ... When you've got a free moment, be a dear and draw me a map of how to get there.' She didn't react and Myles's humour leavened. 'How long is it now, Ruth? I mean, *since* . . .'

'Since?' Ruth laughed at his coyness.

'Since – you know – *Maarten.*'

'It's two years, Myles. Nearly two years since Maarten died.'

The corridor had all the charm of a ventilation duct: caged oblong security lights, no-smoking signs and – in the same anti-incendiary spirit – votive niches with extinguishers and limp bobbined serpents of fire hose. Ruth glanced at the bare concrete and wondered what on earth could catch fire. The air was powdery with latent nightmares of asbestosis. She found herself refraining from breathing deeply.

'You or me?' said Ruth when they got to stores.

'Pearls before swine.'

Embedded in the mullion was the biometric identity verification system. She scanned her ID badge on the LaserCard terminal. The red light turned amber. She keyed in her PIN. The amber began to wink. She inserted her index and middle finger into the terminal's camera unit. Inside the grey box state-of-the-art data-rich vector maps were plotting her live fingerprints against digital templates, bombarding the ridges and valleys and whorls with mind-boggling algorithms.

She held her breath.

The light went green. Digital signature accepted; finger geometry validated.

Ruth breathed freely again.

The door opened with a satisfying click and they walked in.

This was it, the Amsterdam repository of the NK-Collection: Nederlands Kunstbezit, Dutch Art Property . . .

Myles switched on the low-heat twin-tube fluorescent lights.

The stacks went from three tiers of small paintings – each numbered and draped in sackcloth or plastic sheeting – to a single tier for large canvases at the far end of the bunker. The rock-steady needle on the hygrometer showed a relative humidity of fifty-five per cent. Temperature, a constant twenty degrees centigrade, regardless of cold snaps or Indian summers in the great outdoors.

Myles woke up his laptop and double-checked the shelf mark.

The painting was in the small stacks and measured some ninety by sixty centimetres in its fragile gilt frame. They slipped off the corner protectors, unwrapped it carefully and stood it lengthways on an inspection easel. It represented a young woman of about eighteen with dark hair and fair skin asleep on a chaise longue. She was fully clothed in an egg-blue satin dress, but her ankles and bare feet were exposed, her hair tousled, her shoes cast aside on the floor.

She was a beauty.

Behind her headrest, on the floor, there was an enormous bouquet of mimosa in an earthenware pot. The flowers – in catkin clusters – created a canary-yellow halo around her head. The room was narrow with a steeply sloping ceiling and a small window that gave onto a cloudless sky and typical Dutch house tops, centred on a bell gable with curved sides. A man stood in the background, looking out of the window, his back to the painter. His head and shoulder rested against the window frame. There was something melancholy about his posture. A small carriage clock squatted on the mantelpiece over the hearth. The whole was rendered with minute attention to detail. The painting was signed 'Johannes van der Heyden'.

Myles picked it up and spun it round adroitly. On the wooden frame was a new sticker, 'NK 352', and a yellowed sticker that read 'Johannes van der Heyden. Amsterdam. Miedl. K41. RG. 937.'

'That old one looks like an ERR tag,' said Myles. 'Einsatzstab Reichsleiter Rosenberg – The Task Force Rosenberg. Which would mean *confiscated*. It looks like it, but it isn't. The coding's unusual. I'll have to check it out against my list.'

He rubbed the dust off the wood. A Reich eagle and the words 'Linz N° AR 6927' were inkstamped on the frame.

'Interesting,' he murmured.

A further label read: 'Alt Aussee → Munich Collecting Point.'

'Something to go on, at any rate.'

He eased the wedges out of two corners, slipped the wooden back board out an inch and tapped the rear of the picture. 'Copper. Painted directly onto a sheet of copper.' He rubbed his finger against the metal and held it to his nose.

'They used all kinds of supports in those days. Wood, canvas, metal.'

'And someone – presumably Meneer van der Heyden himself – had the good grace to provide us with a date.' He drew her attention to the corner he had exposed, where '1758' had been scratched into the metal. Then he flipped the painting round again and replaced it on the easel. 'What d'you think?'

Ruth took one step back and lingered on the details. She shook her head. 'I don't know what to think.'

'How do you mean?'

'It's a very *accomplished* painting. Detail, proportion, colour, glazes – it's draughtsmanlike.'

'But?'

'But there's something odd about it. Something odd about the composition and – well, the situation itself, really, the situation *in* itself.'

'The angel on the couch, one assumes, is having an afternoon nap.'

'Possible. The thing is, this kind of interior, showing middle-class life, nearly always tells a story. I'm thinking of Jan Steen's *The Sick Lady* – you've seen it in the museum? The lute hanging on the wall in the background suggests abandoned pleasures. The little details have narrative significance. Even the posture.'

'Do you think she's sick?'

'Maybe. There's that other painting, by Gabriël Metsu – *The Sick Child*. Recumbent or semi-recumbent means sick. It's part of the semiology of the times.'

'Like the Victorians who had their dead children laid out and photographed as if asleep. Yuk! The only give-away detail is the rosary between the hands.'

Ruth shrugged, dubious now at her own conclusions. 'Of course you also lie down if you're dead drunk – Steen's *After the Drinking Bout* being a case in point. Or, as we said at the outset, if you're asleep. Viz *Jacob's Dream* by Frans van Mieris the Elder.'

'So what's the story here?' asked Myles, rubbing his chin.

'I've no idea. What do you think?'

'The mimosa suggests February or March to me. That's when the florists are chock-a-block with the stuff.'

'You're turning into a proper Dutchman.'

'Actually, we English know a thing or two about *bloemen* as well. The name mimosa has the same root as mime. Its leaves are sensitive to light and touch. They close up and droop in darkness, or if you touch them. People used to think it drooped its branches to greet passers-by.'

'I'm speechless. Except to say that it's not just February. There's a second flowering, I think, I can't remember when. If the weather's fine, you can get it earlier too. The girl hardly

seems dressed for winter, but the fire's been going in the grate,
so she may have just taken her coat off. Now mimosa . . . There's
a big Bonnard painting, come to think of it, of his own studio
with mimosa seen through the window. It's in the Pompidou.
There's something about mimosa, isn't there? It's pure sunlight.
It's nature's own Impressionism.'

'*A toi*, clever clogs. '

'Okey-doke,' she said. 'Well, we're in good old Amsterdam,
I reckon, given the view from the window. An attic room in a
traditional canal house. Look – you can just see the hook from
the hoist beam. Some time after two, judging by the clock.
Notice the light falling on the girl and the flowers seems to be
coming from above, rather than the little window – ergo, a
skylight. The girl's well to do. A gorgeous satin dress. Diamond
necklace. As for the man – .' She peered closely at the dark
figure by the window with his back to her. For some reason it
perplexed and grieved her. It was an obstruction, a false note.
Like a child failing to accept the two-dimensionality of picture
planes, she wanted to nip round the other side to catch his eye,
to see what he was thinking. 'He's *contre-jour*, so we can't make
out so much detail. Youngish. No wig. Quite an ordinary
dresser.'

'And the clock?'

'Don't ask me. Either symbolic – the passing of time, he's
waiting for her to wake up – or else it's just there. A naturalistic
detail. Wait a sec. Look – how odd! It only has one hand.'

There was a moment's silence.

'There's something opaque about this painting,' Ruth went
on. 'It doesn't quite add up. I mean, narrative painting should
just get on with the job and tell the story. This one doesn't. It's
holding something back. Even the composition's bad.'

'It's not exactly bad,' said Myles. 'It just lacks the usual
symmetries and balances and decorum. It's artless. It's modern.
Know what I mean? Casual – off-centre, somehow. A slice of
life. Things going on out of frame.'

She laughed and nodded. 'True! D'you think it's a fake?'

'Could be.'

'It's not typically eighteenth-century. Not Frenchified – like Cornelis Troost or those garden scenes by Hendrik Keun.'

'And Jan van Huysum would turn his hooter up at those flowers. Too simple. Too natural. They haven't been arranged.'

'Nevertheless,' Ruth concluded, 'if it's not a fake, then a bona fide product of the Decadence.'

'Quite. Scurvy times. Peregrine Pickle times.'

'Huh?'

'Peregrine Pickle. The hero of an English novel by Smollett. He comes to Amsterdam and loafs around in the docks and brothel area. Goes to dance halls. Coughs his lungs up in the smoky coffee houses. Oh – and ends up dancing the night away with a French trollop. Not the Dutch Republic's most glorious days . . .'

'But fun. Sounds all too familiar, if you ask me.'

'Yeah, it does, doesn't it?' He squinted at her with mock renewal of interest. '*Plus ça change* . . . You and I must frequent the same fleshpots, my dear. It's a wonder we haven't bump-danced into each other in the torrid heat of the night.'

Ruth pulled a face and stared at the painting again. She still couldn't make sense of it. It was provocative, resistant. 'Myles, where can I find out about this van der Heyden character?'

'Christ knows. We'll check in the museum records, OK?'

'Now?'

He showed her his watch by way of answer.

'Yeah, I guess it can wait.'

They picked up their coats and left the museum.

She rolled the wheels to open the combination lock on her bike – five, two, one – and walked alongside the Englishman in silence across the frozen canal and down the Weteringschans.

A single heron stood on the pristine blanket of snow that

covered a little garden near the Casino. They stopped to watch it until it ruffled its feathers and moved stiffly – prudishly – away.

Ruth was elsewhere.

The image of the man by the window in the little eighteenth-century painting hadn't left her. It was the way he turned his back. It was the way his head and shoulder rested against the window frame – mopey, listless, heavy-hearted. It was the way these details spoke to her. She knew now why the figure touched her with an emotion that was in excess of the facts. It reminded her of Maarten. It reminded her of his disconsolate soul, a part of him that always turned away. Towards the end, there had been times when he'd lean by the window, hands clasped behind him, just like that, and she wouldn't know whether his eyes were open or closed, she wouldn't know how to reach him, she wouldn't know if she could ever reach him in any of the old ways again.

They gave up on the heron and continued on their way.

'So,' said Myles, 'tell me about this brand-new bicycle bell of yours.'

Three

The following Saturday afternoon, Ruth noticed a slow puncture in her front tyre. She left her bike at a repair shop and picked Jojo up at their regular cafe. They walked the short distance to Maarten's family home on the Entrepotdok canal to the north of Artis park.

Jojo's family came from Ghana via Suriname. Her parents had emigrated from the old South American colony to the Netherlands in 1975. With her mocha skin, obsidian eyes and braided Afro hair, she was petite and compact like a child gymnast. She spoke in quick, inflected sallies – junk talk, chuck-away chat, as if anything she said couldn't possibly matter ultimately, so it was best to rattle it off and have done. She fixed her gaze on the pavement as they walked, except to flash cautious glances at Ruth to gauge her mood, monitor her reactions.

When things had finished between Ruth and Maarten a year before the accident, Ruth had found Jojo for him. She saw her waitressing in an Indonesian restaurant, befriended her and presented her to her ex. Jojo was Ruth's goodbye gift. She had a quick wit and a frank sense of humour. Of course, she had her faults: there was a dark, voodoo side to her – a fragility that expressed itself through defensiveness, sometimes verging on paranoia, and an alarming tendency to take everything literally. But Maarten would lighten her up: in this, she needed him as much as he needed her. True, she was studying hard, back then, to be a social worker, but family life and a job weren't incompatible. She would adore Maarten, she would have his babies. A smooth and easy relationship, free of intellectual conflict. A marriage of simple, uncluttered love. Nobody ever found out that Ruth had set it up. It was a good turn, a gratuitous act of kindness. Who was to know then that a motorbike jaunt would end all that, leaving two bereft instead of one?

'So these pilots, see, they fly over the king penguins as a tease,' Jojo said. She was describing a TV documentary she had seen about the South Atlantic. 'First they fly from side to side, making the penguins turn their heads like they were at a tennis match or something. Right? Then they zip overhead to get them to crane their heads back and fall over.'

'And do they fall?'

'Dunno. The phone rang when it got to the important bit.'

'Damn.'

Maarten's father, Lucas Aalders, was a senior university lecturer in chemistry. He lived with his wife on the top floor of a converted nineteenth-century warehouse near the old Kromhout shipyard. He opened the door and ushered them in. A big, bald, formless man. The teatless udder of his double chin juddered beneath his face when he spoke or cleared his throat.

As they trod on the Welcome mat, an electronic voice chuckled out: *Ho, ho, ho! Merr-eeee Christmas!* The tree was still up, dangling toffees – nuggets of silver and gold in their shiny wrappers – lights winking, the fairy scintillating with fairy benedictions.

Clara, the mother, came out of the kitchen, wiping her red hands on a tea towel. She hugged them both. There were tears in her eyes. She asked them to take their shoes off and gave them each a pair of flat, one-size slippers of the type office cleaners wear.

It was a spacious open-plan apartment – a *salle de danse* of barren varnished parquet. They sat on high-tech furniture of black leather and chromium tubing, forming three sides of a rectangle. The parents were in the middle on the sofa, the girls on the side armchairs. The polish on the smoked-glass coffee table between them was so high that a single thumbprint took on ludicrous proportions, an indictment of imperfection, a prosecution of humankind.

Ruth crossed her legs.

She positioned her body sideways so that she could look out of the window and watch the herring gulls bickering in the starved winter sky as Maarten's parents plied Jojo with questions – Jojo, their son's intended, the never-to-be daughter-in-law. Jojo was the promise of Maarten's unfulfilled future. Ruth was the faithful retainer of his past. They were bookends or brackets, parenthesizing empty space, the vacant side of the rectangle.

As if to confirm this impression, there were photographs of them both on the sideboard, Ruth and Jojo, facing each other, even – apparently – looking at each other, a fortuitous exchange of complicit smiles that was actually nothing of the sort, given that the photos were taken on separate occasions.

Ruth ate the canapés and Unox cocktail frankfurters that were passed round, slipping the wooden sticks into her sleeve because she didn't know where to put them. The door to Maarten's room was slightly ajar. In there, they had made love for the first time within a few days of meeting at the university. She remembered the luminous toy-shop stars he had stuck to the ceiling, a careful reproduction of the northern constellations, and wondered if they were still there.

Now it didn't seem real, it didn't seem true.

And behind Clara, on the white laminated shelf, an old stereo with an LP player had stood. They would listen to the Doors and the classical piece that Maarten was crazy about – Ravel's Pavane, wasn't it? When the music centre conked out, Lucas replaced it with the latest Bang & Olufsen. Beside it stood an equally impressive giant flat-screen TV.

Ruth sniffed.

The bare brickwork in the apartment gave off a distinctive odour, slightly acrid, not unpleasant. The same smell had lingered round Maarten's jackets and shirts. She sniffed again, thought about it, as she never had before – and then she got it. It was the smell of caps from a child's cap gun. She supposed it was saltpetre. It took her back to Maarten, but also to her own childhood. Christ knows why a flat should smell of caps, but it did.

Jojo had been telling one of her stories. When she finished, Clara turned to Ruth. 'Are you coming down with something?' she asked.

'What – me?'

'I thought—'

'It's this apartment.'

'Is it cold?'

'Yes – I mean, no. It reminds me of Maarten.'

This was the first time the son's name had been uttered. Clara, puzzled by Ruth's non sequitur, glanced at a black-and-white photograph of her only child on the wall for reassurance. Other eyes followed. There he was, in Buddy Holly glasses, adopting a Hamlet pose with a brain-like cabbage in his hand.

Larky Maarten, the faculty wag.

Lucas cleared his throat and glared at the reflections in the gleaming table, as if gathering his thoughts to deliver a sermon. In the end he said nothing. Perhaps he'd changed his mind. His face prickled with redness. The muscles hardened round his jaw above the plump bellows of the chin. Ruth watched him, eerily aware of the dead son in the father.

They sipped mulled wine, each alone under the cool lights.

Lucas and Clara broke the deadlock simultaneously. He said, 'We all know why we're here . . .' She said, 'It was so good of you both to come!' The double false start was an embarrassment. They laughed it off with forced gaiety, but the atmosphere didn't slacken. If anything, it tightened a notch.

Clara picked up the thread. 'We're here because of Maarten,' she said firmly, soberly. 'We're here because it's two years, two years to the day.' Despite herself, the tears welled up in her eyes once again.

'To Maarten,' said the father, raising his glass with grim ceremony.

They all followed suit.

'We thought it would be nice,' said Clara, recomposing herself, 'to share a few memories. Memories of our son. The bereavement counsellor said it was a good idea. The thing is, everyone has different memories. You get used to your own and you forget that there are other perspectives on things – on people – that you hadn't quite suspected. And there are other people's stories – things you didn't know. Jojo, would you like to start?'

Jojo smiled, treating it like a party game, and told a shaggy-dog story in which Maarten absent-mindedly walked out of a hardware shop with a bicycle padlock for which he hadn't paid. Luckily for him, there were no CCTV cameras or store detectives to catch him out. 'A theft to stop a theft,' Jojo concluded, repeating Maarten's words, his punchline to the tale.

When she finished, all eyes turned on Ruth.

She sighed and bit the tough right angle of skin at the corner of her thumbnail.

'I remember that Maarten always used to turn his jacket collar up,' she said.

She sipped her wine. It left a taste of cinnamon on the back of her teeth.

The others waited.

'And?' said Clara.

'Just that. It didn't matter whether it was winter or summer, an overcoat or a lightweight jacket. Come rain or come shine, he'd always turn the collar up. I never knew why.'

The parents eyed each other.

'Like Elvis,' said Jojo and giggled.

Ruth nodded. 'It's true there's something fifties about it. The hound-dog look. I used to think it was calculated.'

'To do what?' asked Lucas.

'To get women, if you really want to know. I mean, when girls see guys with turned-up collars, they have this irresistible urge to say something, or even to go up to them and turn the collar down. Know what I mean? It was a gambit. But whenever a woman pointed it out, he'd just shrug and leave it there. I promised myself I'd never ask him about it – as if he was challenging me, defying me to ask him, just by doing it. And now I'll never know. My other theory was that it gave him a sense of protection round the nape of his neck. It's a vulnerable part of the body. Some dangers come from in front. Others come from behind.'

As soon as she'd shared this thought she regretted it. The mention of vulnerability and danger revived the ache of Maarten's fate. Maarten had been a fanatical skater. He was riding north for the Elfstedentocht, the 199-kilometre skating tour that took in eleven Frisian towns, with over 14,000 skaters. And a little patch of black ice did for him. She saw the coastal road, where they had planted the wooden crucifix and laid the flowers. She heard the wind and the sea, recalling the dense mass of migratory birds that flew under one impulse, a giant pointillist kite on an invisible string. She sensed that she had brought them all back to the tether of this cross through her thoughtlessness. If only she had said something light and wistful, something to conjure a joyful ghost.

The miniature pizzas and vol-au-vents had gone cold. Clara put them on a baking tray and went to the kitchen to reheat them.

Lucas, who rarely initiated a conversation, asked Ruth about her job.

She shrugged noncommittally. 'It's OK. It'll do for a time. But I'm beginning to wonder what I'm doing there, to be honest.

You know the way kids chew paper at school? That's how I feel. I'm munching on paper all day long. Pap. Pulp. Dirty old paper, dirty old history. I don't see that it does anyone any good. I'll probably go back to the galleries. What about you? How's the university?'

'I've got some good students this year. One of them's helping me research a book. But, come June, it's gold-watch time for me.'

'You're jacking it in?'

'Early retirement. Like you, my heart's not in it any more – or rather I'm just plain clapped out. Clara and I thought we might move away. Maybe get a little property in France, in the Lubéron.'

'Oh.'

'Do you know it? Charming region – expensive, of course. We used to go there on holiday with Maarten when he was little. We rented a house each year. It was what they call a *mas*, an old farmhouse, that is – walls this thick, you know!'

'He may have mentioned it once or twice,' said Ruth.

'The name of the house was *Ça me suffit*,' said Clara, sailing back in on a wave of buoyant humour. 'Painted on a big flat stone. Roughly translated: *This is quite enough for me!*'

'Or *I've had enough!*' said Lucas, pulling a dour face. 'Enough of the rat race, that is!'

'It was a beautiful place. Maarten loved the garden. There was a little stream where he floated paper boats. In fact – ' She nodded, deferring to her husband as if on a prearranged signal.

'We used to shoot home movies. Eight-millimetre stuff,' said Lucas, taking up the baton.

'And—' Clara over-eager, smiling, feeling awkward. She thought better of it and held her tongue.

'I had them transferred onto video,' said Lucas. He sounded bashful too, as if apologizing for breaking a vase. 'They're not very long. No sound. Though I did dub music onto some sequences.'

'We'd love to see them,' said Jojo. 'Wouldn't we.' She turned to Ruth.

Ruth felt a look of interest, of enthusiasm, on her face. Her head was nodding. It was a coin-op reaction. Despite years of wear and tear, her social reflexes were extraordinarily intact.

Inside she was as cold as charity.

Inside she was a numb blonde.

The wide flat-screen TV flickered into life and colour like an aquarium, and there was Maarten – scaled down to a guppy, a swordtail, a black phantom tetra. This was a pre-Ruth Maarten, their relationship teasing her with its latency. Ruth stared in disbelief at the time machine. How could she be reminded of things that were prehistoric? Come on, Maarten! That's enough of your pranks! Get out of there and grow up for once!

She stood up and went to the toilet.

'Are you all right, dear?' Clara was waiting, edgy, outside the bathroom door.

Back in the living room, Maarten had been put on pause. He was on a swing, soaring high in the air. His grip was so tight that his little fists were white and there was a gasp of fear or panic in his eyes – those eyes that were now beyond all fear, all panic. In the background of the picture, Clara was approaching with her eternal tray of snacks and drinks. The pause feature was defective. Instead of holding, the image ticked forward a fraction at a time, flicking through those bygone pages of time. Clara advanced with an airy, unchanging smile. *Flickety-flick, flickety-flack.* The swing wobbled, reversed direction. *Flick, tick, flickety-flock.* Maarten's eyes shut tight almost in prayer as his longish hair blew back across his face, closing over it, the tendrils of a carnivorous plant.

Ruth made her excuses and left.

Four

*O*utside, the Entrepotdok canal was frozen hard, scattered and skidmarked with slabs and splinters of ice where kids had thrown them. She tugged her black woollen beret down over her ears, did up the top toggle on her navy duffel coat and blew into the conch of her cupped hands.

At one end of the road was the long facade of the Oranje–Nassau barracks, at the other the square tower of the General Union of Diamond Workers.

Apart from a muddy salted channel on the pavement, a glassy crust of snow clung everywhere. She made a small geisha shuffling motion on the sea salt, then headed off.

Opposite the Hortus Botanicus, the entrance to the Wertheim-park. Two winged, smiling sphinxes, each with an iron lantern poised above its head. On the spur of the moment, she slipped in and jogged along the winding gravel paths, from which the snow had melted away. She touched her toes, clapped her hands together and slapped her sides. She trotted past the glass memorial, 'Nooit Meer Auschwitz', and round the ugly dry fountain, a brown marble column rising out of a dish on legs.

There was no one else about.

She sat down on a bench and lit the slim spliff of Kashmir black she had prepared for just this occasion: post-Maarten, post-Aalders, post-Memory Lane. Wacky baccy ... It wasn't strong. Just enough to get her head together. Just enough to shake the world's dust off her wings.

Adrian Mathews

Later a number fourteen tram trundled up to its stop. She boarded, gripped her coat sleeve and rubbed a porthole into the miasma of human breath on the window to watch the familiar landmarks roll by: the unremarkable modern Stopera concert hall, the flamboyant Blauwbrug bridge, the Rembrandtsplein – seedy but endearing – and the bleak wind-tunnel of Rokin, leading up to old Dam Square.

When they reached Mint Tower, where the Singel and Amstel rivers met, there was a sharp explosive crack. The tram jumped a few centimetres sideways and came to a rough, shuddering halt. A fat woman lurched forward over the wheels of a push-chair and bumped her head on a handrail. The baby in the pushchair began bawling. The driver clambered down and inspected the wheels of the tram, the trolley boom and overhead power cables.

'Why don't you watch where you're going?' someone shouted when he came back.

'Did he hit someone?' another voice piped in.

'It's kids!' the driver yelled back, livid. 'Those little buggers have derailed the tram! If I get my hands on them . . .'

'Blame it on children, that's right!' said the fat woman.

'It *is* the bloody kids!' he protested. 'Look!' He held up a piece of mangled red plastic. 'They stuff empty shotgun car-tridges with match heads, hammer down the open end, and ram two or three into the rail. Along we come, and Bang! You wouldn't believe it, but that's all it takes to nobble a tram!'

The driver handed the plastic cartridge to Ruth, who hap-pened to be sitting at the front. She sniffed it warily. Sulphur, charcoal, saltpetre. *Caps again*, she thought – the second time that day.

The acrid odour nestled into her sinuses.

'You might as well all get off,' said the driver. 'We're not going anywhere now.'

Ruth lived on a houseboat in the Jordaan. The walk was not unwelcome. She set off through the shopping precinct of

Kalverstraat, then took a left – on impulse – into the maze of transverse side streets, away from the Saturday throng, the clearance sales, the piped music and the aromas of coffee, hot chestnuts and warm poppyseed bread.

She thought she knew Amsterdam, but it was precisely at such moments of unshakeable conviction that the city sprang its surprises – and now was no exception.

She came out onto an unfamiliar street corner, where a busy 'brown' cafe, its windows plastered with ads for Hoegaarden, Grolsch, Ridder and Kriek, plied its trade beside a humpback bridge. Here, in the hot heart of the city, the waters of the canal had not yet curdled and clotted into ice. The sky was marbled with the tints of encroaching night: lavender, foxglove, heather, amaranth. The colours ran down and soaked into the deep mulberry shadows of basements and alleyways.

The old-fashioned street lamps flamed into life as she stood there. Instead of chasing them, the intimate artificial light lent greater depth and secrecy to the shadows. A festive arch of light bulbs tripped on along the lower rim of the bridge, forming a flaming circus hoop with its swaying reflection in the canal.

Ruth hesitated a moment and tried to get her bearings.

Some kind of argument was going on outside the cafe. Her instincts told her to ignore it, to cut back or circle round. She crossed to the opposite pavement, but the row was growing in volume and scale. It drew in a nucleus of cheerful onlookers.

One voice emerged with shrill, cantankerous energy above all others.

'I don't really care what you think, young man! It's downright inhuman, that's what it is! How would *you* like it? How would *you* like to be chained to a ventilation grille and abandoned in the snow, in the freezing cold?'

Ruth doubled back and joined the bystanders. Her ears had not deceived her. The black astrakhan coat, the woollen rapper's cap, the glasses and, of course, the carriers. It was Bags. In hawkish spirit too, by the look of things. She was tearing a strip off a lean, whey-faced man in rolled-up shirt sleeves who looked like Buster Keaton. He and his cronies were enjoying the fun. They seemed to be arguing about a dog.

'And what about the smoke?' said the man, winking at someone over the old woman's head. 'He'll get hooked on cigars if I take him in there. I can't afford to keep him in Monte Cristos for the rest of his days! He's expensive enough as it is.'

'Plus there's the old lungs,' someone chipped in to a chortle of beery laughter. 'You shouldn't take any chances with his health. It wouldn't be right.'

'Don't you make fun of me! You're all drunk. Stinking drunk. It's disgusting! That dog is cold, and there are laws in this country to protect animals – *and* to deal with brutes like you!'

'Take a look at him, lady,' said the young man, changing tack. 'What breed of dog is he? Can you tell me that?'

'His breed is irrelevant. He is a poor, dumb creature in distress. That much I know, and you should be ashamed of yourself! A dog is not a toy or a status symbol. A dog is for life, not just for Christmas.'

'Actually, the breed is not irrelevant,' the man came back with in earnest. 'He's a husky, see? Know what a husky is? That's an Eskimo dog to you. His great-great-grandaddy took Amundsen to the South Pole. Huskies pull sledges. They *love* ice and snow! Christ – at home he sleeps in a kennel in the garden. If the temperature goes above zero, he nips in, opens the deep freeze with his nose and kips down there for the night! I mean – ' the man held out his hands – 'be *reasonable!*'

Bags was not in the mood for reason.

She dropped her carriers and began busying about, untying the dog's leash. The husky gazed at her with its unreal eyes of arctic blue. The young man pulled the leash out of her hands.

'OK! OK! You win, Grandma! But only because I'm the one who's frozen stiff out here! Holy Moses, it's as cold as a well digger's arse!' He faked a shiver and dragged the dog into the bar, dismissing Bags with a flap of the hand and the queasy expression of a diner who's overdosed on the dessert trolley.

The other men trailed back in, laughing among themselves.

The door closed behind them, muting the hubbub of voices, the jazz music, the chink of billiard balls.

'I should think so too!' the old woman muttered to no one in particular. She frowned, gathered her wits and glanced around at the pavement. One of her bags had tipped over in the commotion, spilling carrots, a packet of Parmesan, a box of eggs, a couple of tubs of cheap lumpfish caviar. Ruth bent down and picked up the bits and bobs.

'Thank you! Thank you so much.' Bags peered, surprised and intrigued, at her helper. 'You have to *fight* for what you want in this world. You realize that, don't you?'

'I suppose you do.'

'I know you. Don't I know you?' Bags in close-up now: the whites of the eyes like milky oyster flesh, the sharp nose pinched with cold, grey tufts poking out from the pilling wool of the headgear. She scrutinized each detail of Ruth's face in turn. 'I do know you, my dear, don't I?'

'I work at the Rijksmuseum. You dropped by last Tuesday.'

'That's right. So I did.' A rip tide of anger overtook the old woman. Her voice started shaking. 'You had me th-thrown out! Thrown out like a c-c-common vagrant! It was *you*! And you dare to address me now, in the street!'

Ruth tensed. Blood coloured her cheeks. 'Actually, it wasn't me.'

'How is *that* – it wasn't you? Then who on earth *was* it if it was not you, young woman?' Warm flecks of spit caught Ruth on the forehead. A muted clicking started in the old lady's throat.

'It was Cabrol. My boss, I mean. I couldn't exactly stop him.'

Bags inspected her again. The click cleared and her anger collapsed as swiftly as it had arisen. 'Yes, of course – but of course! You were the *nice* one. I'm sorry, my dear. I'm so sorry. Forgive me. Naturally I remember you! They shouldn't have done that, though. It was wrong. I only came for what was mine in the first place, you understand. People don't want to know any more. They don't want to listen.'

The cold was beginning to bite into the bone.

'Look – can I help you with those?'

'With what, my dear?'

Ruth pointed at the plastic bags, busting at the seams. 'Your – your shopping, I suppose.'

Ruth was expecting a short walk to a tram stop. The walk was certainly short, but – to her surprise – Bags came to a halt on the ultra-chic Keizersgracht, the emperor's canal. The imposing edifice that loomed in front of them was a traditional seventeenth-century canal house with handsome neck gable, fine sash windows, a basement servants' entrance and worn stone steps leading up to the main door.

Above the door was a stone plaque representing the head of a gaping or yawning man, his tongue poking out with something stuck on it.

Ruth looked down the canal.

A man in a chesterfield coat and grey, snap-brim trilby leaned on the railing of the tiny bridge that crossed the Leidsegracht to take in the view. The cold didn't seem to bother him and he was in no great hurry. In the gathering gloom, the high lit windows on the elegant street glowed bullion gold, framed glimpses into centuries of good taste and the cultured mercantile affluence to support it. The hearths of a dauntless tribe, at once open to the world and impregnable. The houses were a regimental parade of well-bred old Dutchmen, making up in height for what they lacked in girth. Some leaned woozily forward or backwards, their timber piles sinking into the damp, sandy undersoil, but the shoulder-to-shoulder solidarity of their neighbours helped them pass muster. Bags's place was a fine upstanding example.

'You rent a flat in this place, or a room?'

'Rent? Oh no, this is my house. It's all I've got. And as for rooms – too many, my dear, too many. Just look at it. What sort of place is this for an old trout like me? I ask you. I can't get up and down the stairs like I used to, and you know how narrow they are in these old houses. A death trap! That's what Sander always used to say – he was my brother – and Lord knows he had a bad enough fall the day he tripped on the stair carpet.'

Ruth's gaze travelled slowly up the elegant facade. It was some time since she'd consulted the real estate ads, but an approximate calculation was not beyond her. She was fairly confident, at any rate, about the number of zeros. She could almost afford it herself: she had the zeros – it was the other number that went in front she hadn't got.

Three separate locks. The old woman fumbled with her keys and eventually opened the door. It was Amsterdam Green, like practically every other door on the Grachtengordel.

'Don't just stand there,' urged Bags. 'Come in!'

'I shouldn't really. It's getting late.'

Bags grabbed Ruth by the scarf and hauled her in, with a cackle of laughter at her own audacity.

'Just for a minute, then.' Ruth relented.

Together they lugged the shopping down the dimly lit hall to an ugly kitchen at the back and Ruth helped Bags unpack: a fairly representative basket of groceries, though cat food and jenever gin were obviously high on the domestic agenda.

'You're all alone, then,' Ruth said.

'All alone now. Apart from my cats and my ghosts! But I won't be around for much longer, you know.'

'Oh, come on – you're not in bad shape. Apart from that little spot of trouble with the asthma.'

Bags stopped what she was doing and froze. She stared, affronted, at the younger woman. 'What on earth do you mean?' she asked after an emphatic pause.

'I mean you're not exactly at death's door.' Again the blood rose in Ruth's cheeks.

'Whoever said I was?' Bags was the dowager once more, ratty and impatient.

'*You* did.'

Bags pursed her lips and frowned, then pushed an inner play-back button to give the young woman the benefit of the doubt. Slowly the mental exercise bore fruit.

'Oh no! Was that it – me saying I wouldn't be around? You've got hold of the wrong end of the stick, my dear. Goodness! I won't be around because I'm going to emigrate. A fresh start. I'm going to Pittsburgh.'

'Pittsburgh?'

'Certainly. As soon as I get my things sorted out. As soon as I make the necessary arrangements. It's just a matter of time and finding good homes for the cats.'

'Ah.'

'Now stop fussing around, will you, and make yourself comfy back there, I'll be along in just a minute. You can light the fire to take the chill off the air.'

Obediently, Ruth went back down the hall. She switched on a table lamp in the front sitting room.

She held her breath.

A frowsty pong of old age, chronic damp and cat's piss. There was a saccharine sweetness to it that you couldn't ignore. Two mangy felines promptly reared up to use her legs as rubbing posts, their tails erect like bishops' croziers.

A handsome room with a big old fireplace and high stucco ceiling, but the old biddy had made a mess of it. Flaky foam-rubber furniture from the sixties draped in tartan travelling rugs, an old TV in a shiny teak-effect cabinet, a bed pushed up against the wall and a little bookcase stuffed with cardboard boxes, pulp fiction, whodunnits and self-help manuals. Free small-ad papers and lottery coupons littered the floor, along

with a bottle of cough mixture, a plastic medicine spoon, a tub
of bronchodilators and a magnifying glass.

Pity to let such a classy place go to rack and ruin.

Some sticks and coal were piled up in the grate. Ruth found
the matches and got the fire going. She stood, coming face to
face with a large statue of the Virgin Mary that reared up to one
side of a yucca plant beside the hearth. The statue reminded her
of the plaster angel on the wine counter at Stoop, her favourite
bistro. The thought alone was enough to conjure up the fragrant
smell of *carpaccio de Saint-Jacques*.

The odour here was something else . . .

She spotted a bowl of potpourri on the mantelpiece and
threw a handful onto the fire. It camouflaged rather than dispelled the gamy niff in the air. Already the dancing flames lent
a cosy illusion of warmth to the austere, uninviting room.

She took off her coat and began closing the curtains, she
could hardly say why: the natural Dutch instinct was to leave
them open, proudly displaying the spotless interior. Outside,
the snow was dappled with evening's purple vapours and
puddles of lamplight, yellow as butter. The snap-brim hat on
the bridge was still there, still mooching about, watching the
world go by. He turned his back, crossed to the other side and
lit a cigarette. After a couple of puffs, he glanced at his watch
and looked both ways down the pavement. Waiting for someone. He made her think of a surrealist statue in the Vondelpark
– a fellow in a dark overcoat, the collar turned up, carrying a
violin case and raising his hat to passers-by. But beneath the hat
there was nothing, not even a head.

The invisible man in person.

She tugged again at the curtains. They rucked and jammed
midway on the plastic rail and she gave up.

Ruth sat down on the sofa, but shifted her position almost
immediately. A hardness under her left thigh.

She felt around.

Adrian Mathews

The offending article was a rubber hot-water bottle.

Bags was shuffling down the corridor now, getting closer. For a moment it crossed Ruth's mind that she shouldn't really be there. Regulations, remember? No personal contact between researchers and claimants. But hell, it was just a chance encounter and who would ever get to know? She'd have a drink, a chat – the poor thing probably didn't get much company – and that would be that.

Bags was so far gone she wouldn't remember anyway.

Ruth began yawning, resigned to the situation, but the sight of a large tourist poster next to a phosphorescent crucifix over the bed caught her eye and scuppered the yawn just as it was getting up steam.

Pittsburgh! Why Pittsburgh? Bags probably didn't even speak English. And at her age too!

Ruth tried her yawn again, this time seeing it through.

Bags came in with a tray, advancing like a tightrope walker so as not to spill the goodies – jenever and eggnog, biscuits with Leiden cheese that was encrusted with caraway seeds.

'So what's wrong with this place?' asked Ruth. 'Why d'you want to leave?'

'I don't like the view,' declared Bags, glancing at the half-curtained window with a superior air. The comment was blunt and brooked no contradiction.

Ruth grinned inwardly, seeing the funny side. No doubt about it, the old duck was as daft as a brush.

Sad, she thought – but true.

Five

'So this is Sander?'

Ruth picked up the framed snapshot from the mantelpiece. A boy in his late teens. Black hair. Sporty grin. An echo of Bags in the prow-like angle of chin and nose.

Something about the picture niggled Ruth. Which angle was the American Hotel being viewed from? Then she spotted it. The buttons were on the wrong side of the jacket. Either he was wearing a woman's jacket or the photograph had been printed from a negative that was the wrong way round. The second explanation seemed more likely. She was seeing him as he'd have seen himself – in a mirror – the facial asymmetries inverted. To get him the right way round, she'd have to hold him up to a mirror, flipping him back into reality, though she would have felt silly going quite that far.

'There were four of us,' Bags continued. 'Sander was two years older than me. Then there were the little ones, Elfried and Asha.'

'Got any pictures of them?'

Bags shook her head. 'They're all gone, all gone.'

'They died?'

'They never came back, my dear. And as for photos, we lost everything. Everything except the house and a few papers and baubles that Papa hid behind a wall brick before the police came for us.'

Bags pincered the small ice-cold shot glass of jenever between arthritic thumb and forefinger, tweaked it back in one practised action and carefully poured a refill. Her fingers left watery streaks on the bottle. It was beginning to lose its stiff frosting of condensation.

A Hannukkah menorah on the mantelpiece – a candelabrum with eight silver branches. It stood near the kitsch plaster-of-Paris statue of the Virgin Mary. Things weren't adding up.

'But you're Dutch,' said Ruth. 'Van der Heyden's a Dutch name.'

'Papa was Dutch. Mama was Jewish. Their names were Hendrick and Rachel. We children were *halfbloeden*, you see. Goodness knows we weren't the only ones. There were a lot of mixed marriages at that time. And you had to register, the Nazis made you – you were either full, half or quarter Jews.'

Ruth got down on her knees by the fire. She jabbed at the embers with the coal tongs. One log cracked like a pistol shot and she jumped. The sap bubbled out of the smoking bark where it had split. She glanced over her shoulder.

'If you don't want to talk about it . . .'

The old woman laughed. She rocked back and forth like someone in a loony bin, her arms clutched around her abdomen.

'I'll talk about anything, my dear. Anything! What's your name again?'

'Ruth.'

'Talk? Just give me half a chance! Talk is all that's left to me. I have memory lapses, but some things you don't forget.' She tapped her forehead and winked. 'I wasn't a kid at the time. When the Germans came I was eighteen. I knew what was what. I knew what was going on around me. The "cold pogrom", some people called it. They kicked the Jews out of public office first, that's what they did. Non-Jewish government clerks had to sign declarations – Aryan declarations, they called them. Jewish businesses were taken over by some commissariat or other. Things happened little by little, so as you'd hardly notice where they were leading. And we were stupid – let's face it – we were trusting.'

'You trusted the Germans?'

'We did! We thought we'd be safe. We thought if we were good, law-abiding citizens, nothing could happen. If the worst came to the worst, our Dutch neighbours would help.' She gave a scornful laugh and turned her head sharply away. 'The next thing we knew, we were no longer Dutch. Banned from public places. Banned from trains and trams. Children banned from school. Like dogs, lepers and pariahs ... We had to wear the Jewish Star. Nineteen forty-two, that was. We were allowed a maximum of four, and we had to pay for them ourselves, I remember. Four cents apiece! Then there were the confiscations. Aktion M – M for Moebel.'

'Rosenberg's Special Operations Staff.'

'Eh? Oh, I expect you're right. I forget the names – those long German tongue-twisters. I forget what they called themselves. They took everything they could lay their hands on. Furniture, cars, money, radios. Even bikes. Bikes! After the war, whenever a Dutchman saw a German, he'd whisper, "I want my bike back!"'

'They still do sometimes. To the German tourists.'

Bags cackled, then hacked up some catarrh into a paper tissue.

'But your father, Hendrick – he was a Dutchman. Couldn't he have done something?'

'Use your eyes, you foolish girl!' Bags barked, clearing her throat raucously. 'I'm here, aren't I? Sander and me, we survived. That was Papa's doing. He worked for a bank. The Lippmann-Rosenthal Bank.'

'The Liro,' Ruth murmured.

Her face was warm from the hearth, but a nasty chill now slithered down her spine. She and Myles knew all about the Liro. There was scarcely a single claim on the NK-Collection that didn't have a Liro connection. The pre-war Dutch-Jewish bank had been taken over by the Nazis. It was the respectable front for the marauder's swag bag, the kleptocracy. Jewish accounts, cash holdings, cheques, jewellery, gold, silver, bonds, insurance properties, house deeds – all were turned over to the Liro. From there it was one small step to the Nazis' Office of Property Administration and Pensions. Even stamp collections, even trinkets and antiques, ended up in the Liro's subterranean safety-deposit vaults. The Jews queued up at the Liro's head-quarters in the Sarphatistraat to surrender their goods and chattels for safe keeping. In return they were given worthless receipts.

The establishment was notorious in banking history. It ran a one-way operation. You could make deposits, but sorry, folks – no withdrawals.

As thousands disappeared to the transit and death camps – 'volunteer workers' for Westerbork, Vught, Sobibor, Hooghalen, Auschwitz – all private accounts were lumped together into one central 'Jewish account'. The cash funded the trains and the camps themselves. It was the final irony. The Jews were paying for their own deportations and deaths.

Bags picked up the thread of her thoughts. She hugged and rubbed her upper arms. 'The round-ups began in 1942. It was springtime. The trees were coming into leaf and bud. I remember it all so clearly. It should have been a time of joy, but it was a time of fear. We could see them out there.' She gestured with a jerk of her chin towards the uncurtained window. 'The Green Police, the Volunteer Auxiliary Police. They weren't Germans, my dear – oh no. They were Dutch! They scared us out of our wits. They came after dark like sewer rats, in military trucks. Green and grey they were. It was very quiet. They'd wait in the street, the motors still running. And in a few minutes it would be over. That was the last I saw of my schoolfriend, Nadia, and Jozef, and Golda . . . Then the next day the removal vans rolled up. They'd take everything – everything! – if your charming Dutch neighbours hadn't got in there first, that is.'

She downed another jenever, sucked in her cheeks and glared at Ruth.

'I don't get it,' said Ruth. 'Your father, he was – well, the Liro was a *Nazi* operation.'

'Papa hated the Liro. He detested it. He would come home in tears.'

'Then why stick it?'

'Stick it? He wanted to save us! He thought he could use his influence. There were nearly a hundred Dutch clerks at the bank. *Insight* was the word Papa used. They had a special insight into the movement of funds. They saw how stocks – securities, or whatever you call them – were secretly sold off. They had more than an inkling of where things were going. More, at any rate, than the rest of us.'

'And they had to toe the line.'

'They had to *what*?' Bags squawked, cupping one ear.

'They had to do what they were told.'

A sad nod came in reply.

Ruth felt a powerful uprush of sympathy. All the same, she told herself, these sorrows were old sorrows, out of the history books. They didn't have much to do with the here and now. People should try and get over things. They should put the past behind them, let bygones be bygones.

Ruth checked herself by glancing at a wall clock above the Pittsburgh poster, casting a grappling hook back into the present for her own safety, her own peace of mind. Bags noticed the gesture and got to her feet, standing there like a lopsided scarecrow.

'We shall eat. I have wintergreen pea soup and some mashed potatoes, kale and smoked sausage. It won't take long to heat them up.'

'No, really . . .'

'Nonsense.'

Bags shambled off to the kitchen, returning in less than a minute and taking up her former place. One of the cats homed in, prospecting, on the make. Bags patted her knees. The creature pounced up and curled into a vibrant ball. It stretched its front legs and sank the barbs of its claws into the chunky fabric of the old woman's skirt.

'Papa was always angry with Queen Wilhelmina. She was in exile in London. We listened to her on Radio Oranje, though it wasn't allowed. She never once called on the Dutch to help their Jewish neighbours.'

'So I've heard.'

'We listened every day, you see, hoping for a word – one word would have been enough.'

'But what happened to you – to your family?'

'Papa knew the worst was yet to come. He never talked about it, but he was making plans. The Germans weren't going to overlook us. There were a lot of half-bloods in Holland at that time – thousands of us, in fact. We could be arrested any day. In theory, they'd let Jews in mixed marriages stay if they were sterilized, but in reality they often got bundled in with the rest. Now the Liro employees, the confiscators, weren't only in Amsterdam. There were others in the camps. Their job was to strip the Jews of their last assets. Rings, valuables, anything they had in their pockets. Papa knew we'd be taken to Westerbork in Drenthe – "work deployment", they called it – and one of the Liro employees there was a friend of his. A man called Janssen. They'd been at school together in the good old days. He asked Janssen to take care of us, to get us jobs in Westerbork. Permanent jobs – skivvying, that kind of thing. It didn't matter what, so long as it kept us in Westerbork. The transit camps were more or less safe, you see. Safer than the final destinations. The important thing was to have a good reason for not moving on.'

'And your father – he was right? I mean, they did arrest you?'

'Oh yes. They took us to the Hollandsche Schouwburg

theatre. That was the first internment centre in Amsterdam. We only spent a night there, trying to keep warm in the orchestra pit. I'll never forget it. We were all very scared. Some of the families were calm – resigned, like unhappy animals. The Resistance smuggled kids out through a kindergarten across the road. Sometimes they'd take them in potato sacks or rucksacks. Really desperate parents would stop at nothing. There was a high wall, I remember, and they threw their own children over, hoping there'd be someone on the other side to catch them. Imagine! That was probably the last they saw of them – flying through the air, over a wall.'

Ruth grimaced and raised her eyebrows.

'War,' said Bags. Her head slumped, her thoughts folded inwards with unusual intensity. 'It's funny . . .'

'What?'

'People. How they'll do anything to save their brats.'

'That's biology. It's how we're programmed.'

Bags looked up sharply. 'Is it?'

'Think of your father.'

'Yes, of course,' she conceded. 'Papa wanted the best for us. He wanted us to live, but it didn't quite work out that way for Mama and the babies. Janssen was a good man at heart. You'd never have thought so, looking at him. A tough, stocky fellow with whiskers and broken veins in his cheeks. We called him the Walrus. Very bossy. Never laughed. But he liked Papa well enough and he didn't like Germans. He was prepared to help so long as he didn't put himself in danger. The fact that we were half-bloods helped.'

'So you skivvied?'

'We worked in the camp kitchens, Mama, Sander and I. There was a storehouse at the back with a little courtyard – dusty in summer, muddy the rest of the time. That's where we left Elfried and Asha to play. There were always potatoes to peel, peas to shell and big cauldrons to scrub out. We had food, you see. There was that. They were eating tulip bulbs, candle fat and stray cats in Amsterdam, but we had food of a kind. But, oh, how Mama hated it! She was never one for cooking and she loathed the endless routine and the calluses on her hands. And unlike Papa, you see, she wasn't convinced of the Germans' evil intentions. Dear Mama, she never thought ill of anyone. For her a camp was a camp. It was a place where you were interned for the duration of the war. It was a bore and a chore. So why not choose the *best* camp, the five-star camp, rather than the two-star one?'

'I don't understand.'

'You don't?'

'You're saying there was a choice of camps?'

'Oh yes. There was for us. The Germans were sending Jews to Theresienstadt in Czechoslovakia. They told them it was a model Jewish city – a new Jerusalem, they called it. Mama wanted to go.'

'Didn't what's-his-name – Janssen – put her right?'

'He did his best, but she was very stubborn. That was her undoing. Sander and I tried to talk her out of it too, but she'd set her mind on it. She wanted a better life for the little ones. She wanted us to go as well, but we refused. So off she went with Elfried and Asha, leaving Sander and me at Westerbork. In her eyes, you see, we were young adults,' Bags added with bitterness. 'All that mattered was the toddlers. They were the ones who needed her.'

'And the camp – the one in Czechoslovakia – it wasn't a model Jewish city?'

'Theresienstadt? My goodness! You young people have all forgotten. But what am I saying? It's me who's foolish, it's me ... Why on earth should I expect you to remember something you've never known? Theresienstadt, my dear, was a transfer camp for Auschwitz.'

She stood up.

They went back to the kitchen and sat under the indifferent neon lighting, heads bowed like convicts, drinking the thick pea soup in silence. When they'd finished, Bags served the *boerenkool met rookworst* and poured out the lees of an old bottle of burgundy.

Ruth looked wonderingly at the dish. 'You eat pig meat?' she asked.

'I eat anything.'

Ruth shrugged. 'Did your dad survive the war?'

Bags shook her head. 'When he heard what Mama had done, it broke him. His health deteriorated. He must have known he was finished, and he was all alone – alone in this big dark house.' She looked up, gazing across the ceiling as if she could see through its crowded molecules – up and up, through every hidden room and chamber, up into each dark cranny of attic and roof where the wind whispered its chill secrets. 'All alone in this place, he was, just as I am today. I don't have to imagine. I know how he felt. There was nothing more he could do for any of us, but he had to protect the property. If he died, and it got out that the house belonged to a family of *halfbloeden*, the Huns would move in and take the bloody lot. Well, he knew he was dying, so he had to put it in safe keeping – for us, for whoever might survive.'

'How could he do that? I mean, he couldn't even trust his own bank to safeguard his assets. Least of all his own bank, in fact.'

'Exactly, my dear. So what the Jews used to do was turn everything over to *bewariërs*.'

'To what?'

'Aryan guards, they called them. Christians. Neighbours. Business partners. Anyone whose blood wasn't tainted. Anyone of good Dutch origin – because the Dutch were *almost* Germans, you understand. Almost, but not quite.'

'A good solid pedigree of merchants, sailors, millers and dairymen.'

Bags nodded and forked a wrinkled leaf of kale into her mouth.

'The arrangement with these Aryan guards – was it formal? Was it contractual?'

The old woman guffawed, almost choked. 'Are you mad? Jews had no rights. They were non-people. You couldn't draw up a contract with a ghost. You couldn't shake hands with a non-being. Besides which, to even think of doing so would be aiding and abetting the Nazis' mortal enemies. Oh no!'

'So it was an unwritten understanding. When the war was over – and won, presumably – the survivors would return to claim their dues.'

Bags smiled cynically. 'We were fools. We were utter fools!'

'It didn't work out, then.'

'Oh, the Aryan guards were wonderful protectors. Wonderful! More often than not, the property was so well guarded that it was never given back. And when you return to your home town from a Nazi labour camp, your pockets aren't exactly bulging with title deeds and bank receipts. You're lucky if you've got pockets at all. So if you can't prove ownership, what can you do?'

'Is that what happened, then?'

'Papa entrusted our house and belongings to a Dutch neighbour. A young businessman with interests in diamonds, very well to do. He was a man who'd helped us out once earlier in the war and Papa thought he was honest. Honest and trustworthy.'

'Wasn't he?'

Bags hugged herself again. For an instant, Ruth glimpsed her solitude, unused to any company but her own.

'When Sander and I came back from Westerbork, no one did us any favours. There was no special treatment for Jews or even half-Jews. We got off the train at Centraal Station with all the others, and that was that. No help. No rehabilitation. We walked back here in the pelting rain and the house was all shut up. The young diamond merchant was at home, and very embarrassed he was too. He gave us the key – so far he was good to his word. But when we opened the door the place had been stripped. It was mostly the furniture and furnishings that they took. They left our silly baubles. But a big chunk of our past had gone.'

'The Germans.'

'Not the Germans, my girl. Oh no! The Dutch! Don't you understand anything? Our neighbours. The people in this street. The decent god-fearing citizens who used to bid us good morning in the queue at the post office or ask after the children. Now they were eating off our plates. Now they were sitting on our furniture. Quietly. Without a word. It was nothing personal, it was just a fact. There was no to-do. But what did we expect? The vast majority of the Dutch never raised a finger to help the Jews. On the contrary, the arrests and deportations were all carried out by the Dutch. They were the police, they ran the railways, the trams – the "work relocation transports", as they called them. It all went like clockwork. The Germans only posted a handful of officers in Amsterdam. They didn't need any more. Our former Dutch neighbours did their dirty work for them. So why should we be surprised when they stole our belongings too? When times are hard, who comes first? Number one, that's who. Charity begins at home. Didn't they ever teach you that at school?'

'How can you be sure of this?'

Bags pointed two fingers at her own face. 'What are these? Eyes. We called on the van den Berg family down the road. The father opened the door. He didn't know who'd taken our property. But I saw what I saw. I saw it with my own eyes.'

'And what exactly did you see?'

'He was wearing one of Father's suits. A smart brown herringbone suit with a Norfolk jacket. English, it was. Papa had bought it before the war, on a business trip to Birmingham. That creature was standing there on his own doorstep, brazenly telling me he knew nothing about Hendrick or our property, and the filthy vermin was wearing one of Papa's suits. I *told* him

Adrian Mathews

– I told him what I thought of him.' Bags subsided into a brooding silence that discharged its destructive static into the room. The air underwent a physical change. Then just as suddenly she seemed at peace again. 'It was a very strange time, my dear. Nobody knew anything, but everybody knew everything. People pulled their curtains and hid behind their flowerpots. Do you understand me now? All we could do was come home – here – shut the door to keep the world out, and thank our lucky stars we were alive. Sander and me, just the two of us. Two peas in a pod. We had to rebuild our lives from nothing, working from within. Then in 1955 Sander had a heart attack and died.'

'I'm sorry.'

'Ha! Why should *you* be sorry? I was angry with him to begin with, but now I've forgiven him.' She touched the frame of her brother's photo with one fingertip and brought the finger to her lips. 'He was sitting there – right where you're sitting – when it happened,' she added quietly.

'The heart attack?'

'He couldn't breathe or speak. He had his hand at his throat. In a few seconds it was over.'

Ruth felt distinctly uncomfortable. Her body was occupying a deranged area of space, once used for the brother's final agony. She tried to shake the feeling off, even – a visceral response – to shift to one side, without drawing attention to the manoeuvre.

'You've been here alone, then,' she said, 'for nearly half a century.'

'Alone, yes – and it damn well suits me to be alone. I've grown used to it, I suppose. I like it. Anyway, I've always had my cats.'

'Four legs good, two legs bad,' murmured Ruth. She frowned and mulled things over. 'You said your father hid things behind a wall brick.'

'Sander came across it when he was replastering. A little

metal box with a few knick-knacks. Mother's jewels, mostly. Some old medals and family letters. A few photos. The papers for this house. There was a note from Papa too, saying goodbye, saying how proud he was of us, saying he loved us and would always love us – forever and ever, no matter what. They were his last words. I still have it somewhere, Lord knows where. The place is such a mess.'

Bags tore off a square of kitchen paper and dabbed at the brimming corners of her eyes.

'So you lost everything. Then eighteen months ago you saw the painting – the one you put the claim in for – at the NK-Collection's exhibition of repatriated art.'

She nodded, brightening. 'I do like old pictures, and I used to draw quite well myself at school. I do like peering into those old, faraway worlds. They seemed so carefree then, don't you think? I go to the exhibitions when they're free. And, oh – I nearly fainted when I saw my painting. My heart started beating so fast! The memories all came streaming back as if it was yesterday, as if it was all a hair's breadth away. It used to hang in the living room, over the fireplace. Papa was a very cultivated man. He loved art. We had a lot of fine oil paintings and drawings in the house in those days. We lost them all, of course, but that one was special to him and all of us. It was part of the family. One of our ancestors, one of the old van der Heydens, painted it.'

'So I gather. And you never learned what happened to it?'

'The diamond merchant I mentioned, the *bewariër*, said the Germans saw it and wanted it. They made what he called a forced purchase, I think, for very little money, and he tried to pass this sum on to us. Sander – silly boy – wanted to accept, but I didn't. You see, I knew better.'

'Oh? What did you know?'

'The *bewariër* was no fool. He knew it was valuable. He knew it was a fine picture, and a special little bit of Dutch history. He undoubtedly did sell it to the Germans, but for a substantial figure – much more money than he ever admitted – for his own personal enrichment. And to think he tried to fob us off with a handful of silver! I still get angry at the thought. Naturally, I would have none of it.'

'I've seen the painting,' Ruth said. 'It's in the collection storeroom. One of the guys I work with and I went and had a look at it. It's odd. The girl – the flowers – they're rather beautiful. And then that man standing in the background, with his back to the painter. We didn't quite know what to make of it.'

'If Sander were still alive he could tell you. There was some kind of peculiar story behind it all. But I forget, I forget. Getting older, my dear – down we all go, down the slippery slope! And I'm never very with it at the best of times, as you may have noticed, though you're far too polite to say anything, I'm sure. I lose track of the most ordinary things. Nowadays I just try to keep myself going, that's all. Sometimes it's a relief to find you've woken up in the morning. At other times it's a dreary pain and a bore. But each day that passes is a small mercy, a little victory over circumstance.' She leaned closer to Ruth, eyes aglitter, conspiratorial. 'Shall I tell you something about life, my dear – something I've had to find out for myself?'

'Yes, do.'

'It's just this. Don't believe it's the big faults that get you in the end. It isn't. It's the little ones.'

Ruth sensed highway closures and lengthy detours into cracker-barrel philosophy in the offing. She wanted road-holding. She wanted to keep things on track. She stood up and went over to the window.

'At the Rijksmuseum you mentioned a photo. An old family photo of the painting. May I see it?'

Bags creaked and bone-cracked to her feet. Her eyes were red and bleary, unfocused. She was obviously the worse for drink. She beckoned Ruth to the foot of the stairs. She tried a switch and a dim landing light glimmered on above.

'I never go up there any more. It's my legs. Take a look in the first room on your left. There should be some stuff lying around. I think you'll find the photo there.' She picked up a pocket torch that sat on the bottom step. 'Here – use this. The electrics may have gone for a burton. The damp from the canal gets to the wiring.'

'Damp's something I know a bit about,' said Ruth. 'I live on a boat.'

Six

Ruth climbed the steps. She paused to crane her head up the stairwell. The wooden banisters zigzagged tightly into darkness. Naturally it was cold, but the chill was so much harsher here that it took her by surprise. She shuddered with unexpected violence. A window had dropped open, there was no other explanation.

The torch beam proved marginally brighter than the landing light. She shone it around the upper landing, twitched it back and forth. More old snapshots on the walls: a superior-looking filly with bobbed hair in jodhpurs and hacking jacket; a muscular beau in a striped one-piece thirties' bathing suit posing with a tennis racket, a seagull frozen in mid-flight above his head.

The light beam dropped.

Dinky little mouse turds by the skirting board – so much for those pampered cats! Carpet threadbare, lethal rents where it had frayed clean away. Internal memo: beware when going down. And now the sickly, lived-in downstairs pong gave way to something different and infinitely sad – the dust-furred, mouldy odour of neglect, a smell like desiccated leather or putrefying wood, the unbreathable fug of junk shops and attics and cellars, derelict, wormy places where laughter and footsteps and children were no longer heard, the private quarters of the dead.

She held her breath and went into the appointed room.

Moonlight and the fake gas light of the Keizersgracht street lamps entered through a tangle of net curtains and mingled in glimmering green-gold interference patterns on the walls. She shivered again. Here was the offending window. She crossed the room, pulled it up on its stiff sashes and turned around. Vapours spilled from her parted lips. A feeling of dismay funnelled through her.

The place was a tip.

Tea chests, cardboard boxes, piles of books and papers, bundles of clothes tied up in black dustbin liners and a crate of cheap glassware. Even the remains of a meal – a pick-a-stick clutter of tiny brown chicken bones and wrinkled peas as hard as ball-bearings on a dinner plate, dust fluffing up out of the old impacted grease. The Room that Time Forgot . . .

How long had it been since Bags last came here?

There was no telling.

Ruth bit her lower lip till it hurt.

There wasn't a snowflake's chance in hell of finding the photo in the mad clutter of this time warp, but no sooner had she thought this than the curling, deckled edge of the snapshot rose to greet her eye.

Seek and you shall find . . .

It was on the table, one corner pinned down by a dome-shaped resin paperweight with tiny pink shells, a filament of green seaweed and a baby sea horse locked for all eternity in their sham submarine microcosm. She pushed the paperweight aside. At least she presumed this was the photo in question: a family group and – yes, no doubt now – that nutty painting on the wall. Funny how easily she'd come across it. Eerie, even. As if *it* had been waiting for *her*, as if it had found her and not the reverse.

She turned up her nose at the room's cold comfort and made her way gingerly downstairs.

'God bless you!' exclaimed Bags.

Reeking of gin, she clapped her hands with small fluttering

bird-wing motions like an over-excited child. She seized the picture from Ruth's grasp.

'See – same fireplace! You can tell by the mouldings, and there – that curly streak in the marble. This is me, here's Sander, and that's Hendrick and Rachel on either side of us. Oh, my goodness, look at us! Aren't I a little madam? I was – what? sixteen? So this must have been thirty-eight. Our last happy days . . . And there, of course, is the family heirloom.'

Ruth's gaze entered the little virtual world of the snapshot.

The young Bags was a different kettle of fish from the old one. In fact, she was Lydia pure and simple – not Bags at all. The rot had not set in. Bonny long hair, loose on her shoulders, full-lipped, broad-hipped and wickedly clean of limb. True, there was a sharpness about the cheeks and nose, which half a century had since whittled into asperity. But here it was the sharpness of a ready wit, a brisk physical responsiveness. Here she was a poem of youth, proudly hanging onto her big brother's arm.

And a fine figure of a man he was too, despite the period hair oil: a gent, potential matinee idol and a gay dog to boot, from the days when those were no mean things to be. Undo several decades of cynical postmodernity and she'd make a swing for a chap like that herself. Farewell cruel punks, apaches and brat-pack anti-heroes of today . . . There was an innocence and gentility about Lydia and Sander – their parents too – that was no longer of this world.

'It's small, but a good, clear picture,' said Ruth. 'Something to go on.'

'To go on?'

'I was thinking of your claim. It's just a pity you sent in a photocopy.'

'What should I have done, then?'

Ruth shrugged. 'A laser print? A photographic copy? Certainly a blow-up – an enlargement. For maximum detail in the painting. To beef up your case.'

'I don't know anything about these things, I really don't.'

Bags sounded fretful. 'I'm terrible with anything formal, anything administrative. If only I had someone young and intelligent to help me.'

Ruth knew what was coming.

It didn't.

This was laudable in its way. Even in her present state the
old girl preserved a certain tact – tact, Ruth amended, or
cunning.

'I guess I could do that for you.' She softened all the same. 'I
shouldn't, but I will. Provided you trust me with the original
photo. You'd have to post it yourself. Then we'll see to it that
it's added to your file.'

'You're so kind! I *must* have my painting, you see. I shall
take it with me to Pittsburgh.'

'May I ask, why Pittsburgh? Do you have family there?'

The old woman shook her head categorically. 'No family –
certainly not – no family. Papa used to go to Pittsburgh on his
travels. He would tell us about the palm trees and the ocean. He
said it was the place for us. It was where we should have gone.
In another life. In another world.' She sank into a dream of
wistfulness.

Ruth was none the wiser. She'd never really made the grade
at geography. Nevertheless, she could have sworn that Pittsburgh was closer to Pennsylvania than the Pacific Basin. As for
American palm trees, only the plastic pollution–proof variety
were likely to survive the mid-eastern climate. And, hold on –
wasn't Pittsburgh where the German émigrés went? If so, it was
surely crawling with second- and third-generation Ottos and
Heinies, with or without jackboots and secret pipe dreams of
the thousand-year Reich. Not exactly, she ventured to guess,
Lydia's cup of tea.

Bags looked anxious. She glanced out from the darkness of
her inner troubles and their eyes met. 'I'm not even sure now
if I filled in the forms correctly. Oh, I wish I weren't such a
scatterbrain!'

'Don't you worry. I'll check those through too at the Rijksmuseum. But I'd be grateful if you didn't mention that we met. It could get me into hot water.'

'Of course, my dear. You can rely on me.'

'We'll just make sure you have the best possible case.'

'I was thinking, you know. Perhaps the letters would've been useful too, but I must have mislaid them. I've looked everywhere. I've searched high and low.'

'Which letters would they be?'

'Van der Heyden's – the painter's. Didn't I mention them? Oh, I am a silly! You see, *they* were in Papa's little box as well. A bunch of letters he wrote to someone or other, an important figure in his day. When the important man died, his family returned the letters to our family as a keepsake. I've never read them myself, but Hendrick talked about them incessantly. So did Sander. He said they were our little treasure trove.'

'They were never published?'

'No, no, never. His private letters. Written in his own hand. But, as I say, it's a mystery to me where they've got to.'

'Well, do have another look, won't you? Anything linked to the painting's bound to improve your case, and the painter's own letters – well, that's definitely cat-in-the-bag territory. Have you looked for them properly?'

'Not in the last twenty years, my dear. I've been far too busy.'

'Well, get cracking – or get someone to help you. That's the kind of stuff that really tips the balance. If you were just dealing with the administrators of the NK-Collection, that wouldn't be so bad. With a rival claim, the going gets that much tougher.'

'A rival claim?' Bags brought her hands up to her cheeks. A flash of naked distress, a quaver in her voice. 'Don't say that! Don't do this to me! What on earth are you talking about, my dear?'

Ruth's heart sank. She kicked her mental shins.

There was no going back.

'I don't know anything about it. I mean, I haven't seen the documentation. But there *is* a competing third-party claim in this case. As far as I can recall you're up against some guy called Scheele, I think. Sorry, and all that ... Whoever he is, he figures the painting's his.'

'He was the *bewariër*,' whispered Lydia, after a moment's pause.

Ruth held her breath.

She half-expected an outburst, but the old woman just looked thoughtful. The thoughtfulness lasted thirty seconds. Then she slid forward slowly off her armchair and thudded onto her knees. 'Jesus fuck,' Ruth whispered.

She'd been here before ...

She scrambled down to the floor and gripped the woman by the shoulders for an intimate face to face.

'Lydia? Lydia – speak to me, Goddamn you!'

A click – then another – and another.

That inhaler! For the love of Mike, where was it?

She scuttled to and fro, then dropped to her belly and writhed about like a sloughing snake, sweeping the tips of her fingers through the dark spaces under the furniture, which were clogged with dust and cat hairs. Nothing but handfuls of hairpins and old coins – a *stuiver* here, a *dubbeltje* there – the occasional rumble and thunk of a dead gin bottle.

This was crazy. *Where's your logic, Ruth? Get a grip on yourself.*

Her old giddiness came back, a loss of balance in panic situations that she'd suffered from since she was a girl.

Bags kept the inhaler in the handbag, that much she remembered – but where the blazes was the handbag? Her memory checked off the likely locations with dumbwit slowness. Then it came. She raced down the corridor to the kitchen and returned with the bag, strewing its contents pell-mell across the sofa.

She popped the tube into the gaping mouth, supported the slack jaw with her free hand and hit the plastic button.

A long, pressurized hiss.

Bags's eyelids lowered and closed. A vein on her temple throbbed with blood. Part of her was not present. Part of her was squeamish and had taken off for a stroll round the block while the nasty stuff was going on. But now the blue knot of tension around the temples loosened, broke up and subsided into calm.

Another whack on the button, just for good measure.

The clicking ceased, the breathing eased to a gentle human rhythm.

Ruth let drop the inhaler and rocked back. She squatted expectantly on her heels. Bags still knelt, a limpness in her frame, but her respiratory functions were getting back to normal. For that Ruth was truly thankful. Please God, in a minute she'd be right as rain.

Silence.

Ruth waited.

It was snowing again, phantom nocturnal snow. The flakes fell like the feathers of tiny luminous birds against the darkness, moulting at wide, unhurried intervals. A minute passed and then another.

What was that thunder in her belly? What was that lightning in her lungs?

She felt the muscle of her heart pounding against its cage of bones. It took up the beat where the old woman's spasms had left off. She raked the hair off her forehead and bit her lower lip – hands on head, wide-eyed – waiting for a sign.

'Lydia?' she hissed, 'Lydia?'

The woman moved, but not in response.

Out in the hall, Ruth stabbed blindly at the phone buttons: one one two. Third time lucky, her finger got the sequence right.

The ambulance yowled up, drawing its fair share of neighbourly attention. Lights went on in windows and avid silhouettes peered out from the glowing panes of the Keizersgracht, as if

they'd been sitting in the dark with their empty lives, lusting
after accidents and drama. A woman with a pug, someone
loitering by that tree – all leeching off misfortune with their
eyes.

Ruth glared back. What's up? Nothing good on the telly?

She slammed the door against them.

The paramedics, a man and a woman, crouched over Bags in
their trainers and creaky fluorescent anoraks. They took her
pulse and blood pressure. They checked her breathing. Ruth
found it difficult to watch. She folded her arms into a fender of
bone and elbows and walked down the corridor to the kitchen.

Three cats were on the table, polishing off the remains of
Lydia's and her meal. The male paramedic came down to see
her. Young, cratered skin and a smell of cigarettes about him.
The smart-ass type, she thought, taking one to know one . . .

'She going to be all right?' Ruth asked warily.

He ignored her question. 'What were you two up to?'

'We were talking and she had this attack. An asthma attack
– you know.'

'So the talk brought it on?'

'I think it was something I said.'

The paramedic gave a sour smile and stared her out with the
points of his eyes. 'Nothing to do with the gin, then.'

'Well, she was drinking, sure. I wasn't keeping a tally.'

'She's as pissed as a parrot, lady. That's what's wrong with
her. Not a pretty sight. I hope you haven't been leading our
Lydia on.'

'You know her?' asked Ruth, surprised.

He snorted and raised his eyes to the ceiling. 'Ask anyone.
She's the mainstay of the service. The day Lyd pops off, we'll
all be out of a job. Strong as an ox, of course, but they're the
ones who like to hit the sympathy button. Know what I mean?'

Ruth looked away, angry with herself – with him – the
situation – everything. The paramedic picked up a wine glass
and sniffed at it disdainfully.

'Who are you, anyway?'

'We just kind of bumped into each other. She invited me back.'

'Not like our Lydia.'

'I wouldn't know whether it's like her or not.'

Back in the living room, Lydia lay on her makeshift bed. The woman paramedic was packing up. Her colleague checked his watch. 'We'd better be off,' he said. 'You never know, there may be a few lives waiting to be saved out there. If I were you, lady,' he added sharply, 'I'd be getting home. She's had enough fun and games for one day.'

The comment rankled, but Ruth held her tongue. She saw them out and put on her duffel coat and beret. She pushed open the living-room door and peeked back in. Lydia was coming round. Ruth entered cautiously. She sat on the edge of the bed. She held the woman by the hand.

'All right, then?'

'I must've dozed off. Has he gone?'

'There were two of them. They've both gone.'

Horizontal, swathed in soiled linen, Lydia was frail, small and disoriented. Ruth felt sorry for her. She looked as if she was peeking out of her own shroud.

'Sometimes he comes when I'm out,' Lydia whispered. 'Other times he comes at night, when I'm asleep. He goes through my things. I can hear him.'

'Who? That ambulance man?'

'What ambulance man?'

It was hopeless. Ruth shook her head. 'Who are you talking about, exactly?'

'I'm talking about Sander, my dear. He likes to rummage when he thinks I'm not around.'

'I thought you said he was dead.'

The old woman's eyes clouded with anxiety and confusion. She clutched her hands together against her mouth. 'I'm so tired,' she murmured, 'so tired.'

Ruth thought about mentioning Scheele again, but that would be asking for trouble. She felt sick at heart. She wanted to get the hell out of there, leave the shambles behind. All the same, the woman's state pricked her civic conscience.

'Listen, do you want me to stay?'

'No, of course not, dear. What's tomorrow? Sunday? I've got social services coming. I'll be all right, I promise. I told you, I'm used to being on my own.'

Ruth took a visiting card from her purse and propped it against the bedside light. 'My address and number. Just in case you want to get in touch. I've taken the photo. I'll get it copied properly for you and drop it back. OK?'

'You're so kind. I'd rather you hadn't seen me like this, but what can I do? Perhaps, when I'm up and about again, we could meet.'

'I'd like that.'

Lydia smiled. The fog dispelled and a new clarity shone in her eyes.

'Now *you*,' she said. 'I've noticed something about you. The way you walk. The way you talk. You don't wear your heart on your sleeve.'

Ruth smiled back, but only on one side of her face. 'That's inside-out, Lydia. That's for the fashion victims.'

'You know what I mean. You don't give anything away.'

'Eh? Oh, I don't have any secrets.'

'I'm not so sure about that. You shouldn't bite your nails.'

'I'll tell you about me another time. That's a promise.'

'There's something wrong, isn't there? You don't have to answer, of course. But I can sense these things. I've been around too long for my own good.'

Outside, Ruth took a deep breath and knotted her scarf. It was past midnight and piercingly cold, but the winter air was tonic and disinfecting. It routed the odours of cat poo and old age from her lungs. The blood came back to her cheeks with a prickly, almost sexual sensation.

She paused for a moment to get her bearings.

A big moon slipped out obligingly through a rift in the cloud to help her on her way.

She turned right and set off at a good pace, cutting across to the Prinsengracht, then up and round into the warren of the Jordaan with its familiar junk stores and bookshops, the shuttered stalls of the bird market, nights of sentimental accordion music at De Twee Zwaantjes or the velvet curtains that opened onto the convivial stage set of De Doffer's coffee shop. This was Ruth's Amsterdam – not the stuffy broom-up-the-arse snobbishness of the Keizersgracht a mere stone's throw away. The Jordaan was a one-for-all and all-for-one place, where students, refugees, yuppies, almshouse dwellers and boat people rubbed shoulders and joined forces, successfully petitioning against a second subway line. They had somehow distilled and bottled the quintessence of flower power – that fugitive and much-maligned fragrance of sixties' peace, love and agitprop – dabbing it behind their ears in defiance of hard-nosed times.

But where were they now, the peace-loving hoi polloi? Tucked up in their beds, shouldn't wonder. Only the baker was at work, the throb of the dough machine and the warm dusty aroma of flour emanating from his basement air vents.

Ruth was coming home.

She thought of her barge, her own bed, the cool clean linen of the pillowcase and the longing for sleep flooded her veins like a drug.

The new snow was deep and crisp and even. It gave a nice grip, provided you planted each foot firmly in front of the other. And that's what she did, leaving neat little tread prints, complete with maker's logo in reverse indentations.

The prints were a doddle to follow.

Had anyone chosen to do just that, she would never have seen them, not even if she'd glanced behind. A stalker could slouch and keep his distance. He could hum a tune, backstep, even do a little casual window-shopping or light a fag. There was no hurry. It was a dreamy, restful night. An hour for solitude and private reckonings.

So why worry?

There was all the time in the world.

Seven

Myles was away on bureau business for the best part of a fortnight: Utrecht, Rotterdam, Leiden. The day after he got back was midweek but everybody had upped sticks. The heating in the admin block at the Rijksmuseum was on the blink and no one wanted to freeze their balls off even for art – least of all Cabrol, their spindle-shanked coordinator. The system had conked out on Monday morning. Ruth, Pieter and the other research staff had taken what work they could home.

Myles called Ruth just after nine.

'You've been knocking around with her, haven't you?'

'So what if I have?'

'Can't you pick on someone your own age?'

'Just shut up, Myles. I'm busy. What exactly do you want?'

'I want to see you. Pronto.'

'Can't it wait?'

'Pronto never waits. Anyway, you wouldn't ask that if you knew what I've got to say.'

'Oh, wow – Mr Mystery!'

'It's about your old dear, as a matter of fact.'

'Lydia?'

'Are there others? Don't tell me you're starting a collection.'

'Hardi-hardi-ha!'

His voice dropped a semi-tone. 'It's about the painting, actually, rather than the alleged owner. I'm just carrying out orders, baby. You were the one who asked me to keep my eyes open for red flags in its provenance.'

'And?'

'One o'clock today, De Jaren, on the Nieuwe Doelenstraat. You know – that place full of trendy wankers like us.'

'It's really *that* good?'

A pause. She heard him breathing and imagined a glint in his eye, dragging out the tease for all it was worth. But when he came back his tone was flat and insipid. It was as if he were wiping his nose or trying to speak without moving his lips, for reasons best known to himself.

'It's weird stuff,' he said. 'I've never seen anything quite like it. Look – you'll just have to judge for yourself.'

Ruth had indeed been seeing Lydia.

It began with a guilt-driven phone call to check she was still in the land of the living and just seemed to take off from there. Lunch at Pier 10. A visit to the Piggy Bank Museum. Coffee twice at Schiller's on the Rembrandtsplein. They were becoming new fixtures in each other's lives, still negotiating the novelty with mutual probings of unlikely sister souls. The truth was each had an instinct for the other's unhappiness. They trotted to help like St Bernards, but with different victuals and rescue plans.

Ruth helped Lydia sort out her wardrobe, take stuff to the dry-cleaner's and go through the piles of unpaid bills. There were thirteen cats, by her reckoning, though they never stopped still for long enough to count. Moves were already afoot to diminish that inauspicious guesstimate – to find homes for three at least. Ruth revamped the claim to the NK-Collection, providing a razor-sharp print of the photo. She drafted a formal but forceful word-processed letter to replace the digressive and partly illegible original. At odd moments she poked around, looking for the stash of ancestral letters, but nothing came of her efforts. She tracked down a new doctor, a specialist in asthma and allergies.

For her part, Lydia talked her head off.

The old girl had a cockeyed way of seeing things. She was one of nature's oddballs, a visitor from a parallel world which occupied the same space but a different time. There were days when just the thought of her brought a wry smile to Ruth's lips. But behind all the shabby chaos, Lydia was a hard nut to crack. Whatever you made of the old crow, she'd been out there on the brink – figure-skating on the dangerous edge of things. That nobody could deny. And she shared her vivid memories with her new acquaintance, despite moments when her deafness or forgetfulness played up with suspiciously good timing.

Some subjects, it seemed, were simply taboo.

Up to now the elderly had hardly loomed large in Ruth's preoccupations. *Old person. Distantly related to homo sapiens. Defining characteristic: takes in excess of twenty minutes to buy a stamp in the post office.* Now, in the street, she began to look at them anew. She couldn't help herself.

Were they all like this, just waiting to explode into conversation?

Light blue touchpaper and retire . . .

Ruth stretched, yawned and slipped a hand up the back of her Aran sweater for a wake-up monkey scratch. She wriggled into a pair of stonewashed jeans. She filled her dented camping kettle and popped it on the gas ring, then climbed out on deck, peered overboard to examine the strakes and riveting, then visored her eyes to the sky.

From her berth on the Prinsengracht, she had a view down the Bloemgracht canal. The morning sun hung above the water like a pale, levitating apricot. It pinked the air and trees with its fruity bloom, lending a glamorous fluorescence to the step gables of the Keyser Foundation building.

A low soup of fog still clung to the water, the odd gossamer wisp tearing itself away.

'Tra la!' she thought. 'Tra la!'

She clapped her hands and rubbed them together till they were red.

She cleared her throat and gave full voice to her joy: 'Tra la la! Tra la la! Tra la la!'

The bald, round-faced Chinaman who ran the occult book-shop was out sweeping the step. He glanced up in surprise. She had dubbed him Mr Moon. He had a penchant for psychedelic kipper ties. His eyes were baffling. They looked as if they'd make more sense viewed upside down, like a trick rotational drawing where two faces emerge out of one. He leaned on his broom, gazed around and waved brightly when he saw it was her. Ruth waved back, all palsy-walsy. It was a new day, and new days – like old neighbours – have to be treated with respect. That was a rule with her. They have to be treated with qualified optimism, with generous human expectations on the cumulative basis of past experience.

She sat like a bosun on the edge of the gunwale and surveyed her domain.

In theory, seawater was pumped into the canals from the IJsselmeer and the dirty water streamed into the North Sea during low tide at IJmuiden. The reality was that the canal system was a seventeenth-century open sewer, just one of the functions it was designed to fulfil in the first place. The house-boats, vessels and arks were gradually being connected to the modern sewage system. In the meantime, it was not exactly a life on the ocean wave. A few lumps of raw sewage were bobbing and rolling in the water right now and – she noticed – some colourful new graffiti had materialized on the galley hatch. All the same, the odour of tar and the whiff of wood smoke from her stove's chimney rescued her good humour.

A boat was a boat and there was a heck of a lot to be said for it.

Adrian Mathews

In this country it was the land that was precarious, not the water, a subaqueous plain that would completely vanish if the sea level rose by twenty metres. The words 'sea level', in fact, were rarely used in polite conversation. One said 'NAP' – normal Amsterdam level – instead. 'NAP' was user-friendly. 'Sea level' meant up to your gizzard in water. 'Sea level' meant breathing brine. Remember that, ye putrid landlubbers! All things considered, and given Amsterdam's reputation as a modern Sodom and Gomorrah, having an ark handy was not such a bad idea in the end . . .

Après moi, le déluge . . .

Lydia would have lived through the flood tide of 1953 which had devastated much of the south-west of the country. As for Ruth's father, she remembered saying to him that Holland should never have existed. It was a country that had been dragged out of the sea. 'We were all dragged out of the sea, dear,' he had replied in his characteristically philosophical manner.

Ruth's *woonboot*, the *Speculant*, was a 1935 flat-bottomed Luxemotor barge, a sturdy former aggregate carrier, just over thirty-six metres long, five metres in beam with ninety centimetres below the waterline – an elegant marine beast from her straight proud bow to the graceful swell of her stern, though her years were beginning to tell.

Ruth and Maarten had studied for their pilots' certificates in tandem. They bought the barge in Lemmer, fitted her out with a new 180hp Detroit diesel engine and chugged across the broad expanse of the IJsselmeer, which they both preferred to call by its historical name. They'd lock arms in the wheelhouse, crooning some old song about 'Sippin' Cider by the Zuyder Zee'.

Those were the good old days, when everything lasted forever.

Those were the days that had one day ceased to be.

The *Speculant* was a biggish boat. Three was a good crew, but two could handle her, provided one of the two was a man.

You needed muscle and masculine savvy to live on the face of the waters, as Ruth had found to her cost. There was bright work to clean. There was timber to sand and varnish. There were bilge pumps to fix and winches to oil. At least the boaties stuck together, helping the neighbours out in a fix. The esprit de corps was part of the razzmatazz of it all.

She sighed, checked out the wheelhouse and climbed back down into the galley.

The gas was out, the water for her morning coffee stone cold.

She brought her head down and sniffed at the ring. She couldn't have lit the damned thing.

She struck a match and tried the knob.

Nothing doing. Strange . . .

For safety's sake, the Calor gas cylinder was kept outside. A high-pressure LPG tube fed through a hole in the deck.

Was a kink in the piping stopping the stuff getting through? Unlikely.

She climbed back up and round to starboard.

The hose was new and, anyway, LPG was tough stuff. She ran her fingers down its length all the same. No splits, no kinks. She checked the bulkhead-mounted regulator. Then she spotted it. The hose hung limply from the six-kilogram propane cylinder. It had come away. She rocked the cylinder. Empty, dammit! She rocked it again to make sure. She'd only bought it a week ago and one would normally last her for months. As for the joint, that was a mystery. The hose fitted the cylinder with a female-threaded POL connector and adjustable Jubilee clip. She'd tightened the hose clip herself. Not too much – that was true. If you overtightened, you ran the risk of biting into the hose. But her wrists and hands remembered the firm, steady force they'd exerted to get that thing on. It was a gesture she'd repeated dozens of times.

She couldn't believe she'd ballsed it up.

She straightened her back, put her hands on her hips and bit her lower lip.

Perhaps it was something to do with the cold, though school-book physics would suggest the contrary. She shrugged, went back down into the saloon and phoned through to the delivery company for another cylinder. Twenty-four hours, they said. In the meantime, there was no way she was going to do without her coffee. She climbed back up through the cabin, rounded the wheelhouse, tripped up the gangplank and whistled and waved like Robinson Crusoe to attract the attention of the Jongewaards, who were sweeping the deck of their next-door barge.

Thank the Lord for neighbours!

Ten minutes later she was back home with a Thermos of Illy, the best Italian *caffè macinato*.

She poured out the first sweet shot of the day.

Ruth's passion was old records. The centrepiece of her saloon was a 1962 Dansette Popular four-speed in pink leatherette, with auto-changer, the Rolls Royce of record players. It was hard getting the styluses these days, but she managed. It played vinyl EPs, LPs and the old seventy-eights. She had hundreds of records, most of them in their original sleeves and arranged in strict alphabetical order by artist on high purpose-built shelves. The pride and joy of her collections was an original set of Chet Baker.

She switched on the machine and put on Gladys Palmer singing 'Where the Lazy River Goes By' with the Roy Eldridge Orchestra, a 1937 recording. There was a nice trumpet on that track, which must have been Roy Eldridge himself.

She sipped her coffee, sighed and glanced past the fuel and water tanks into the galley, then back at the saloon, where she was sitting. The carpet and upholstery were on the tatty side, but this had come to be home. Admittedly, there was an element of make-believe in skippering a boat that went absolutely nowhere, but there was poetic justice too.

It just summed things up.

The varnished teak panelling and furniture, the brass fittings, glowed warmly in the wintry sunshine as did the golds and reds of a small reproduction of Rembrandt's *The Jewish Bride* or *Isaac and Rebecca*. The husband held his hand to his wife's bosom, neither meeting the other's gaze, their expressions inscrutable to the last – and what on earth was the woman holding in her right hand? Van Gogh said he'd give ten years of his life just to contemplate this painting, with nothing more for sustenance than the occasional loaf of bread.

Beneath the print and a snapshot of her parents in Driebergen was Ruth's desk, the thumb-smudged screen of her computer and the stack of work she'd taken home. Her chair was draped with an old velvet curtain, burgundy in colour, which she liked for its lost grandeur, its uneven fading, the pigment sucked out slowly by the suns of yesteryear. She'd picked it up for a song at the Waterlooplein flea market along with a box of miscel-laneous cut-glass pendants from a dismantled chandelier. Now there were pendants hanging at all the portholes. They twirled dreamily on their nylon threads, sending tiny rainbows skitter-ing around the saloon. She followed one on its dancing flight. It swung in and out of the corner above the built-in bookcase, catching for an instant on a grotty micromesh of cobwebs.

Ruth scowled.

She was a stickler for spit and polish. Nothing raised her hackles like spiders – the orbatid spider in particular, with its inexplicable fondness for barges and boats. To the microscopic orbatid brain, a barge is the promised land, waiting to be spun into a spidery paradise. It was a wonder that they were around in the depths of winter, but she always kept the barge nice and hot, so it must have buggered up their seasonal body clocks, a small-scale model of global warming.

Ruth tried to think of something else, to focus on what she ought to be doing – anything.

It was no good, a case of force majeure. Her eyes kept flitting back to those cobwebs. There were the tiny orbatid cobwebs that you could simply blow away, but there were large ones too. Big spiders loved the round portholes. They were the perfect size and shape, and the light attracted insects.

She took a stroll down the barge, inspecting the portholes.

Nature's little net curtains hung everywhere.

This was hardly the time of year for spring-cleaning, but nothing could stop her now. For three hours she climbed and crawled through the saloon, galley, forepeak and back cabin, the wheelhouse and her bedroom. She dusted and scrubbed. Her courage only flagged in the grimy shadows of the engine room and workshop.

Half-twelve.

She'd almost lost track of time.

She washed quickly, changed, locked up and took to her bike.

Juddering on autopilot over the uneven cobbles and speed bumps of the Prinsengracht, she passed the soaring spire of the Westerkerk. Its chimes rang out in giddy carillons, scattering pigeons into the air.

She cut back in one block.

The Herengracht?

No. Somehow she'd missed a turn.

Not to worry ... a city of ninety islands linked by five hundred bridges can hardly be expected to obey the laws of Euclidean space. A next right would sort her out.

So far, neither trams, taxis nor red lights had stopped her, but all at once she applied the brakes to get her bearings.

She had a queasy feeling that something or someone had led her astray. Crazy! There was no one to blame but herself. She blew angrily into her hands and perched back on the broad cracked rump of the leather saddle, taking in the scene.

The Leidsegracht bridge, the waters mushy below and waiting for one clean snap to lock into a brittle plane of ice. A flower stall, bright with winter roses, by the bridge. And, over yonder, the large clock tower of the Metz & Co. furniture store.

This was the Keizersgracht, no doubt about it, the emperor's canal.

Why had she stopped?

Then it clicked.

On the other side of the canal was a handsome seventeenth-century house with a neck gable and an unusual cartouche representing the head of a gaping or yawning man, his tongue poking out with something stuck on it.

Her heart skipped a beat.

That house, or Lydia herself, was a bloody magnet, drawing her insidiously off course. She felt like a dupe, taken in by a tawdry magician's trick.

She flipped up a pedal with the tip of her toe, ready to strike off, as the front door of the Bags residence opened. The brass knocker caught the sun and a distinguished elderly man in a fur-collared coat came out: curly white hair, a Shakespearean forehead and the conclusive air of someone who had rounded off a piece of routine business and was now free to take a little breather. He pulled the door shut behind him and held his briefcase between his knees as he eased on his leather gloves. He walked down the steps with cautious, old-man steps and sauntered away.

No sooner had he gone than a younger man appeared from nowhere. He had black hair and glasses and wore a brown Western-cut plaid jacket with the word Cisco embroidered on the back in pale-blue chenille letters. He took the steps two at a time and rang at the bell. He put one foot up on the wall – showing off a suede desert boot – and flexed his knee. He arched his back over the leg like an athlete warming up while he was waiting.

The Cisco Kid, thought Ruth.

Suddenly she felt ill at ease with herself for observing him. There was nothing to warrant the feeling. He was oblivious to her presence. He had not even turned around.

She resisted the urge to move on.

The door opened – a brief glimpse of Bags – and in he went. Show over . . .

Lydia's social life was definitely hotting up. The thought piqued Ruth, as if she'd been made redundant, as if her own services had been summarily dispensed with. Furthermore, there was a weird sensation in the back of her neck.

She turned round abruptly.

At a semi-basement window on her side of the canal, a venetian blind shivered slightly as one flexible slat snapped back into parallel.

Eight

At De Jaren, Myles was eating pickled herrings. Ruth lifted one by the tail and lowered it expertly into her mouth.

'This city,' she said, still chewing, 'was built on herrings. Not diamonds, not dope, not wooden poles.'

'How come?'

'It was founded by the herring fishermen of the Amstel, wasn't it? Even the damn Portuguese migrants came here because they were bringing salt from Portugal.'

'Salt for the herrings?'

'Salt for the herrings,' she confirmed, swallowing hard.

'I've got some fresh unsalted red ones for you here,' he said, tapping his case.

'Huh?'

'Forget it. English idiom. Doesn't compute.'

From the street the sound of a barrel organ reached their ears, the wheeze of mechanical valves and pipes. Ruth strained to make out the tune. It was an old sea shanty that reminded her of childhood and the gesture of tossing a coin wrapped in a ball of paper from a window to the organ grinder below. She rested her head on the cup of one hand and Myles, noting her distraction, bided his time.

Even in stillness, there was a quiet grace and the discretion of poise in this young, sloppily dressed woman with her short blonde hair. He responded to it with the fat man's special sensitivity to physical beauty, an admiration that verged on pain.

The music moved on.

'Still with us?' he asked.

'You bet.'

She began to rouse herself.

The big, airy cafe – a steep well of light, all glass and sleek pale wood, the sun shimmering up from the river outside – was only half full as yet. Solitary men in corduroys leafed through the morning papers. Girlfriends chatted over low-calorie pasta entrées draped with ribbons of smoked salmon. Some kids from an office were messing around with a mobile phone.

Ruth hailed a passing waiter and ordered hot chocolate and a side dish of *Poffertjes* pancakes.

'Come on, Myles. Stop pissing about. Get to the point. Why are we here? Tell Mummy all.' She crossed her arms on the table and frowned.

He crossed his arms too in unconscious mimicry.

'Serious?'

'Serious.'

He leaned forward towards her and straightened out his voice.

'I had some time on my hands in Rotterdam and Leiden, Ruth. Like I said on the phone, I looked into the van der Heyden provenance. Not just for you or the old girl. Professional curiosity. There was something about the docketing on the back of the picture that was eating at me. I couldn't get it out of my mind.'

'Go on.'

'Think back. There was an old tag – right? – that read Johannes van der Heyden. Amsterdam. Miedl., followed by a classmark of some kind. Up against it was a Nazi Linz stamp, along with another classmark. Then there was what looked like a transportation tag, saying the thing had been shifted from Alt Aussee to the Munich Collecting Point. That's a lot of labels, and you and I know what lies behind some of those place names, right? But it still didn't add up. Then I looked into the Scheele claim on the painting, the one Cabrol filed, and suddenly everything fell into place. Well, nearly everything. A logical sequence, shall we say.'

'Lydia called Scheele a *bewariër*. The painting was in his safe keeping during the war, but he sold it on. For his own profit, she says. A forced sale, according to Scheele himself. After the war he offered the van der Heydens token compensation. Lydia wouldn't have any truck with that, but her brother Sander accepted.' She shrugged and raised her eyebrows. 'It's a story we've heard a few times before, or something like it. She reckons he made a lot more out of the deal.'

'I guess from a sceptic's point of view Scheele's case is airtight. Who can prove a sale was forced? But that's what he's claiming, and there's no particular reason to treat his claim with cynicism, even though he can't produce receipts. After all, as you say, Lydia couldn't even agree with her brother over whether to accept Scheele's offer. OK, under Dutch law, all transactions with the Nazis are considered illegal. But forced sales are grey areas, legally speaking. They did happen, with varying degrees of coercion. It's not so much of a sticking point, in my opinion. You just have to work through the evidence cold-bloodedly and see what it tells you.'

'Rather you than me.'

'Quite. You being in cahoots with the old lady must compromise your objectivity.'

'Hold on!' Ruth slapped the table petulantly with the flat of her hand and Myles flinched.

Conversations stopped.

Heads turned.

'Let's get this straight. I didn't seek her out. We crossed paths purely by chance. All I did was tidy up her claim. She's *old* – know what I mean? Maybe in London you push little old ladies under the red double-deckers to save on pensions, but here we try to behave like human beings. For all I know, she could have Alzheimer's. Anyway, she's not up to these things and there was no one else around to help her.' Ruth frowned suddenly in confused consternation at herself. She'd just remembered the changing of the guard at Lydia's palace, not half an hour before. 'It's out of my hands, Myles. Cabrol's the coordinating officer. He and the committee will weigh it all up. What I mean is, I didn't doctor her evidence. I didn't load the die. I just helped her present her case. It was secretarial – nothing more.'

'Scheele has a case too.'

'I've no doubt. Dutch Gallery Owner Made Forced Sale. As you say, it may or may not stand up in court. What d'you want me to do – type his letters out too?'

Myles sighed and no-no-ed. 'You're jumpy.'

'Sure I'm jumpy. It's the heat and the low wages.'

'Let me put you right on one matter. Scheele isn't a gallery owner and never was. He's a businessman. Alois Miedl, however – the name on the first label, remember? – Miedl was a dealer and a close acquaintance of Scheele's.'

Ruth's ears pricked up.

'*Alois* Miedl?'

'Sound familiar? German businessman and banker living in the Netherlands. Jewish wife. Mixed up in lots of shady stuff. Diamond smuggling, for instance, or trying to buy the coast of Labrador to keep the Fatherland supplied with timber.'

'Small-time,' Ruth shrugged.

'Right. Nowadays, he'd sell World Trade Center rubble in perspex souvenir boxes, or diddle Joe Public out of his life savings in some time-share villa scam. The Canadian government soon put the kybosh on his plans for Labrador.'

'You mentioned diamonds. Isn't this Scheele's territory? Lydia said something to that effect.'

'*Was*. We'll come to that. He's moved on to higher things. Let's get back to Miedl. What do you know about him?'

The hot chocolate had arrived but not the pancakes. Ruth squinted round, wondering what had become of them. A morning spent clobbering spiders had left her feeling murderous and fazed. She tried to point her brain at the question.

'He was hand in glove with Seyss-Inquart and Mühlmann, wasn't he? The Chancellor and the State Secretary for the Arts. A loose cannon, all the same. He got the Jewish dealers to sell to him by putting on the frighteners. Sell while you can before the evil fascists confiscate your stock. He and Pieter de Boer were the really big buggers when it came to shunting Dutch art into German hands. Am I right, or am I right?'

Myles leaned in, approving. His ginger ponytail bobbed against the collar of his tartan lumberjack shirt.

'Just so. The smart dealers, like Vecht or Goudstikker, got their best stock out of the country early on and tried to save their bacon. But Miedl's big safety net in all his dealings was Reichsmarschall Goering. He knew Goering's sister and he'd visited Carinhall, the Goerings' posh hunting lodge outside Berlin. Goering, of course, was an art enthusiast.'

'A man of dubious tastes, they say.'

'Oh, sure. I mean, his favourite Vermeer painting, *Christ with the Woman Taken in Adultery* – that was a blatant fake. But he liked Cranach, Jan Breughel, Rubens and Rembrandt too. Old, classy stuff. If you think about it, the one thing Nazis never collected was official modern Nazi art. The truth is, they all knew it was a load of old cobblers, Adolf included.'

'He should've stuck to his watercolours,' said Ruth, stirring her chocolate.

'That's what my aunt Ivy always says. Let's get back to Goering. Amsterdam was one of the places he liked to drop in on for a spot of shopping. You know – a little retail therapy, to get you through the wars. Mühlmann's Dienstelle office opened art-purchase accounts for Goering and Hitler, and Goering would send his curator, Walter Hofer, in ahead, then nip over on a tour of inspection once the goodies had been set up. Like in May 1941, just before going to Dunkirk. Buy a few piccies, then take in a nightclub or two. Wine, women and song. That was the bottom line. So Goering had Hofer, and Mühlmann's office was helped out by Edouard Plietzsch, the Berlin expert on

Dutch art. Like Hofer, he analysed collections to be bought or confiscated.'

'What happened to Miedl?'

'I was getting to him. Miedl tagged along with Hofer on his May 1941 trip and put him onto various collections. Hofer advised. Miedl bought. A whole stack, for example, from Franz Koenigs, the non-Jewish German banker. Koenigs had money problems, and nine paintings by Rubens – amongst other goodies – helped bail him out. Goering had first refusal on Miedl's offerings and Hofer got kickbacks on resales. That was the deal. In this case, Miedl was also in the process of buying out the Liro bank. So Hofer was Goering's advance guard and Miedl was Hofer's advance guard. Miedl kept Hofer two steps ahead.'

'Ahead of whom, exactly?'

'Ahead of the Führer, for one. Goering and Hitler both fancied themselves as culture vultures, didn't they? So Goering was constantly rushing around trying to get to the best pickings first. It was Miedl who got Hofer Cranach's *Madonna and Child*. His big coup was the Goudstikker firm when Goudstikker and family did a runner. Remember Cabrol going on about that deal? They rubbed Goering's nose in it at the Nuremberg trials. Miedl got the Goudstikker name and all the property: Castle Nyenrode, the Villa Oostermeer, the Amsterdam gallery. But the signatory to the contract of sale was Hofer. Why? Because Goering had put up some of the cash and got six hundred paintings to keep him happy in return, including the Cranach I mentioned earlier. Miedl ... That's the name that crops up everywhere. A proverbial bad penny.'

The waiter had an insolent way of gazing askew whenever he passed.

Ruth grabbed him forcefully by the elbow.

'You haven't forgotten me, have you?' she asked sweetly.

He made the appropriate assurances and backed off.

'You're bogging me down in detail, Myles. What's all this got to do with the van der Heyden?'

'Johannes van der Heyden. Amsterdam, Miedl. K41. RG. 937. That's a Hofer classmark. Miedl's the middleman, of course, having put the screws on Scheele – or so Scheele would have us believe. And RG. is the purchaser.'

'RG. for Reichsmarschall Goering.'

'That's it. Goering himself. The porker in the fancy white suit with the shiny buttons. Inconspicuous bloke, wasn't he? There's no bill of sale. Scheele says there wasn't one. Says he got a thousand florins cash.'

'Not too bad for those days, I guess.'

''Spose not. For an unknown painting by an unknown eighteenth-century Dutch artist. But that's assuming the valuation's just. Miedl had evidently seen the van der Heyden in Scheele's place and did the dirty on him. For some reason, he thought the picture was class. Class and spondulicks, naturally. There's no bill of sale, as I said, but Scheele's dates for visits and the sale check out. Miedl, Hofer and Goering were all in town at the time.'

'He could've mugged that up in the local library.'

'He could have. But if we just go along with him for the time being – and those labels seem to bear him out – the question is: why should this unknown painting by an unknown and frankly mediocre eighteenth-century Dutch artist be of such capital interest to the commander-in-chief of the Luftwaffe?'

'Pass. I'll take the money.'

'It gets worse, dearie. Let's look at the second marking. Remember? An ink mark. The Reich eagle and the words Linz N° AR 6927. Linz for . . .?'

'Linz for Linz. No acronyms there. A charming Austrian city on the Danube not too far from Salzburg. Cosy place. Snowy alpine views in winter. The peaceful clunk of cowbells in summer. All it lacks is a really mammoth art museum.'

'Right.'

'With, say, seven-thousand-plus major paintings plundered from every public and private collection in Europe, which constitute a third of the cultural wealth of the Western world?'

Adrian Mathews

'Atta girl! A Breughel here, a Leonardo there ... Linz was Hitler's childhood home, right? And Linz was where old Adolf was going to plonk his Führermuseum. The centrepiece of a vast cultural complex. No contemporary art, as we said. That would go to the Haus der Deutschen Kunst in Munich. Just the expensive old stuff. In his bunker, Hitler spent the last days of the war poring over a tiny architectural model of his dream museum. It was his pride and joy. The day before he topped himself he made the Linz collection over to the German nation. He thought the Brits and Yanks were really after the Russians. He never dreamed Germany would be sliced up like liverwurst, nor did it occur to him that the major spoils of war would be repatriated. Somehow, Christ knows how, his glorious museum was going to rise like a goose-stepping phoenix out of all those ashes.'

'He was one crazy fucker, Myles, you have to admit. They all were. It's funny how those barbarians thought of themselves as cultured.'

'That's what gets me too. You have to remember the cultural policies were part and parcel of the genocide, the imperialism. Hitler, Goebbels, Himmler, Goering, Rosenberg, Ribbentrop – all those pseudo-arbiters of culture – they communicated through symbols and myths. The Linz collection was the final revision of the new cultural canon, a huge reshuffling of the icons of history.'

Ruth smiled and shook her head. 'So let me get this right. You're telling me that Lydia's little van der Heyden painting was earmarked for Linz? I must be hearing things.'

'That's what the ink stamp says. You saw it yourself. Linz was Hitler. It was also Dr Hans Posse, Hitler's special emissary. Together, through their agents, they spent a hundred and sixty-three million Reichsmarks on artworks for the new museum. No crap. Just the crème de la crème. They were the biggest art collectors in history. Your Lydia's van der Heyden was one of the works they were after. One of thousands, it's true – which makes it less incredible. It's pretty odd, all the same, that it came in for Goering's special attention, if my scenario holds water. First Goering, I should say, then Hitler.'

'Hey, come on, Myles! You mean they even fought for it, Marquis of Queensberry rules, an' all that?' She pummelled him playfully on the upper arm. They'd look like Laurel and Hardy! Or Chaplin – you know, *The Great Dictator!*'

'Hitler was – well, a bit of a Hitler, to put it bluntly. He got what he wanted. Nobody stood in his way. But there was one incident this reminds me of. I'm thinking of the Kröller-Müller Museum. Goering was very taken by three paintings there that the museum's benefactors had bought in Germany. A *Portrait of a Lady* by Bruyn the Elder, a *Venus* by Cranach and another *Venus* by Hans Baldung Grien. He reckoned the price had been set too low and they ought to go back to Germany – to his own private collection, natch. So he sent in Kajetan Mühlmann to deal with the museum's director. Goering got his pictures, but he had to let one of them go. Hans Posse, the Linz director, wrote to Martin Bormann saying the Baldung Grien *Venus* was one of the masterpieces of the German Renaissance. When Hitler got wind of this, he snapped up the painting for Linz. There was nothing Goering could do.'

'So?'

'I know there's not a lot to go on, but suppose – just suppose – something similar happened here. That would explain the purchase of the van der Heyden for Goering via Miedl, then its pre-emption for Linz.'

'Hofer didn't get his foot in the door first this time round.'

'Apparently not.'

'But why *that* picture – why the van der Heyden? I still don't get it.'

'Well – just thinking aloud here – but van der Heyden was Dutch, of course. As far as the Nazis were concerned, Holland, Flanders and Luxembourg were the Nordic Reich. Rosenberg led the Combat League for German Culture, and Dutch artefacts were particularly easy to pull in under that blanket term – easier than Grecian urns and Italian frescoes, at any rate. They were Low German, but at least they were German. So the great Dutch art of the seventeenth century, for example, was a good starting point for the new order, the new orthodoxy.'

'Van der Heyden was eighteenth century. We know that. Nothing particularly great about the age or the painter.'

Myles sat back heavily and shrugged. 'Like you, I don't get it. There's something we've missed. But I haven't quite finished yet. I turned up some other weird stuff too.'

The waiter circled smoothly, served the *Poffertjes* and tacked off in one seamless impersonal motion, like a child imitating a plane.

The mini-pancakes, dusted with icing sugar and swimming in translucent melted butter, gave off a hot floury fragrance. Ruth tucked in with a vengeance.

'You've really been putting your back into this,' she said admiringly through full cheeks.

'Stick with me, kid. It ain't much fun, but it's educational.' He watched her eat with fascination, then made his excuses and went to the toilet.

As he got back, Ruth's mobile rang. She fished it out of her duffel-coat pocket and fumbled for the button. 'Lydia told me there was a story behind that painting,' she said. 'Sander, her brother, knew it. I guess he took the secret to his grave.'

'No problem. We'll just dig him up.'

She glanced at her phone, swore and jumped back, staring wildly around her.

'What is it?' asked Myles, alarmed.

'Will you look at that?' She held up the screen. A flash SMS text:

Bon appetit, Chickenshit.

They both swung round and surveyed the cafe's clientele.

'Someone you know?'

She glared at the LCD again.

'Damnation! Some kind of practical joke, I suppose.'

She scanned the room methodically now, pausing on each face. If a head was turned away, she waited till it came into view. She stood up, strode across to the bar and stalked back again, fuming. A few diners shrank over their cutlery, waited for her to sit down.

'Well?' asked Myles.

'Nobody I know, as far as I can see.'

'Don't those things tell you who the message is from?'

She glanced back at the screen and scrolled down.

'It's just a number. Look.'

---

47 107.8682

'Weird,' she added. 'Forty-seven could be a country code, I guess.'

'Yeah – Santa Claus or the Grinch, calling from the frozen wastes of Norway. But I doubt if that's a phone number. Be logical. It's lunchtime. Your prankster wanker isn't necessarily here. He's just counting on the fact that you're eating a meal somewhere – anywhere – in town.'

'What makes you think it's a he?' she snapped.

'OK, he or she. Someone with a smattering of French and English, though.'

'Huh?'

'*Bon appetit* and *Chickenshit*.'

'Jesus wept. Hark at Sherlock Holmes here . . .'

Myles played wounded.

'I'm just trying to be helpful, dearie. As I said, it's perfectly possible your message was sent by someone who isn't here.

On the other hand, maybe it *is* someone here. How would I know?'

Again they both looked around, half-expecting the anonymous messenger to call it a day and break cover.

They were out of luck.

No one turned a hair.

'Tap out the number,' he said. 'The number on the screen.'

She did, but there were no telltale ringtones in the restaurant. She put the phone to her ear. 'Dead. It's not a real number, Myles.'

'The word *Chickenshit* doesn't mean anything particular to you?' he ventured.

She scowled. 'What d'you want, a dictionary definition? *Faecal matter excreted by a notoriously dimwitted domestic fowl . . .* How's that?'

'That's not quite what I was getting at. It could be a term of endearment. At a pinch, I mean. In a backhanded kind of way. '

'Look – I don't know what kind of friends or lovers you have, but if *Chickenshit* is a term of endearment in your book then I must be getting seriously out of touch with the latest trends in gay slang.'

He shook his head. 'Jesus. It must be hard on you.'

'What?'

'Being trapped in a woman's body like that.'

She clammed up, putting the chat on hold. She pushed away the rest of her pancakes, uneaten, and sulked. She was fidgety and bad-tempered.

'Shall we get out of here?' she asked after a while. 'I don't feel too good about this.'

'Having a bad hair day?'

'Words *can* hurt, you know,' she chipped back earnestly. 'Besides, it's all this talk of dead Nazis. Holy shit, Myles, I'm getting the creeps, it's so damn doom-laden. Know what I mean?'

'Satan wants you for a storm cloud, baby.'

'Huh?'

'We're dancing with the devil here, Ruth.'

'I think I'd feel better if we were somewhere less public. That's what I think.' She looked up, caught his eye and remembered herself. 'Oh, and Myles . . . sorry?'

They walked down Oudezijds Achterburgwal, past the Hash Marajuana Hemp Museum, the Tattoo Museum and the Erotic Museum, pausing to comment on the window displays of bongs, body art and dildos respectively. She took him by the arm and fell in step with his heavy, rocking gait.

By the canal some children were tossing bread to the gulls. The gulls hung motionless in the air, then lurched down and forward like expert yo-yos to seize the crumbs on the wing.

Further along, Myles covered Ruth's eyes and made prim maiden-aunt twitterings as they passed an old moustachioed drunk blithely pissing into the canal. He was wearing the traditional Dutch costume of red striped smock, black breeches and the black pillbox hat.

'OK,' said Myles decisively. 'You said you wanted a quiet spot, right? Well, I know just the place.'

He steered her towards a nondescript house on the margins of the red-light district.

'Our Lord in the Attic,' he whispered. 'No one ever comes here.'

'What?'

They paid an entrance fee, climbed a series of wide and narrow staircases and pushed open a door into a tiny church, the nave flanked by two tiers of galleries.

The church was empty.

'You shameless tourist, Myles! What is this place?'

'What does it look like?'

'A church, of course!'

'And that's what it is. A clandestine church in a house. Built secretly in this attic by the Catholics at the time of the Alteration in 1578. The city council became Protestant and the Catholics went underground.'

She wrinkled her nose. 'Not really the most appropriate expression, don't you think?'

'Well, no – quite . . . overground, I suppose, or just plain up.'

'Closer to God, Myles. Pulling a fast one on those Protestants. And not exactly discreet either. I mean, they've even got a fucking organ. Look!'

Myles held a finger to his lips.

'A little less of the fuckings if you please, sweetie pie.'

Ruth resisted a genuflection she felt coming on as they passed in front of the altar. The impulse displaced. She watched aghast as her finger described a sketchy cross on her chest. It had a life of its own. *I'm turning into a Catholic*, she thought. *I wasn't even brought up a Papist, I'm not even a rotten backslider, but here we go.*

It must be the incense – something in the air . . .

They sat down on three red chairs in the first row, Ruth on one, Myles spreading his ample buttocks across the other two on the flying-buttress principle. She glanced behind her, then up at the two wooden galleries on either side.

No one about.

'So where were we?' she said.

'The third label.'

'Remind me. What did it say?'

'Alt Aussee to Munich Collecting Point. Mean anything to you?'

'Sure. Linz didn't exist, except on paper. Hitler had to store all the clobber he pinched somewhere. And it had to be somewhere safe, what with the Second World War raging on all over the place. It had to be safe, it had to be difficult to find, it had to be dark. And the temperature and humidity had to be constant, if you didn't want to end up with a mountain of soggy, mouldy canvas.'

'Somewhere like a salt mine . . .'

'Somewhere like Alt Aussee. Near Salzburg, isn't it? Come to think of it, the name of the town itself must mean salt mountain.'

'Near Salzburg, yes. The Salzkammergut, a swanky summer resort way up in the Alps. Alt Aussee's a giant complex of chambers nearly two kilometres inside the mountain. When Hitler's henchmen first investigated the place they even discovered a little secret chapel in there – just like this one – with religious oil paintings. The pictures were in good condition, so they knew they were onto a good thing. Of course, they had to kit the place out and everything. Then along came the Führer's stuff on little choo-choo trains that ran in and out all day long. The Ghent altarpiece, the Bruges *Madonna*, the St Florian Altdorfers and later the Naples masterpieces from Monte Cassino. Some seven thousand oil paintings in all.'

'What happened when they started losing the war?'

'With the German armies retreating, Hitler had a scorched-earth policy. The local Gauleiter at Alt Aussee, a guy called Eigruber, took the policy a little too literally. He tried to blow up the mines along with everything in them. Kaltenbrunner, the SS intelligence chief, only managed to stop him in the nick of time. So instead of blasting the world's art treasures to kingdom come, they blasted the mines shut, sealing the stuff in.'

'The third label's a US army label, right?'

'The American Third Army. They were the guys who stumbled on Alt Aussee. They also found the Einsatzstab Reichsleiter Rosenberg records for the collection in Neuschwanstein castle. It wasn't just paintings. There was sculpture, armour, furniture, books – you name it. They commandeered the old Nazi Party buildings in Munich, calling them – your starter for ten?'

'The Munich Collecting Point.'

'Correct! All the stuff was bundled off there. A massive task, and it took bloody ages. They created three classes for works of art works. Class A for works stolen from public and private collections. Class B for works where some compensation had been paid by the Nazis. Class C for works belonging to the

German nation in the US zone. The Yanks tried to take the Class C works back to the States for safe keeping.'

'Hey – *safe keeping* – haven't I heard that word before somewhere?'

'You certainly have, dear. Our old wise custodian again. They were stopped in their tracks by a protest called the Wiesbaden Manifesto. The last thing the Americans really wanted was to be seen to be behaving in precisely the same way as the naughty Nazis, even though some dickheads were sorely tempted.'

There was a slight creak in the gallery above.

They both looked up, waited for it to repeat itself.

It didn't.

The coast was clear.

'These timber buildings are alive, I'd swear,' he said. 'All it needs is a little temperature difference and you get these tiny shifts and shivers in the joists and beams. Expansions, contractions. Crick – crack – creak!'

Ruth rubbed her chin. 'The van der Heyden – Lydia's painting – ' she began.

'The NK-Collection painting, sweetie. It's nobody else's for the moment.'

'Point taken. But, whosever it is, in the American classification system it ranks as Class B, right?'

'Yup. Where some payment had been made, the idea was that receipts could be settled at a later date, possibly as a charge against war reparations payments. In the end Class B goods were mostly restituted, though it took time.'

'Quite. Here we are over half a century later, still trying to clear up the goddamn mess.'

'The funny thing is,' he went on, a new note of intrigue in his voice, 'by Hitler's standards – or those of Posse, the Linz director – the van der Heyden wouldn't have been a Class B art work at all.'

'How come?'

'Remember the Linz classmark? Linz N° AR 6927. I looked into the Linz and ERR records and that's not a classmark they used for paintings at all. Remember, Hitler didn't just have paintings in the Alt Aussee salt mine. AR 6927 was part of a small private hoard of artefacts that the Führer was keeping to one side.'

'What kind of artefacts?'

'That's what I'd like to know too. The key records for this were found in a storeroom at Schloss Banz near Bamberg after the war, kept there by Baron Kurt von Behr, one of Rosenberg's jackals. To crack this particular little nut, either you or I will have to get onto any surviving members of the OSS or the MFAA.'

'The what?'

'Sorry – more codes ... The Americans' Office of Strategic Services and the Monuments, Fine Arts and Archives Section.'

Ruth went over to the side of the altar and lit a votive candle, dropping a coin into the tin box. She placed the candle in the little cylindrical sconce.

'I think it's time we took another look at that painting,' she said, turning to catch Myles's eye.

'So do I. And I'll tell you something else. Remember we said that Goering was the first to take an interest in the van der Heyden, via Miedl? Well, Goering, of course, committed suicide at Nuremberg, but his wife didn't. In April 1951 she turned up in her best Sunday frock at the Munich Collecting Point, in Lane Faison's office. He was the American director of the Collecting Point. She wanted to claim a little fifteenth-century Flemish *Madonna*. She made out it was a gift to her and not her husband, from the city of Cologne. And while she was at it, she mentioned the van der Heyden. Claimed it was hers too.'

'Our van der Heyden? – Sorry! I mean *nobody's* van der Heyden?'

'None other. The whole thing's down in black and white in Faison's diary. Nothing came of it, of course. As far as they were concerned, the whole incident was just a bad joke.'

'Conclusions . . .' said Ruth. She came back to her seat and sat sideways on, tucking one leg under the other. 'Miedl, Goering, Hitler, Frau Goering – they all knew something we don't. That would seem obvious. However, they're not going to be much help to us, unless we invest in a ouija board or the services of a Nazi-friendly medium. Scheele, on the other hand, *is* alive and here in Amsterdam, though he must be pretty long in the tooth. And if he's so keen to get his hands back on the painting, he might just have an inkling what it's all about.'

'Maybe your Lydia does too.'

Ruth shook her head categorically.

'It has sentimental value for her, that's all. We've talked the whole thing through and I'd swear to it. After all, it was painted by her ancestor, wasn't it? I've been trying to track down his letters, by the way, but no joy. I'm beginning to think she just dreamed them up. Hey, Myles, weren't you going to tell me something about Scheele? About what he does?'

'Oh, sure. It's no longer diamonds. That whole industry's in turmoil, anyway, with Angolan blood diamonds fouling up the market. No, he got out of that some years ago. Liquidated his assets. He's one of the big investors in the docklands regeneration scheme here in Amsterdam. Conference centres. Marinas. Parks. Museums. Housing blocks. You've seen what's going up?'

'Sure. I went to the official opening of the new passenger terminal in the harbour. Pretty impressive. A lot of stackola must've gone into that.'

'The whole development adds up to some half a billion euros, no less. Presumably Scheele isn't short of pin money.'

'Rich enough to have a chauffeur?'

'His chauffeur could have a chauffeur.'

Ruth clapped her hands and held them clenched together to

her breast. 'Hey, aren't we serious here today, Myles? I mean, listen to us! None of the usual office banter about hanky-panky in the photocopying room, or who ground Viagra into Cabrol's coffee. I feel so grown up, all of a sudden. I just wish I'd brought my camera. We're being *serious*!'

He looked at her in surprise.

'If we can't be serious in a church, where can we be? By the way, who'd you light that candle for?'

'I dunno. You – me – Lydia – the world. I keep getting these inexplicable religious impulses. Some kind of genetic twitch, a throwback to my forefathers. Are you a believer, Myles?'

'I've been vaccinated. Tell me, did you find out anything about van der Heyden himself?'

'Nope. I will now, though. I can't wait. Just as soon as we're back at the Rijksmuseum.'

'You might make some headway from home. Try the Documentation Information System on the Intranet. You've got an access code?'

She nodded. 'Should we tell Cabrol?'

'He's away at one of those CODART congresses. A curators' do in The Hague. I don't know that it's a good idea to say anything right now. He'd wonder what the hell we're playing at. The van der Heyden's not part of our current remit. We're only up to E.'

'That's discrimination.'

'What is?'

'Discrimination on grounds of alphabetical position. If Lydia's painting had been a Dürer, she'd have got it back much sooner.'

'True, or Scheele would've got it back. Perhaps that's a point worth making. In the meantime, let's just see what we turn up. Somehow, I don't think Cabrol would take too kindly to the idea of having a couple of lone riders on the team.'

Nine

$\mathcal{M}$r Moon leaned forward as far as his pot belly would allow and inspected the galley hatch. He had been glancing at it all morning from his bookshop window in a desultory kind of way and at last curiosity had got the better of him. Despite the angle of his upper body, his loud tie remained firmly in place, fastened with a sterling silver crocodile clip to his well-laundered sky blue shirt. This was the attitude in which Ruth found him when she cycled back to her barge.

Her brakes squeaked as she pulled up alongside.

She followed the direction of his gaze.

Together they studied the new graffiti that had materialized in the morning, but which she had only seen from a distance and at an acute angle. It was the usual cellulose spray paint, the ugly red of ox blood, but instead of standard tags or cartoon goofs, an odd symbol met her eyes: a six-pointed star, in the centre of which was a circle and, within that, a smaller circle.

Her first thought was of the Jodenster.

'Fascists!' she murmured. Her blood was still curdled by the tales Myles had been telling. She scanned the hull and superstructure from prow to stern.

No swastikas. No slogans. Nothing to confirm or deny her initial impression.

Mr Moon slowly shook his head. 'I don't think so,' he said with his round, lingering vowels. He turned the impassive spectacle of his round face upon her.

'Six points,' she insisted. 'That's the Star of David.'

'You Jewish?'

'No.'

'See what I mean. Not yellow, neither. Then you got two little circles. That's an old one, that is.'

'An old what?'

'Symbol, an old symbol. Not same as Star of David. A circle on a hexagram. An' sometimes you got a cross thingy on top. I got plenty pictures in shop.'

'Show me, will you?'

'Sure thing! But not now.'

'Are you closing early?'

'No, not me. It's you – you got visitors.'

He raised a dumpy forefinger perpendicularly, the flesh pinched in above the knuckle by an exotic silver ring, then aimed it forwards like a flintlock.

The wooden hatch-board to the back cabin was gaping open.

She cursed and pushed her bike against a tree.

'You want I come with you?'

They crept up the gangplank, craning to peer through the skylight and ducking to take in the portholes. She signalled silence and listened at the open hatch.

At first nothing, then running water and a metallic clatter.

She and Mr Moon exchanged a glance.

'I call cops?' he whispered.

'Maybe – maybe in a minute. First, let's see. If it really is an intruder, we'll just slam the hatch shut and padlock him in.'

She lay down flat on her belly and poked her head through the hatch. 'Come on!' she yelled. 'Who the hell's there? What are you doing on my boat?' Her voice shook, surprising even herself. She felt an unpleasant tingle of fear and outrage.

A smallish figure appeared silhouetted in the galley doorway.

The person was drying a cup on a tea towel.

'Don't you ever do the washing up?' said a woman's voice.

'I promised myself I wouldn't, but then I had to in the end.' She moved forward into the light. 'Ruth – are you all right?'

'What on earth are you doing here, Jojo?'

'You said I could! I told you I loved your boat and you said I could come here whenever I want, day or night. Don't you remember anything? You gave me a key.' She climbed one step of the ladder and spotted Mr Moon. 'Oh, hi there! Ruth – aren't you going to introduce me to your friend?'

Below deck, two plump black girls in identical sloppy joe homeknits perched on the narrow leatherette saloon sofa. They giggled nervously in unison when Ruth came in.

'I brought the twins, my brother's girls. I hope you don't mind. They were just dying to see inside! They've never been on board a houseboat before.'

'Be my guest,' said Ruth wearily and plonked herself down.

This little incident had given her an unwelcome shot of adrenalin that now had nowhere to go. She wanted to say something mordant but couldn't bring herself to.

Jojo was just being Jojo.

There was something so unDutch about dropping in unannounced – letting yourself in, making yourself at home – that it was positively flattering. It implied a depth of friendship that cut across all divides. It was as if she'd been accepted into the great black sorority that proliferated outside the inner-city limits in the gritty quadrant called the Bijlmer or simply Zuidoost – south-east – in Reigersbos or Ganzenhoef. And, as ever, Maarten's shadow was between them, his arms slung lazily round both girl's shoulders, the undying link in the human chain.

It was funny how history, writ large and small, went about making more history. If the British hadn't given the Dutch Suriname in exchange for Manhattan island; if the Dutch hadn't shipped their slaves there from Elmina Castle in Ghana; if Suriname hadn't suffered political and economic troubles since independence – well, New York would be New Amsterdam, and Jojo wouldn't be here.

If, if, if . . .

This was history on the back pedal. Paradoxically, Zuidoost had become like an American ghetto now.

Jojo's work at the community centre was in the social vanguard, fighting prejudice and mastering the delicate balancing act between immigrant assimilation and the preservation of ethnic identity. The last time she was on the barge she'd thrown a paranoid fit, ripping up Ruth's copy of *De Telegraaf* before her very eyes: unbeknown to Ruth, the paper had a history of immigrant bashing.

Yes, Jojo was one of the climbers, the idealists, the militants. She was so unlike the two dozy lumps on the sofa, so unlike Ruth herself. Her small, athletic body and agile mind were built for decisive action, for getting things done – most recently, lobbying for democratic consultation over the new urban renovation project in the Bijlmer.

Ruth put 'Whistler and His Dog' on the Dansette, a 1913 recording by Arthur Pryor's Band. It was a catchy tune that most people got into. The twins just looked bored. They began scanning through the CDs, heads cocked sideways, but nothing seemed to grab them there either. 'Ain't you got any Youssou N'dour?' one of them asked. There was a note of teasing, of adolescent mockery. Ruth's musical tastes were being stamped uncool. Discrimination, she thought, takes a thousand forms.

'Used to,' she replied. 'I really liked the new version of 'Thiapa Thioly'. But, you know – when he wrote the official soccer anthem for FIFA – that was so naff. I just felt he'd kind of sold out.'

The girl sat down again and shut up.

Ruth beamed.

'Pepsi, anyone?' she asked.

They drank and Ruth sketched out the Lydia situation, play-acting the old girl in such a way that Jojo was in stitches. They talked boats and visited the engine room. They turned the pages of the old photo album, showing the Luxemotor's refurbishment, 'Before' and 'After'. Maarten hard at work with the wire wool. Ruth scrubbing the deck. 'Home at last!': the happy couple, hugging and clutching a magnum of champagne, waiting unblinkingly for the lazy self-timer on the camera. That was the day, nearly a decade ago, they finally berthed at the Prinsengracht.

The twins got bored and sidled back to the CDs.

Ruth closed the album and squeezed Jojo's shoulder affectionately.

'I never thought of showing you these before,' she said.

Jojo nudged her in the ribs and laughed dryly. 'We're getting as bad as his poor old mum and dad! But don't you think it's about time we – you know – moved on? Decent intervals, and all that. Not that either us could ever find another Maarten, of course . . .'

Ruth sighed. 'It's not Maarten that's stopping me. It's me. I can't explain it. My clock's just kind of stopped.'

'I'd noticed. You haven't exactly been burning the candle at both ends.'

'That always struck me as impracticable. I mean, to light both ends you'd have to hold the candle horizontally and then you'd just get hot wax all over your knees. See what I mean?'

'So what do you do with the candle?'

'Don't ask. Frankly, Jojo, I'm turning into some kind of hermit. I mean, I live off hard-boiled eggs and potato crisps, and I don't seem to be destined to meet anyone these days apart from geriatrics and pansies. Anyway, I always thought you weren't supposed to force these things. Isn't that what they say? The trouble is, the less you force things, the less there's anything left to force. Maybe I have moved on. On . . . out . . . one step beyond . . . Maybe I've just got used to being a free spirit. *I think therefore I'm single . . .*'

'You do what you like, dear,' said Jojo, 'but just remember, God helps those who help themselves.'

'If God could give me a little money tree in a plastic tub, that would be just dandy. *Please*, darling God?' Ruth raised her eyes and put her hands together in prayer.

'Problems?'

'The usual. Too much month left at the end of the money. I've maxed out my credit card and – as you know – the pay's zip all. I'll get over it. My fault, I guess, for going half-time.'

'Tell you what. Kill two birds with one stone. Why not find yourself a rich sugar daddy?'

'Now you're talking. What about you?' She tickled the black girl under the chin. 'Come on now, tell all! How's Jojo's little love life?'

Jojo buried her face in her hands then looked up. She managed to grin broadly and bite her lower lip at the same time. Some big news was in the offing. There was a dramatic pause before she spoke. 'Well, dear, as it happens I *have* met this man . . .' she began huskily, drawing the confidence out for all it was worth.

'A real live one?'

The black girl nodded eagerly.

'Jojo, you sly little flirt!'

'No, don't! Stop it! Don't say anything!' the black girl pleaded, gurgling with unstoppable laughter. 'Nothing's *happened*! I've just met him, that's all. At work. He's got a certain *je ne sais quoi*, I have to admit.'

'Is he one of ours or one of yours?'

'Oh, one of yours definitely. I wouldn't want to hold up the integration programme, would I?'

'Well, come on then! Tell me all about him!'

' 'No, I won't, Ruth! Really, I can't! I've said far too much already. I'm so stupid. And, anyway, I don't know anything about him. Not a thing. I don't even know if the guy fancies me.'

'But of course he does, Jojo. You've got that special whatsit about you that they all go for.'

'What – tits?' Jojo cupped her own breasts as if she were weighing mangos.

'Oh, now look, scumbag! You've made me spill my Pepsi.' Ruth rubbed the spillage into the knees of her jeans and sucked her fingers. 'Let's get to the point. Am I going to meet him or not?'

Jojo took an operatic breath to regain her composure and geared back to her low confiding tone. 'We're having a *parrr-tee.*'

'A party?'

'Yes, a parrr-tee. Remember parties? Music – laughter – letting the good times roll? Next Wednesday at the community centre offices. It's not going to be anything special. There's a boring old meeting first, but you can skip that. I do hope you'll come, Ruth. You need to get out of yourself a bit more.'

'Don't say that. If I got out of myself, I wouldn't know where to go.'

'Well, get *into* yourself, then. Oh God, that sounds so New-Age, doesn't it? I didn't mean it to come out like that.'

The excitement was all too much. Ruth reached back for a pre-rolled spliff from her tin on the narrow ledge under the porthole. Jojo stayed her hand and nodded in the direction of the twins.

'We don't want to go corrupting modern youth, do we, now?' she said in her spoof Mamma-of-the-Savannahs drawl. 'Dey got *all* deir lives ahead of 'em, and dey'll need all de help dey can get. Lord knows, I should never have brought dem to dis sink of iniquity in de first place!'

Later, when they'd gone, Ruth put on Count Basie, plugged the phone line into her computer and accessed the Intranet. The Institute for Cultural Heritage, ICH, was in the process of compiling a database of possessions and acquisitions on the Netherlands Collection Network. She keyed in 'van der Hyeden' and 'No Matches' flashed up. She was about to give up when she noticed her mistake. Amazing how literal search engines are, how archly intolerant of human error.

She tried again, correcting the letter reversal: 'van der Heyden'.

Johannes van der Heyden (1731–90)

NK-collection: *Recumbent Woman with Mimosa*
 (oil on copper, 91 x 63 cm, NK 352)
Portfolio of sketches (Rijksmuseum Library, Van Jl. 3051)
Works in other collections: No data

Little information about the life of Johannes van der Heyden has come down to us, and few of his works. His family appears to have originated in the province of North Brabant. His father, Arnoldus, moved to Amsterdam to become a relatively well-to-do pharmacist and supplier of artists' pigments and binding media. Johannes was expected to take over the family business, and did so reluctantly. Passing references to him in the papers of successful contemporary artists (van der Mijn, Jan van Os and Jan Ekels) suggest that his true ambition was to live by his painting, though he lacked the necessary skill and training to fulfil this aspiration – to which, moreover, his father was vigorously opposed. He is known to have admired the work of the wealthy painter, timber merchant and collector, Cornelis Ploos van Amstel (1721–1798) and to have engaged in a now lost correspondence with van Amstel. *Recumbent Woman with Mimosa* (his only extant oil painting) is executed with a meticulous, if cold, realism reminiscent of Hendrick Keun or Isaak Ouwater, but the composition is descriptively diffuse and unresolved. The surviving handful of earlier sketches are naïve and of indifferent quality. A marginal figure at best, van der Heyden's ambitions apparently came to nothing in the clannish, competitive and sophisticated professional art world of eighteenth-century Amsterdam. Nothing is known of his later career.

Bernard Cabrol

Ruth stared at the name at the end of the article and rubbed her chin.

'Little information.'

'Nothing is known.'

The sudden growl of a passing motorbike roused her and she clicked through to her email browser. Two new items.

First:

Dear Ruth,

Things are very quiet in Driebergen. The garden's thick with snow and we put out bread and nuts for the birds and squirrels twice a day. They're so grateful. One little robin even pecks at the window to get attention! Mum had the endoscopy and got the all-clear, thank God, but they still have to remove the gallstones. They hope to slot her in some time in early March. We went for a trudge in the woods last week and found a barn owl that had tangled its foot in some old fishing line by the lake. It was dead, poor thing. You wouldn't believe the wingspan of those creatures! Since then we've hardly been out, except to the shops. The wind is bitterly cold. One thing I will say for these long winter days is that we've vastly improved our backgammon! Would you fancy coming over for a weekend? We both miss you and Mum gets so restless. The logs are nice and dry in the woodshed and we had the chimney in your old room swept, so we could get a good blaze going. What do you say? The Verbruggers just called byyyyy. (Sorry! The keys stick from time to time, and the Delete key's buggered!) They send their best wishes and Max whimpers when-ever we show him your photo on the mantelpiece. I think he's got fleas again. Those damn collars never work.

Love, Dad

She glanced at her wall calendar and its grid of little white squares. They were virtually all blank apart from the phases of the moon and one dental appointment (which she'd missed accidentally on purpose). There was Jojo's knees-up the following Wednesday – not as yet pencilled in – but the rest was a stony silence. Why not? One measly weekend of domestic boredom was hardly a huge bite out of her precious solitude, and in Holland distance was never an issue. Everywhere abutted onto everywhere else, as if the country's founding topographers – Gerardus Mercator and company – had cavalierly ditched the problematic dimension of space.

She fetched a cheese cracker from the tin in the galley and turned to her second email:

I know your little game, Chickenshit. You dance barefoot on the razor's edge. You wander in the labyrinth without Ariadne's thread. Seeing, you do not see. Hearing, you do not understand. Get out while you have the chance. Visit the old woman at your peril. Remember this: like produces like. The elder tree does not produce pears, thorns pomegranates or thistles figs. Man engenders man and beast beast. I beget the light, but darkness too is of my nature. We are approaching the 5th density. Will there be another war in heaven between the angels? Obscurum per obscurius, ignotum per ignotos. Your soul is fouled with corruption, and still you lust after the blackest secret. Not a few have perished on that road. Next time you'll lose more than your precious fucking appetite. Sweet dreams, Chickenshit, and fare thee well. No more monkey business, remember. You wouldn't like the kind of games I play.

47 107.8682

She sat bolt upright, rigid.

'Jesus wept,' she whispered.

Who or what in the name of Jumping Jehosaphat was *that*? Her fingers trembled. A nasty fluttering started in her stomach.

She scrolled back quickly to the email's header:

From: mystery@anonymous.com
To: rbraams@hotmail.com

It had been sent less than an hour earlier and the subject line was blank.

She clicked 'shut down' and the machine went through its motions.

Windows is shutting down.

She sat still for several minutes.

She listened to the forlorn sound of an empty bottle clunking slowly against the hull of the barge.

She waited for her breathing and heartbeat to slow down.

She was shaking with anger. She didn't like being called 'Chickenshit' by someone who hadn't the guts to give his or her name. She didn't like it one little bit. She was scared too. She had never been the victim of intimidation before. To further poison the brew, Myles's speculations churned relentlessly through her mind.

The name 'Scheele' flickered subliminally against the back-cloth of her thoughts.

The police?

One email and one text message hardly seemed to merit it. And – who knows? – perhaps it was some kind of impotent hoax, a jest, a prank, though hardly in the best of taste.

Perhaps the problem would simply go away.

But Bags and her goddamned painting were beginning to leave a nasty aftertaste, as if in themselves they were to blame for all manner of misapprehensions. A beautiful woman sleeping on a couch. A bouquet of mimosa. A man looking out of a window. It was dead and gone. It had all happened one afternoon two and a half centuries ago. Yet the picture was real enough and some scrap of the painter's DNA was still knocking around down there on the Keizersgracht, seriously diluted with jenever gin.

On the cusp of a hostile impulse, she phoned Lydia, but – even as the phone rang, even as she could see the old woman rising arthritically from her chair and making her way into the hall in her own mind's eye – Ruth checked herself, reined herself in, rapidly reviewing her tactics with that odd luminous logic that comes to people in moments of adversity.

'Yes?'

'Lydia, it's Ruth.'

'Oh, my dear, I'd been hoping you would call.'

'Nothing wrong is there?'

'No, nothing at all. I wanted to tell you, the new doctor – the one you found for me – he's marvellous. It's the cats! He says it's the cats.'

'What is, Lydia? What is the cats?'

'My allergy, of course. He did all the tests. I'll have to take them down to the cat sanctuary. It's a pity, of course, but there's nothing else to be done about it. I'd been hoping I could keep at least one or two, but he says it's quite out of the question. But just one wouldn't hurt, would it? Anyway, once the cats are gone, I'll have to have a good spring clean – get all the dust and fluff out of the place – and then my tubes should clear up. Not the asthma, but the allergy. The one doesn't help the other. That's what Dr Luijten says.'

'I see.'

Spiders or cat fur, everyone had their little domestic curse.

The fight suddenly drained out of Ruth.

Lydia was just a sweet old biddy, dotty but not unintelligent, one foot in the grave. She deserved a little fellow-feeling in her sunset years. Ruth felt bad about the surge of animosity and suspicion that had swept over her scarcely a minute beforehand.

'Not that I'm asking for your help,' Lydia went on. 'I wouldn't want to be a burden on you. But I would so like to see you again. We had such a lovely time when we last met, such a nice little chat. It seems so long ago now.'

Ruth glanced at her calendar again. 'It was five days ago.'

'Is that all? Oh, my goodness! Doesn't time fly?'

'Tell me,' Ruth asked, 'have you seen anyone since we last met?'

'No – no one.'

'Are you sure? No visitors?'

'Not a soul, my dear. I'm all alone, as you know.'

Ruth was on her guard again. Could this be forgetfulness? Only that morning she'd witnessed the two callers from across the street. Perhaps it was nothing more than an old woman's pathetic fiction of solitude, a crude play for companionship using any old bait that came to hand.

Who could say?

'I *would* like to talk to you, actually, Lydia,' she said after a thwarted pause. She tried to inject a firm, no-nonsense tone into her voice, a cautious neutrality. 'I'd like to talk to you about certain matters.'

'Then come round – whenever you like. Not for the cats. No, I don't want to trouble you with that. I'll get the social services to see to things. That's what they're there for, after all, isn't it?'

When she'd put the phone down, Ruth did ten press-ups and the same number of sit-ups on the floor.

She was starting to get her act together.

There were various things to be seen to on the barge.

She darned a hole in one of her pullovers, changed the batteries in the radio and jotted down a shopping list. The small galley fridge was empty barring one banana-flavoured yogurt that was way past its sell-by date, the foil lid swelling ominously. Then she switched on the computer again, printed out the threatening email and studied its arcane language. It was erudite, possibly biblical, with a fire-and-brimstone feel to it. She had no idea what the Latin meant. She'd have to look into that. But this was tangible. Every human contact leaves traces, as forensic science knows only too well – and virtual contacts are no exception. This bluster or wickedness was evidence and shouldn't be left hovering in the paperless world of bits and bytes. And when grievance strikes, she noted, system, order and method come to the rescue.

Alles in ordnung, shipshape and Bristol fashion.

Whoever her anonymous emailer was, she was now strangely thankful for one thing. He or she had riled her into life – or at least *liveliness.* There were people who simply got to her like that. For, verily, the one with whom we wrestle doth strengthen our nerves and sharpen our skill, she thought, trying out the biblical style herself. That was the theory, anyway, though it didn't work too well for fish struggling in nets. She, however, was no fish. Through opposition, through conflict, she would beat a path to herself.

It was something like love.

Ten

'Your heating back on in admin?' asked one of the librarians as Myles filled in the order slip.

'Yeah,' said Ruth. 'Still waiting for our brains to thaw out, though.'

The girl took the slip away and Myles sat down at the large oak table. Ruth perched tentatively on a hot radiator, warming her hands and buttocks to the point of physical discomfort.

'So that's where you keep your brains,' Myles remarked.

She raised her middle finger by way of reply.

It was morning and no one else was about. Another day of snow, Siberian winds and mute iron-grey skies. The two of them were ahead of schedule by design. Cabrol and Timmermans wouldn't be around for another hour at least.

'Show me again,' he said, in earnest now, with a brisk beckoning gesture. His face was red, his jaw stiff with cold.

She handed him the printout. He read it in silence and passed it back.

'I didn't know you could send email anonymously,' she said.

He raised his eyebrows. '*Moi non plus.* What're you gonna do about this?'

'What would you suggest?'

'Either it's a nutter or someone putting on a pretty convincing show of being a nutter.'

'Helpful,' Ruth commented, 'but it doesn't answer my question.'

'Well, knowing you, you're not going to be swayed by this guy's fancy rhetoric, so the chances are you'll hear from him again. Unless it's bluff, he seems to know your every move.'

'Helpful *and* reassuring, I must say. Thanks a bunch, Myles.'

'You're not alone, dearie. If he's watching you, he's watching me too. Sorry – *he* or *she*, I should say. We're both in the spotlight of that all-seeing eye.'

'What – even as we speak?'

Instinctively, they both looked over their shoulders, then laughed in unison as their haunted eyes met once again.

The librarian returned with a large portfolio. She placed it carefully on the table and untied the black cloth ribbons. 'Eight drawings in card mounts,' she said. 'Usual rules. Hold them by the mounts. No sneezing, no coughing and no ink pens in the vicinity.'

She returned to her desk on a raised dais and peered at them over her half-moons.

One by one, they turned the big card mounts like rigid pages. The drawings were executed in red iron-oxide chalk. There was a landscape with windmills by the sea and a couple of domestic scenes – a woman sewing while a child played by her side and a man and a woman with wooden pails by a water pump. The other five drawings represented a heavily pregnant woman, standing and recumbent. One of the latter was a nude. Each was signed 'Johannes van der Heyden'.

They studied the sketches in silence, then turned back to the first picture.

'Well?' said Myles.

'It's just as Cabrol said in his entry. "Naïve and of indifferent quality." In my humble opinion, they're bloody awful.'

'The best that can be said for them is that they have a certain freedom.'

'Sure. They're loose, undisciplined and free, as you say – free of any saving graces. I'm talking technique, naturally. In other respects, they're not without charm. There's a certain enthusiasm in the movement of the lines and hatching, granted – he warms to his subject – but absolutely no conception of anatomical correctness, don't you agree? I mean, look at this one. The woman's got one arm longer than the other, her face is a mess, the chair's missing a leg and the perspective's haywire. It's all over the shop.'

Myles nodded, thoughtful. 'He can't draw,' he said quietly after a while.

Silence fell again between them.

Myles's words sank in and Ruth snorted and shrugged her shoulders. 'That's it, exactly! He can't draw. Or he *couldn't* draw, we should say. Because later, when he came to do our *Recumbent Woman with Mimosa*, he *could*. That's the thing. There are lacunae here. This stuff's obviously juvenilia. At some point, Johannes went and got himself an education. Maybe from Cornelis Ploos van Amstel, if he was still around at the time. I'll have to check the dates. But all we have to go on is these eight sketches and the one oil painting. The rest is gaps and holes.'

'Empty frames,' mused Myles. He glanced at his watch. 'Shall we?'

A few minutes later, in the Rijksmuseum stores, they placed the small painting on the inspection easel. Myles found a halogen clip light and trained it directly onto the surface of the picture. The colours of the oils burned forth with a new intensity.

The soft pale blue of the young woman's satin dress was extraordinary. It radiated a sheer silvery sheen where the light caught it from above and fell in such a way over her sleeping form that you could sense rather than see her hips, thighs and knees – the exact alignment and overlap of her slender legs – beneath the elaborate folds.

The texture of her tousled dark hair was equally realistic. It picked up the yellow flames of mimosa in its highlights. There was even one hair that levitated spookily with, Ruth assumed, some kind of static charge.

To her, the picture had changed since they'd last seen it. It had gained in complexity of detail and richness of latent emotion, as if the two characters had gone away for a coffee break and then come back to resume their former poses with slight, barely discernible variations.

She could feel the warmth of the girl's face, the heat of blood and beauty in its deep repose, the vulnerable delicacy of the small naked feet. She could hear her breathing. She guessed at the man's melancholy abstraction, his back to the painter, gazing out wistfully on a street in old Amsterdam. She felt the exact pressure-point on his shoulder where he leaned against the window frame as if she herself were there.

And other details now rose up to seize hold of her attention, her imagination: the grain and knots in the dark wooden floor-boards; the sleeping pigeon on the bell gable across the road, its head sunk into the hollow of the clavicle; the charred log and ashes in the hearth; a stained glass alembic on the mantelpiece.

She got the digital camera out of her bag, took several photographs of the painting and stood back, perplexed.

'Quite a contrast, huh?' she said. 'With the drawings, I mean.'

'You bet. Whatever you think of it compositionally, he's come a long way. The copper support's dead smooth. That's good for fine detailing. He couldn't have done this with canvas or wood. The crudeness of the warp and weft, or the grain, would've got in the way.'

Their eyes met.

'It kind of grows on you, doesn't it?' she said.

He turned the painting round on the easel, scrutinized the tags once again, then wiggled loose all four wedges from the corners, tapped back the wooden back board and lifted the whole paint-ing out of its gilt frame. He put the frame aside, stood the picture back to front on the easel and adjusted the halogen lamp in such a way that the light grazed the surface of the copper plate from one side.

'Well, how about that!' he exclaimed.

Ruth moved forward, straining to see.

'We missed this last time, dammit. I just levered off part of the back board, remember? If I'd had my wits about me, I'd have gone the whole hog.'

The date was there, as before – 1758, scratched in one corner. But in the middle of the copper rectangle was an unusual design: a six-pointed star in the centre of which was a circle and, within that, a smaller circle. To one side of this symbol was a crescent moon; to the other, an oblong bisected by a straight horizontal line. A lengthy sequence of numbers was engraved in a spiral around this central group of symbols and there was another pyramid of numbers above the star.

Ruth gasped and Myles shot her an enquiring look.

'I've got one of these star thingies at home,' she said.

'What – on the barge?'

'On the galley hatch, to be precise. Graffiti. Our local taggers are getting pretty esoteric. Next thing you know, they'll be billing me for royalties.'

'Does it mean anything to you?'

'Sweet FA. I was going to ask Mr Moon, but what with one thing and another I never got round to it.'

'You were going to ask Mr who?'

'What do you make of those figures?' she asked, ignoring his question.

'Christ knows. As you say, it all looks somewhat esoteric. Cagliostro woz 'ere. Take a picture of it, will you?'

Ruth obliged, but twisted her mouth with a look of dissatisfaction as she glanced at the LCD viewfinder. 'Not much resolution, even on Macro.' She took a couple of pictures all the same, then studied the finely scratched design and numerals once again. 'Got a pencil, Myles – an ordinary pencil?'

'Sure.'

She took the painting over to a table and placed it face down. Beside the table, on a wall bracket, was a large roll of silky tissue paper, used for protecting fragile items before storage. She pulled out a length and cut it away with the pair of nail scissors she kept to correct the ravages of her nail biting, then covered the back of the painting with the paper, smoothing it out with the palm of her hand.

'Tape?'

Myles shook his head. But in her bag she found some sticking plasters. She cut them into small adhesive squares to hold the tissue paper in place. Then, using the side of the lead, she depressed the pencil and shaded softly, taking care not to miss a thing.

'Brass rubbing,' said Myles, admiring her inspiration.

'What?'

'I used to do this with my dad on our hols in Norfolk. It's one of those queer English pastimes, like train-spotting or dropping live ferrets down your trousers.'

'I'll have to take your word for that, Myles.'

When she'd finished, they both examined the rubbing. The symbols and digits were clearly visible. Ruth untaped the paper and folded it up neatly. Myles turned the painting round and replaced it on the easel. Then Ruth sat on the floor and hugged her knees while the fat Englishman leaned on the table, gazing down at her.

'I know what you're thinking,' he said after a while.

'Oh yeah?'

'You're thinking: Scheele.'

'Wouldn't you? Who else would warn me off Bags? Apart from the grey bureaucratic machine of the NK-Collection itself, he's the only one with a stake in this thing. But it doesn't make sense.'

'What doesn't.'

'His tactics. They're so off the wall. And anyway, in his place, wouldn't you wait for the outcome of your claim?'

'That might be too late. Especially if you got wind of the fact that one of the supposedly impartial researchers promoting the great cause of restitution was privately hobnobbing with a rival claimant and sharpening up their case.'

'Oh, sod it!' She shook her head in despair. 'So you think I should steer clear of her, do you?' She bit nervously at the nail of her little finger.

'No, I don't,' he said. 'If you want my personal opinion, I think you should stick in with her.'

'Why?'

'To turn up those letters she told you about, for one. The letters van der Heyden wrote himself.'

'Jesus, I've tried, but you haven't seen the state of her place. A tip! That's needle-in-haystack territory, I'm telling you. Oh, and by the way – she's getting shot of her moggies, if you'd like one to keep Sweekieboude company.'

'God forbid.'

'You know, Myles,' Ruth added, gripped by a sudden after-thought, 'Sweekieboude's a really kinky thing to call a cat. I'm not surprised she's always playing up. Where the hell did you get that name from?'

'I've no idea. I just invented it one day. It seemed to fit the cat.'

Ruth stared at him, unconvinced. 'I wonder what she calls you?'

'The Can-Opener, probably. You're changing the fucking sub-ject, dearie.'

'Where were we?'

'Lydia. Is she totally upfront, would you say?' he asked, probing.

'I used to think so. Now I'm not so sure.'

He turned the broad expanse of his back on her – the tartan shirt, the elephant cords – and, taking a handkerchief and penknife out of his pocket, started tinkering with the painting.

'Look, Myles,' she added after a moment's thought, 'cats and OAPs aside, I think we should see Cabrol. At least put some of our cards on the table. There's no harm in us having made certain discoveries. You turn stones and what do you find? Creepy-crawlies. That's part and parcel of the job. The harm arises when you keep the finds to yourself. I mean, OK, there's a devious and possibly significant historical dimension here. And OK, we – or *I*, if you prefer – have apparently put some anonymous weirdo's nose out of joint. But the bureau's designed to handle that kind of resistance, isn't it? The NK-Collection, the Institute for War Documentation, the Ekkart Committee – the whole restitution business is about doing justice before it's too late, and undoing the injustices of the past. We rake over the ashes. We take from some; we return to others. It stands to reason there are going to be losers, and it stands to reason those losers are going to be seriously pissed off. What I mean is, that's legitimate procedure. Why are we nervous about this? Why are we keeping it to ourselves?'

Myles still had his back to her.

He slipped an envelope into his trouser pocket.

He switched off the halogen lamp and looped the flex round his hand. His shoulders hung slack. She couldn't see his face; only the small Romany earring that hung from his right lobe, the sagging hamster pouch of his cheek.

Myles turned and leaned heavily against the wall, as if he were supporting it rather than the other way around.

She noticed that he had reframed the painting.

'On the face of things,' he began slowly, 'you're right. You could lay out your wares. You could even try Cabrol for clearance to collate this case officially. Trouble is, then you really would be jeopardizing yourself. Especially if you went on cosying up to the old girl. Alternatively, you could stay in the shadows and let me put in for this one. Not that there's any particular glory in it, I should add. I mean, we're not exactly

Carl Bernstein and Bob Woodward, are we? Nor, let's face it, is this Bags-gate. Another possibility is for both of us to sit tight, to ride at anchor.'

He looked away, mulling things over.

'Is something wrong, Myles?'

Their eyes met. She'd never seen him so moody.

'Maybe,' he said guardedly.

'Well, what?'

'You said you think we should see Cabrol. What makes you think he can't see us?'

'Huh?'

'There's something not quite right about all this, Ruth. Cabrol's au fait with the territory. The ICH Intranet entry on van der Heyden was by him, right? Plus, he did the docketing. I checked on claim schedules and this one simply hasn't been assigned. It's in some kind of eerie administrative limbo. What if he's keeping it for himself?'

'Why would he do that?'

'Your guess is as good as mine.'

'You could always ask him,' she pointed out.

He folded his arms and half-closed his eyes as if trying to view a ship on the horizon. 'I might just do that.' He sighed eventually. 'Oh, and by the way I found out something else that may just interest you.'

He pulled a small card out of his briefcase.

'What's that?'

'Scheele's address.'

Ruth chuckled and stood up, raking the hair back off her forehead. 'What d'you want me to do – knock on his door with a "Chickenshit" conference badge on my lapel? Assuming he's the nutter, of course.'

'You do what you like, sweetie. I just thought it might amuse you to know where he hangs out.'

She glanced at him doubtfully and took the card.

It was an address in the Keizersgracht.

'Hell's bells, Myles,' she whispered. 'He's Lydia's next-door neighbour!'

'Opposite,' he corrected. 'The other side of the canal.'

'No wonder . . .'

'No wonder what?'

'Huh? Oh – just something she said.'

Ruth thought back to her first time at Lydia's. 'Why do you want to leave?' she'd asked the old girl. 'I don't like the view,' she'd replied.

Eleven

Wednesday, 6 February, 7.35 p.m.
Line 52.

Ruth pulled the beret down over her ears and buried her nose in her cashmere scarf, recycling the dewy warmth of her breath.

On impulse, she began running to warn him but soon gave up. Now there seemed no point. A higher power had decreed things thus. And, anyway, Maarten would have laughed at her childish forebodings, her unsubstantiated fears. 'Ruth, baby,' he would have soothed, 'don't get yourself in a stew. Trust me! I'm a big boy now. I can take care of myself.'

His pride and joy was a vintage Brough Superior SS100, the Silver Ghost of motorcycles. It was the same model that had done for Lawrence of Arabia on the road to Clouds Hill. His pet name for it was George VII. Wide open, it went like a cannonball out of hell. The legendary Englishman claimed to have raced Bristol fighters on the beast, as Maarten himself was fond of informing people.

Ruth stopped in her tracks and bent down, hands on thighs, to get her wind back. Her knees nearly gave way. Her forehead was prickly with sweat. She had a stitch in her side and the tears welled in her eyes. She straightened up again and her breath condensed into whorls of vapour that flourished and died on the air.

A breeze chafed in from the North Sea and blew back the

spiky marram grass that crested the dunes. It flung waves of fine sand across her path that stung her cheeks.

The black dot of the bike disappeared forever round a bend in the road. Maarten had neglected to fasten the buckles on the leather panniers. Now his papers were everywhere, strewn and flattened on the icy road or frolicking in the wind like maddened flocks of white geometrical Escher birds. She grabbed one as it looped the loop in front of her. It was covered in numbers and hastily scrawled emblems. It made no sense and only served to deepen her frustration.

There were certain doors that would remain shut fast to her till the crack of doom.

A perfect pillar of black smoke had begun to rise over the dunes, undisturbed by the wind. It shot up with improbable energy. It was like one of the tropical twisters or cyclones she'd seen on TV, but, crazy as the thought was, this was no mere weather phenomenon, however freakish and extreme – of that she felt sure. It was alive, it was brutal and it was coming her way. At a certain altitude it hit an invisible ceiling and rolled out fast in all directions while losing none of its density, like coloured oil accelerating through water. Then the lukewarm winter daylight was snuffed out and the sounds of man and nature, of which she had been half-aware – the sepulchral bassoon of a ship's foghorn, the bleak cries of gulls and oyster-catchers – suddenly stopped, dumbfounded.

Despite her exertions, a chill penetrated her bones.

Should she go on or turn back?

The horizon was slashed by a final sword of light. The road itself was now barely visible. She was a child again, ignorant and bewildered. As the panic rose in her breast, a hand seized hers. It tightened on her wrist.

'Come with me,' said a thin voice, and she followed.

In the twilight, she saw that her guide was wearing breeches, spatterdashes, a rough scarlet frock coat and a grey wig and was carrying a three-sided cocked hat under the other arm.

'Where are we going?' she asked.

The head turned and Lydia's wizened features – the watery marbles of the eyes, the thin blue nose – emerged like a bad joke from under the eighteenth-century man's wig. The wig had been pulled down over her woollen rapper's cap. The old woman was grinning, baring her stained dentures.

'The question, my dear,' hissed Bags, 'is not *where* are we going? but *who* is going *where*?'

Her breath smelled of gin and rotting meat. A jewelled brooch in the form of the crescent moon glittered at her throat.

Ruth wriggled and shook her wrist free from the old crone's clutches, then scrambled away up the slight sandy incline on the bank of the road.

Somewhere in the gloom she heard voices.

Lucas and Clara Aalders pushed past her, unaware of her presence. They were arguing in harsh whispers, gesticulating angrily.

Then Myles appeared feet first from above, his considerable bulk floating down under the splendid cloche of a pale blue satin parachute. He made a textbook landing and bowed ceremoniously. As the fabric of the parachute crumpled to earth behind him, he opened his clenched fist and a tiny clockwork Hitler goose-stepped and Sieg-Heiled around the palm of his hand in a slim bar of light that broke for a few seconds from the canopy of smoke.

He closed his fist and opened it again like a magician.

The spotlight tripped back in.

This time he held a miniature dead owl with slashes of blood on its white feathered breast.

Ruth heard cries of dismay and recognized her own parents' voices. She looked about, but no one was there.

Myles took one step back, smiled and toppled into a pit in the ground.

Behind her there was a scream, a thud, then a clattering sound. She spun round on the ball of her heel.

She strained to see what was coming.

A huge rickety staircase rose up into the sky towards the central column of smoke, and something or someone – a nondescript boulder of flesh and bone – was tumbling down it. The object thundered to a halt at her feet and unrolled. It was Lydia again. She was no longer in period costume. She was stark naked. Her wrinkled paps sagged down to the loose white skin of her belly. A six-pointed star, within which nestled two concentric circles, had been branded between them.

Lydia stood up and steadied herself with a hand on the newelpost. Her face and limbs were bruised. She was panting. On closer inspection, her hair and eyebrows were crawling with tiny orbatid spiders. There was a look of glee in her bloodshot eyes. She pointed a bony finger up the stairs. Her voice crackled with excitement. 'He's up there, my dear! He's there!'

'Who?' Every muscle in Ruth's body clenched.

'Who do you think – the man in the moon? He's been up there all along. I told you before, you silly goose! He creeps in at night. He comes when he thinks I'm not there. He's up to no good. He comes for a good old rummage.'

'And what's he looking for?' asked Ruth.

Lydia opened her mouth but there was silence.

Her mouth remained open, exposing her blotchy tongue and tonsils.

Then a single glottal click echoed sharply around her. It was closely followed by another, and another.

Click, clack, clickety-click.

A-one, A-two, A-one-two-three-four . . .

Soon there was regular rhythm to it, a snappy jazzy syncopation.

Clickety-click, clickety-clack; wick-wock, wickety-wack!

The tempo faltered and collapsed. Ruth felt a tug like inertial deceleration. The clicking slowed, deepened and opened out in pitch. Her body rocked with a loose motion. Her head lolled sideways and tapped up against something hard and cold.

There were people milling everywhere. She heard their voices. She felt the warmth of them, their patient waiting. All around was the odour of their damp winter clothing, their individual smells. They swayed against her. They bumped and rubbed her knees. A great multitude, whom no man could number. And someone, Christ knows who, bent close to her ear.

She could feel the breath, the hand on her shoulder, the urgent shake . . .

She blinked against the invasive neon light.

The shaker was an elderly black man with curly grey hair and an apologetic smile.

The train was at a standstill.

'Terminus, lady! It's the end of the line. If you stay sitting there, you'll end up back in town.'

'Oh, thanks!' She drew the palms of her hands down over her face, stirring the blood. 'Shit! My body clock must be telling me to hibernate.'

Some of the standing people smiled at her and at each other. She put on a brave front, though the little hell of her dream was still nagging her back.

The train doors opened and the crowd surged off.

The sign over the platform read 'Zuid/WTC'.

She got up, yawned and followed the stairs and passageways to Line 50.

She was just in time for the connecting train.

RAI – Overamstel – van der Madeweg . . .

The old picture-postcard Amsterdam had been left trailing behind. A satellite metropolis took its place under the amber grids and necklaces of sodium lamps. It had mushroomed on an old polder of reclaimed land in the late sixties and seventies. Road bridges. Viaducts. Underpasses. And the first zones of slab blocks, honeycomb repositories for humanity, rectangular concrete boxes for the living, dropped haphazardly from the developers' cranes onto the featureless terrain.

This was the Bijlmer or Zuidoost, the city's south-eastern extension.

It was the most notorious failed housing project in the Netherlands, a monument to group-think, a place without rhyme or reason, where thousands of poor saps had been cast down to live out the rest of their days, not knowing quite what had hit them.

This was where Dutch society touched bottom.

Housing-wanted ads in the Amsterdam papers always ended with 'Geen ZO': No Zuidoost.

The train rumbled on: Duivendrecht–Strandvliet/ArenA . . .

The floodlamps were burning white at ArenA, the new 50,000-seat Amsterdam stadium, home to the Ajax football club, and here investment had poured in unstintingly. A state-of-the-art development zone now extended its electronic tentacles: American-style clusters of high-rises and business parks, urban-fringe tech industries, designer plazas and atriums, the Pathé, the Heineken/Mojo concert venue, theme shopping in the malls and megastores of the Arena Boulevard and Villa Arena, the Transferium commuter car park, and so it marched on. A brave new digitally specced world, magicked up from the architects' and planners' neo-platonic imaginations and graphic interfaces into glass, concrete, steel.

Ruth had cycled out this way one summer's day and was familiar with the principal landmarks: the KPM Telecom centre, the Sparklerweg zone, the glitzy BMW dealerships and the six towers of the Bijlmer 'can' or prison, which were only a little more forbidding than the district's infamous ten-storey deck-access housing units.

Yes, here it was, somewhere in the vicinity: the dear old Bijlmer. Behind the window dressing were some seven square kilometres of instant dysfunctional ghetto.

Just add a few thousand immigrants – preferably those who had never wanted to live there in the first place – stir, bring to the boil and serve.

She got off the train at the elevated station. A smell of chewing gum in the air from the Sportlife factory. She walked a few blocks, hurried through the muggers' paradise of a rundown shopping precinct and took the lift to the community centre offices on the top floor of an unpretentious block.

She crossed the threshold and someone whisked away her coat, scarf and beret.

Thanks.

A plastic beaker of mulled red wine materialized in her hand.

Thanks again.

A quick sweep told her Jojo wasn't around.

She made a beeline for the buffet and nibbled a pretzel then picked at the tab on the foil wrapper of a cheese Apericube with the stump of her nail.

She felt suddenly glum and uneasy.

As parties go, this one didn't augur well. It was an open-plan office and nothing could disguise the fact. The furniture had been shunted up against the walls and a few token balloons and paper garlands hung optimistically from the ceiling. But what had she been expecting, the Gatsby mansion?

A couple of dozen ordinary folk lounged around talking shop and the Xerox machine was still churning away in one corner. Its green scanner strobed back and forth under the smudged plastic lid.

Nobody paid her any attention.

She circulated.

She glanced at the little melting pot around her – Surinamese, Moroccans, Turks, Chinese, Dutch – but shied away if eyes happened to meet. An old Marvelettes number jingled out of the sound system. She sucked her cheeks against her teeth. She felt like a gate-crasher.

Self-effacement and protective colouring seemed the right

survival strategies under the circumstances, at least until Jojo deigned to clock in.

She hovered around the cork-tiled walls, pretending to be interested in the in-house petitions and posters. One of the posters showed three figures dressed like astronauts picking through the rubble of a building. The caption read: *The Men from Mossad: they're not looking for daisies.* Another, also against a background of debris and flames: *Depleted Uranium: the Disaster after the Disaster. When will the stonewalling stop?*

She took a few steps back and surveyed the whole wall.

All the notices seemed to be harping on much the same theme, though she couldn't be bothered to give the matter much thought or search for a common denominator.

She helped herself to salted cashew nuts.

She sipped the warm cinnamon-flavoured wine.

She looked round as another mini in-crowd bustled into the room. Jojo wasn't amongst them. A dark unshaven man in the group of newcomers was chatting to several people in turn. He argued a point with one, made polite noises to another. He turned round to help a woman off with her winter sheepskin coat.

Ruth lowered her head and picked thoughtfully at the chunk of pink-tinted lemon in her wine. It sank, then bobbed up again. She fished it out and bit off a corner of the tart peel just for something to do. She didn't quite know what was happening. Her face felt hot. There was no doubt in her mind at all.

It was him.

She glanced over once again, trying to be casual about it.

The mop of black hair, the lean unshaven face, tortoiseshell glasses and tired deep-set eyes; the Western-cut plaid jacket, rust brown with wide mouton-trimmed collar and lapels and the word 'Cisco' embroidered in pale blue chenille letters on the back.

The Cisco Kid in person.

She put him in his late thirties.

He took off his jacket and draped it over a wire hanger on the clothes rail beside the door. He looked ill at ease now, in his white polo-neck, black jeans and suede desert boots, as if the event called for smartness and he'd risen dutifully to the occasion, but this wasn't really his bag at all.

A large black man in an ill-fitting striped suit started talking to him in a confidential manner, conducting his monologue with big orchestral motions of his arms. The Kid stared abstractedly at his boots as he listened, hands in trouser pockets, one shoulder held higher than the other, as if he was afraid of something. The thought struck her that there was something defeated about this man, some slight infirmity or flaw which accounted for his reserve. His attention was undivided, but the rest was rationed, withheld. Her sense of him was presumptuous and based on no more than a few seconds' observation, if that. But it came in such a flash that she felt compelled to believe it was true.

She remembered him distinctly from the last sighting: the leg-warming exercises, the way he'd run up the steps. Whoever he was, they had one thing in common: Lydia van der Heyden.

But who the hell was he and what was he doing here?

He was still lending an ear to the black man, but his attention had begun to drift. He scratched his neck and slowly reconnoitred the room.

Ruth nipped out to the toilets for a pee.

She studied herself with objective hostility in the mirror above the washbasin as she pumped out a dollop of green liquid soap.

Her nails were gnawed to the quick, her hair was a disaster and the darning wool on her jumper was obviously a poor match, though it had definitely looked OK on the boat, goddammit.

Let's face it, she said to her reflection, *if grunge were an Olympic sport, you'd be representing Holland.* 'Slovenly' would be her mother's term, but what the heck? An office party in Zuidoost didn't exactly call for best bib and tucker.

She splashed her face and shook her head back. The water coursed into her lashes, her scalp, the roots of her hair. It felt good and cleansing, a surprise shower of rain on an oppressive day.

A toilet flushed behind her. A shuffling of feet, a fumbling with buttons, belts or zips. Someone was about to emerge. She dried herself quickly on the roller towel and returned to the bright, uninviting room.

Still no Jojo . . .

She tried her mobile and the message service tripped in. 'Where are you, ratbag?' she hissed and hung up.

The ratbag's party was living up to her worst expectations.

Behind a curtain, a sliding glass door gave onto a balcony. She slipped through and rolled a skoofer in the vague hope of rounding her edges and sweetening her frame of mind.

She rested her elbows on the iron balustrade and breathed deeply.

Stars prickled against the darkness.

The brash steel-and-concrete Bijlmer skulked in its own shadows, except where the late traffic crawled along beyond a huge futuristic billboard that looped through ads for ISPs, Amstel beer and DVD players.

Across the plaza a monolithic residential block reared up like a four-square multimedia installation. Each lit window was a thumbnail movie about some aspect of domesticity: The TV Dinner, Making the Bed, Junior Zaps the Aliens, Baby's Bath Time. Some movies were in duplicate; there were even a few identical triple bills.

Wherever your head was, wherever your thoughts and dreams might fly, it was amazing how everyone's physical life could be parsed in the same way – hour by hour, day by day – reduced to the same repetitive grammar of functional rituals.

The insect-like, mathematical replication of everything fascinated and repelled her, a facsimile world of glimpsed mirror-selves, swarming clones, going about their business. The idea that you were individual, unique and special – even, Ruth baby, if you live in a boat – was a hollow myth.

Her heart skipped a beat.

On a balcony opposite, a woman rested on her elbows against a balustrade. She was lost in thought, contemplating the sweep of the night sky. She didn't seem to notice her alter ego.

'Maphepha,' said a voice, booming out of nowhere.

Twelve

The large black man stepped gingerly over the raised aluminium rail of the sliding door.

The Kid followed.

'Maphepha?'

The black rubbed thumb and forefinger in the international money sign and chuckled drily.

Ruth made herself small. Neither man had noticed her. They seemed relieved to be out of the aggressively synthetic atmosphere of the office with its strip lights and warm ergonomic moulded plastic.

'Money recognizes money,' the black man went on. 'It spots it a mile off.' He drew a sight line from the middle of his broad, flat nose. 'In the street, it stops, takes off its kid gloves and says hello. "Hello, my friend. Nice to see you. Now where did we meet before?" Look over there.' He gestured towards the office blocks by Bijlmer station. His belly strained against the fully buttoned jacket. 'Men in suits. The guys who build that stuff. They know what it's all about. It's about turning a profit. It's about making your pile. Either you're bankable, Thomas, or you're not. No two ways about it.'

The other man sighed. 'You don't give up, Cameron,' he said.

The black laughed. It was a peculiar, high-pitched laugh that contrasted with his booming voice: slightly manic, as if there were a tiny cartoon character inside him producing it. 'No, I don't! The day I give up is the day I lay me down to die!' He tossed a peanut into the air and threw his head back to catch it in his mouth. Then his humour suddenly expired. 'You're pissing your life away, man,' he murmured. He turned his head aside and crossed his arms in peevish disgust.

The Kid didn't respond and the black's irritation increased exponentially.

'The reason *they* have no clout,' he added, jerking his thumb back over his shoulder to indicate the assembled partygoers, 'is that they're just a bunch of poor saps like you. No offence, Thomas. Nobody listens to them, and nobody listens to you neither. Know what I mean? You're one of the little people, one of the Munchkins. Always were, always will be.' He indicated just how little with the caliper of thumb and index finger.

The other man still didn't react, but there was a rigidity in his unresponsiveness that was an act of pure will. He wasn't going to snap at the bait of provocation.

The black realized he'd overstepped the mark and relented. He threw a bear-like arm around the Kid's shoulder and the twittery absolving laughter bubbled up in his throat once again. 'I told Isma that babysitting story of yours,' he said. 'It slayed her, man! I mean, fuck – babysitting for a dog!' He slapped his thigh loudly and shook his head. 'You made up that shit, didn't you? Confess it.'

'No, Cameron, I didn't,' said the Kid quietly. His own mood lightened, though something in his manner remained taut and guarded. 'What was I supposed to do? She asked me to babysit and when I got there it was a dog. A big one, too. Alsatian. And it had to be waited on hand and foot because that's what his lordship was accustomed to.'

'Dining on lambs' bollocks, huh?' said the black.

'Well, yeah – *rognons blancs*. Sounds better in French. The whole works, barring the vintage claret.'

'A fucking dog, man. It could only happen to you!' He leaned over, a giant hand on the Kid's shoulder, and whispered loudly,

'They don't know what to do with their beans! All withered up inside, but what they want is dolls, comforters, surrogate babies – the old oochy-koochy-koo – know what I mean?'

A breeze caught Ruth's sleeve and the black noticed her.

His shoulders stiffened a mite, then he straightened up and slipped back into the old bonhomie. 'Talking of which,' he said, tapping his nose, 'remember the low-down on the little fox, right?' He pulled the peanut trick again, glancing at Ruth once more out of the corner of his eye. 'Smitten, man. That's breaking news, straight from our man at Reuters, OK?' He gave a theatrical shiver, making his jowls wobble. 'Dunno about you, but my assets are frozen solid. It's bastard cold out here. You think things over, Tommaso.' He pointed a finger at his temple and wiggled it in little circles. 'Tick, tick, tick. Let me know if you change your pig of a mind.' He did a spoof karate routine, chopping and slicing into the Kid's gut, and backed away through the sliding window.

The other man was about to go in too when he spotted her.

A look of embarrassment, almost humiliation, crossed his face like the shadow of a cloud. He seemed to change his mind about going in. He picked up his plastic beaker of mulled wine from the floor and cupped it in his hands, resting his elbows on the balustrade in imitation of Ruth's own pose.

'That guy's nuts,' he said after a while. He turned to face her and shook his head, laughing at inanities. 'Completely barking mad!' He was speaking half to the air, half to her.

She didn't know what to say.

'Larger than life, I guess,' she managed.

'Yes, he is, he is!' Suddenly he looked taken aback. He ran the fingers of one hand through his shagpile of black hair. 'You've been here all along. I didn't realize.'

'I came out for a smoke but, as they say, *no smoke without fire.*'

'Wait there.'

He went back in and came out again with a book of matches.

She lit up and offered him the matches, but he gestured her to keep them.

'Do we know each other?' he asked.

She shook her head.

'Should we know each other?'

'Maybe,' she replied, surprised. 'Maybe we should.' She'd made her mind up not to mention Lydia, but the opportunity was now wide open. It was too good to lose. 'Lydia van der Heyden. She's kind of a friend.'

'Oh, God,' he exclaimed. 'Lydia!' He extended a hand. 'Let's be slaves to convention – Thomas Springer.'

She introduced herself.

'Yes, of course . . .' he said, piecing things together. 'Lyd goes on about you all the time. She hit a bad patch some weeks back, feeling down, then she pulled through. It was thanks to you. You've worked wonders for her, really. The business of the painting, I mean. Not that that's over. But, hold on – you, me – me, you – ' He narrowed his eyes, making a quick metronomic gesture with his hand. 'How did you know who I am?'

'I didn't . . . I mean, I don't.'

He stared back at her now, on his guard.

'I saw you a few days ago. You were calling at Lydia's place. It's as simple as that. I saw you from across the street. I've really no idea who you are. Lydia never mentions her gentleman friends. If she were to be believed, she never sees a soul.'

His eyes relaxed back into a confiding smile. 'That's old folks for you. They're sharper than you think. They know exactly when and how to make you feel sorry for them.'

He produced a card: *Thomas Springer. Amsterdam Officer, Stuurgroep Experimenten Volkshuisvesting (SEV).*

She'd never heard of the Netherlands Steering Committee for Experiments in Public Housing. It existed, he explained, to promote independent living for older or disabled people. Living care centres were provided for those who found it harder to cope and there were other solutions for Alzheimer's patients.

Wherever possible, the elderly were helped to stay in their own homes. So far, Lydia had been one of their shining stars. She was fiercely independent. He'd first got to know her in the course of his house calls some five years previously and they'd hit it off. Nowadays he dropped round whenever he could for a chat, just to see how she was getting on. From a professional viewpoint, she was an interesting test case. The tall, narrow canal houses with their steep old staircases were far from ideal for the elderly. Either you lived on the ground floor or in the semi-basement, or you took your life in your hands. A chairlift was a possibility, but Lydia would have none of that. It would amount to admitting she was infirm. And chairlifts were not without their own dangers.

'Have you ever been upstairs in that place?' asked Ruth. 'I have. Just to the first floor, mind you. It's mind-boggling, the stuff she's got up there.'

'Yeah, Ali Baba's cave. Trouble is she's losing her grasp. There's the upkeep on a place like that, not to mention the bills. Financially, she's riding for a fall. It may not be long before we have to sort her out.'

They opened up a pair of folding plastic chairs that had been leaning in one corner of the balcony. Ruth sat with her legs raised, resting her chin on her knees. The Kid spun his chair round and straddled it, planting his folded arms on the backrest like a hip theatre director. The pose seemed a conscious attempt to hide his diffidence.

He told her about his childhood near the Bijlmer. The confidences soon flowed. She listened without a word, trying to size him up.

He remembered the time when the polder was within walking distance. He remembered the glassy waters of lagoons and marshes, mirroring the clouds. He remembered the song of curlews and lapwings, the rustle of reeds and swaying, heavy-headed bulrushes.

In the old days the loudest sounds in winter were the cries

of white-fronted or greylag geese in flight. Then, in summer, there were migrant waders, sandpipers and grebes. He collected plovers' eggs or fished in the Waver river, where dragonflies hovered under summer suns and some of the windmills were still operational. The old fellow with the retriever who worked the pumping station by the river dyke sat out and whiled away the hours by telling him tall stories, pausing only to clean his meerschaum, blowing sharply through the stem like a whistle, or to shoulder his gun and take potshots at the rabbits who dared trespass among his runner beans. That's when the Kid had started listening to the old folks, to the crazy yarns they'd tell.

Nowadays it was nothing but women.

Amongst the over-eighties, there were three times as many women as men. With a few exceptions, they simply outlived their menfolk, as they did the whole world over, and that's why they were all alone. Not that Lydia had ever married.

'Was there ever a special somebody, do you think?' asked Ruth.

'She never mentions anyone.'

'She never mentioned you and you exist.'

He fetched two more beakers of mulled wine and they talked about Lydia, her past, her father's work at the Liro, the transit camp, her family. If Lydia had outlived them all, the vagaries of war were largely to blame. She was a barnacle, a hard-carapaced creature from another epoch, still clinging to life and the hull of the modern world. Old Scheele was another.

Ruth stopped him. What exactly was it with Lydia and Scheele?

He seemed surprised at the question.

'They hate each other. Of course, they haven't spoken for decades. But the hate goes on and on. It's what keeps them alive. It's their fuel, their juice, their renewable energy. Surely you knew that?'

'The painting must be so important to her.'

'It's more than the painting. There's some kind of principle at stake. I don't pretend to understand.'

Scheele was a cipher.

He was pure empty space, a void. But the Kid had met him, albeit once, and Lydia had told the Kid all about him. Little by little, as the Kid talked, a rudimentary profile of the *bewariër* was beginning to emerge.

She listened closely.

The Kid had a hesitant way about him, as if thought came more naturally than speech. Occasionally his eyes met hers. When they did there was a shy, unexpected humour dancing in them.

He was telling her about Scheele, Lydia's bête noire, and he warmed gradually to his subject. As Myles said, the old man was out of rocks and sparklers. Now he was an investor. Now he made money make money. In particular, he was a major stakeholder in the docklands regeneration scheme. He was in his eighties, the Kid explained, a misanthropic old bugger who buried himself away in his house across the Keizersgracht from Lydia's. He kept the world at arm's length, rarely going out even for business meetings. On the one occasion when the Kid had called on him – a courtesy call on behalf of the SEV, to see how he was coping – Scheele had cut him dead in mid-spiel and slammed the door in his face. A brief encounter. Enough to leave its mark.

A thought occurred to Ruth. A long shot, but worth a try.

'What's he like? Physically, I mean. Curly white hair – a high forehead, like Shakespeare?'

'Who are you describing?'

'The day I saw you call on Lydia, there was an old fellow who left her place just before. Smart, professional looking – briefcase. Come to think of it, he was more late sixties, early seventies.'

The Kid shook his head. 'That's not Scheele.'

'So who was my Shakespeare?'

Adrian Mathews

'When was this?'

'Last Friday. She didn't mention any other callers?'

'The only visitor she ever mentions is you.'

Their eyes met and there was a moment's silence.

'A very circumspect lady, our Lydia,' he said, raising his eyebrows.

'So it seems.' Suddenly Ruth gave in to a surge of resentment. 'But – dammit! – if she expects people to help her, if she expects people to take professional risks on her behalf, the least she could do is be a little more above board.'

'You've taken risks for her?'

'Perhaps risks is the wrong word. I've maybe bent some rules. Nothing dramatic. What I'm talking about is this constant evasiveness. It's slightly insulting. If people make an effort, it's courteous to meet them halfway.'

'Sure, but it's understandable after all she's been through. She's lost everything in her time – everything except the house. It's hardly surprising if she's got a thing about betrayal. On her bad days the world's just one great big conspiracy against her.'

'Hey, Tommaso!'

There was a rap on the window and someone pulled back the sliding door. Their intimacy was broken.

The mingled scents of warm, milling bodies wafted from the room.

A group photo was in the offing, just for the record. Some were cross-legged on the floor, others perched on a row of chairs. Ruth and the Kid were corralled in at the rear, shoulder to shoulder regimental-style, standing room only.

Eyes left. Eyes right.

Still no Jojo . . .

The red bulb of the auto-focus, the set of facial muscles – anticipating immortality – and a white dazzle as a fraction of a second was snatched out of the flux of time. The group broke up into smaller clusters, reconfiguring into the old patterns before the demands of posterity. Ruth watched the tired faces float past her. She too would be in that group snapshot. Maybe some observant person would point her out, wondering who the hell she'd been.

The flip side to this thought occurred to her too.

'Who *are* these people?' she whispered. 'Social workers? They look more like stretcher cases, if you ask me.'

The Kid scratched the back of his neck and looked down at her. He was almost a head taller. 'You weren't at the meeting?'

She shook her head and put on her goofy face.

'And nobody told you? I mean, you didn't even see the posters?'

She glanced across at the noticeboard again. 'Is something eluding my razor-sharp mind, Thomas?'

'OK – we're in the Bijlmer, right?' he began, shifting into explanatory mode. 'A putrid old slum, in other words – or new slum, if you prefer. Anyway, no one outside Amsterdam had ever heard of it. Not until the fourth of October 1992, anyway.'

'Oh, right!' said Ruth, seeing the light. 'The crash! The cargo jet. But what's that got to do with this lot here?'

'They lived here then. So did I, come to that, near the Kruitberg and Groeneveen flats – the ones that were hit. And,' he added, 'they live here still, God help them.'

'They survived,' she said.

He dipped a ladle into the big saucepan of mulled wine and topped up their beakers. 'Try telling them that.'

October 4th, 1992. The city's worst day in living memory. The El Al Boeing 747 crashed into the Bijlmer apartment blocks, killing forty-three people. The rest of the story – the sequel – she was not really up on, though scraps had got through to her from the papers or the odd news bulletin.

They went over to the posters and the Kid filled in the gaps.

The accident started a small inferno. A sweet smell invaded the area. The plane's cargo contained perfume and flowers, or so the Dutch and Israeli governments maintained. But men in white protective suits appeared among the rescue workers and took things away with them. Six years later the real cargo manifest was leaked: the sweet smell had been dimethyl methylophosphonate, one of the chemicals used to make sarin nerve gas. Three of the four chemicals required to make the gas had been on the ill-starred plane. The consignment was destined for the Israeli Institute for Biological Research.

But it was not this, or not this alone, which had sounded alarm bells, and it was not this that accounted for the walking wounded who now surrounded them.

According to unconfirmed reports, all the sniffer dogs used by the emergency personnel had died within six months. Then local people began to suffer: headaches, tiredness, skin rashes, pains in joints and muscles, giddiness, breathing problems, cancer, auto-immune diseases. The number of miscarriages increased, as did the rate of birth defects such as six fingers and hydrocephalus.

In the Bijlmer, one prime suspect emerged for their collective ills: depleted uranium.

It turned out that the chemical had been used for counter-weights in the plane's tail rudder and, some thought, the wings. In the kerosene fireball caused by the crash, the DU oxidized rapidly and the strong north-west wind that was blowing at the time bore the dust clouds far and wide. Anyone who was around while the fire burned was inhaling micro-particles of uranium oxide in greater or lesser concentrations. In 1999 a government inquiry held by the Meijer Commission admitted the contamination, but concluded that it was unlikely that large groups of citizens and rescue workers had suffered significant uranium poisoning.

'File closed?' asked Ruth, once the Kid had recapped the facts.

'Not yet. So long as this lot are still alive, at any rate. They want justice and compensation. The first step is to recognize the scale of the problem. Files close when people are dead and buried, when no one's left to put up a fight.'

Lydia and her precious heirloom came to mind. Scheele too, come to that. 'While there's life, there's hope,' she said, raising her eyebrows.

'You took the words right out of my mouth.' He sighed and put his hands into his trouser pockets, bunching his shoulders as he did so. 'So who – I mean, what exactly brings you here?'

'A friend. The Judas didn't show up. She didn't tell me what kind of party this was going to be either. If I'd known, I'd have brought a Geiger counter.'

'It's not their fault. They haven't got much to celebrate.'

'A bong, then.' She relented. 'And my Disco Inferno double CD. Guaranteed to wake the dead.'

The Kid didn't know how to interpret her humour. He took her hand, shaking it warmly. 'I've got to go,' he said. His eyes wandered away from her, as if part of him had already left the room and the rest had to catch up.

'Did I say something wrong?'

'There's some business I have to see to. Do you know about fyke nets, by any chance?'

'Huh?'

'Fyke nets, or vertical jigging? No, no – you wouldn't,' he added to himself. 'But eels – you like eels?'

'Eels?'

'I can get you one, if you want.'

'An eel?'

Her mobile buzzed in her bag. The Kid moved away. A text message from Myles:

Monday at 10. Plenary bureau meeting with Solomon Cabrol. Van der Heyden on agenda. Be there, Poppet.

She made a note in the diary she kept in her back pocket and caught up with the Kid at the coat rack.

'Listen, I'm going to duck out too. You wouldn't happen to

have a sleek black Lincoln Continental waiting down there, would you?'

'Where's home?'

'The Jordaan. And you?'

'You're on my way.'

The limo was a mud-spattered VW Dormobile Camper. Ruth glanced over her shoulder as they made their way up the A2. There was a bed in the back, along with heavy outdoor clothes, wader boots, cooking facilities, an oil stove, various bags and boxes of equipment and trays of postcards. The *Men from Mossad* poster with the white-clad spacemen was taped to the rear door.

'May I?' Ruth lit another spliff, toked a couple of times and crushed it out. 'Some find themselves through suffering, some find themselves through joy,' she intoned philosophically. 'Me, I've only tried this stuff so far. I swear to God, I don't know why I bother. It doesn't do anything for me any more.'

He gave her a quick ironical look. He had a cool, film-star way of driving, his left hand draped over the top of the steering wheel. 'You're a stage-five weedhead. Immune. The pleasure's dropped clean out of it. No hit. All that remains is the gesture, the ritual of rolling up.'

'How many stages are there?'

'Five.'

'Funny, I had a feeling you were going to say that.'

He grinned broadly. 'What else d'you do in your spare time, apart from funny cigarettes?'

'Me? Oh, you know – I blow the wrappers off drinking straws, pop bubble wrap, twiddle my thumbs, practise flower arrangements. I'm a bit of a rebel, actually. If the girl at the florist's tells me to cut the rose stems diagonally, I go home and cut them straight. Don't ask me why. I haven't come by my blonde hairs lightly.'

At intervals, pockets of low-lying fog reared up across the road, giving back the yellow light of the headlamps in cotton-wool cones. It was like coming in to land in a noisy turboprop at night. The Kid slowed down, then hit the gas again when they were through the clouds.

'What about you?' asked Ruth.

'Huh?'

'What do you do?'

'Me? I chat to Lydia and the other oldies. I put out fyke nets in the polders. That's illegal. I collect old picture postcards. And I go race-cycling.'

'Who do you race?'

'Myself. And Old Father Time. Here – ' he opened the glove compartment and handed her a book: *De Renner*, by Tim Krabbé – 'know it?'

She shook her head.

'Borrow it.'

It was too dark to read. She flicked through the pages to get the feel of it, to show her appreciation of the loan.

'I've got this theory,' he said after a while. 'Eighty per cent of people are weird shits.'

'I guess I'd go along with that.'

'I haven't finished. Eighty per cent are weird shits, but there's another twenty per cent who are weird without being shits. See what I mean? The big test in life is telling the two groups apart, because there's good weird and bad weird. That's my theory. By the way, you're one of the good ones.'

Ruth glowed.

'Probably,' he added as an afterthought.

It was one in the morning when he dropped her by the barge.

'I'm trying my best to curb my curiosity,' she said as he opened the camper door for her, 'but I think you promised me an eel.'

'I'll drop it by on Saturday.'

'Make it Monday, if it can keep. I'll be away for the weekend. I'm going to see my folks in Driebergen. Jojo's agreed to house-sit the boat for me.'

'Jojo?'

'A friend – the one who stood me up tonight, in fact. Come to think of it, you could bring the eel round any time this weekend. Jojo's going to be there.'

'Damn, I know Jojo,' he said. 'We work together. You should've told me it was her. She had to stay behind to help someone who was taken ill at the meeting.'

'Is that so?' Ruth ran her hand round the nape of her neck, thinking things through. 'The funny thing is, she desperately wanted me to come. She was going to introduce me to some Gay Caballero she's sweet on.'

He was lost in thought for a moment. He lowered his head. He shifted from foot to foot.

Oh, my God, thought Ruth, *it's* you, *isn't it? It's* you! *The Gay Caballero in person!*

Eventually he placed a hand on his heart and raised it in the air. 'Listen – nice talking, an' all that. Salaam. See you Monday.'

Thirteen

'Let's have a look, then,' her father said.

It was Saturday morning. In his workshop, he pored over the van der Heyden photos, the rubbing and the books and pamphlets from Mr Moon's occult bookshop, some of which Ruth had browsed through the previous day on the train.

She left him to it.

She chatted to her mother as they warmed up the pea soup and sauerkraut. She listened to a holiday programme on the radio.

It had snowed throughout the night. In the long hillocky garden, a single raven alighted on her father's short-wave mast. What was it about those creatures that made her think of pall-bearers? It flapped its wings like a wet umbrella before clenching itself into a kind of half-sleep.

Ruth ventured out into the dazzling whiteness to clear the driveway. Her shovel scraped against the gravel, violating the quiet. Her lungs ached with the effort and the cold. She paused to catch her breath. Birds, foxes and other animals had left their signatures, a tracery of prints to chart their scavengings. By the frozen pond there was evidence of a scurry, a conflict and – further on – a single grey feather and three scarlet drops of blood.

The world sparkled in the pale sunlight and now a slight thaw was audible. A faint, crystalline creaking and settling, the dribble of ice-cold water in pipes and guttering, the drip of spindly icicles beneath the eaves, the sigh of collapse as a stooping conifer branch suddenly shrugged off its burden.

In her old room, Ruth found a suitcase full of school exercise books, dolls, a jar of baby teeth, tiny woollen bedsocks and other ruins of infancy. There were two pictures in coloured crayons she clearly remembered drawing: a gaudy, smiling prima donna with a diadem, a magic wand and butterfly wings, and a strange red woman with yellow hair – eyes agog, limbs akimbo – who was either singing or screaming.

She sat on the child's bed and caught a glimpse of herself in the wall mirror.

Then was then; now was now.

The days, months and years between fell away, disposable fragments of the infinite. It was hardly a cause for regret. When she was ten the family moved to a flat in Amsterdam, but they kept on the Driebergen house near Utrecht as a weekend retreat. The house always stirred up the ghosts of her old selves. Her parents had aged and were ageing, true. Each visit brought this home. Her father, Joris, was slower on his feet, for example. But his slowness was as if time itself had decided to relax and take things easy. As for her mother, Maaike, it was the tint and perm that did it. It was worse than a cattle tag, earmarking her for coach trips to folk museums, Klaverjassen card-game tournaments and church hall coffee mornings. Ruth tried to ignore the hairdo, but couldn't. It looked like fibreglass or candyfloss rather than hair.

At the same time her parents had become more themselves, like caricatures. Their habits, mannerisms and quirks of speech grew more pronounced. They were always together – grousing, reminiscing, plotting, eternally playing off against each other – a marital Tweedledum and Tweedledee.

Her mother still checked the electrical fittings and gas taps obsessively before going out. She had a horror of draughts and always fiddled with a single strand of hair that the hairdresser hadn't succeeded in neutralizing.

Her father smelled of cloves. He chewed them non-stop as he read or listened to his short-wave radio. The clove-chewing was a habit he'd adopted when he gave up smoking, though he still allowed himself a slim panatella after lunch. He wandered round the house, talking to himself, with his grizzled beard, open-neck shirt, leather waistcoat and sarong – a bolt of blue cotton, printed with lotus flowers, that he'd taken a shine to on a trip to Malaysia and which was now constantly knotted round his waist, making him look like a New Age swami or guru.

'Crazy stuff,' he growled, looking round sharply as she came into his workshop. 'In future I'll stick to my crosswords.'

Ruth curled up into a ball in the leather armchair.

The room was a mess of clamps, soldering irons, wires, plugs, circuit boards and computer paraphernalia. Joris's passions were electronics and radio. Before retirement he'd worked for Mobil Oil. Like his wife, he'd travelled widely and was a readaholic – novels, biographies, philosophy. Books, magazines and ring binders of bank statements and domestic paperwork were piled everywhere. He took a couple of bulldog clips and attached Ruth's brass rubbing to the back of a folding screen.

'Make anything of the numbers?' she asked.

'What?' He was slightly hard of hearing.

'The numbers,' she repeated, raising her voice. 'Make anything of them?'

'Nope. I phoned Lucas and emailed them to him. Two heads better than one, eh? He said he'd look into it.'

'Lucas Aalders?'

Here was another relic of the past. Maarten's parents and her own had bonded. They met up two or three times a year and even holidayed together. Ruth no longer felt entirely comfortable with this situation, but there it was, take it or leave it.

'Some kind of code, I reckon,' Joris went on. 'Probably not very sophisticated. Not like modern cryptography. Just a simple number-for-letter substitution. You've got twenty-six separate band-pass filters, each highly specific. That should be a cinch.

Adrian Mathews

You just have to work out which number stands for which letter. It's based on letter frequency and word rules. For example, all words have at least one vowel. I've been tinkering with this in old Dutch, but so far no joy. Of course, it could be a cyclic cipher. You know – every few letters the digits get rotated, the filter changes. That would be trickier. To get this right, you'd have to know what codes were doing the rounds in the eighteenth century, wouldn't you? Mind you, it ain't always easy. You've heard of the Voynich Manuscript?'

'No.'

'A scientific book, at least four hundred years old, written in code. No one's ever managed to crack that one, not even you modern whizz-kids.'

'And the symbol in the middle. I found it in that big book there. It stands for the philosopher's stone, doesn't it?'

Joris opened the volume to where he'd marked it with a silver jeweller's screwdriver slipped between the pages. 'Yup. Here we are – the philosopher's stone. The mad dream of the alchemists.'

'Turning base metals into gold.'

'That's the bit everyone knows,' he conceded, 'but it goes further according to this. I mean, it wasn't just a medieval get-rich-quick scheme. What they were really after was the elixir of immortal life. Transforming metals was just part of the process. The gold was a metaphor for the source of life. They were early chemists, see. They must've had their fair share of crackpots, of course, and they certainly had their own dotty language – an esoteric way of talking about things. But in their hit-and-miss way they made important discoveries. Alchemy and chemistry only really began to go their separate ways in the seventeenth century.'

'I saw an exhibition of paintings of alchemists once,' said Ruth. 'It used to be a popular setpiece. There was one I liked by Joseph Wright of Derby – of an alchemist who'd accidentally discovered phosphorus. He's just crouching there, staring in amazement at his test tube or alembic, or whatever you call it. A bloody good painting, actually.'

'There you go, then. Those old fire-and-brimstone codgers paved the way for modern mineralogy, chemistry, medicine, pharmacology. Even gunpowder – even fireworks. Name Cornelis Drebbel mean anything to you?'

'There are schools named after him, aren't there?'

'A Dutchman, of course. Inventor of the first recorded submarine. Also an alchemist.'

There was a phonebook and pen on the arm of her chair. Ruth doodled. She glanced at the rubbing and copied the six-pointed star with its two concentric circles.

'But why a stone? Why the philosopher's stone? What was it exactly?'

'Listen to this.' He followed the print with his finger.

We call the Philosopher's Stone the most ancient Stone of the sages, the most secret or unknown; incomprehensible in natural terms; celestial, blessed, and sacred. It is said that it is true, and more certain than certainty itself, the arcanum of all arcana – virtue and power of the divinity, hidden from the ignorant, end and goal of all things under the sky, definitive and marvellous conclusion of the operative work of all the sages. It is the perfect essence of all the elements, the indestructible body that no element may damage or harm, the quintessence; it is the double and living mercury which has within it the divine spirit – the treatment of all the weak and imperfect metals – the sempiternal light – the panacea of all ills – the glorious Phoenix – the most precious of all treasures – the greatest possession in all of nature.

'That's from the *Musaeum Hermeticum*, 1625.'
'Sounds great,' said Ruth. 'I'll take a six-pack.'

Adrian Mathews

Her father peered dubiously at her over the top of his reading spectacles in that intense, silent way of his which – as a child – she'd always found intimidating.

'What I mean,' she relented, slightly exasperated, 'is how can a mere stone be all of those things at once?'

'Panvitalism. They believed everything was alive, right? Including stones. Stones had life and mystery. It says here that when Cortez asked the Aztec chiefs where their knives came from, they pointed upwards.'

'Meteorites?'

'Exactly. Stones were also fertile and sexual. Ask any of your diamond cutters in Amsterdam. They still sex the diamonds, according to their brilliance.'

'The brighter ones being—'

'A girl's best friend, I suppose!' He laughed softly, sidestepping her trap. 'Think of it this way. The alchemists came out of the fiery professions – goldsmiths, enamellers, foundry workers, glass workers. In Phoenicia, ancient Egypt, Greece and the Near East, they were linked to the priesthood. They worked in the temples. And what were they doing, those old metal smelters?'

'Mixing metals, I suppose.'

'Mixing metals. Making amalgams. Generating new mineral alloys. That's where the sexual bit comes in. You take two opposite or different things and create a third thing, something new. It's what they called a *hierosgamos*, a chemical wedding. Here's another bit.' He pulled a slim volume from the pile and found his place. '*The Book of Morienus*, an old Arabic work. A description of the alchemical operation, or the making of the stone. "Marriage, increase, pregnancy, birth and nourishment are necessary to you in the conduct of this operation. For when conjunction has happened, conception follows, and pregnancy arises from conception, and birth follows pregnancy." The alchemists thought all metals came originally from mixing up sulphur and mercury. That's why so many of them went barmy. The sulphur must've been bad enough, but inhaling mercury fumes definitely drives you nuts. Nowadays we get the stuff straight from our dental fillings. That's progress for you. But to get back to the alchemists, there's a further point here on the subject of amalgams. If you make alloys of silver and gold, at the end of the process you appear to have more silver and gold. See what I mean?'

'The Midas touch. Something for nothing.'

'Another age-old dream. But remember they weren't all money-grubbers, though there may well have been a hard core of budding venture capitalists among them. The serious ones were holy men because alchemy also has its roots in religion and mysticism. It's about harnessing celestial powers. You destroy to create. There's marriage, passion, death and resurrection. They talk of killing monsters, of dismembering a man with a sword. Strange motifs – you've seen the crazy pictures in these books. Sometimes the philosopher's stone is represented as a virgin or a child, sometimes as Christ or a phoenix. And the process of producing it is one of purification and redemption – like a Calvary, like the steps up a mount towards the supreme arcanum. You have calcination, sublimation, solution, putrefaction, distillation, coagulation, tincture, and so on. Those are the words they use for the steps. And your raw material survives destruction. It's transmuted, born out of ashes. That's the big stone-nativity theory, anyway. See now why it's also the elixir of life?'

'I guess so. But I still don't get what it is. A stone? An elixir? Gold? Silver? What?'

'Well, I don't know any more than it says here,' he admitted, 'But, where are we ... Here, listen again.' He nudged his spectacles up onto the bridge of his nose. 'Revelation. St John the Divine. "To him that overcometh will I give ... a white stone." There's a list here ... it's the Stone of Fire in Ezekiel. It's the Stone with Seven Eyes upon it in Zechariah. It's the biblical stone rejected by the builders in Psalms. It's green vitriol. It's a dead body. It's urine. It's tail of the dragon's milk. It's Brazil.

It's a fugitive servant. It's chaos, a toad, an adder, a green lion – you name it, Ruth. This old guy, Petrus Bonus, says it can be compared to just about anything in the world.'

'Which doesn't exactly help anyone pin it down. But what do I know? Maybe that's the whole point. It's unpindownable.'

Joris took off his reading glasses and left them to hang by the cord round his neck. A strip of buttercup sunlight fell across his beard and bony chest. In the darkness above it, his sharp eyes shone.

'Maybe that's it. It's all things to all men. It's whatever you want it to be. And each historical epoch has its own forbidden fruit, its torment of Tantalus.'

'What would ours be?'

'I dunno – DNA? The genetic code – the new secret doctrine of all life? The more they find out about it, the more they'll be able to cure disease and prolong life, after all – at least in the rich countries, but that's another issue. Yeah, DNA. A suitable candidate for the new elixir, don't you think?'

'If you say so.'

'They're changing the world,' he added. 'Virgin births and all that. They reckon they can create a child direct from the mother's egg. No male intervention. I knew they'd find a way of getting rid of us in the long run!'

Ruth winced.

One of her feet had gone to sleep. She massaged it, then stood up and went over to the bookcase. She was intrigued by people's museums of little objects, the things they'd been drawn to in life's journey and that it pleased them to have around. She picked up an old coin. It was soft, worn and warm in her hand. The profile of some bygone king or emperor was just discernible, more to the fingers than to the eye.

'What's it all about?' Joris went on in his dreamy, rambling voice. 'What's the universe made of? Where do old things go to? Where do new things come from? Metamorphosis and mutability, slow change, violent change, new life and the death of what's gone before. That's the stuff they were interested in, the be-alls and the end-alls. Everything must change.'

'You're beginning to sound like a George Benson song, Dad.'

'Who's George Benson?'

'Never mind.'

'Bring the elements into balance and you get the philosopher's stone – the clue to it all, the secret of immortality. And the one thing they all agree about is that their famous stone is made out of something that's as common as dirt. Something that everyone turns their noses up at and rejects. That bloke Morienus again.' He returned to the book. '"Matter is unique and everywhere rich and poor possess it; it is unknown to all; it is before the eyes of everyone; it is despised by the vulgar, who sell it cheaply like mud, but the philosopher who understands it holds it as precious."'

'Garbology,' Ruth commented.

'You what?'

She raised her voice. 'Garbology. It's the study of a culture by examining what it chucks out. A bunch of modern artists have made a big thing of it. There's a photographer who tips up the dustbins of the rich and famous and takes pictures of their trash. But what d'you reckon this tells us about the philosopher's stone?'

'Well, look at silicon chips. Our computers depend on them. But silicon's nothing but sand. Everything's dirt, come to that – dust, clay, ashes, whatever you want to call it. The mystery's in the transformation, in getting diamonds from carbon, oil out of fossils, or life itself out of a ball of muck floating around in the cosmos. I mean our earth could've turned out like the moon, then where would we be?'

Ruth was pacing around the room, picking things up at random, blowing dust from the tops of books, helping herself to Jaffa cakes from the box Joris had left on the table. There was an edge of impatience to her, a shutdown that happened whenever her father slipped into philosophical mode. It was probably her education. She was hard-wired for specificities, not his airy-fairy generalizations.

'What about the painting itself?' she said. 'What's that got to do with your great arcanum?'

'Christ knows.' He shrugged. 'Maybe someone just needed a convenient place to hide some secret information. Not necessarily the artist himself, either. Nice little picture, though. Almost makes me want to take up my sketchbooks again.'

'So for you there's no obvious link between the painting and the symbols on the back?'

'There's a glass alembic on the mantelpiece that looks vaguely alchemical, but apart from that nothing. Your guess is as good as mine.'

'Look at this photo.' She pushed one of the digital snapshots towards him. 'See those labels? Myles – that's the English colleague I told you about – he's the expert on Nazi docketing. He figures that Goering was after this picture but Hitler's buyers stole a march on him. It ended up in the Führer's private collection. What we're trying to fathom with our slow-track arty brains is: if that's true, why did he want it? The painting's pretty enough, but it's mediocre. It isn't great art by a long chalk. So that leaves this stuff on the back. Is that what they were after? Is that what caught their eye?'

Joris pulled a face. 'I hope you're not expecting me to answer that.'

'Well, somebody's got to!' she snapped, bringing her hand down on the table with an unintended bang.

'So that somebody's got to be your poor old dad, has it?'

Her anger melted at his hangdog surprise. She kicked herself for her bossiness. She perched on the edge of the table and ran her hands through his tangled grey hair – Daddy's little princess. With both thumbs she rubbed at the furrows on his forehead, hoping to smooth them away.

'You know, I was only a kid at the time,' Joris said. 'Adolf used to give me a bell occasionally to let me know how things were going on the Eastern Front. But oddly enough he never mentioned his artistic pursuits. Funny, that. In all other respects, we were great buddies, always in cahoots. Pity it all had to end up the way it did for him.'

'Shut up, Dad!'

'See what Lucas says,' he growled. 'Crack that number code and you'll be one step closer.'

'Why the hell don't people just say things? What do they need all these codes and jargon for?'

'It's like those Rosicrucians, the Freemasons, the Church. If you have specialist knowledge, you don't want other people to get their hands on it. Not necessarily for dog-in-the-manger reasons. It could just be that you don't want it vulgarized. Anyway, what's so different nowadays? Which profession doesn't have its technospeak or gobbledygook? Microsoft, for example. I bet you art historians are no different. The alchemists leaned on the Bible and liturgy. They loved speaking in paradoxes and riddles.'

Ruth tipped up the empty biscuit carton and caught the last spongy crumb in the cup of her hand. 'I've got a new penpal who does that too,' she said.

She had told her parents about Lydia, but not about the email or the curse that hung over the whole affair. The previous evening she'd accessed her server and another mad, garbled message had come her way. It had fouled up her sleep, eating its way into her dreams in which – she now remembered – the Cisco Kid had also made a guest appearance, complete with nose-diving 747 cargo jets.

Her father was fiddling with his short-wave radio. He had not heard her remark. She remembered with a jolt that the printout of the email was in her cardigan pocket, following her around.

She took it out and read it over once again.

✉

Chickenshit: will you never learn your lesson? You women live
by your fucking lies. The truth has become a stranger to you.
You wish to receive, but you give nothing in return. And how
does Nature learn to give and to receive? The copper man gives
and the water-stone receives; the thunder gives the fire that
flashed from it. For all things are woven together and all things
are taken apart and all things are mingled and all things combined and all things mixed and all things separated and all things
are moistened and all things are dried and all things bud and all
things blossom in the altar shaped like a bowl. Corpus infantis
ex masculo et femina procedit in actum. The floods are risen, O
Lord, the floods lift up their voice: the floods lift up their waves.
I warned you, Chickenshit, I warned you. Now you have made
me angry. That was a bad thing to do.

47 107.8682

Numbers again. That weird numerical sign-off.
Her throat tightened.
Immediately she wanted to tell her father, but a kindly
impulse held her back. She was a woman, not a child. Joris and
Maaike were at an age when their personal anxieties were
bothersome enough. She'd be doing them a disservice to burden
them with her own. Two things, however, were now clear. First,
her emailer was – or purported to be – a male of the species.
Second, he'd been onto the alchemical slant from the word go.
He'd got the lingo off pat.
Whoever he was, she had to admit, he left her at the starting
block.
'Listen to this,' said Joris, cocking his head and turning the
large black dial. 'Forty metres band.' He fine-tuned out the static
and the daffy pitch on the voices. 'Bloke in Christchurch, New
Zealand, talking to another bloke in Latvia. What d'you think of
that, then?'

She shook herself out of her reverie and tried to look suitably awestruck. Her father belonged to the Meccano generation that was still impressed by reel-to-reel tape recorders and bulky nuts-and-bolts technology. If she preferred anything, it was the miniaturized, prosthetic gizmos. There was a kind of Stalinian grandeur in creating your own full-blown broadcasting station along with a colossal garden transmission tower, granted, but it was like swatting a fly with an oar. *For crying out loud, Dad,* she wanted to say, *what the hell's wrong with the phone?* Besides which, all the old radio-ham geezers ever talked about was ohms and watts and the latest variable capacitors. The really salty stuff – sex and drugs and rock 'n' roll – was banned by the rules of the game. The whole potty business was an elaborate ploy to get away from their nagging wives.

The lunch gong rang out from the dining room.

Joris pulled a soggy clove from between his yellow teeth and dropped it into an ashtray.

'For Pete's sake don't start talking to your mother about philosopher's stones,' he said.

'Why not?'

'She's just had the gallstone thingy, hasn't she? – the endoscopy.'

'Dad!' Ruth exclaimed. 'That's ridiculous! Trust you to make a bizarre connection like that.'

Lunch was a quiet affair.

Afterwards, they all drove out to get some diesel and a box of firelighters. They stopped for ten minutes at an antique store. Ruth bought her mother an old coffee grinder built around a Delft earthenware pot for her collection.

Back on the road, the glare from the flat white vistas of snow was blinding. Ruth felt a pinching pain behind the eyeballs. Her parents' complexions were drained of colour. Her mother's perm was a ball of dead tumbleweed stuck to her head.

Ruth pulled down the sun flap and examined herself in the little mirror. Another whey-faced ghost. Her lips were chapped and bluish, despite the gusts of hot air from the blowers. Her pupils had contracted to pinheads. Luckily, there was a pair of flashy red and gold sunglasses in the glove compartment. She applied some lipstick and put them on. Now the world was a serene hyacinth blue.

With an inward sigh, she retreated into the tunnels and grottos of her thoughts.

A roadside sign caught her father's eye and he veered off down a private lane bordered with electric fencing and the occasional hangar in which hulking agricultural machines slumbered through the winter months. At the end of the track was a pheasant farm – unusual, in what was otherwise dairy country. Joris and Maaike had visited it once before in the previous winter. They thought it might interest Ruth. More to the point, it was the only local sight they could think of. Another characteristic of the ageing process was feeling that they constantly had to entertain.

Ruth gave in, hiding her indifference behind the big limousine panes of the dark glasses, an anonymous starlet chilling out between takes on the Italian Riviera.

The farmer's wife remembered Joris and Maaike and shook them by the hand. She led them into a superheated brooder coop. There was a flurry of straw and wings, a panic of cheeping, as they entered. The young birds flocked to the far side of the enormous pen under the dusty orange glow of overhead radiators, then tentatively ventured back towards the feed outlets. There were explanations. Here the pheasants were raised to the age of eight weeks before being weighed and banded. In other coops and feeding stations elsewhere on the farmstead, grouse, woodcock and partridge were reared. Some went straight to the dinner plate, others were returned to the wild, by special arrangement with the local game-hunting association. The farmer himself was a keen huntsman.

She invited them back to the farmhouse kitchen for cake, coffee and business.

Joris and Maaike didn't want a pheasant, live or dead, but they asked for a dozen hens' eggs, a punnet of fresh button mushrooms, some duck pâté and home-cured ham. The deal done, they down-geared to convivial mode, drank their piping-hot coffee and chatted about this and that. Joris dropped in his latest theory about telephone masts dressed up as plastic trees. Ruth said she'd heard of a company that made fake plastic trees, and soon they got on to the new criminal vogue for four-barrel .22 pistols disguised as mobile phones, which the Arrow Team of the Amsterdam police were currently having to deal with.

'Apparently,' the lady of the house was saying, 'they fire when one of the numbers is pressed. I wonder which number it is?'

'Dial M for Murder,' Ruth murmured.

Her cellphone rang.

Ruth slipped out and into the sitting room, clicking the door shut behind her.

'Everything all right?' asked Maaike when she came back.

'Yeah,' Ruth breathed with a light, reassuring smile. The strain in her eyes, a tiny pulse in the muscle of one lid, told a different story. She waited until the three of them had left the farmhouse before making her announcement.

'I've got to go back.'

'Back?' said her father.

'Back home. Back to Amsterdam.'

Maaike turned on her in alarm. 'Right now?'

'I'm afraid so.'

'I knew it! I knew something had happened! What did I tell you?' She gripped her husband by the crook of the arm.

'Nothing's happened, Mum. It's just a friend. She's got herself into a spot of bother.'

'What sort of bother?'

'The whole lot, actually – emotional, financial. The bumper

variety pack. Don't make me go into details. She's got nowhere to stay. I'm the only one she can turn to.'

'Well, tell her to come out here if you want to.'

'This is really something I've got to deal with by myself. We need to be alone.'

Maaike hugged her daughter with feeling. 'She's lucky to have someone like you, that's all I can say. You always were headstrong, Ruth, and a bit aloof. That's Clara's word for you. Not a criticism, mind. But your heart's in the right place – isn't it, Joris? – and that's what counts.'

'What?' said Joris.

'Her heart's in the right place.'

'Oh yes – right place!' He nodded, not quite certain what was being discussed or what was expected of him.

'And that's what counts,' Maaike repeated.

Ruth was relieved.

The lie was over and done with. Minimum collateral damage. How would she have fared hooked up to a polygraph? Her mother's compliment left a twinge of unease, but the fib was her parting gift to them, a little protective reality-screening. And the alleged friend was just a roundabout allusion to herself. The question of where her heart was located would have to be put on hold, pending developments. It could wait for her day of reckoning, however far off that happened to be.

Her father consulted his timetable. 'There's a train at five thirty-five, if the gods are willing. You'll need to change. It'll get you in at around a quarter past six. If we make a move now, we'll just have time to nip home and pick up your bag.'

'Oh, Ruth, love,' her mother gushed, 'we'll miss you so! Promise you'll come back soon . . .'

Fourteen

*O*n the train, Ruth had time to think.

The fact of the calamity didn't preoccupy her. That was an event, a practicality, something to be dealt with later. She was edging round the obstruction, hoping to see what lay behind. She tried Jojo's number all the same. She even tried the Kid. No damn luck. Her one channel of communication was unproductive.

Left to her own devices, she couldn't relax. It was impossible.

She bummed a cigarette and moved to the end of the railway car.

Dusk was drawing in.

The flat, repetitive landscape streaked past on a seemingly infinite but gradually darkening loop.

A couple of elderly gay men held hands in the corridor, their portly bodies swaying with the motion of the train as if to music, as if quietly crooning some old sentimental ballad by the light of a tinfoil vaudeville moon.

A woman with a young daughter came out of the loo. The girl lurched and bumped into Ruth's leg. 'Mummy, that lady hurt me! She did it on purpose.' The mother gave a despairing smile and pulled the child away.

Ruth drew nervously on the cigarette.

There was a foldaway seat in the wall by a fire extinguisher. She flopped down on it and pressed her cheek against the cold, vibrating window.

I fucking knew this was coming, she thought. *It's always the same. When everything's sailing along merrily, you get it slap in the face – customized shit, your own special number stamped on it – a warning against taking the good times for granted.*

Did some bad part of me make this happen?

She blew against the window and drew a cross in the dwindling halo of mist. When no one was looking, she stuck her tongue out at her own reflection and banged the back of her head twice against the wall. *Take that, crazy woman! It's an accident, that's all. It isn't the end of the world. It isn't even the first time it's happened. Look at it this way – when your life's a millpond of sweet solitary tedium, one little pebble kicks up a hell of a lot of waves. Lesson one: life keeps moving. It's a question of fluid mechanics. And* you *have to move with it, otherwise Thump! Sorry, lady! Nothing personal. Just don't hold up the traffic!*

At Duivendrecht she changed platforms and boarded the Utrecht–Leiden express. The city was only minutes away.

A guard with a cleft chin examined her ticket for an inordinate length of time. She braced herself for some kind of wrangle, but in the end he passed it back without a word, smiled faintly and moved on. No doubt his thoughts had wandered into the sidings.

What do Dutch railway guards dream of? Things that stay put. Things without wheels and tracks. Windmills on windless evenings. Huge feather beds riveted to the floor. On the other hand, why seek complications? Maybe the poor sap simply fancied her. One of the tongue-tied, unassertive, stealthy ones.

'We will soon be arriving in Amsterdam. For passengers alighting here, please make sure you do not leave any belongings behind.'

Her thoughts had free-floated. They now locked back on target. The train pulled into the city and the grimy whale-belly smell of the railway station filled the air.

Now for the tram . . .

She made the switch on autopilot, walking across the station concourse in a hollow dream. The lights, the shops, the cars, the crowds. Nothing was real. It was a cardboard show that a breath of wind would collapse, but it was all bringing her closer. A stranger's voice on the phone. The sudden overthrow of plans. The motionless motion of public transport, when she lost all sense of time, and – all the while – her mind fluttering helplessly over things, blown and buffeted off course.

On the tram unconnected flashbacks popped into her head.

A skating trip with Maarten out on the polders. As usual, he'd shot ahead. And suddenly she was alone, her head spinning, her legs giving way. She'd seen something dreadful and unforgettable. Beneath her feet the body of a drowned dog was locked into the ice. Only its black, bloodied nose and muzzle stuck out from the milky surface. She realized with a start why it was blood-raw. The blade of her skate had sliced clean through.

Another image gasped out of the past.

Her first boyfriend, Frank, the way he'd hold her close by the waist. He held her so tightly it was difficult to walk unless they synchronized their steps. She remembered the possessive pressure of teenage fingers on her right hip.

At school he sat behind her and blew on the back of her neck. It tickled. It made her smile. Then one day the history teacher asked what she found so amusing and she didn't know what to reply. 'The burgemeesters,' she said – the only word she remembered from the lesson – and everyone sniggered. There'd been a punishment, Frank had gone off with another girl, and ever since – even in adulthood – whenever the word 'burgemeester' cropped up in conversation, on TV, or in a book, it made her squirm, a fat, fur-trimmed, port-guzzling little devil of a word whose specific mission was to fuck with her emotions at unexpected moments in her life.

A bell clanged. The tram was stopping.

She realized she'd been staring at the ground. 'You're thinking of the past,' Maarten would have said. 'When people think

Adrian Mathews

of the past, they look at the ground. When they think of the future, they look up into the sky.' Or was it Frank who had said that? No – too young. Perhaps her father, or someone else entirely. What did it matter? She'd forgotten, she forgot.

She was in a daze.

Words detached themselves from people like leaves from the trees, and who ever bothered to stick the leaves back onto the trees?

She walked from the tram stop to the Bloemgracht. For hours her mind had been over-stimulated, firing off at wild tangents. Now she was close to home, the physical presence of the city brought her back to realities.

Night had come.

The trees that flanked the canal were jagged sketches of darkness, their primitive metabolisms in suspended animation. Bright garlands of white and blue light bulbs hung from their dank branches. In Driebergen it had snowed. Here the temperature was a critical few degrees higher. Either it had rained while she'd been away or the last snow and sludge had melted. The waters of the canal were high and turbid. The road and pavement glistened with mirrorlike depth. Dark, broken shapes shifted against the stippled patterns of reflected coloured lights.

The first thing she saw was the striped plastic tape that barred the gangway to the *Speculant*. The word POLITIE was printed in fluorescent red letters on it at the same repeated interval.

The big Luxemotor barge was low in the water and listing sharply.

A fire-brigade vessel was moored nearby and people were moving around with pumps and hosing.

The police had phoned to tell her it was flooded, but there were floods and floods. She'd hoped it would be one of the more manageable varieties. For example, if all four thousand-litre fresh-water tanks had emptied into the vessel, there'd be four metric tonnes of water slopping about fore and aft, coming to about three centimetres above floor level. Her physics was not too hot, but that was the mental calculation she'd made on the train. The boat would never sink because the total weight of water would be the same before and after the accident. Inside it would be a bit wet, but at least it would be clean water.

The cop's description, however, and what she saw now with her own eyes, told a less optimistic story.

The slight thaw could be a clue. Ruth had fresh water piped in and on Friday it had been very cold. What if she or Jojo had turned on a tap, found there was no water and accidentally left the tap open and the sink or bathtub plugged? Then, when the ice in the pipe melted, the water would flood the boat. This was one of the known hazards of barge-dwelling. It would be clean water, but the effect would be disastrous, unless stopped in time.

The golden rule was: find your leak and pump out the vessel immediately.

She ducked under the plastic tape and went down the gangplank. She unlocked the wheelhouse, where she dumped her weekend bag. She rummaged around in the utility box, found a pair of waders and pulled them on. A man who was working the pumps came to see her and shook her hand. He introduced himself as Laurens Driest, an emergency worker from one of the shipyards on the IJmeer.

'Been away?'

'Yeah. Just my luck, eh?'

'These boats are touchy. They don't like being ignored. We caught her just in time. Another hour or two and you'd have been the proud owner of one antique submarine.'

'Fresh water or canal water?'

'Pure Amsterdam Perrier, straight out of the frog pond.'

'Shit.'

'In a word,' he said. 'That's the trouble with boats. They're surrounded by water. And all that water's only got one idea in its head. It wants to get in.'

'Don't tell me. I've been here before. How much longer d'you reckon?'

'Another four hours maybe. There's no telling. When we started, it was about a metre deep. We're sucking up about ten centimetres an hour, but we don't know where it's coming from.'

'Taps not running?'

Driest shook his head. 'The old question with leaks. Has it stopped? No way of telling till we find out where it is. If the hull's punctured, we'll have to get her out of the wet stuff and into a dry dock for some double-plating. Are you going to hang around?'

'I'll take a look inside. I'll be back in a sec.'

'Watch your step. And don't try to switch the light on unless you fancy a little electrotherapy. Got a candle or a paraffin lamp?'

'Somewhere, I can't remember where. It doesn't matter. I'll manage without.'

The hatch-board to the back cabin was open.

She climbed cautiously down the wooden steps. On touching bottom, she could guess at the water level: some forty centimetres in depth.

She swore under her breath.

Gone was the usual fragrance of Tibetan joss sticks. The whole place stank like a bad egg.

Her eyes adapted to the gloom.

There was just about enough light from the portholes to see her way around. Some of the portholes were open to allow the sucker tubes to pass through. The pump motors throbbed on deck.

Time for damage assessment.

Her first thought was for the Dansette Popular and her collection of records. She was in luck. The record player was just above the waterline, and the old records had all been stacked high up on purpose. Once bitten, twice shy. In the last flood, she'd lost some of her best. But something would have to be done with them. She picked up a loose record and held it at an angle to read the title: Trixie Smith singing 'My Daddy Rocks Me'. Its sleeve was damp and pulpy. She'd have to get the whole collection to a dry place soon.

The worst damage was down below.

Her old velvet curtain was sodden and ruined, as were most of her clothes. Papers, books, CDs and photos floated around her. The engine room would be flooded, the *Speculant*'s wood-work would have to be repaired or replaced.

It didn't bear thinking about.

Wherever you are, Maarten, don't look now! She could just imagine his expression. The boat would be uninhabitable for a while and it would smell for even longer.

She climbed up on the leatherette sofa in the saloon and snatched a file off an upper shelf. Her bank and insurance papers. *I hope to God I'm up to date on the instalments.* She splashed through to the kitchen and found a dry plastic carrier bag for the papers and anything else she could rescue, including a few clothes.

So far, so good.

A spirit of practicality had come to her aid. It was only human. When the earthquake stops, when the flood recedes, when the volcanic dust settles or the guns fall silent, the sur-vivors pick their way through the rubble and debris and wreck-age. A chair leg here, a first communion certificate or bundle of love letters there. The flotsam and jetsam of the old ways – the ways that will never return.

Suddenly she was dog-tired.

She opened a drawer and tossed a gold watch and a few bits of jewellery into the carrier, along with a plastic frog that hopped when you squeezed a rubber bulb. She'd had the frog since childhood. She lifted the print of Rembrandt's *The Jewish*

Bride off the wall and put that into the bag too. Then she clutched the carrier to her breast and perched on the narrow sofa just above water level.

She started to cry.

Her nose ran. She wiped it on her coat sleeve. The tears kept coming. There seemed no end to them. She sobbed in fits and starts that took her breath away, like hiccups. Then just as suddenly the sobs turned to laughter.

Was it imaginable that part of her could actually be happy that this had happened?

She could hardly believe it. It flew in the face of reason. It was simply a backlash or boomerang effect, a nervous reflex. It was seeing things bottom side up, a freak symptom of stress and fatigue.

The *Speculant* was her home. It was everything she had. She loved its nooks and crannies, its romanticism, the noble sweep of its bow, its jaunty anchor and spruce little galley, the way it fitted her to perfection. She'd grown into it. It was her.

'Perfection.'

The word seemed to sum things up.

She wiped her nose again. The daemon laughter that didn't belong died in her throat as abruptly as it had come.

Something was nagging her from above.

She glanced up at the skylight.

A man was squatting on the deck.

The sight of him made her jump.

His arms were crossed on his knees and he was observing her. It wasn't Driest. He wore a heavy dark car coat and a Russian chapka that looked like a cat sitting on his head. The fact that she'd seen him didn't make the slightest difference. There was nothing furtive about his attitude. On the contrary, he gave a one-finger salute, like someone hailing a waiter.

Myles? It wasn't his build. The Kid? Again, wrong profile.

There was a new guy on the block.

They stared at each other for several seconds, then Ruth

made to get up. The man got to his feet faster. He wasn't running away. He held up one hand to tell her to wait. He spoke to someone just out of sight. A few seconds later he clumped down the back-cabin steps. He was also wearing high rubber boots. When he got to the foot of the stairs, he turned round to face her, removed a small battery-powered torch he'd been holding in his mouth and said, 'Ahoy there.' He pointed the torch at her, resting his buttocks against the stair and rucking his coat up so it didn't trail in the water.

He cleared his throat with a noisy mid-tone, then switched to a deeper tone to round the operation off. 'Braams – Ruth Braams?'

The torchlight hurt her eyes. She turned side on. He let the beam drop onto the surface of the water. It reflected up onto the roof of the saloon, creating dreamy abstract patterns.

'Andries Smits. Cop ... I'm the one who called you.' His phone buzzed. 'Excuse me a sec.' He held the device to his ear and listened.

A tough, lantern-jawed man in his fifties with dark rings under his eyes and a protruding lower lip. With his Kremlin fur hat and bulky car coat, he looked like an animal cooped up in a shoddy provincial zoo – a nondescript marsupial that visitors couldn't quite put a name to who'd gradually gone apathetic after a life of sticky buns, rotten cabbages and rainy afternoons. Ruth had a rough idea that detectives were supposed to look like this. If so, at least he had the merit of being true to type.

He lowered his head slightly to avoid bumping the ceiling.

'Tell De Vries to talk to the Filipino,' he said quietly. 'And put an APB out for the guy from Ouborg, the one with the Harley. If he shows, check for needle marks. See if he was in room two-one-two. What? Read the manifest, Nico. Pennsylvania, not Transylvania.'

He switched off the phone and brooded a moment.

More footsteps. Someone else was coming down the stairs.

A young female cop in uniform. No waders. She turned

round and sat on the steps, just above the water level, shifting her belt and holster so they didn't snag on her hips. Shirt and tie. Black leather bomber jacket, fur-trimmed collar, leather gloves. Dark blue peaked cap, with the Dutch police insignia on it, a gold flambeau. She was shapely and pretty good-looking for a dickless Tracy, with dark hair tied back in a bun, noble features and gentle eyes. *Star quality*, thought Ruth. Her lips were a beautiful woman's lips too. They smiled sympathetically at Ruth.

Ruth smiled back.

'This is Bianca,' muttered Smits. 'Bianca Velthuizen.'

'I didn't know we were going to meet,' Ruth said lamely.

'Me neither.' He looked around, unimpressed. 'This place yours?'

Ruth was suddenly anxious. 'Jojo, the girl who was here. Is she really OK?'

'I told you on the phone. She slipped and broke a leg in this stuff. Compound fracture. Mild concussion too. She's laid up in hospital.'

'I have to see her. I want to see her.'

'Really?' He smiled inscrutably.

The woman police officer seemed troubled. She looked down sadly and started playing with a small rectangular electronic device.

'Any reason why not?' said Ruth.

The smile fell away through an invisible trapdoor. Smits sniffed. 'Please yourself. Prinsengracht 769. She'll be there another day or two. She's in an odd state of mind – emotional. You'll find out for yourself.'

He waded towards her, still holding the hem of his coat up as if it were a skirt. In the half-light, he brought his face up to hers and examined her. He cupped a hand over the torch. It shone blood-red through the flesh of his hairy fingers.

'So what about this, then?' he asked, spreading his arms in

theatrical astonishment to take in the disaster zone. 'Quite a mess, eh?'

'It's a complete fucking shambles. Excuse my French.'

'We were concerned at Police HQ in the Marnixstraat. We thought this lump of old iron would end up at the bottom of the canal like the wreck of the *Hesperus*. You met Driest from the shipyard? We pulled those guys in double-quick. They still haven't got to the bottom of it. You know about boats. What d'you reckon happened?'

'I was hoping it'd be the fresh-water tanks. No such luck.'

He took out a handkerchief and blew his nose loudly. 'So where's the leak?'

She explained her theories. Together they checked out the kitchenette with the torch. The sink extension hose hadn't popped off. They checked out the toilet too. Nothing out of the ordinary.

'Beats me,' said Ruth.

Various misgivings were shuttling through her mind. She didn't feel like sharing them with the marsupial cop or his handsome confederate for the moment: there was no firm evidence. That last email was still in her pocket:

The floods are risen, O Lord, the floods lift up their voice: the floods lift up their waves.

But if this was sabotage, how had it been done? The simplest way was to drill or blowtorch through the hull, which was about five or six millimetres thick. Not so easy to drill underwater, but there were other ways of going about these things. Drill at the waterline, for example, then shift the furniture inside the boat to that side, so the hole dips below the waterline. This brainwave was a technical variation on her last flooding, back in the good old days. It'd be easy if the boat was empty and there was no one around – out near the polders, for example. But fuck it, Jojo had been on board and the *Speculant* was sitting in the heart of old Amsterdam, overlooked by houses and streets. A maniac drilling into a barge hull wouldn't exactly go unnoticed.

Ruth felt the cold. She pulled her coat tight around her.

Something caught Smits's eye. He leaned across and plucked a piece of fluff from her hair. He turned the torchlight onto it. It was a tiny pheasant's feather. He held it for a moment under his nose and the downy tendrils at the base of the quill trembled in the downdraught from his nostrils.

'So where exactly were you, Miss Braams?' he wanted to know.

'I was in Driebergen, with my parents. I told you on the phone.'

'I called your mobile. By definition, a mobile can be answered anywhere.'

She stared at him. 'What are you suggesting – that I'm lying?'

'I'm just trying to establish verifiable facts.'

'That's what we'd all like to do. I don't know what went on here any more than Driest does. I couldn't get through to Jojo. You've spoken to her. What's her story?'

Smits acted as if he hadn't heard. He waded over to Bianca and tucked the little feather into the band of her peaked cap. She was tinkering with the device again. He sat down beside her and looked at its screen.

'Nice,' he murmured. 'You're getting detail in these conditions?'

'These conditions are ideal,' she said. 'It often works that way. The worse the conditions, the better the image. The low-light sensor kicks in and compensates. Which one, sir?'

'This one.' He pointed to the screen.

Bianca tapped a button, then snapped the device shut and pocketed it. The two cops turned and climbed back up on deck as if on a signal. Ruth followed him.

'Well?' she persisted.

'Well what?' said Smits. His patience was frayed. He was barely polite.

'I was asking you about Jojo.'

'Your friend?'

'Yes, my friend.'

'She was asleep. It was night. She woke up and got an unpleasant shock.'

'I'm not surprised.'

'She was.'

'Exactly,' Ruth flashed back. 'I'm not surprised she was surprised. I've had floods before. You don't know the water's building up until it reaches floor level unless you pick up the smell. If she was sleeping, she wouldn't have noticed a thing.'

Smits scowled and shivered. He raised his shoulders up to his ears for at least ten seconds. 'If it had only been the water. That would've been bad enough.'

'There was something else?'

'What did I tell you? I can't remember.'

'You told me about the flooding, that was all.'

'I didn't tell you about another thing?'

'No.'

'Then what makes you think there was another thing?'

'Jesus!' Ruth exploded. 'You implied it. Just now! Didn't he?' She turned to Bianca for moral support. The woman cop didn't know which way to turn. She looked down in tense confusion at her shoes.

'Cool it, cool it,' said Smits. He rested his heavy hand on Ruth's shoulder. She shook it off and faced him. 'As it happens,' he went on, 'your intuition's right. There was something else. Apart from the leak, that is. There was something she saw. We don't know exactly what it was. She was rattled. She didn't go into detail and her judgement may have been impaired. It was something she saw before the flood. Whatever it was, it upset her a great deal. Let's hope she isn't of a nervous disposition. Let's hope she gets over this psychological trauma in the fullness of time.'

'Are we talking mouse or rat here?' asked Ruth.

Rat was unlikely: her mooring ropes were well greased and fitted with disc-shaped baffles. The steel spars that held the boat away from the bank wall were decorated with spikes. That, of course, didn't always stop them. Sometimes she heard them at night, scampering along the gunwale, as she heard ducks nibbling at algae on the hull. But never indoors.

'Which do you keep?' said Smits.

Ruth looked at Bianca in disbelief. 'Is this what they teach you guys in interrogation school?' She turned back, in a different mood, to Smits. 'No pets. OK? Unless you include orbatid spiders. I've got bucketfuls of them. But they don't count. Their breast stroke's crap.'

'It was not an animal. It was a thing. But we'll have to wait for the young lady to regain her wits. Let's hope she can give an accurate account of events. We'll have to file a report in due course. We have her initial statement. It was far from coherent, though the main gist of it didn't leave much room for doubt. That's standard police procedure. We start with the gist, then we fill in the details.'

'Holy cow,' Ruth whispered under her breath.

'Nope, it doesn't look good.' Smits shook his head. 'You and I should talk.'

'I've got to see Jojo.'

He eyed her with his level gaze, judging, evaluating. Then he held his head back and relaxed. His nostrils flared as he drew in the damp night air.

'Got anywhere to stay?'

'I haven't even thought about it.'

'It's not too late to check in somewhere. There aren't so many tourists at this time of year. There's always the Grand Hotel Krasnapolsky. That's where we put the visiting top brass. They do a good breakfast in the Winter Garden, I'm told.' His gaze latched on to her again expectantly.

'Why not? The Krasnapolsky's my idea of emergency accommodation too. I take it the police are paying?'

'Ah!' said Smits. 'If it weren't for those budgetary restraints . . .'

'Then I guess I'll just have to settle for the hotel over the road. One star, no lift, but very comfy. I happen to know the owner.'

'Bianca will wait for me in the car. I'll come with you.'

'No,' said Ruth.

There was now a specious ease in her exchanges with Smits that made her feel uneasy, as if he were limbering up for a new assault, a delicate war of nerves, each comment or question a tiny but destructive self-guided, heat-seeking dart. She sensed that he didn't suffer women – or maybe simply *people* – gladly.

They walked down the gangplank and ducked under the plastic tape.

The two cops reached a white Fiat Panda that was evidently theirs and Smits turned his ringed eyes and saggy jowls back to the *Speculant* with an expression of tender affection. 'A lovely vessel,' he enthused. 'And old too. A vintage model.'

'Thirties,' said Ruth. 'A Luxemotor.'

'How long have you lived here?'

'Nearly four years.'

'And what's your philosophy?'

'I'm sorry?'

'Your philosophy – your system of metaphysics. Is that a stupid question? I'd always assumed that someone who makes a conscious decision to adopt an alternative lifestyle does so for a reason. To live alone on a boat is a kind of retreat, isn't it? Now to me – the layman – that means one of two things: disillusionment with society or withdrawal for meditative purposes. Are you a cynic?'

'I'm on a sliding scale. Buddha at one end. Kierkegaard at the other.'

'And where are you on the scale?'

'Still sliding. Look,' she went on, tired of playing games, 'I moved onto this boat with my boyfriend. We split up three years ago. A year or so later he died. Since him I've been alone. That's all. In case you hadn't noticed, a lot of people live on boats in this town. It's fun. It's a little unorthodox. It can even be cheap.'

He stared glumly at the damaged vessel and Ruth found herself doing so too.

'Of course, sometimes it isn't fun,' she admitted, 'and sometimes it's far from cheap. Sometimes it's a pain in the butt.'

'I take your point.' His voice had reverted to conciliatory mode. A thought occurred to him out of the blue. He chuckled. 'Funny, isn't it? You know, if I asked you that question – about philosophy – it was because I really wanted to know. You see, secretly I've always wanted to live on a houseboat. It's a kind of dream, a missed opportunity' – he tapped his temple – 'somewhere in the back of my mind. That's Amsterdam for you. Us flat dwellers are always looking out enviously at you boat dwellers. If I hadn't married, if we didn't have the mortgage to pay off, I'd have probably given it a try. But there you are. Like that poem by the American poet Robert Frost, "The Road Not Taken". We never know if we've taken the right path in life. And we never will know – that's the point. You, for example.'

'What about me?'

'You did it. You set yourself up in a houseboat. You fulfilled my dream. But you'll never know either. It will always be a secret to you.'

'What will?'

'Whether you've taken the right path. You'll never know, any more than I do.'

Ruth rubbed her hands and did a little jogging motion with her feet. All at once she was famished and desperate for warmth and light.

'Well, dreams have a way of turning into humdrum realities,' she bitched. 'And anyway – look where it's got me. Homeless and flooded out. The only thing I've got to be grateful for is the insurance. Without it, I couldn't even afford the pumping and repairs.'

Smits glanced at Bianca. His eyes lit up for an instant the way slot machines do a fraction of a second before the payout. Ruth was just in time to detect it. The woman cop blushed and looked away, fiddling with the press stud on one of her gloves.

Smits seemed hugely satisfied.

'The insurance!' he breathed. His bushy eyebrows shot up under the chapka, forming a couple of wrinkles on either side of his forehead. The wrinkles were freshly coined punctuation marks that might have been custom-built to deal with a brand new human emotion.

Suddenly Ruth didn't like Smits at all.

She glanced round at the hotel sign and took a couple of steps backwards. 'Goodnight, Inspector – Detective – whatever,' she drawled. She pulled her scarf up over her mouth and nose so that only her eyes were visible beneath the beret.

'Cop,' he replied helpfully.

Shitface, thought Ruth. *That's who you are.*

Bianca came over. 'Will you be all right?'

Ruth nodded.

'You mustn't worry.'

'Me – worry? Why should I worry? Nothing will happen to me. Nothing ever does.'

The policewoman touched Ruth's hand. 'Oh my!' she whispered. Her voice was soft and tender. A tragic expression fled across her face. 'Your skin is so dry!'

'Is it?' Ruth ran the back of her hand against her cheek automatically, surprised.

'Yes, it is. Really! Do you use a moisturizer?'

'No. Should I?'

Bianca nodded. She seemed to be taking the matter seriously.

'I will,' Ruth promised.

Close up, the policewoman was even more of a cutie than

she'd thought, in a unique, thoroughbred Junoesque kind of way. She was really rather special. There was a comforting police smell about her too: shoe polish, leather, pistol grease. So pretty, so clean! How could she work with that hog?

Smits got into the car and raised a hand in a lazy gesture which, like everything he said or did, seemed to carry a blurred foreign language subtitle. This one read *au revoir*, or something like that.

Definitely not *adieu* . . .

She gave a one-finger salute, just as Smits had done spying on her through her skylight in her private moment of distress.

Then, as she backed off and turned, she felt suddenly sick at heart.

It was all so hopeless! Where on earth are your friends when you need them? If Myles were here, he'd give me one of his cuddles, the Heimlich manoeuvre ones that squeeze the wind out of you along with half your breakfast. And what would he say in the circumstances – the homely Mylesean voice of reason? 'Well, chuck, we *have* got our arse in a sling, haven't we!' or 'Goodness! What a pickle!' Something of the kind. Something British. But that was him all over, the incorrigible old fairy. 'Cuppa tea an' a digestive?' – his universal panacea.

If only he were right!

The world, thought Ruth, would be a better place . . .

The sickness twisted and turned inside her.

It was a good question: where exactly were her friends?

Fifteen

The Hotel van Onna occupied three canal houses on the Bloemgracht.

Ruth was on nodding terms with Trip, the man who ran the place. He showed her up to a vacant double room under the rafters on the third storey of the smallest building and they discussed her plight. He found a couple of suitcases in a broom cupboard. Together they made a return trip to the barge to pick up her weekend bag and anything else they could salvage. When they were done, Ruth locked the hatch and returned to her room.

She started fussing around.

She draped damp clothes over the radiators. She stood *The Jewish Bride* on the bedside table. She got out the plastic frog and squeezed a couple of times on the bulb. She unpacked her photos of the van der Heyden, the rubbing, the books from Mr Moon.

She was jumpy, unfocused.

Her mood annoyed her. Despite herself, she kept stopping halfway through whatever she was doing to start something else, then she stopped halfway through that in turn.

She swore and ordered herself to stand still.

Her arms dangled limply at her sides. The attic room was dotted with evidence of her partial initiatives. To cap it all, she was starving. Her stomach howled like a wolf. Trip had said she could find some cold cuts in the fridge downstairs, but food would have to wait. Why? Because one thing was crying out to be done.

What time was it, anyway?

Nearly nine.

Prinsengracht 769, Smits had said . . .

She had to see Jojo.

However crazy the circumstances, indirectly she was the one who'd got Jojo into this mess. It wasn't her fault – she'd simply asked her to boat-sit – but there she was all the same, an innocent link in the chain of events.

Poor Jojo!

The broken leg was a bummer. And concussion? How long would she be laid up? She imagined her waking in the night to the eerie slop of water – not outside, Jojo would slowly have grasped, but inside, almost level with the bed. The scene dissolved into murky browns and greys. The weak lamplight through the portholes, the dawning realization. Cut to the struggle out of the bedclothes, still half-stunned with sleep, trying to find a footing and slipping backwards, probably banging her head. The gasp, the smack of water flooding the mouth and nostrils, blindness, flailing limbs and thumping heart. Just as suddenly she would have surfaced, spluttering for breath, with the searing pain of the broken bone. And then there was the 'thing' she'd seen before the flood. What the hell had Smits been alluding to? Ruth hated the guy. He used words to say nothing, to do the opposite of communicate. It was a subtle form of police torture: knowledge deprivation, insanity through insatiable curiosity.

She wouldn't fall for it.

She felt a sudden shimmy of panic.

She'd imagined the flood scene too vividly, like a cheap horror film, almost down to the breathless soundtrack. Jojo had become Ruth. More to the point, Jojo should have been Ruth. She was the intended beneficiary. And what had so far been a loose gut feeling was now a hard little cyst of certainty.

The boat had been sabotaged.

Someone had done this, just as someone – she now felt sure – had disconnected the LPG tube from the Calor gas cylinder. Someone was trying to make a point. So far that someone was only a number, but the name 'Scheele' was a little horseshoe magnet, tugging all the iron filings into radiating patterns.

What could she do?

Rash accusations would only backfire. She needed Myles. She needed proof. She needed to shape up her case. This was one reason for seeing Jojo. Some tiny detail might clinch it. The other was her unquiet conscience, her self-reproach. Jojo had been her stand-in, her body double – almost a guilt offering, a sacrifice. Absurd! There was no way Ruth could have known. But the thought alone brought her out in gooseflesh. There was something screwy at the bottom of this situation that rang a little too true. She shied away from this secret pocket of knowledge as if it didn't exist.

Practicalities . . .

The air needed to be cleared.

She couldn't sleep until she and Jojo had spoken.

She left the hotel and called by at the boat. The men were still manning the bilge pumps. Laurens Driest spotted her and came over.

'We may have found the problem,' he said.

'Oh?'

'Have you used your washing machine recently?'

'I left town on Friday. There was a friend staying here. I did put a load of washing into the machine, come to think of it. I didn't see my friend in person. She has her own key. But I left a note telling her to add any laundry of her own and switch the thing on. Why?'

'Come with me.' They walked round the wheelhouse. A light rain was falling. He talked on the way. 'Your washing machine's below water level, right? In itself, that's OK. As you know, the outlet pipe for the dirty water goes up, through a hole in the side of the hull, then hangs down over the canal.'

'Sure. I rigged that up myself. What's the problem?'

They crouched down on deck and looked over the side of the barge.

'That's your problem,' said Driest. 'The outlet pipe's too long. Maybe you or your friend tried to feed it up through the hole. The result is that the pipe hangs down into the canal water. Here's where a little elementary physics comes in. The machine finishes its cycle and empties out the dirty water, so the pipe's full. But because the pipe dips into the canal, you get reverse suction, a siphoning effect. Get it? The canal water starts flowing up the pipe and down into the washing machine, below water level, quietly flooding the boat. That's what we found it doing.'

'Shit. Who'd have thought?'

'A tip. If you want to avoid that in future, just punch a hole in the hose overhang. If the water siphons up, it'll go out of the hole instead of into your barge.'

'There's one thing I don't get. How come it's never happened before?'

'As I said, before the pipe never touched the canal. Someone must have fed it through.'

'Impossible. It isn't long enough.'

He held her arm and helped her lean further forward. 'It isn't touching the water now because we pulled it up to stop the flooding. But it's definitely long enough to reach the water. Look for yourself.'

She strained her eyes in the half-light. A car passed on the opposite bank and for a moment its headlamps caught the side of the outlet pipe.

'That's two pieces of pipe, not one,' said Ruth. 'Fuck. Someone's added an extension. Look – it's the same kind of hose but a new extension. You can just see the join.'

He looked at her, wondering. 'It wasn't you?'

'No, it wasn't. I should know. Why would I want to do a thing like that?'

They both stared down into the water.

'The curse of the phantom extension-hose donor,' he said.

'That just about sums it up.'

They stood up and walked back to the galley hatch.

'At any rate,' said Driest, 'that seems to be your main problem. But leaks are bitches – you know that. It may be something else as well, like a hole in the hull. Do you have your records?'

'They're downstairs. I'll go and get them.'

She fetched the boat's records and he glanced through them.

'Know when the hull was last inspected?'

Ruth shook her head.

'When you bought the boat. Eleven years ago. That's pushing it. You're not going to get your permit renewed at this rate.'

'You're telling me I should dry-dock her?'

'We'll see.'

'In the meantime, what about all my gear?'

He rubbed his chin. 'We're going to wind up the pumping soon. We'll check to see if she's still taking on water. If everything seems OK, we'll leave her till Sunday. We'll be back at around four tomorrow. That'll give you time to do whatever you have to do. Then tomorrow, by daylight, we may have a better idea of how things stand.'

He handed her his card.

'By the way,' he added. 'I couldn't help noticing the old seventy-eights. I'm an amateur collector myself. You've got Nan Wyn in there.'

'Yeah, "On the Bumpy Road to Love". Nineteen thirty-eight, isn't it? With Teddy Wilson.'

'Wow, I love that stuff. Listen, I'll get some plastic sheeting down there and see what I can do to keep them out of harm's way while we're pumping. But do try to shift them tomorrow. That's history, that is. It's irreplaceable.'

*

Ruth set off briskly along the Prinsengracht.

The rain started lashing down again and she had no umbrella. A spiteful wind made it fall diagonally at her, stinging like sleet on her face. She hugged her coat around her. She batted her eyes.

The city was a friend turned stranger. It seemed to be carved out of basalt.

The fine facades, the Golden Bend, where the canal veered south-east at Leidsegracht as if it – rather than she – was in motion, the bright boutiques, the cafes, the stalwart old warehouses, the Pulitzer Hotel, the purring cars that crawled and bumped on soft suspension over uneven cobbles, the glimpse of an elegant middle-aged woman pouring ruby wine into a crystal decanter in a beautiful chandeliered room, a sad tune played on an oboe – it all felt unreal. A nameless divinity had shuffled the pack. It was the same shudder of disconnectedness that had struck her at the station. Either it would all suddenly plummet away into the sludge below or the waters would rise: Atlantis, Lemuria, Amsterdam.

The city itself hadn't changed. This was business as usual. If anything was coming unstuck, it was her. The good citizens of Amsterdam could be trusted to be themselves, lulled into inner stupor by the reliable clockwork of routine.

Their time would come . . .

Today, it was she who'd drawn the short straw in the *Minor Calamities: Damage to Property Only* stakes. Alas, alack! Poor old fucking Ruth! Today she'd got the rough end of the pineapple. Statistically, into every life a little acid rain must fall, or – if you're really unlucky – a Boeing 747 or a cloud of depleted uranium. Statistically, everyone gets to walk into life's shit-on-a-string sooner or later, later or sooner. Today it had been her turn.

And so what?

She was just shaken, that's all. Physically, she was intact.

There was time to rebuild . . .

Across the canal, a scooter passed by with a deafening roar.

Faulty exhaust? A burglar alarm was triggered somewhere and the rain hardened a notch, if that was possible – rebounding from the cobbles to create a fizzy, boiling effect a few centimetres off the ground. People were running in all directions, taking shelter in doorways, flattening themselves against walls as if from sniper fire.

She reached the hospital just in time, making a dive for the warmth and light.

There was no one at reception, but the hospital was relatively small. She'd been here before several times. Once she'd nicked her hand on the blade of an electrical sander and needed stitches. Another time she'd come to see a consultant. He'd recommended psychotherapy to come to terms with the loss of Maarten. 'What terms am I supposed to come to?' Ruth had asked. Most recently, she'd seen an endocrinologist, who'd put her on a course of cute little pills to debug those maverick hormones: up and down they went, up and down.

She knew the place like the back of her dry-skinned, nail-bitten hand.

Finding Jojo would be no problem. A little gumption was all that was called for.

She nipped round to the back of the information desk. A register was lying open. 'Recent Admissions'. That would be it.

Cuijper, Geerssen, Obermeijer, Wiltenbroek . . .

Jojo's family name was the last on the list.

No time for indecision. Whatever the visiting hours, they were sure to be over. If she was going to buck the system, she'd better get going.

She took the lift to the second floor. An orderly spotted her as she came out. 'You look like you need one of these,' he said cheerily.

He tore off a paper towel from a roll on his trolley.

'Thanks,' she replied. 'It's still bucketing down.' She took off her beret and mopped her face and neck as she moved on down the corridor.

He doesn't care that I'm here, she thought.

She came to the room. The handles to the double doors were fastened with a chain and padlock and a red No Entry sign had been taped up. A pale violet glow emanated through the small panes of frosted glass set into the doors.

Strange!

But no – she was mistaken. This was room 212.

Jojo was in 213, the next one along.

It was a single room. The door was open and nobody was about.

Ruth peered in.

Jojo was lying twisted on one side, her back to the door. There was a dressing on her head and a traditional Guatemalan worry doll on the pillow beside her. Ruth recognized the doll from Jojo's home. It was her totem, her talisman. Jojo's right leg was in a plaster cast and raised off the bed with wires and pulleys, just like in the cartoons. One naked black foot poked out of the end of it. The cast had already been scribbled on by well-wishers. A few cards and a glass of water stood by the table lamp. The lamp shed a warm, pearly light up and down, but left a dim buffer zone across the middle of the room. A television stuck out from the wall on a heavy black bracket. The picture was on. The sound had been killed. A documentary about the war: the arch, troll-like face of Goebbels, barking inanities at one of the rallies; apple-cheeked Rhine maidens, decked in flowers; boys in lederhosen practising archery; a *bierfest*, complete with oompah band.

Days of wine and roses . . .

She moved in quietly and pushed the door shut behind her. She leaned forward as if her eyes were trying to get somewhere before the rest of her body, so as not to disturb Jojo.

Jojo was asleep.

She snored lightly. The glass on the bedside table buzzed like a bug and tiny widening ripples shivered out on the meniscus of the water. At first Ruth thought it was the snoring. Then she realized that a faintly audible vibration from a piece of equipment elsewhere in the hospital was being picked up like a tuning fork by the table and transmitted to the glass. The glass moved a couple of centimetres supernaturally and she moved it back. She sat cautiously on the edge of the bed and waited for her breathing to slow down.

'Jojo!' she whispered.

No reply.

She glanced at the cards. *I wanted to make you chicken soup, but someone wouldn't cooperate!* (picture of disgruntled chicken), *Love, Mum. A big hug from the Get Well Fairy.* Lucas and Clara, that one. *A kiss to make it better* ... No name, just an initial, T – Thomas?

She turned her attention to the leg.

There were three or four blue felt-tip autographs on the plaster. Someone had drawn a hand doing the Peace and Love sign. An inevitable Smiley, and then . . .

She looked closer, leaning over the cast.

It was just below the knee. So small she had almost missed it. She parted her lips. There was a tremor in her breath and her heart fluttered for an instant, like moth wings whirring against glass.

Two concentric circles within a six-pointed star.

It was a different colour from the other inscriptions: red ballpoint to all appearances.

She sat up rigidly and hugged herself.

A sensation of nakedness gripped her.

What's happening? Am I safe? When and how will this nightmare end?

Outside a Saracen moon, so fine as to be barely visible, slit through the clouds.

She was briefly aware that the downpour was over.

Jojo stirred.

She grunted faintly and rubbed the back of one hand against her eyes. A hair, thought Ruth – the tip of a single hair had caught on her eyelid. A tiny pressure point, but enough to trouble her. In her half-sleep, the girl tried to shift her body but the immobilized leg left little margin for manoeuvre. It was this resistance that eventually woke her up.

She opened her eyes, frowning.

She became aware of Ruth.

'Jojo?'

She was aching to ask about the alchemist's star and the washing machine, but they were hardly the right place to begin. The right place to begin was with compassion. It was Jojo who'd had a bum trip. She realized that now, looking down at the unlucky girl. She herself had got off lightly. She'd dodged the bullet. It was real compassion that Ruth felt, not the bogus oh-you-poor-little-thing variety, but she was not too good at expressing herself. She'd lost the knack. What was more, she was blocked by her suspicion of displays. And Jojo's eyes were getting in the way. They were very red. *Red eyes*, thought Ruth, *always look more startling on a black person than a white person.* Now why was that? Like wounds ... like flesh turned inside out, the veiny, liquid flipside of the eyelids.

She tried to arrange her expression to hide her macabre thoughts.

Jojo leaned over with drowsy deliberation and pressed a button on a wire that dangled beside the bed. An electric motor whirred. The head of the bed rose about forty degrees and stopped. Jojo elbowed herself up so that she wouldn't slide off the pillow. Ruth wanted to help, but the girl's intent self-help attitude told her not to.

When she was comfortable, Jojo tried to speak. There was not much left of her voice. It was not even a whisper. Ruth had to follow the shape of her mouth to get what she was saying. It was like reading lips through a plate-glass window.

'You ...' mouthed the girl.

Ruth leaned forward. 'Oh, poor Jojo! Yes? What is it?'

Jojo strained. There was darkness in her eyes, something

struggling to get out. She took a breath and recycled the air. It moved along the windpipe, bringing the words up with it.

'You're . . . going . . . to . . .'

'Yes?' Ruth tried to hold Jojo's hand, but the girl snatched it away.

'Burn.'

'Jojo?'

'Burn. You're going to *burn* . . .' Her voice landed abruptly on the last word. The corners of her mouth twitched with suppressed emotion.

Ruth stared in incomprehension.

'Burn?' she questioned, in a trance.

'In hell,' Jojo added quietly, matter of factly. She gave a deep, ugly sigh. Her cheeks seemed to collapse. With a supreme effort, she managed to reproduce the whole phrase. Each word came out like a small emphatic burp.

There was a peculiar serenity about her. 'Yes,' she breathed when she had finished, 'that's what I want. I *want* you to burn in hell.'

She'd said her bit.

She'd got it right.

Her body relaxed, the dark cheeks caved in and she closed her eyes. When she opened them again the eyeballs didn't look human. They were moonstones or opals. They were the bead eyes of the little Guatemalan doll. The person behind them had taken a few steps back.

Ruth stood up.

She balled her hands and bit her lower lip. She glanced at the door.

For an instant there was fire in her veins. She wanted to thrash this thing out. She wanted to vindicate herself. But from what? She was desperate for explanations. Her mouth opened, but Jojo's face lit up again with a fierce electricity of hate.

Ruth caught her breath.

She turned and fled.

She stumbled out of the room, hardly knowing where she was going. She bumped into a nurse carrying a blanket. The nurse said something cutting, but Ruth didn't hear. The blood was beating in her ears. A sweat had broken out on her forehead and chest. She made an automatic response. The nurse shrugged. Ruth moved on.

The lift. Reception. And out. Out into the freezing darkness. Out into the open.

She was on stage. The rain had virtually stopped, giving way to a spittled wind. The houses opposite were watching her, holding their breath, wondering what she'd do next.

A late tourist boat puttered slowly down the Prinsengracht, churning the reflection of a street lamp. She watched as the waters stilled and the lamp fragments wobbled together again and docked into wholeness.

She gasped and brought both hands up to her mouth.

Nothing made the blindest bit of sense.

Was it the concussion? Was Jojo delirious?

If only she could think straight herself.

Three nuns in identical blue trench coats and pristine white wimples were coming arm in arm down the road. Two walked in perfect sync. The third was a little shorter. She kept giving a little half-skip to fall in step, like the last of Snow White's dwarves. One of the taller nuns was telling a story and the other two were laughing. Ruth thought she heard the word 'burgemeester'. Their heads turned like soldiers at a regimental parade as they passed her. She felt the ache of distress on her own face, but the nuns' stride did not falter.

'Excuse me!' she called after them on an impulse.

They stopped uncertainly, broke ranks and turned round.

'What is it?' one of them asked.

Ruth felt herself blushing. 'You wouldn't happen to have a cigarette, would you?'

The nuns looked at each other in amazement. She might have just pulled a fully illuminated Christmas tree out of a hat.

'I'm desperate for a smoke,' she explained.

They broke into light peals of laughter as if she'd cracked a good one, turned and walked on regardless, falling back into step. The three starched wimples bobbed along and disappeared around a corner, where a white Fiat Panda was parked at a bad angle on a zebra crossing.

The cold penetrated her to the bone. There was a tension at the back of her neck. The trapezius muscles seemed about to tear apart. Her lips were dry. Her hands were trembling like a wino's.

I must not be weak, she thought.

I must harden myself to the world.

Don't stand here as if the sky has fallen on your head, even if it has – at least one chunk of mouldy cosmic plasterwork, the girlfriend fiction. Keep moving, that's the important thing. Keep moving until the illusion of purpose turns illusion into purpose, indirection becomes direction, lost becomes found.

First, put Jojo out of your mind.

Something has just happened that's marginally beyond your ken. Accept this. You aren't equipped with the necessary facts to comprehend it. The correct response isn't panic. The correct response is surgical logic. The trouble is your intuition: 'feminine logic', Lucas calls it, with the slightest curl of the lip – not quite a sneer. No time for maps and compasses. You women just don't have the patience. What you want is direct, unmediated perception of the truth, nothing less. As if, by simply concentrating and introspecting, it will come to you in the manner of divine revelation. Shazam! That, Ruth thought, depends where the truth is: out there in 'reality', in the hot, cabbage-shaped labyrinth of this overpopulated town; or in here, in this cabbage-shaped brain.

For a bizarre instant her mind backflipped inwards, observing the hypothesis of itself. As if a blind man had knocked something over and frozen to the spot, assuming another living being (friend or foe?) was lying low in the room.

Keep on moving, baby . . .

She crossed the road, followed the canal, then over a hump-backed bridge and down one of the transverse side streets that debouched onto the Prinsengracht. A gloomy, narrow thoroughfare.

She glanced behind her.

The man she knew would be trailing her was there, making no effort to conceal himself. The Fiat Panda was his. Only cops got away with that kind of parking. Would he give up and get lost? No, not him. She'd known he'd be outside the hospital. He was a relentless mechanical device, built for reconnaissance, data-mining and sample analysis. He was also a prick – no offence to real pricks.

For a second, she had the tactical advantage. A motorbike wobbled up the street towards him with its bright headlamp. He raised an arm, as if fending off a blow, to shield his eyes. She slipped round a corner and leaned against a wall. She thrust her hands into her pockets. Her eyelids fluttered shut.

What to do next . . .

Head home?

There was no 'home'. The hotel, then. If so, what the hell was she doing in this poky alleyway? Her life was turning into a goddamn Möbius strip. She had started at point P – as, indeed, she'd been taught and brought up to do – then continued in a straight and unwavering line. But by some topological aberration she'd ended up on the other side of P. Where had she gone wrong? Where hadn't she gone right?

She looked up at the street name. Her internal map of the city kicked into slow-zoom mode and a connection formed. She wasn't far from the bar that was advertised on the book of matches the Kid had given her at Jojo's abysmal party. She fished the book out of her pocket. She held it up in the dim streetlight and read the address.

And why not?

A place to rest, a place to shake off the law. The name – Jade Beach – had a strange, narcotic pull.

The motorbike disappeared from view. The wet slap of
footsteps approaching. She pulled herself together and made off
down the street and round another corner – and another – and
another . . .

The bar was nearer than she thought, a cursive neon sign
buzzing erratically over the black doorway.

Inside, a tight spiral staircase going down. Quiet music, no
hubbub, a peppery, attractive heat that rose as if from a flue.
The choice was: out or in. Maybe it was a private joint, but what
could she lose? In a worst-case scenario, she could play the
innocent wayward. She'd simply be asked to leave. But even
that much forward planning seemed a waste of time.

The music was getting louder. Lowered voices, friendly
sounding. Cigarette smoke. Ladies' loos to the left, Gents to the
right. Remember, get your bearings . . . And a perpendicular
sliver of green light where two heavy black curtains just failed
to meet. She took a deep breath, entered the bar – or club – or
dive – and sailed airily across the floor.

Perfect.

No hesitation. She removed her coat, scarf and beret and
took a seat at a vacant table as if it was hers and hers alone, as
if she'd just been out to powder her nose or toot foo-foo dust –
depending on the status of the establishment.

Nobody rugby-tackled her. Nobody intercepted her. Nobody
even registered her appearance.

Safe.

She settled into the luxurious velvet-upholstered chair,
elbows on the table, and took in her surroundings. The warmth
invaded her drained, ice-cold skin, her numb fingers and toes.

A dim stone-walled cellar decked out in mottled shades of
green. The colours were seaweedy, submarine, reposeful. It
wasn't shrill, it wasn't a knocking shop and it wasn't a rat fuck,
smoothly skinning the flush tourist trade with killer spiked
cocktails and turbo-hiked bills. The place had class in a shabby-
genteel, démodé kind of way, a relic of another age. It was a

dreamy reef for elegant old wrecks, a hidey-hole for quiet, owlish souls. It was probably also the kind of spot where you could lose the odd weekend without really noticing or caring, Bermuda Triangle style – the odd weekend or, please God, a persistent cop.

A dozen or so punters, solitary and in pairs, blended into the brickwork. The staff consisted of two starched and doddery bow-tied waiters, an equally obsolescent bartender, who was slowly folding napkins into complicated shapes, and a young Asian cat in satin floral tunic and Mao collar who made Ruth think of opium dens. In one corner, on a raised dais against a draped backcloth, a man was quietly strumming a blue guitar. He wore evening dress and had slicked-back hair, fifties style. His eyebrows looked plucked.

The lazy guitar chords set the tone of the place, even the easy rhythm at which the waiters tottered back and forth, even her pulse. The soft-edged disc of a spotlight lingered on the performer. He was hunched over his instrument, oblivious. Apart from the spotlight, the only illumination was from the candles, one on each table, and an electrical sign over the quilted pelmet of the bar that read *JADE BEACH*. The letters were cut out of transparent green Perspex like big jagged pyroxene crystals. She'd never heard of the joint.

A giant papier-mâché dragonfly dangled from the vault beside a motionless ceiling fan.

So much for the surroundings . . .

There was a guy she recognized at the bar.

They'd struck up a conversation once at De Doffer's coffee shop in the Jordaan. He prepared aeroplane lunches at Schiphol airport. That's all she could remember. Their eyes met, but his gaze travelled through her and drifted off. The recognition was only one way.

The other patrons also kept themselves to themselves. This seemed to be the house rule.

In a little niche, directly opposite her, two Goths slumped

against each other, the girl's head nestling between the man's shoulder and chin. They talked. They kissed, taking their time about it. Their black lips stuck together slightly each time their heads parted. They both wore black shirts and had short, cropped black hair, forget-me-not eyes, chalky complexions and jewelled crucifixes on velvet ribbons around their necks that clunked into each other. Ruth stared at them as if she was at an identity parade. *They love each other*, she thought. The idea ambushed her.

Love! What is love?

Two strangers suddenly get a whiff of one another, lock tackle, then gradually the outline goes. Like soft wax, the wax of this candle. They melt, they drip, they meld into each other, back and forth, until they're pure, indivisible oneness. It's fun too – while it lasts. Example opposite, in flesh and blood. Had that ever really happened to her? She used to think so.

Now she began to wonder.

Zany thoughts, Ruth, get a grip!

She forced her concentration away.

She took a plastic toothpick out of its paper sheath and poked at the clogged holes in the salt shaker.

One of the ancient waiters pulled by for a pit stop.

'Martini bianco. Bags of ice. Second thoughts, make that a double,' she instructed. 'Hey – come back! Can I eat here?'

The Asian girl breezed up as if she'd been waiting for the opportunity. A wind-up doll: raven hair, cherry lips, lean, small-breasted body with smart multi-directional articulations. One hundred per cent synthetic, factory perfect apart from the cratered skin around the high cheekbones, the vestiges of teenage acne. She carried an aura of patchouli around with her.

'Hi, my name's Cheetah. Is there problem?'

'No problem,' said Ruth. 'Unless hunger's a problem.'

'Hunger a big world problem everywhere 'cept here. You wanna eat?' Cheetah smiled. 'That no problem.'

'Is there a menu?'

'This is Jade Beach. You can have anyfing you wan.'

'Anything?'

'Anyfing. So long you no take it way wiv you!'

'How about a fillet steak, flash-fried in salted butter. Possible?'

'Possible! See that guy?' She pointed to the guitarist. 'That Mister Shine. He got two jobs. He play guitar an he do cookin. You wanna eat, you gotta choose: music or steak?'

'You're joking?'

Cheetah laid a hand on her shoulder and arced back like a reed, tinkling with amusement. 'Yeah, jus kiddin! I doan wan no static!'

'What about smokes?'

A fakir look came into the woman's eyes. She reached out a hand, fumbled behind Ruth's ear and produced a cigarette.

'Magic,' said Ruth.

'Is only menthol. Never mind. Low-tar. Like smokin' toothpaste. Enjoy the show, lady!'

She swept off, head erect and one finger in the air to answer another customer's summons.

Ruth lit the cigarette from the book of matches and let the smoke do its stuff. She checked her mobile. No coverage. That figured in a cellar.

She listened to the guitarist. He stopped the soft strumming and pulled a microphone towards him.

'An old Sam Theard composition now, à la Django Reinhardt. "You Rascal You". This one's for all you incognito bandits and desperadoes out there.'

It was a catchy tune that soon got her foot tapping. The blue iridized guitar, its nacre scratchplate and chrome headstock, looked great with its showbiz spangle in the spotlight.

Ruth wet her whistle on the Martini.

The steak came – just the steak, nothing else on the plate apart from a single radish carved into a fluffy thistle shape. It was pretty artistic. Did kitchen staff take courses in creative radish whittling? The meat was practically raw, the way she liked it, straight off the bone.

Food aside, now she had a dilemma.

Someone was watching her.

Sixteen

A man had sat down at the table right behind her, not a couple of metres away. She had seen him from the corner of her eye, but resisted the impulse to turn round.

It was a proven fact that people could tell when they were being eyeballed from behind, an old atavistic preservation thing. She'd read about it in one of her parents' *Reader's Digest*s. What sensation you felt depended on who the person was and how they were sizing you up. She felt it now, a coldness on her neck as if she were sitting with her back to an open fridge. Then, when he cleared his throat – exactly as he'd done earlier on the barge, first in a mid-tone, then in a deeper tone that sounded like a slow-speed, crunching collision between two small cars – she knew it was Smits.

Smits was a new problem in her life, sticking his nose into her business, setting her up for that foul encounter with Jojo, even though he must have known she had a gripe and things were bound to turn ugly.

Ruth didn't like being put through his hoops.

But cops were a boring fact of life, like dog shit or income tax. They were one of her phobias. She'd come up against them once before when she was with Maarten: a dawn raid on the boat that nearly gave her a stroke. They were rough, armed to the teeth and looking for an amyl-nitrate factory, though all they found was a wilting pot plant and half a bottle of Baby Bio. Anger, outrage, resistance – none of that stuff really worked. It just got the stormtroopers more excited. Now was the same. She had to decide on her attitude. Unfazed was best. Play it by ear.

She knocked back her drink and chewed the last of the meat. The plate was swimming in warm blood. She mopped it up with a slice of baguette, ate the dripping pink bread and wiped her lips on the napkin.

A lull in the music.

'That was a small steak,' said Smits, just loudly enough for her to hear. 'No garnish. A tad on the mingy side, if you ask me.'

'Enough's as good as a feast,' she said without turning round. She could feel him smile, mentally approving her culture.

'Me, I don't touch red meat. High blood pressure. Have to be careful.'

'Is that so?' She gave him her bored voice. She glanced round ironically now, crossing her legs as she did so. The all-new, shatterproof Ruth, hard as nails. 'Don't you have a home to go to either?'

'I changed my mind and decided to catch up with you outside the hospital. Earlier on, when we parted, I thought you were kidding me about wanting to see the girl.'

'Jojo? Why should I kid you?'

'Suspicious mind,' said Smits, tapping his temple with a forefinger. 'An occupational hazard. To tell you the truth, I wanted to see if you'd go through with it.'

Without the overcoat and chapka, he turned out to be a snappy dresser. She was reluctantly impressed. Good-quality dog-tooth suit, bespoke shirt the top button flipped open, and a nice silk necktie pulled open too, like the man wanted to get out of a noose – the *I've been working my tail off, but now it's time to relax* message. The outfit was colour-harmonized by the green effect from the bar.

An old-fashioned sleuth with old-fashioned self-esteem, though the white Reeboks were not such a good idea.

He had pale blond eyelashes, eyebrows and curly blond hair, which she hadn't noticed before in the half-light of the barge. They gave you an idea of the kind of young man he'd once been. That said, she wasn't inclined to upgrade him. He was still a marsupial. The stocky frame, the heavy eyes, the fat lower lip. He was still a gumshoe. Given the choice, she wouldn't touch the soap in his shower.

Ruth flagged down her waiter, asked for a fresh Martini.

'May I?' said Smits, pointing to the vacant chair next to her. She shrugged noncommittally.

He moved in, ordered a Chivas Regal.

'My boat was nobbled,' she said.

'Driest called me. He told me about the washing machine. A little problem with hydrodynamics, eh?'

'That hose never reached the water. Somebody added an extension. He told you that, I hope.'

'Sure,' said Smits, smiling. 'We'll just have to take your word for it.'

Since the morning, at her parents' place, she'd had the last email in her cardigan pocket. She took it out, unfolded it and passed it over to him without a word. He read it through.

'That's the shit who did my boat,' she said when he'd finished.

'Sounds like you upset him.'

She turned round sharply. 'I don't go through life upsetting people. I don't even know for sure who this is.'

'So you have an idea?'

'A hunch. He's messaged me twice.'

'This stuff about lying,' he gestured at the email. 'It sounds specific.'

The comment riled her. She didn't know how clued up Smits was concerning Lydia and the painting. That would depend on how long a chat he'd had with Jojo, who was the only one who could have apprised him of the facts. Ruth dodged the prompt for the time being.

'Is it really possible to send email anonymously?' she asked.

'A cinch. Emails carry headers that show the path they've followed. Crooks or scammers use remailers – sites that automatically resend email anonymously. That's what this guy's done. The only source address you get is the remailer. Theoretically you can issue a warrant to the service provider. That takes time. And if your friend's daisy-chaining – hopping from one remailer to another – then he's really got his back covered. See what I mean? The cops go to the trouble of raiding the records of three, four, five, six remailers – who could, incidentally, be anywhere in the world – only to find that the first mail came from a cyber cafe in Timbuktu or some wormhole out in the dark net.'

'The dark net?'

'Data sources that've simply disappeared. Why? We don't know. Wrongly configured routers. Weird routing structures. Old addresses that no router references any more. In your case, the only move you can make is to block any further messages by informing the front-line remailer.'

She raised her eyebrows. 'Is cyber-crime some kind of speciality with you?'

'Not exactly. I listened to some talks, I read a couple of books. I try to keep up with the criminal mind.'

'So there is such a thing?'

'Sure. It's the same as my mind or yours. It just has a different agenda and considers a broader variety of means. Risk is a stimulant. How do you feel about risk?'

'Me? I don't even buy those scratch cards any more.'

The drinks arrived. Smits peered gloomily into his whisky and picked out a fleck of ash that was floating there. 'Where's your computer?' he said, getting things back on track.

'Where d'you think?'

'The boat? It's probably fucked then.'

'Yeah, but that won't stop him. He sends text to my mobile too. Or did – once.'

'Nice.' said Smits. 'What about regular post?'

'I got a chain letter – not from him, I guess. It said I'd drop dead if I didn't send six exact copies to everyone I knew and a cheque to some mailbox in Rotterdam.'

'Did you?'

'Nope. Somehow I survived. I'm not superstitious, Smits. I reckon it brings bad luck. Unless you're like the guy in the blues song.'

'Tell me about him.'

' "If it wasn't for bad luck, I wouldn't have no luck at all," ' she crooned.

He grinned, showing long teeth the colour of old accordion keys. He looked down and skimmed the email again. 'Some kind of religious nut, maybe? How's your Latin?'

'Non-existent.'

He folded up the printout and left it on the table. 'This doesn't say a lot to me.'

'Oh?'

'Someone likes writing to you. So what?'

'So what? So he also tampers with my Calor gas cylinders, sprays graffiti on the galley hatch and sneaks on board and tries to sink the tub. That's so what.'

'Your story . . . There isn't a single thing there you couldn't have done *by* yourself, *to* yourself, and that includes the anonymous emails.'

Ruth stared at him, trying to figure him out.

'The girl, Jojo, thinks you had it in for her. She may press charges. Then there's your insurance company. They'll be taking a lively interest in developments. Jojo mentioned cash-flow problems, said you'd overshot your credit. Don't get me wrong. I'm not taking sides. I'm just letting you know how things are stacked.'

Ruth's hackles were up. She flushed, hoping Smits wouldn't see this in the overall greenness. She got her temper from her father. Paradoxically, he'd lost his. Old age had smoothed him out, unruffled him, turned him soft and genial. She alone was now landed with the family curse. She smouldered but tamped down the embers.

The guitarist was at it again, but Smits had managed to louse up her peace of mind to the extent that the music had lost its entertainment value.

'I think I need a foghorn here,' she said. 'In the hospital Jojo wished me to hell. She said it like she meant it. She was in no mood for a cosy chat, so we couldn't talk things through like grown-ups. What's going on? What's up with her?'

'Thomas Springer. Name mean anything to you?'

'Yeah – the Kid. That's what I call him. We met at a party in Zuidoost. He gave me a lift home.'

'She talked about the party and Springer. She's strong on him.'

'I know. She was the one who told me, as a matter of fact.'

'She reckons you muscled in on her act. Says it wasn't the first time, either.'

'What? Come on!' Ruth shook her head in disbelief. When was the other time? Jojo could only have meant Maarten. 'Listen – years ago I introduced her to the guy she was going to marry. Going to, but never did. OK, he was my ex – the one I told you about, the one who got himself killed. But she took over from me, not the other way round.'

'So now it *is* the other way round,' said Smits, unconvinced, 'and that's supposed to make everything OK? That's supposed to make you quits?'

She stared at him again. 'Where do you cops learn to reason, some terrorist camp in the Hindu Kush?'

'There's a group-psychology phenomenon whereby a woman's drawn to a man because other women are too. It's a herd instinct. Herd valorization.'

'I don't deny it. I'm simply telling you I *gave* my ex to her. I was the one that brought them together. There was no rivalry. It was a succession. They were happy. Then he died.'

'So that's when the depression started,' he said.

'I wouldn't say Jojo was depressed. Not clinically, anyhow.'

'I'm not talking about Jojo. I'm talking about you. His death must have got to you, if you felt for him.'

'Well, of course it did,' Ruth said hesitantly.

'So it's normal – I mean, getting depressed. Especially all alone on a boat. It takes years to get over that kind of thing. I know. I've lost some too in my time.'

Ruth froze, a look of consternation on her face. Was she supposed to sympathize?

'What exactly is all this about depression?'

Smits smiled faintly. 'You said Jojo wasn't depressed, and I suggested that maybe *you* were. It seems kind of presumptuous, if you don't mind me saying, to think that she wasn't depressed. She loved him, after all. They were going to get married. You seem to underestimate the depth of her sentiments.' He pulled a pad from his pocket. 'His name?'

'Who?'

'The dead boyfriend.'

'Maarten – Maarten Aalders.'

Smits wrote it down. He was a boring, perfunctory cop again. His little digression had run its course.

'As for Springer,' Ruth went on, thawing slightly and letting some of this weirdness pass, 'I knew she'd got her sights on a new man. Of course I did – as I said, she told me herself. We were friends, remember? *Were* being the operative word. But she didn't give me a name and I didn't know it was him. Not when he and I met, anyway. We got talking by chance. Then he gave me a lift home in his van. It was only when he dropped me off that the penny dropped.'

'He offered you a lift?'

'No, I asked him. What does it matter? It was cold, it was late and he was going my way. I didn't have a chaperon, but this does happen to be the dawn of the twenty-first century. I mean, a girl can take a ride with a bloke without having to plight her troth, unless I've totally misconstrued the courtship rituals of my life and times.'

She uncrossed her legs, then crossed them again in the other direction – away from Smits. She turned her head too, averting her anger. The Cheetah woman had been hovering round in her shiny tunic. She tuned in to the body language and sidled up.

'Everfing OK, sweetheart?'

Ruth nodded and smiled a warm woman-to-woman smile, grateful for the concern.

'Good! Keep it that way. Doan wan no static!'

Cheetah tacked off with a reassuring backward glance.

'I guess Jojo misread the situation, then,' said Smits.

'How could she misread it? She got held up at a meeting, looking after someone who was taken ill. She wasn't even there.'

'She knew people who were. They told her there was a look between you and Springer, as if you were clicking, as if you were hitting it off.'

'Holy hollyhocks!' Ruth snapped. 'Excuse me, but I can't believe I'm listening to this tripe. A *look*? Shouldn't you be out there, Inspector, Hoovering the Batmobile or waxing the Bat-pole? I mean, who's keeping the good citizens of Gotham City safe in their beds tonight? Commissioner Gordon and Chief O'Hara must be shitting bricks without you.'

Smits went broody, taken aback.

He raised his Chivas Regal and sipped philosophically – the lonely marsupial once more, relegated to his dreary zoo.

Something was happening on-stage.

The guitarist twiddled the buttons on a small synthesizer and a slinky bossa nova rhythm got going, brushes swishing on the virtual snare drum. Cheetah stepped up and took the hand-held mike, swirling the lead around her feet as if it were her own angry big-cat tail. The guitarist started his strumming and in next to no time she was singing her heart out. It was 'Besame Mucho' – odd-sounding at first, delivered with an Asian accent, but you soon got used to it.

When the song stopped, Smits blew his nose as if he had a cold and clapped his hands twice as enthusiastically as anyone else in the place. He raised himself off the chair, knees crooked, wanting to give a standing ovation but – eyes twitching left and right – wary of being the only stander-upper. The applause petered out, Cheetah flounced back to the bar with a big Queen-for-a-Day grin and Smits plonked back with heavy satisfaction in to his seat. He turned to Ruth, suddenly remembering she was there. His gaze was still blurry with emotion.

'All right?' she asked nicely.

He nodded and sniffed like a kid after a rough day at school. When he spoke his manner was gentler. The music had tenderized him. 'I wish I could understand Italian,' he sighed.

'It was Spanish, actually.'

'Oh.'

'I sometimes think it's best not to understand,' she added to soften the blow. 'You just get the raw vocal melody, the emotion.'

'And you? Are you an emotional person? Are you ruled by your head or your heart?'

'Oh, heart, definitely,' said Ruth, tongue-in-cheek. 'The weaker sex and all that.'

Smits looked worried. 'That's what I thought . . . This jealousy thing, you – Jojo – the ex – Springer. Believe me, it happens. It leads up to situations. I see a lot of that. You gotta stop it before it gets to the situation stage. I know it's hard. We have feelings we can't control, feelings we sometimes regret. We make the wrong decisions in life. If you don't mind me saying so, you're an attractive woman. You've got good bone structure.'

Ruth wrinkled her nose. 'I don't trust men who tell me I've got good bone structure.'

'Why not?'

'Who's interested in bones? What's wrong with my flesh?'

'OK, OK, you've got attractive flesh. Your friend too. All right? Men are – how can I put it?'

'Attracted?' she helped out.

'Yes, attracted. Exactly. That's what leads up to the situations. The attraction wouldn't be so great if you were less – you know—'

'Attractive?'

Smits nodded. 'Of course, women are attracted to men too.'

'You don't say?'

'When that happens, when you get the two-way thing' – he made a quick back-and-forth movement with his forefinger to dramatize his point – 'there's potential for conflict, friction – you name it.'

'More situations, I imagine.'

'Uh-huh. Good ones and bad ones. There's no telling how things can work out. So it's important to get things into perspective. You need a scale of values. A system. Something bigger than yourself that you can measure yourself against. I mean, when it comes down to it, in life you can allow the godhead to remain in exile, Miss Braams, or you can invite him back. Back into your heart. Do you understand what I'm saying?'

On the outside, Ruth nodded slowly. Inside was another matter.

'As someone once said, "It depends what you mean,"' she said slowly.

'I mean what I say, Miss Braams. The godhead must be within you. You're an empty husk without the godhead.'

'I try to stay on the side of the angels,' she replied, smiling and opting for a politic response.

He threw up his hands in despair. 'Trying's not enough. I know this is a personal question – and I'm truly sorry for it – but do you have difficulty accepting who you are?'

Her anger had gone. She felt as if she was listening to this conversation from afar, holding a long cardboard tube or a yogurt pot to her ear. *Conversation* didn't seem quite the right word for it. She'd met a few space cases in her time, but Smits definitely took the biscuit.

'Did you say what I think you said,' she asked slowly, 'or have the batteries conked out on my hearing aid yet again?'

'We're following a new training programme at HQ,' he confessed reluctantly. 'Psychopathology, motivational studies, personality profiling . . . They encourage us to study the thresholds of human behaviour.'

She tapped her forehead and nailed him with her eyes. 'I have a voice that speaks to me in here,' she said with quiet conviction.

'A voice?'

She nodded. 'It speaks to me when the going gets tough. When it speaks, I listen.'

Smits stared at her intently. His teeth were clamped together. The knobs of his jaw hinges stood out just under his ears.

'Do you know what it's saying right now?'

He shook his head.

'It's telling me we need a little reverse-engineering, you and I. You want me to explain?'

The cop looked wary but tempted.

Ruth leaned forward.

'It's like this, Smits – *nice* Mr Smits . . . Putting aside, for a moment, whether I'm possessed by demons or angels – putting aside whether I am now, or have ever been, psychotically depressed – putting aside whether my steak was too big or too small, my radish crisp or soggy, my Martini shaken or stirred – and putting aside the question of whether or not I can accept – or indeed even *know* – who I am and what the hell is going on in my little shitcake of a life – I did *not* try to scupper my own boat. Crazy, isn't it? I'm so damn stupid, the idea never even occurred to me. Between you, me and the gatepost, if it had done, I might've given it a try. Why the hell not? Barge-dwelling, as I was telling you earlier, isn't all it's cracked up to be and, frankly, the cash would've come in handy, especially with the spring sales coming up. I've been thinking I could do with a new wardrobe, and one of those clockwork radios they

give away to African tribesmen would be nice too. However, as
I say, I'm such a hopeless muttonhead I never thought of it.
Shame! Another fucking missed opportunity! I obviously don't
have one of those devious criminal minds you were telling me
about. Nor – to tackle that other little matter – did I ever think
of putting Jojo out of the alleged romantic picture with Thomas
Springer, for a reason that's extraordinarily simple, though you
seem to be experiencing some difficulty grasping it. The reason
being that there is no romantic picture, nor has there ever been
a romantic picture, between any one of the three of us. Period.
Furthermore, she is – or was – a friend. In other words, that
neat little triangle you've got in your head has far more to do
with Jojo's lively but misguided fantasy life – or, dare I say it,
your own – than it does with anything I personally have ever
said, felt or done. And while we're at it, Smits, there's another
thing. It's true that you haven't shown me any ID, but you led
me to believe you were a cop. Not a shrink, not a missionary,
not a priest. And, innocent that I am, I took your word for it.'

She glanced across at the Goths. They did look like priests,
come to think of it – cabaret priests, with their clunky crosses,
wantonly flaunting their vows of celibacy.

'Now, I'm no expert in criminology,' she went on, frowning
slightly and turning back to the detective, 'but it seems to me
a fair assumption that a crime fighter's first task is to know a
crime when he comes across it. Right? First, know your enemy.'
She spread her hands and smiled at the luminous logicality of it
all. 'Otherwise there's no crime to fight, or you end up fighting
something that isn't a crime, which would just be downright
daft. Either way, a regrettable waste of time and resources – all,
of course, at the taxpayer's expense. Now a moment ago we
were talking about situations. Personally, I couldn't give a stuff
what you or the entire police force do in other situations. But
this particular situation – the emails, the graffiti, the flooded
boat – happens to involve me. So, frankly, I'd like to exercise
my statutory right to a fair hearing on this occasion. Little me,

Ruth Braams, single and unattached, thirty-two years of age, no previous criminal record – unless talking back to police officers has recently been made a treasonable offence. So who am I? Well, for one thing, I'm a Dutch citizen. One of sixteen million, it's true. Nevertheless, right now I need help. And, as a Dutch citizen, I'm entitled to ask for it from the appropriate authorities. That means you. Some weird little fucker's threatening me. That person has carried out an act of deliberate criminal damage against my home and property, very possibly with the intention of causing me physical harm as well. An ex-friend took the rap instead of me, but that doesn't change the fact of the matter, whatever hare-brained persecution theories the young lady in question may have cooked up on the spur of the moment, whatever the chips on her shoulder. You are a Dutch policeman. Do you want me to teach you your job? This is the person you should be looking for.'

She pushed the folded email towards Smits across the table and crossed her arms in defiance.

'You've been practising that speech,' he said after a pause.

'No, I haven't. It just kind of came out like that.'

'It was good. I mean, there was energy, emotion and strong development of ideas. I'm impressed.'

'Thanks.'

He looked down ruefully and tapped the folded document with his fingertips. 'Why didn't you come to the police before?'

'Nobody tried to drown me before. I thought the emailer was just a harmless crank.'

'And now?'

'Whoever he is, I bug him. Wherever he is, I get up his nose. What I do know is that he's potentially dangerous. What I do know is that he doesn't like me being on friendly terms with Lydia.'

'Lydia?' he asked in an odd monotone.

So Jojo hadn't got round to that . . .

'It's a longish story.'

She glanced at Smits, then at her watch. The second hand wasn't moving. Did he really want to hear this? He was waiting with that bored opossum face of his. She took a deep breath and began. She told him about Lydia turning up at the Rijksmuseum, their chance encounter and companionship, Scheele's rival claim, the anonymous threats. Instinctively, she put down mental roadblocks at certain junctions: saying nothing, for example, about the painting's unusual past beyond the issues of the Aryan guardian and the forced sale.

She needed Smits like a hole in the head, but you never knew. If things took a turn for the worse, his questionable skills and privileges might come in useful.

The synopsis was minimal. Events, key players, chronology.

Smits listened moodily, his jaw clamped shut. Occasionally he dipped a plastic swizzle stick into his whisky and took out his sulks on the last remnants of his ice cubes, battering and submerging them to accelerate the melting process.

'I think I've heard of this guy Scheele,' he said when she'd finished.

'He's old. Must be older than Lydia herself. Unlike her, he's rolling in it. Big investments in the eastern docklands development, so I hear.'

'What's he want with the little painting, then?'

'That's what I'd like to know. The reasons may not be financial. After all, Lydia's aren't.'

An expression of slight distaste alighted on Smits's face. 'It doesn't seem quite ethical, I must say – you working for the Inspectorate's bureau and teaming up with the old lady. If I were Scheele, I'd see his point of view.'

'If anyone were Scheele, they'd see his point of view.'

'You know what I mean.'

'I told you the circumstances. She came to the museum, then I happened to bump into her in the street. If an old person needs help, what do you do? Say, "Sorry, dear, I'd be transgressing my professional code of ethics by carrying your shopping home for you"? There are still a few human beings left out here in robotland, Smits. So to answer the question you're about to ask: no, I won't stop seeing her. She's a crazy old biddy, but I like her company. I'm not looking for trouble and, as far as the painting goes, I'm not trying to load the die in the old woman's favour. I'm also not in the mood to be intimidated.'

'Fair enough.'

He picked up her mobile phone from the table and began inspecting it with absent-minded thoroughness, even to the point of removing the sliding hatch to the battery compartment. He seemed slightly disappointed to find it was just an ordinary phone.

'So how do we stand?' she asked, wanting to bring things to a conclusion.

'We'll have to wait and see whether the Jojo girl decides on charges. With regard to the incident on the boat, you can come to the station and make a signed statement, if that makes you feel better about things. But you can't go round making unsubstantiated accusations against complete strangers. This Scheele guy's in his eighties, right? Would he really go around spraying graffiti and trying to sink boats?'

'The same thought had occurred to me.'

'Can I keep this?' He held up the email printout. 'Send me the other email you got, if your computer's still working, and let me know if you get any more anonymous communications, whatever form they take. What else? Keep a log of anything out of the ordinary. That's always a good idea. I guess it'll be a few days before you get your home back in a habitable shape. What're you going to do? Friends?'

'I don't have the kind of friends you can blow in on like that.'

'Get on to the insurance people. They ought to be able to put some money upfront to tide you over. In the meantime, can I give you a lift?'

'No thanks. I want five minutes here, on my own, then I'll walk it. I need the air.'

Smits left some coins on the table and stood up. He gave her his card.

She watched as he put on his coat and hat, then climbed the narrow spiral staircase, one hand on the rail.

A thought occurred to her. 'Smits! So what was it? That "thing" Jojo saw?'

But it was too late. The detective had gone.

She drank down the last of her Martini and mulled things over.

She kept seeing Jojo in the hospital and hearing her evil words. It's a hard thing when a friend turns against you and you have to be hard to stomach it. You have to draw in your horns and bow before the storm. At the same time, all the old unspoken grievances suddenly rear their ugly heads. Ruth's white liberal conscience got to work on the matter. *Why did I choose Jojo for Maarten and not a white girl? Why did I feel I had to nominate my own successor in the first place? What went wrong between me and Maarten? Was it my fault, his fault, or a bit of both?*

God . . .

If there was any nugget of truth to be sifted out of the dust, it was this. She had never really given herself to Maarten, body and soul, nor he to her. And giving yourself was love, wasn't it? She looked around, but the amorous Goths had gone. Love! She didn't even trust the word. It was a crutch. It was the desire to be desired. Realism or cynicism? She couldn't make up her mind. Maarten had felt the same way. They were two rationalists, sharing the bland fruit of their rationalism. Neither admitted as much, but both knew it. There was never a moment of abandon, a moment when their egos were not in full control. All their shared projects, the biggest of which was the barge, were designed to camouflage this sobering fact.

Now that Maarten was dead, she was left to figure it out for herself – the dumb own goal, the colossal crap-out, the miserable flopperoo of their relationship. That was the poisoned chalice she'd passed on to Jojo, hoping a little old black magic would sort Maarten out. He had not been a gift. Quite the contrary. Like so many men, he was just a boy who'd never grown up, the kid on the swing in the video, shit scared but putting a brave face on things. Ruth had simply given up on him. She'd tendered her resignation. She'd found Jojo and passed the buck.

She went over to the counter and paid Cheetah.

She felt in her pocket, but the book of matches had gone. Smits must have taken it.

'Do you have a card?' she asked.

'No card, sweetie.' said the girl. 'This is Jade Beach. You find us when you need us.'

A row of colour snapshots were taped up under the bar's pelmet. Ruth's gaze fell on one particular picture.

'That our Chrissmas party,' said Cheetah. 'Is no exackly a rave, but we whoop it up OK. You shoulda come.'

'May I?'

Cheetah unstuck the picture Ruth was looking at and handed it to her.

'This guy,' said Ruth, pointing to one of the partygoers in the photo. 'I've seen him around somewhere.' A black man with a big smile, his white teeth flashing, a Tahitian-style garland of flowers round his neck.

'That's Cameron,' said Cheetah.

She knew it was Cameron, and she knew exactly where she'd seen him, and with whom. A balcony in Zuidoost, with the Kid. The coincidence of the photo knocked her off balance for a second.

'He come here time to time,' Cheetah added. 'He one crazy fucker!'

'What does he do?'

'Arty,' Cheetah called out to the guitarist, 'what's Cameron do?'

'You should know,' said Mr Shine.

'Hey – back off!' said the girl, playing offended. 'I mean his *job*.'

'I know what you mean. That's what I mean too.'

Cheetah gave up on him with a skittish pout and turned back to Ruth. 'Cameron's always fulla big-shot schemes. He has this company that make slots for slot machines.'

Ruth stared at her in disbelief. 'How can he make slots? The slot's empty space. It's a hole.'

'That the slit. The slit in the slot.'

Ruth shook her head. 'The slot *is* a slit.'

'I mean the slot wotsit, lady – the mechanism,' Cheetah came back with a note of irritation.

'Oh. That doesn't exactly sound like a big-shot scheme to me.'

'It was when the euro come in. New coins, new shapes. They go change all the slots in the slot machines. Or the slits. Hey! Now you got me at it!'

'Sorry! So I guess he was in the right business at the right time, eh?'

'Sure. Cameron made a fuckin' fortune. Now he wanna expand. Get into other business. Last I hear, he blew nearly all his cash on a big ol' grain silo on Java Island, eastern docklands. Doan ask me why. Some kinda conversion. It's gonna be big cos they buildin' a bridge out to the island, bring all the people. That's what he keep goin on about. He's a man, baby. Jus' another fuckin' pig! Chasin' money, chasin' skirt – is all the same to him. What bout you? We ain' introduce usselves.'

'Perhaps another time, OK?' said Ruth, handing back the photo. 'I've got a date.'

'Now?'

'Yeah. With my bed. I've had a shit day, frankly. I just want to spark out.'

'Awright, honey,' said Cheetah, laughing. 'Come on a Wednesday next time. That's karaoke night. You know where to find us.'

She began wiping a glass out on a towel.

'Jade Beach,' said Ruth, looking up at the green sign. 'I'll be back. Oh – and I liked the song!'

On the way home, she stopped dead in her tracks. The sheer oddity of finding Cameron's photo at Jade Beach had been sinking in and now the fog was beginning to blow clear.

Was it really such a coincidence?

At the party the Kid had given her the book of matches, advertising Jade Beach. But the Kid didn't smoke.

Remember, Ruth . . . reconstruct . . .

He'd gone indoors to get the matches and who did he get them from? She hadn't seen, but she could make an intelligent guess. His pal, Cameron, of course – that's who. They'd been talking together only a few minutes before. So it was only natural that Cameron's snapshot should be here, among the many other Christmas partygoers. This was one of his favourite haunts. The book of matches was a cardboard hinge between the two events, one of the commonplace mechanisms of destiny. She imagined it passing from Cheetah's hand to Cameron's, Cameron's to the Kid's, the Kid's to hers, and now – well, Smits had got it, hadn't he?

She sighed and started walking again.

That was that sorted out.

Nevertheless, for the past few minutes she'd felt as if she'd been standing at the brink, peering into a wormhole of cosmic weirdness.

She shook her head, wonderingly. All she'd done was ask for a light.

Seventeen

'Why don't you come and live with me?' said Lydia.

Looking back, the whole morning had been leading up to just that. Perhaps it had all been hatching even longer.

Ruth had got up late.

The attic room with its timber beams and white sloping walls had several windows. Angular sunlight flooded the room. It was the splendid, crisp light you get on certain unbargained-for winter days. It sent the spirits soaring. There was a sparkle to it, like ice-cold spring water high in the mountains.

Ruth climbed out of bed and peered from the window at the canal down below and the long, slanty shadows of cars, trees and pedestrians. There was Mr Moon, outdoors on a stepladder. His shop was closed, but he was cleaning the window with big scalloping motions, waving in slow motion to his dusty piles of occult books, pendulums and packs of Tarot cards. There was her trusty bicycle with its new bell, chained to a tree, miraculously unstolen. And there was the boat, a little sorry for itself, its roof rimed white with hoar frost.

It was not just an oblong heap of scrap iron. It was her previous life, or the waterlogged remains of it.

It was good, if bewildering, to wake up in this crow's nest.

She lingered a while, leaning against the wall, thinking things through, then showered and weighed herself on the bathroom scales. Sixty kilos. The scales must be wrongly set. She stepped off. The pointer hovered just above zero. She tweaked the serrated wheel in the base till it sat just under the zero – for some reason she couldn't get it spot on – and tried again. Fifty-nine. A slight improvement, not ideal. Of course her hair was still wet, which added to the weight, she was wearing her silver Ethiopian ring, and there was yesterday's fillet steak to be considered.

Yeah, well . . .

She stood to attention like a guardsman, naked, facing the mirror.

Mens sana in corpore sano.

Yesterday had been a mad hallucination, a horror-stuffed trick of the mind. *And* the wrong time of the month to boot . . .

Today she was rested. Today she would get her life in hand.

That minge bag over there in the mirror had to be seen to. She squeezed the flesh at the hips. Exercise, for those unloved love handles. The tow-head hair was a mess. A cut, then. Something drastic. Clothes, make-up, manicure – a total relook – and where, dear girl, was the money coming from?

She wrapped a towel into a turban round her head and went back into the well-heated bedroom. She sat in the wing-backed armchair with her feet up, hugging her knees. CDs, tampon wrappers and other junk littered the floor around her. The body care would have to wait. There were practicalities to be sorted out. She knew what they were. In her half-sleep, she'd got it all planned.

Today began with phone calls.

She rang the insurance company and got the robotic voice. What did she expect on a Sunday? She tried Driest from the shipyard on his mobile. The boat was OK, but he wanted to talk. Their four o'clock date still stood. She rang Myles, told her tale of woe, asked him to pass the tidings on to Cabrol and promised not to miss the bureau meeting on Monday at ten. She rang her parents with a truthful but toned-down version of events. Her mother listened in silence, then let loose a barrage of questions. Ruth did her best to deflect them with gentleness, humour and style.

'But how are you doing for money?' her mother pleaded.

'Mum, don't worry, OK? I'm all right. If I ever do really get stuck, you'd be the first I'd come to see – you know that.'

Reassured, Maiike passed the phone to Joris. Her father was more easy-going. Ruth realized he'd been listening in on the loudspeaker, silently taking in her various reassurances. Lucas, he said, wanted to get in touch.

That over, she thought of calling Jojo's family to set the record straight, but that might be easier said than done. This one she'd save for later, once everyone had calmed down.

She rang Lydia.

No reply.

She went down the steep stairs to the breakfast room and helped herself to toast with ham and cheese, a bowl of muesli and a soft-boiled egg from the buffet. High fibre, low fat and low salt would have to wait. She washed it all down with orange juice and a couple of mugs of piping hot Costa Rican coffee, opting for brown sugar over the sachets of sweetener.

A French couple were sitting by the window with their daughter, a girl of about four or five. Tourists. The parents were in their early forties. *They had her late*, thought Ruth. The little girl was dressed in vintage forties style – grey woollen leggings, a warm brown dress and green jacquard sweater, her mousy hair in coiled plaits, held in place with coloured hairgrips. She had a cute smile, shy and pert at the same time. She was telling her parents some convoluted story, swinging her legs to and fro. When she finished, the parents laughed indulgently and the woman kissed the girl on the forehead.

Motherhood. Now that was another life . . .

The family finished their breakfast and left.

Ruth was alone.

Where the hell was Lydia?

The question kept popping back, as if she – Ruth – were responsible for the old girl. What if something had happened? It was Sunday morning. She wouldn't be shopping and it wasn't like her to go out for a constitutional promenade. She was far too homey and set in her ways.

Ruth wanted to talk to her about Scheele. She had to know what was going on. There was also the question of those missing letters. Lydia tended to clam up or change the subject when certain topics came along.

That was going to stop. Things had gone too far.

Then she remembered. Lydia was a Catholic – well, a kind of Jewish Catholic, the Judo-Christian tradition, as her mother once called it, getting her cassocks and black belts confused. Anyway, Lydia was bound to be at mass. But where? The Westerkerk was a beautiful church within easy walking distance, with its lovely chimes and Rembrandt's grave, but it was Protestant. Lydia had said something once, hadn't she? Ruth remembered it was De Krijtberg where she went, the church of St Franciscus Xaverius on the Singel, not far from the flower market. Why? For the Latin mass, that's why. Perhaps it reminded her of the old days before Vatican One, or Vatican Two. Ruth wasn't too up on that kind of thing.

She phoned enquiries and then the church. The mass had begun half an hour ago, at eleven a.m.

If she was quick she'd catch Lydia.

It was a short ride.

She chained her bike to a lamp post. Two octahedral towers, lancet windows, gables and needle spires – the facade of the nineteenth-century edifice was austere, a cliff of dull brown stone.

Inside, she ran a finger round the rim of the holy-water stoop and walked to the back of the nave. The church was about half-full, the congregation packed up at the front towards the altar to get a grandstand view and, probably, accumulate a little body heat. Long streamers of incense hung high in the air and the choir was singing the Agnus Dei.

Ruth rubbed her hands (she'd forgotten her gloves) and walked slowly forward.

Everything was brown and gold, with a brown and gold smell about it. The oiled brown wood of the Gothic double-doored confessionals, the high gold pulpit, with its baroque turret of a canopy. The place was a forest of tree trunks, rising through the colours of autumn leaf mould to the cool aerial tints of the clerestory windows, a high tracery of stone foliage, all so unlike the cosy little attic church that Myles had taken her to see. And everywhere there were pictures and statues of the Virgin. Mary seated, with her infant son, *Sedes Sapientiae*. Mary supporting the dead Christ on her lap, a Pietà. Mary standing, devout and alone.

Ruth started counting the Marys, but soon gave up.

She edged through the empty pews to the side aisle and clocked the backs of the congregation.

No Lydia . . .

Then she spotted her: unmistakable, really, the sharp wicked-witch nose under the pilling woollen hat, the old coat and – naturally – the carriers. The curve of the spine and asymmetrical slope of the shoulders were also distinctly *Bags*. She was in a side chapel, well away from the entrance, kneeling in front of another statue of the Virgin, her hands clasped in prayer. The statue faced the entrance. Ruth hadn't seen it immediately because the pillars were in the way.

She moved in quietly, sat behind Lydia and glanced round. Only one other person in the chapel. A guy in a chesterfield coat – head bowed, grey combed-back hair – his hat beside him on a chair at the back. He and Lydia were both mumbling to themselves.

The statue was more impressive than the one Lydia had by the fireplace at home. Mary was standing, holding the baby Jesus up in her hands, and the baby was holding something in one hand, maybe an orb, and raising the other in benediction. The Madonna wore long white, red and gold robes. The dominant colour was gold. They both had spiky gold crowns and wavy golden hair that fell over their pink lacquered skin.

Something formal about the poses and neutral in the expressions stopped you responding with tenderness, as you might to a real mother and child – the ones in the breakfast room that morning, for example. The figures were ritualized, symbolic. Ruth was more at home with Dutch domestic art and landscapes than religious works, but it struck her that this pose and the Pietà stood in parallel. The infant Jesus and the dead Christ were one and the same to her, the Virgin, the all-suffering mother. A saint, yes, but also the archetypal mum. She brought her child into the world and she saw him out of it. That was the essential pathos.

Lydia's prayers distracted her.

She leaned forward to listen.

'I did say,' Lydia was muttering, 'that you weren't to go with Asha. She's got her nature study to do. And, anyway, it's far too windy. The weather vane blew off the foundry in Vondelstraat this morning. That cap's not enough. Where's the new scarf I bought you for Christmas? It was damp. I told you to leave it in the airing cupboard, but, oh my, you're such a scatterbrain! The coupons are in the drawer, Sander. Now take care and don't forget the butter. She'll tell you there isn't any, so you'll have to remind her. She promised to keep a little wrap to one side for me, under the counter.'

Holy Moses, thought Ruth, she's off – talking to her dead brother – a one-way ticket to the funny farm.

The Goldilocks Madonna gazed down serenely, bending an ear to the stream of nonsense so she could pass on the message, back in the abode of the shades, back in kingdom come.

Ruth tapped her on the shoulder.

Lydia jumped and turned round, squinting. She didn't have her glasses on.

'Oh, goodness, my dear, it's you! You gave me quite a turn.'

'Sorry, Lyd.'

The Gregorian chant had finished. The high mass was coming to a close. Lydia shut her eyes and crossed herself hurriedly – 'In nomine Patris, et Filii, et Spiritus Sancti' – then came back to Ruth, switching out of prayer mode.

'Where have you been? What have you been getting up to? I've missed you, you know.'

A peremptory cough. Ruth glanced over her shoulder. The man at the back of the chapel was staring at her furiously.

'Shall we go?' said Ruth. 'If you're ready, that is.'

Outside, Lydia found her spectacles and put them on, Ruth unchained her bike and they walked and talked on the bank of the canal, pausing only when a tram swished past. Ruth helped Lydia with her carriers. She attached them to the panniers with an elastic strap. They were full of potted heather plants that Lydia had bought for one of her windowsills.

The cold began to bite.

They crossed the Singel to Cafe Dante in Spuistraat. The big art deco establishment, under the Steltman art gallery and the Herman Brood collection, was quiet at this time of day. The only other customers were a couple of young fogeys smoking sweet tobacco in pipes and leafing through the weekend papers. Ruth and Lydia ordered a warming snack, bouillon with seasonal vegetables and waldkorn rolls.

Bags wiped the drip off the end of her nose and listened, all ears, to her friend's story. She looked worn, more fragile than when last they'd met. Her skin was the colour of cold ashes.

'So, you see,' said Ruth, 'it must be Scheele. Your painting's more than a painting. Don't ask me what, just more. Are you sure your brother or parents never said anything – even a hint, a clue?'

Lydia shook her head.

'Well, whatever it is, Scheele must have a pretty good idea. After all, it was his for a time. He's seen the stuff on the back.

And now he's decided he wants it for keeps. I'm the gremlin in the works, the one who might just foil his well-laid plans. That's how he figures it, anyway. Somehow, he's got to get me out of the picture.'

'But you're not in the picture, my dear.'

'What? Oh no – not *that* picture, Lydia! He wants to get me out of the way is what I mean. He doesn't like me having anything to do with you.'

'Confounded man.' Lydia let her spoon drop with a splash into the bowl.

The two fogeys glared, then returned, frowning, to their papers.

A thin trickle of soup spilled from the corner of the old woman's mouth. She tore off a crust of bread and wiped her lips on it.

'I'm not saying it *is* Scheele,' Ruth backtracked, embarrassed. 'But it kind of looks like it. Everything points to him. There's no incontrovertible proof, that's what I'm saying.'

'Incontro-what?' Lydia cupped an ear.

'No proof – no certain proof. To tell you the truth, I'm not sure of anything any more. What do you think? You know him, or knew him. Would he be capable of that?'

'Why not? He cashed it in once, though it wasn't his to sell. I'm sure he'd be delighted to cash it in again. Even if he didn't intend to sell it, he'd be more than happy to stop me getting my hands on what's rightfully mine.'

'OK, but what I really meant was would he be capable of this intimidation I mentioned? I had my doubts because he's – you know – old. Not that I've ever clapped eyes on him. Older than you, I suppose. I reckoned he'd be past it, past these kind of shenanigans, psychologically as well as physically.'

'Past it? Am *I* past it? No! Then why should he be? Of course he's not past it. He's been waiting for this all his life. He'd leap at the opportunity to get at me.'

'So you think I'm right? You think it is him?'

'Not a shadow of doubt,' proclaimed Lydia in the exalted dowager tone.

'What is it, then, that's eating him?'

'Greed,' said Lydia. 'Possessions and money are all that matter to him. He was one of the unscrupulous individuals who used the war to get rich, exploiting other people's misery.'

'Surely he was a friend of your father's? I mean, the house was entrusted to him, and you got it back.'

'Empty.'

'Granted, but he didn't empty it. You told me so yourself. To the degree to which he was trying to protect your property – Jewish, or half-Jewish property – he was sticking his neck out on your behalf. Correct me if I'm wrong.'

Lydia's expression foreclosed further debate.

Ruth sighed. 'All the same, there's something I can't quite wrap my otherwise all-encompassing mind around. OK, the painting's a big bone of contention between you. But if you hate the guy so much, how can you bear to live opposite him?'

'Don't you see? That's the way things have always been. Him over there, me over here. I can read him like an open book. I know his every thought. I'm not afraid of him. I'm not intimidated, to use your word, or weakened. On the contrary, his presence gives me strength. Of course, very soon now I'll be off. Very soon I'll be shot of him.'

'Pittsburgh, huh?'

Lydia nodded. 'Then I can settle down, forget about all of this. In the meantime, this is the way things have to be. At least until my painting's returned to me.'

'I've seen the police. They imply that I can't do a thing – not unless he really comes out into the open. In other words, you're allowed to lodge an official complaint only if and when you've got a bullet lodged between your eyes.'

'The man's a coward. He wouldn't have the guts to attack you.'

'He had the guts to flood my boat. He had the guts to scare

the living daylights out of Jojo. Assuming for the moment that it was him. How much more guts do you need?'

'Where's the safest place to have your enemy?' asked Lydia with an enigmatic smile.

'I wouldn't know.'

'Well, where do you think?'

'Like you said, I suppose. Where you can see him.'

'Just so. And my enemy is your enemy now, so that's where you should have your enemy too.'

'What do you mean?' asked Ruth after a pause.

Lydia had the smug look of someone who's been dealt all the right cards. 'I mean that you're out of a house and home. You can't go on paying for a hotel.'

'So?'

'Why don't you come and live with me?'

Ruth's first thought was of the smell. Her second was the mess. At the same time she felt bad about reacting so selfishly, so fastidiously, to the old lady's kind offer. Her face must have shown some of this.

'I mean out the back, of course, in the *achterhuis*,' said Lydia with a certain formality and hauteur. 'It's where Sander used to have his den. You'd have your own privacy, away from me and my unsightly clutter. Nobody's used it for a long time, but it's clean dirt, as they say, and there's even a bed and few sticks of furniture. I heat it from time to time to stop the damp getting a hold.'

'I couldn't,' said Ruth.

'Is it the cats that are worrying you? They all went to the refuge, my dear. All except one. I kept Principessa, if you remember her.'

'Oh, the cute black fluffy one.'

'I felt that, of all the cats, she was the one I needed the most, and the one who needed me.'

'To wait on her hand and foot, I suppose.'

'She is a little demanding, I grant you, but I'm sure you'd get used to her, and me, for that matter.' There was a pause with awkward things going on in it. 'I don't want you to think I'm trying to lure you into my lonely old woman's clutches. I just want to help you out. Temporarily, that is, until you can live in your nice old boat again.'

'That could be some time,' said Ruth, still in two minds. 'It may have to be dry-docked for a check-up, but when I get it back it's going to stink. Plus there's furniture and bedding. The last time I had a flood we were out for a fortnight.'

'It doesn't matter to me how long you stay, my dear. Anyway, that's my offer, take it or leave it. Lord knows, it's not often I get the opportunity to make myself useful.'

Ruth nibbled at her thumbnail.

'That's a very bad habit, you know,' said Lydia.

'What? Oh, sorry! Listen, Lydia – I don't know what to say, really I don't. It's so sweet of you. I'd have to pay rent.'

'I wouldn't hear of it.'

'Something to cover the bills then. Heating, and light.'

'We can discuss that later. In the meantime, come and have a look at the place if you're undecided. I don't think you've ever been out back, have you?'

The three-storey *achterhuis* was separated from the *voorhuis*, where Lydia lived, by an inner courtyard housing the toilets and a low wooden door that led to the underground utilities. They walked down a corridor that ran alongside the courtyard between the two buildings. Ruth had never visited this part of the canal house before. The corridor was decorated with heavy stucco ornamentation and floored with worn marble slabs. It led to a wooden door, also embellished with mouldings.

Lydia turned the big old-fashioned key in the lock with both hands.

The door opened onto a beautiful parlour, as wide as the whole front house.

Ruth felt a frisson when they went in, as if she was burgling the place. She imagined the spectre of Sander confronting her or looking up angrily from the substantial mahogany desk by the window.

The parlour had a broad decorated fireplace, a grisaille over the door, and above their heads was more pastry, as Ruth thought of the stucco. It framed a faded old ceiling painting of angels disporting in the clouds, all pastel pinks and whites and blues. At the back the windows gave onto a small garden. There was a broadloom carpet, almost as big as the room itself, and a tatty antique kilim hanging on one wall. The other walls were lined with old books.

It dawned on Ruth that Sander's den had remained almost untouched since his death nearly half a century before. It was obviously cared for and cleaned, but so were museums. Everything in the parlour dated from the late forties or early fifties, with the possible exception of the light bulb – which didn't work – and the electric heater, which Lydia was now trying to chivvy into life. There was even a page-a-day wall calendar, which had stopped on 3 June 1955. Sander's bits and bobs were everywhere, preserved against the ravages of time and fashion.

Ruth had heard about a room that was found in 1980 above a deserted synagogue in London's Whitechapel area. Its occupant, a Russian Jew called David Rodinsky, had walked out some time in the sixties, leaving a time-capsule of his life. What had become of him? There was a dent in the pillow where he'd slept, a cup of tea beside the bed, porridge on the stove, books and mysterious cabbalistic writings. Had he been murdered? Had he accidentally tumbled into another space–time dimension? Nobody knew. The room was all that was left of him. Rodinsky had no loving sister to cherish his memory in her heart. The curators of his museum went by the names of chance and neglect.

Ruth looked at Lydia's bony back, hunched over the heater, her fingers twiddling the dial. She was quite a phenomenon – the last scion of the van der Heydens, the lone leaf at the end of autumn, all dried up, crackly and half pegged out, still clinging by some trick of fate to the topmost branch of the tree, come rain or shine.

As for the dead man, his presence could be felt in little details. An old aquatint of the seafront at Menton, the books – works on ornithology, optics, architecture, travel – the ivory letter opener, Bakelite fountain pens, a large blotter and draughtsman's implements in a long velvet-lined box with a gold clasp, which lay open on the table. The room was the projection of a literate, cosmopolitan mind with a technical rather than artistic bent. A thought occurred to her, which translated instantly into a tingling sensation on the skin. Could the painter's letters be hidden here? The brother was the one who had hidden them; suddenly she realized how little she knew about the man.

'What exactly did Sander do?' asked Ruth.

'Sander? He wasn't one for banking, like his father,' said Lydia, a little short of breath. She'd got the heater working and was now pulling off the big dust covers. Ruth helped her fold them into neat squares. 'He was interested in chemistry and physics and making things work. When he was a boy, he used to build go-carts out of wood and old pram wheels. He made about five or six, I remember – each one with a better steering or braking system. After the war he trained as an oph—, an eye doctor. Oh, now what is that word?'

'An ophthalmologist, I guess.'

'Of course ... Sander always got angry with me because I could never remember the word, and the more he got angry, the more difficult I found it to remember. But where was I? That's what he was going to be until he decided to give up his studies. He got bored. Then he just sort of drifted, as people do. He worked as a technician in the margarine industry, when they started importing copra. He worked for a cigar manufacturer. He even worked for a nearby confectionery company, then he packed that in and ended up doing odd jobs for people. A jack

Adrian Mathews

of all trades. Welding, carpentry, mechanics, electrics – anything he could turn his hand to.'

'A practical man.'

'Definitely. Always taking things apart and putting them together again, fixing old things and designing new ones. It's a family trait. Our father was like that too. There was no end to Sander's ingenuity. He lived in a little world of his own.'

That little world was here, thought Ruth. Lydia had become wistful, possibly thinking the same thing. After a while she came back to the job in hand with a businesslike air.

'Now, my dear, you can either sleep here on the sofa or upstairs. There's a little bedroom. It's up to you. The bathroom's upstairs too. I've just turned the boiler on so the water should be hot in a couple of hours. If you want to cook, you'll have to use my kitchen, and I'll clear a shelf for you in the fridge. Help yourself to anything you find there. But what am I saying? You haven't told me whether the arrangement suits you.'

Ruth wiped a sleeve against her forehead, then put her hands on her hips and looked around. 'It's fine, Lydia, really fine. I accept your kind offer, and I'm very grateful – truly.' Lydia beamed and Ruth gave her another hug. 'Now shall we look upstairs?'

'If you could get the Hoover from the house – oh, and a stepladder. We'd better change this mantle before it gets dark.'

'Mantle? That's what we call a light bulb, Lydia. Gas went out of fashion some time ago.'

'Oh yes. Silly me! And I forgot to mention – don't worry about the colour of the tap water. The iron's good for you, but it's not very pretty. Just leave it running. It'll soon flow clean.'

By the time they'd finished, it was half-past three.

'I'll probably get a taxi to bring some of my things. The rest will have to stay on the boat,' said Ruth. 'And I've got to see the guy from the shipyard. Will you be here when I get back?'

'I'll be here,' said Lydia. She was gazing at Ruth in a peculiar way, her eyelids blinking.

'Is everything all right?' asked Ruth.

'Yes, my dear. I was just thinking. It's soppy, I know, but I feel like a little girl again. Oh, goodness, should I tell you? I was thinking we shall be like sisters, living here together. But Ruth, I'm embarrassing you. Forgive me. You mustn't pay any attention to an old woman's ramblings. *Meshugge*, you know. That's the word my mother would have used. She used to speak *Jodenhoeks*, the language of the Jewish quarter. Lydia, she'd have said, stop your nonsense at once. You're going soft in the head.'

Eighteen

*O*ne, two, three . . .

Ruth braked hard and rang the bell on her bike.

Driest, Myles and the Kid had been chatting together beside the barge. They turned round to face her.

'Well, well, well,' she said, slipping forward off the saddle, 'Three gentlemen for one lady.'

'It's all right, dear. I'm just going to watch.'

'Shut up, Myles, you maniac. So where shall we start? Thomas! What are you doing here?' she asked the Kid.

'I came in the van. Lydia gave me a ring. She said you'd signed out of the hotel and brought one suitcase, but that you might need a hand with the big move.'

'Funny, I've just left her. She didn't say anything to me about calling you.'

'That's Lydia.' The Kid shrugged.

'Well, thanks. I won't say no. Damsel in distress and all that.'

Driest turned away to talk to one of his men.

'You're moving in with her now, are you?' said Myles with a sly smile.

'Temporarily. I'm de-homed as you can see. She offered to put me up for the duration. Anyway, Myles,' she pursued in a harder tone, 'your turn. To what do we owe this unexpected honour?'

'I'm just one of those postmodern voyeurs who are drawn to disasters. Car accidents, fires, sinking boats, plane crashes – any

of that stuff turns me on. I can't get enough of it. Disasters are
the real cultural infotainment of the times.'

Ruth caught the Kid's eye and they shared a no-hope look.

Driest came back. 'The boat's pumped,' he said. 'You can
shift your stuff now, if you want. It's not exactly bone dry, of
course.'

'Sounds to me like rehab time for postmodern voyeurs,' said
Ruth.

'Yeah, yeah,' said Myles. 'I'll help you load the van.'

Myles and the Kid worked in relay, passing things up
through the galley hatch and stacking them in the van.

Driest took Ruth to one side.

'The dry dock?' she said.

'Looks like it. First thing we spotted was some dodgy riveting behind the washing machine, then we tapped the hull. It
isn't holed, but at this rate it will be soon. We're not sure, but it
seems to be under three millimetres in places.'

'So you double-plate?'

'We've got a sonar gizmo back in the yard. We map the hull
to find the weak points, then – as you say – double-plate. While
it's dry-docked, we might as well clean the hull and retar it too.
If you want to get your permit renewed, that is. All in all, a
three-day job.'

'Shorter than I thought.'

'Don't forget you'll have internal repairs. Nothing structural,
just getting your furniture sorted out, waiting for the damp and
the smell to go. It could be longer.'

'And the damage? The other kind, I mean.'

He handed her an envelope. 'Here's our quote. We'll take the
boat now. There are two guys down in the engine room, checking the mechanics. The machinery's been out of action for some
time. Post the quote off straight away to your insurance company, along with the claim. Given the circumstances they ought
to be able to OK it provisionally, even if they haven't had time
to make their own assessment. It's called good faith.'

'Oh, good faith. I remember that.'

'Right now, your big problem's going to be the records, especially the seventy-eights. You can't just let them skid around loose in your friend's van. Frankly, it looks like a rust bucket.'

'Vintage rust bucket,' said Ruth. 'Pre-sprung suspension, pre-shock-absorbers and pre-internal combustion.'

'That's what I thought. So they need to be tightly boxed, bubble-packed and reboxed. I've got what you need in the car. Want me to do that?'

'Would you?'

'I'll do my best. No liability for breakages, and all that . . .'

'Just look out for the Americans. Benny Goodman, Tommy Dorsey, Bix Beiderbecke and Chet Baker, in particular. Also the Dutch. I've got some classic one-offs in there. Hannes, the old comedian, Max von Praag, Kobus Robija.'

Anything that was unsalvageable stayed on the boat or was dumped in a skip that builders were using further down the street. The rest was packed into the van. Ruth made coffee and caught up with the Kid in the wheelhouse when he took a break.

'I knew about this,' said Springer, 'before Lydia called me.'

'How come?'

'I called by on Saturday, as promised. Remember – the eel?'

'How could I have forgotten?'

'I was going to leave it with Jojo, like you said I should. Then, when I got here, the place was crawling with cops and firemen. I thought, maybe this is not the time.'

'For what?'

'For the eel.'

'I take your point.'

'The guy from the boatyard told me what'd happened and said the cops had already called you. He also told me where I could find Jojo. I called in on her at the hospital.'

'So you know,' said Ruth. 'You know Jojo's big conspiracy theory of what happened.'

'I don't know anything. She was out cold, under sedation.

The nurse let me in for a second so I could drop off a get-well card. That was it.'

'There was no one else with her?'

'No one.'

Ruth turned things over for a moment. 'The leg. Did you see the leg?'

'The leg in plaster? Sure. It would've been hard to miss it.'

'There were things written on it.'

'There usually are.'

'Not just written. Drawn. Someone drew that damn symbol.'

The Kid looked ill at ease. 'The star, you mean, with the circles inside?'

'You saw it too? So whoever drew it visited her before you. What time were you there?'

'Just after twelve. But, listen, that star thingy – it was me.'

Ruth stared him out. 'You painted that on my galley hatch too?'

'Your galley hatch? I don't follow this. I mean, didn't *you* paint it on your galley hatch?'

'No, I didn't.'

'Well, neither did I. I drew it on her leg, that's what I'm telling you. I don't know why. I wanted to make some kind of mark on the cast, but it seemed corny signing my name. I'd just come from your barge and I'd seen the star. It was in my mind. I was wondering what it was. So I drew it on her leg. It was more for my benefit than hers. I wanted to see if I could reproduce it.'

'Jesus,' breathed Ruth. 'The irresistible human compulsion to scribble on plaster casts. When shall we ever get to the bottom of it? Someone should write a psychology doctorate on the subject. There must be parallels with cave art.'

She topped up the Kid's mug from the coffee pot and leaned against the boat's wheel, arms folded. 'You know this was all your doing, don't you?'

'What was?'

Now he looked distinctly nervous.

'The flooded barge, Jojo in casualty.'

'Me?'

'OK, you didn't actually do anything physically, but you were the apple of discord, so to speak. Think back to the party, where we met. Remember? Jojo invited me, then got held up. Little did she know, but I was going to steal you from her. Prize bitch Ruth had got it all planned. For years she and Jojo had this jealousy thing going between them. Then along comes eligible Thomas Springer. Not that you were Jojo's in the first place, but she'd kind of earmarked you for herself. Know what I mean? Your own opinion on the matter was completely irrelevant. Ratbags, these women! Then just to push Jojo completely out of the running, Ruth got her to barge-sit, flooded her own barge, breaking Jojo's leg, knocking her half out and scaring the shit out of her into the bargain.'

'Sounds like you over-reacted.'

'Not really, because I had my eye on the payback too. A little background here. Poor old Ruth was as good as dished. The boat was becoming a liability. Might as well cash in the insurance chips, mightn't she? So the accident was rigged to happen while she was out of town. Cunning, eh? It was the perfect crime, straight out of Patricia Highsmith. A heady blend of cool calculation and burning passion, with high financial and romantic stakes. I still don't get it. Where did I slip up?'

'You're having me on. Somebody really believes this stuff?'

'That's how Jojo's sussed it, and there's a nutty cop called Andries Smits who's already got me tabbed as a hardened felon, though I've managed to throw a little fairy dust in his eyes. In the meantime, my one hope of reprieve is if darling Jojo turns out to be concussed, recovers, sees the light of day and doesn't press charges.'

'Jeez. I've got a feeling I've seen this movie before.'

'I wish you'd tell me how it ends.'

'Listen, would you like me to talk to her to straighten things out?'

'No, don't bother. This is girls' stuff. It's going to be tricky, though. I didn't get a nice reception from her in the hospital. Frankly, she really spooked me out. I've tried to ring her once or twice since, but they say she's unavailable.'

'You'll keep trying?'

'I'll keep trying. But the worst thing is, this isn't just an almighty farce. There's a grain of truth. This wasn't an accident. The boat was scuppered – deliberately.'

'You're serious?'

'What do you know about washing machines and drainage pipes?'

'Not a lot.'

'Then I'll skip that bit till later.' She glanced at her watch. 'We'd better get on with the move. I'll tell you this much for free, though—'

'What?'

'The lady never got the eel.'

'How d'you know?'

'I saw the trailer.'

'Well, you're wrong,' said the Kid. 'It's in the fridge at Lydia's. I put it there an hour ago.'

Myles came up. 'Go,' he said.

'What d'you mean, "Go"?'

'I mean go, now. To her place. If you don't go now, you can't come back.'

The pink Dansette Popular looked good on the desk in Sander's parlour. Ruth opened it up and took a seventy-eight out of one of her cardboard boxes.

'Here we go,' she said. She lowered the tone arm, positioning the needle over the edge of the disc. 'Jimmy Bertrand's Washboard Wizards. "Easy Come, Easy Go Blues". Chicago, April 1927. Louis Armstrong on trumpet and the immortal Jimmy Bertrand himself on washboard and blocks.'

'Just in case you've been on Mars for the last three-quarters of a century,' Myles remarked to the Kid.

Ruth and Myles locked hands and waltzed around for a bit, then unlocked and Charlestoned face to face. When the music stopped, Myles flopped into the armchair, red and sweaty.

Lydia produced a bottle of Asti Spumante and the Kid popped it. Together they all raised their glasses in house-warming.

Ruth picked out a more sedate record and this time the Kid took Lydia for a whirl. The old lady put on a superior air, as if she were at a *thé dansant* in the old days. The one remaining cat, Principessa, sat on the desk, following the record going round, ears cocked forward, uncertain whether she was supposed to try and catch it or not.

'Thomas seems like a nice boy,' said Myles when he'd got Ruth on his own.

'Don't tell me you're after him as well.'

'As well as whom?'

'As well as the whole of womankind, apparently.'

'Alas, no. I have Rex, for my sins, not to mention Sweekie-boude.'

'Myles, I have something to ask you. Am I doing the right thing? What's your honest opinion?'

'If I knew what you were doing, I might be able to answer that.'

'I'm talking about coming to stay here.'

Myles looked uncomfortable. 'Shall we get some air?' He led her into the inner courtyard. When they were completely out of earshot, he spoke again. 'You took up the old lady's offer. What's wrong with that? It'll only be for a few days, anyway. Of course, in the unlikely event that Cabrol gets wind of this, it could cost you your job. That's the downside. If, on the other hand, you really want to get a line on van der Heyden, as I think you do, then fate's setting things up rather nicely for you.'

'I know, I know – the letters.'

'Look for them, Ruth.'

'I do, whenever I get a chance, but even Lydia has never laid eyes on them. It's all hearsay. Added to which, it's not a brain she's got, it's a scrambling device. She hardly knows which century we're in. What is there to prove that those letters even exist?'

'Let's talk about this later. Did you make any headway with the numbers?'

'Shit, I was supposed to ring Lucas . . .'

'Do that. In the meantime, we've got Cabrol tomorrow morning at the bureau.'

'Any idea which way he's going to go?'

'If I knew that, I'd certainly be at one with the powers of darkness. He's so suspicious he doesn't even confide in himself. But his judgement's one thing and the groundwork we're doing is quite another. Agreed?'

She nodded.

'To be honest, I'm half tempted to confront him head on.'

'You think he knows more about the painting than he's letting on?'

'I simply haven't a clue. But when I consider confronting him, I get this red warning light flashing in my primitive brain stem. He's too damn snaky. All I'd be doing is selling us both down the river.'

'So what happens tomorrow?' Ruth asked.

'I'd like you to be there to back me up in certain requests I'm going to put to Cabrol, and also because there's someone I want you to meet afterwards. You're not winging off after the panel meeting?'

'No. Who's the someone?'

'A visiting dignitary. I thought we could show him around the Rijksmuseum. There are a few paintings on the walls that he hasn't seen since he was in the MFAA.'

'That damn acronym again. You told me what it meant but I've forgotten.'

'Tomorrow.' Myles held a finger to his lips. 'Be there.'

Ruth gestured at Myles to go in, then called Lucas. She looked up at the little flag of sky between the front and rear houses.

'Hello, Ruth.' There was a remoteness in Lucas's voice that she didn't like. 'What can I do for you?'

'Dad said I was to ring you. About the numbers.'

'Oh.' There was a pause in which he breathed heavily. He was like a peculiar amphibious creature that kept disappearing underwater just when you thought you'd got it in sight. 'I'd almost forgotten about that, what with the other thing.'

'The other thing?'

'I'm referring to Jojo.'

In her haste to ring him, Ruth had overlooked the Jojo connection.

'We went to see her,' said Lucas, still breathing heavily, 'and we were very upset by what we saw and heard. Do you understand what I'm saying, Ruth?'

'I understand.' She heard her own voice coming out coldly, steeling itself and her.

'Naturally there are two sides to every situation,' he went on, 'and we would want to hear what you have to say in your defence rather than jump to conclusions.'

'Jojo's a mile wide of the mark,' said Ruth. 'And she's concussed. I've been trying to phone her, but I can't get through. However, I think you should know that I had nothing to do with the state she's in now.'

'I didn't think that you had. It all seems so far-fetched.

Nevertheless, you'll forgive me for saying so, but Clara and I couldn't help feeling that some of the things she told us rang true. I'm referring to a certain rivalry between the two of you over Maarten.'

'Someone told me Jojo felt that way. She and I have never discussed the matter. But if it's true, well, that's her problem, I'm sorry to say. Personally, I've never seen our relationship in those terms.' Ruth was still looking at the rectangle of sky. A seagull flew into the centre of it, looped lazily, then sailed away. 'If you want my opinion, I think Jojo was jealous of the fact that Maarten and I had a past together. When he died, there was no future left for her with him, only the past – and I'd had a bigger bite of that past than she had, if you see what I mean. It was as if I'd stolen him from her in reverse, in time running backwards. Shit – I know that's crazy, but I think there's something to it. You see, she loved Maarten, and I didn't. Not really and truly. Of course I felt affection for him. What I mean is, we wanted to love each other, but we didn't know how.'

There was no reply.

The breathing faltered a little, then came back thick and laboured.

'I'm sorry if that's a hurtful thing to say,' she added.

'I won't repeat what you just said to Clara,' said Lucas after a while, 'and I'd be thankful if you didn't take it upon yourself to do so either.'

'No, of course not.'

'Still, I suppose I should be grateful to you for this confidence, after all these years. I now have a better idea of how things stand or stood. If what you're telling me is true, it might explain Maarten's long-standing frustration.'

Ruth tried to decide how to take this. You never could tell with Lucas. He was as capable of refined bitter irony as he was of a bald honesty that was so frontal in impact that it was almost worse than his ironies.

'Frustration?' said Ruth, trying to sound him out.

'And frustration,' Lucas went on, as if he hadn't heard her, 'can lead to recklessness.'

Now it was clear.

She was being held responsible for Maarten's death.

This she would not let pass.

'At the time of the accident, Maarten was living with Jojo,' she said firmly. 'You know that, Lucas. He was on a roll. Everything was upbeat. Remember? I was already history. I admit I was a disappointment to Maarten, but he had had plenty of time to get over that. Things never really clicked between him and me. I don't know whether you guys talked about it, so maybe Maarten never confided in you. Maybe you're hearing this for the first time. If that's the case, I'm sorry. I was almost certainly a disappointment to Maarten – though these things go both ways, as I'm sure you well know – and now I'm proving to be a disappointment to you.'

There was a lull with nothing in it but a crackle of static on the line.

'The truth is not something one withholds to avoid disappointment.' Lucas spaced out his words as if he were physically laying them down in a row. 'The truth has a value over and above one's visceral reaction to it. In most circumstances, I believe, it's preferable to falsehood. Things should be told as they are. I'm encouraged to see you have the audacity to do just that.'

Why was it that his sentences always felt like traps slowly closing over her? They were close-knit meshes of reasoned and reasonable argumentation, free of redundancy or hesitation. They could neither be faulted nor avoided. Invariably, she saw them coming and played doggo. The poor man, it wasn't his fault. It was the way they talked at the university. There was never a breath of frank emotion about them.

The logic was impeccable but extraterrestrial, the product of a thought system that was as tightly closed as a superglued

Tupperware box. He was a man with his head full of chemical formulae, where everything had to balance everything else and did. He couldn't understand why life and ordinary language, which should be easy, failed to square in the same way. She felt sorry for him, really she did. He had never got over the death of his son. His mind went on turning in ever-decreasing circles, like Erskine Tate's Vendome Orchestra in the other room. In the end, there was nothing left but a scratchy silence.

The Kid opened a window and put his head out. 'We're going to make something to eat. Will you join us?'

'Yes, Thomas, I will,' she replied, 'that'd be nice.' She brought the phone to her ear again.

'Would that be Thomas Springer?' said Lucas, a new edge to his voice.

'Yes, do you know him?'

'Jojo told us about him, as you can imagine.'

Ruth's heart sank.

'It's not what you think. He and I just happen to have a friend in common. An old lady, not Jojo. He also has a van. He helped me move my things out of the boat. If you want him to confirm what I'm saying, I'd be happy to pass the phone over to him.'

'That won't be necessary,' said Lucas stiffly. 'What you do in your private life is your own concern. However, I feel it my duty to tell you that Clara was very upset to see Jojo in that condition and to hear what she had to say. I don't want to force your hand, but I think it would be nice if, out of common kindness, you called round some time to put her mind at rest, whatever small price the effort may cost you. Your friendship with Jojo, you see, means a lot to Clara.'

'Do you think it means nothing to me?'

'You're putting words in my mouth, Ruth.'

'Sorry.'

'As for those numbers,' he added, relieved at being able to shift to factual matters, 'I believe Joris was right. It's a code, of a kind that was quite common in the eighteenth century. A number-for-letter substitution. Like your father, I'm afraid I've drawn a blank for the time being. He probably explained to you that there are letter-frequency rules we use to crack these codes, but none of them corresponds to Dutch.'

An idea came to her in a flash. 'Latin,' she said. 'Have you tried Latin?'

It seemed so obvious. Johannes van der Heyden was an eighteenth-century pharmacist. Latin would have been second nature to him. The names on old apothecary's jars were always in Latin, weren't they? She'd been getting quite an earful herself, what with the mass that morning and her anonymous emailer's habit of slipping in the odd tag.

'It's an idea,' said Lucas. 'I'll give it a go. You never know, it might work.'

'Thomas set your computer up,' said Myles when she came back in. 'It works, you'll be delighted to hear, though the speakers sound a little on the soggy side. He's taken an extension lead off Lydia's phone line, so you can surf to your heart's content. You pay a forfeit, don't you?'

'Sure.'

'We wouldn't want the old lady footing the bill.'

'No, quite.'

'As for me,' said Myles, 'I'd better be off. Listen, dearie, I'm glad to find you're your usual scintillating self, despite all the slings and arrows of outrageous fortune. Just don't let the buggers get you down.'

'I'll remember, Myles. Won't you stay for one last dance?'

'Do you take requests?'

'Name it. If I've got it, I'll play it.'

'There's an old Inkspots number I'm rather fond of. "Someone's Rocking My Dreamboat".'

Ruth kicked him in the seat of the pants.

'Take a hike, you scurvy varlet!'

Ruth, Lydia and the Kid picnicked in the parlour on smoked ham, cheese and baked potatoes. As ever, Lydia cracked open a bottle of jenever. She sat enthroned on the one chair, while the others squatted on the floor. Principessa was in fact just a kitten, a sleek black creature with three white socks. She reduced them all to tears of laughter, walking sedately round the room, then suddenly catching a glimpse of her own tail and tearing after it, with increasing frustration.

'I know how Principessa feels,' said Ruth. 'She's what the philosophers call a futilitarian. She recognizes that what she's doing is pointless, but she does it all the same. It's a kind of ideological statement.'

'Yeah,' said the Kid. 'I caught her reading a copy of Sartre's *Being and Nothingness* the other day. That cat's just too damn smart.'

Ruth finished her ham and hugged her knees to her chest. 'Don't you miss the others, Lydia?'

'To be perfectly honest, I haven't even given them a thought. To me, Principessa is all of them rolled into one.'

'The very quiddity of cathood.'

Lydia frowned and sipped her gin. 'I wish you'd use words I understand. You remind me of Sander. He was always trying to blind me with science.'

The kitten stopped her antics and sat between them, licking her paws. For a moment she was distracted. Her head twitched around, following the flight of an imaginary insect, then she returned to her toilet with the same self-possession as before.

Lydia fumbled in the pocket of her cardigan and brought out a screw of paper that she'd tied to a length of pink wool. She dangled it in the air. The kitten responded in time-honoured fashion, rearing up and batting the plaything with both paws. Eventually she tired of the game and walked away like someone leaving a tedious conversation to answer the door.

There was a quiz show Lydia wanted to watch on television. She made her excuses and left.

The Kid stood up and looked through Sander's books. He opened one, glanced at a couple of plates and put it back.

'If there's anything else I can do for you,' he said, turning slightly.

'Thanks. You've been a great help. You never did tell me where you live.'

'I've got a room in a block of flats near the Vondelpark. It's not far. When I'm in the polder, I just camp in the van.'

'I thought so. It has a lived-in feel about it.'

'I've been thinking about what you said,' he began. 'The things we talked about at the party. All of this, I mean.' He spread his hands and looked around, encompassing the whole house with the gesture. 'Lydia, the painting, Scheele, and the rest of it. If I can do anything to – you know – help.'

'You've never seen any old letters lying around here, have you? I mean very old, written by Lyd's painter-ancestor.'

The Kid bunched up his chin muscles and shook his head. 'She never mentioned anything.'

'She did to me. One of these days, we'll have to put our heads together and tell each side of the Lydia story. Sort out the information and disinformation. Know what I mean? And this – the parlour, the brother museum – been here before?'

'She gave me a tour. It's completely wacko, but there's some great stuff here. She showed me a sketch of a bicycle-gear system the guy designed. It looks really good and I've never seen anything like it in the real world. No idea if it works, either, but it looks feasible on paper.'

For a moment, she remembered Thomas the first time she'd seen him, on the balcony with the black. She liked the Kid. He was a nook-and-corner person. The goods were not all thrust out on display in the window. They emerged unexpectedly from behind the counter, one at a time. He was also an oddball, and she wasn't quite sure how deep the oddness went. She thought of mentioning Cameron and the snapshot she'd seen at Jade Beach, but didn't know how to broach the subject. She decided to put it on ice. The black had stifled him. There was some kind of business between the two of them.

Right now, she didn't feel inclined to mess with the Kid's good humour.

He was still standing by the bookshelves. 'Have you got everything you want?' he asked.

'Sure. This is fine. Lydia and I can take care of ourselves.'

A minute or two later, after he'd left, she replayed what he'd said. 'Have you got everything you want?'

She wondered . . .

Was it possible? Had he meant something else by that?

Surely not . . .

She tried her computer. The email worked, but there was nothing but spam mail.

She changed into her striped flannel pyjamas and wandered out into Lydia's kitchen.

She checked the fridge.

The eel was there, as promised, all bar the head. It was chopped up into Swiss roll lengths and wrapped in clingfilm. She pulled a face. There was no way she was going to eat that slimy mess. Principessa, on the other hand, was weaving round her shins, trying to tell her something. Ruth unwrapped one of the chunks and chopped it up into manageable portions. The kitten ate them up with quick, jerky head motions – nature's way of ensuring that no other kitties could muscle in on the action.

The TV was still blaring in the living room.

Ruth put her head round the door.

Lydia was in her nightdress, fast asleep and snoring in bed. Ruth crept in and switched off the television and the standard lamp. She shut the door on her way out and was about to go back to the *achterhuis* when she saw Lydia's torch at the foot of the stairs.

She looked up.

The banister rail zigzagged into darkness. On impulse, she switched on the torch and went up.

Principessa followed, jumping lightly from step to step.

On the first floor she peered into both rooms: the one where she'd found the old family snapshot with the painting in the background, and the rear room, which she hadn't visited before. They had evidently been used for storage until such time as Lydia had ceased to go upstairs. Ruth had no idea how long ago that had been. One thing was certain. Sander's mausoleum, where she was housed, was in much better nick than these forgotten quarters.

She tiptoed up to the next floor, wary of making the steps creak, though it hardly seemed necessary. Lydia was dead to the world. If she did happen to wake up, though, Ruth didn't want her thinking she had intruders. She remembered the old lady's fantasy that her dead brother still rooted around up here in the middle of the night, looking for some prize possession he'd mislaid in the dim and distant past.

Two rooms again on the second floor, front and rear.

The dust climbed further up the nose here, though the rooms were relatively bare. She flashed the torch around the front one. Stucco on the ceilings, curtains hanging loosely, minus a few curtain rings, an old tapestry of a unicorn and a collection of fire tongs and iron dogs by the big sooty fireplace.

In the back room there was only a simple kitchen table and a plastic bucket with a dirty floor cloth draped over the rim. She opened the drawer in the table. It was lined with yellow sticky-backed plastic and held a rusty pocket knife, five dried-out conkers and a tobacco tin with some old keys and seashells in it.

She looked out of the rear window, down across the courtyard and in through the lit window of what was now her own room – the parlour.

She could see a few of her boxes and one corner of the pink Dansette record player. She still hadn't decided whether to sleep there or in the upstairs bedroom. It would depend on whether the upstairs room had been heated properly.

Something brushed against her leg.

Ruth gasped . . .

She took two steps back and looked down. It was Principessa.

The kitten was so light of foot that you scarcely realized she was there.

Up again.

The third-floor rooms were smaller. A mattress slumping against the wall in one.

Some boxes of books full of old illustrated magazines, beer mats and knitting patterns in the other. Ruth contented herself with peering round the doors.

One more flight of steps . . .

Up she went, to the top.

Two doors again, front and rear.

The rooms were similar to the attic she'd occupied at the Hotel van Onna, the walls and beams sloping up to a ridged point and, at the front, a smallish window overlooking the canal. Here there was nothing but a rickety wooden chair and a few folded newspapers on the floor. She shook one of the newspapers and placed it on the chair seat.

She sat down in her pyjamas.

The torch beam picked out the small hearth and mantelpiece. Through the window, she could make out the bell gable of the house opposite with its curved sides. It was either Scheele's place, or one of the buildings flanking it.

She sat quietly for a moment and Principessa leapt up onto her knees.

She liked the sleepy silence of this old house. It didn't creak and move like her boat. The ceilings were high, even the central section in this attic room. Though the overhead clearance served no practical purpose, psychologically there was more *Lebensraum*, a sense of space and freedom. And, though Lydia complained of the damp, it felt dry enough to Ruth.

The cat shut its eyes and purred as she stroked it under the chin.

Yes, it had been a long time, but she could get used to house-living, however amazing your friends thought it was to live on a barge. A house was like another species, with a different skin, heartbeat, entrails and eyes. In this particular house, Lydia's personality and clutter were concentrated like sediment on the lower floors. The upper storeys were progressively clearer of recent history.

Most of all, Ruth liked being high up.

She enjoyed the sense of detachment from the world in this garret with its square window like a picture frame, such a change from the poky cobweb-clogged portholes. At the same time, the room had an odd vibration, something she couldn't quite put her finger on.

She soaked in the silence, realizing that all these spaces would have to be searched for the letters, then took the kitten up in her arms and went back downstairs.

Lydia was still snoring.

Ruth went back to the parlour, then climbed the stairs in the *achterhuis* to the bedroom. The sheets were clean and fresh. The electric heater had taken the chill off the air.

Yes, she would sleep here.

As for Principessa, she chose to stay in the parlour. Ruth had left the table lamp on and the kitten curled up on the desk top under the warm bulb. An old wall clock, which Lydia had wound up, ticked gently. And next to the sleeping kitten was the little screw of paper that Lydia had produced from her cardigan pocket for the cat to play with, trailing its length of pink wool.

Maybe it was the lamplight that did it, but that paper looked old and yellow and written on. Not that Principessa would have noticed. The tip of her black tail reared and flinched from time to time in her sleep.

Her mind, no doubt, was on higher things.

Nineteen

*R*uth slipped in late and sat next to Myles, avoiding Cabrol's timekeeper glare.

The plenary session was in a boardroom at the Stedelijk Museum hung with large abstract canvases. It overlooked Museumplein and a lawn where a temporary ice rink had been set up. A lot of people were skating.

The van der Heyden was at the far end of the room, dwarfed by the big wooden easel on which it stood.

Ruth scanned the faces of the bureau committee. In addition to her immediate colleagues, there were representatives from the Inspectorate of Cultural Heritage, the Institute for Art History, the Institute of War Documentation, the Jewish Historical Museum, the Ministry of Education, Culture and Science, the Netherlands Office for Fine Art in The Hague, among others. About thirteen heads in all on the panel, including the secretary who was taking minutes.

A couple of faces were unfamiliar to her.

Cabrol, she noticed, was wearing his red silk cravat – the one he pulled out for formal occasions.

Myles slid a copy of the agenda over. She'd missed the latest episode in the debates concerning the former Mannheimer, Lanz, Koenigs and Gutmann collections. They'd now moved on to 'NK 352', Lydia's heirloom.

'Provenance conclusive, then,' Cabrol was saying as he leafed through the file. 'There are ownership lacunae, but we're left in little doubt where the painting came from and we know a good deal about its wartime wanderings. A quick recap?'

There were nods of agreement.

'Being half-Jewish, the painter's descendants entrusted the work to a custodian during the Occupation. The custodian – name of Emmerick Scheele – sold it on to the Nazis. A forced sale, says Scheele. Next stop, the Linz collection at Alt Aussee. After hostilities, the Allies moved it to the Munich Collecting Point. This is confirmed by the labelling on the reverse of the artefact.'

'We also have internal registration forms,' Timmermans pointed out, 'and the records of the De Gruyter transport firm. They worked directly for Dienstelle Mühlmann.'

'Thanks, Pieter. It came back to Holland in 1946, and this is where wires start getting crossed. After the war, Scheele offered the proceeds of the forced sale to the van der Heyden family. He maintains that Sander van der Heyden accepted his offer of a thousand florins cash. Sander has since died. The only surviving van der Heyden, Sander's sister, claims they refused Scheele's offer on the grounds that he was withholding the major part of the sum he'd received from Hofer or Miedl. Unjust enrichment, in other words. The painting was assumed lost by both parties until the viewing day last year, when both the direct descendant of the painter, Lydia van der Heyden, and the wartime custodian, Emmerick Scheele, identified the work and filed rival claims.' Cabrol looked up from his notes. 'Voilà, voilà,' he said.

A skinny man with a goatee beard from the Institute of Art History spoke up. 'If the provenance is clear, how come the whole procedure's taken so long?'

Cabrol sucked in his cheeks and meshed his long fingers.

'When it was returned from Germany, it was put on view in the Mauritshuis, The Hague, then in the Central Museum, Utrecht. That was in 1946. Wrong towns. The sales were publicized in Amsterdam, but, frankly, if you didn't work in the art world you were unlikely to get to hear about them. That was one factor that stood in the way of claims. The other was the obligation for claimants to refund sales commissions and other costs. Some former owners were deterred from claiming their property. We're more sensitive to these issues nowadays.'

A woman from the Inspectorate of Cultural Heritage raised a finger to interrupt. 'I've read through the file. I don't see exactly what the strength of the Scheele claim is here. At no time did the painting become his property.'

'That's how it looks if you follow the van der Heyden version,' Cabrol said. 'The issue of whether the sale constituted a voluntary or involuntary transaction seems irrelevant here. Anyway, the SNK expressions *voluntary* or *enforced sale, theft* and *confiscation* have never been defined satisfactorily.'

'The Ekkart Committee recommends all sales of works by Jewish private persons in the Netherlands from 10 May 1940 be treated as forced sales,' Timmermans interrupted.

'Quite, said Cabrol, 'but Scheele isn't, and wasn't, Jewish. What's more, as I said, he claims that Sander van der Heyden accepted his offer of payment of a thousand florins in cash in lieu of the painting. Needless to say, there's no record of this transaction, just as there's no record of the forced sale. Scheele says that a thousand florins was precisely the sum he received. The picture had since passed out of his hands, of course, but he'd bought it retroactively.'

'He sold the painting first,' said Timermanns, 'then bought it later.'

'In effect, that's the back-to-front logic of the case. And since the allegedly forced transaction was later deemed to be illegal, how much he was paid – and, indeed, whether or not he was paid – then became immaterial. What mattered was that he had title to the painting and, under the terms of restitution of mis-appropriated art works, it should be returned to him by the custodial museum, in this case the Rijksmuseum itself.'

The distant sound of piped music reached the room. Ruth

craned her neck to look out of the window at the ice rink. There was a festive atmosphere out there, not unlike some of Breughel's winter scenes. Three teenage skaters had linked arms and were sweeping round the rink like a human bulldozer. The less confident skaters swerved out of the way.

'There are a lot of imponderables, if you ask me,' said a woman called Anne Gelder from the Institute of War Documentation. 'Did the sale take place under force, duress or improper influence, direct or indirect, of the enemy? Did the post-war undocumented transaction between Scheele and Sander van der Heyden actually occur, and – if it did – what sum of money was involved and what validity did that transaction have? I'm just speculating, but imagine a situation in which Scheele knew that the work had been repatriated in 1946 and the van der Heyden family didn't. He could have been aware of The Hague and Utrecht viewings. It seems unlikely because he'd then have insisted on an official bill of sale for his transaction with Sander, but it's not impossible. What do we know? Maybe he did have a bill of sale. Half a century's a long time. Documents disappear. See what I'm getting at? This kind of narrative seriously compromises Scheele's credibility. I think I'm right in saying, Bernard, that the committee hasn't come up against a case of quite this kind before. Resolving these questions goes a long way beyond the scope of our mandate.'

'It's beyond the competence of our researchers as well,' said Cabrol.

'Ouch!' Myles whispered, tapping Ruth with his foot.

'One or other of the two claimants isn't telling the truth,' said the man from the ministry. 'So who gets the benefit of the doubt?'

'Perhaps neither,' said Cabrol. He doodled abstractedly on his agenda.

'Neither?' said Myles.

'There's a further possibility to consider, which hinges on the forced-sale issue. Scheele's Dutch. He didn't belong to any of the persecuted population groups. This makes him an unlikely victim of forced sale. Time for another narrative, to borrow your buzzword, Anne ... Let's suppose it could be proved that Scheele sold the painting voluntarily and at the going market rate. Suppose we also accept that he paid off Sander van der Heyden. Retroactively, as we said, this would make Scheele the legal owner and seller of the work. There'd then be no reason for his claim to be taken seriously, since he'd have freely and voluntarily disposed of his own property for appropriate payment. In fact, there'd be no legitimate grounds for a claim in the first place, since claims only relate to the involuntary loss of property.'

Ruth pricked up her ears. Was Cabrol arguing for Lydia?

'As such,' the coordinator went on, 'when the painting was recuperated it came into the custody of the Dutch state perfectly lawfully. It's therefore perfectly lawful for the painting in question to remain in the custody of the Dutch state. Not only lawful, but rightful. From all points of view the painting is the rightful property of the Dutch state and people.'

There was a pause while everyone took this in.

'I don't agree,' said Myles.

'There's nothing to agree or disagree with,' said Cabrol coolly. 'As I said, this is pure hypothesis, one possible narrative.'

'I don't agree with one of the premises of your narrative.'

Cabrol raised his eyebrows, waiting.

'You implied that because Scheele was non-Jewish he couldn't be the victim of a forced sale. There's a precedent here in the Gutmann case. A July 1952 judgement by the Council for the Restoration of Property Rights. They reversed the SNK Council's judgement that sales made in 1941 and the first quarter of 1942 couldn't have been forced because there was no direct coercion.'

'The sale of the van der Heyden took place later,' said Cabrol.

'Granted, but the same principle applies. Coercion doesn't have to be direct. An occupying power's a coercive entity. It's a threat in itself. A specific threat doesn't have to be made. It's implicit in the political predicament.'

Cabrol wore a perplexed expression. 'Are you saying that Jews, gypsies and gays were not specifically targeted by the Nazis under the Occupation?'

'Not at all. I'd risk being specifically targeted myself if I did.' A ripple of mild amusement passed round the table. 'What I'm saying is that, in addition to the obviously persecuted population groups, the occupiers represented a threat to the entire native population. If you don't accept that, you're effectively suggesting that the non-Jewish, ordinary straight Dutch people were somehow complicit in their own Occupation.'

'Heaven forbid,' said Cabrol. 'So according to you, everyone was persecuted?'

'I wouldn't use the word persecuted. I'd say that most Dutch men, women and children were the unwilling victims of a foreign invasion and Occupation. If they failed to obey the occupier, or if they actively disobeyed the occupier, they'd be putting themselves at risk. So they weren't free citizens. Pax Romana. They make a wilderness and call it peace.'

'I'm lost,' said Cabrol. 'What was the point you were hoping to make?'

'That anyone, not just a Jew, could be the victim of a forced sale.'

The coordinator smiled dubiously, mulling over the ramifications of this position.

'It's also a question of where your sympathies lie,' added Myles.

'It's a question of justice and law.'

'Aren't we forgetting the findings of the Scholten Committee?'

'Namely?'

'That the strictly bureaucratic approach of the old SNK days was inflexible, legalistic and callous. We have to bear in mind the exceptional position and interests of the victims of spoliation.

I'm referring to the need for compassion. I'm referring to Lydia van der Heyden.'

Another pause and all heads turned to Cabrol. He looked less self-assured now.

He tapped his pencil against his front teeth before speaking. 'Naturally, the question of what happened to the revenue from the forced sale is important here. But if we accept, for the time being, that the painting was sold into Nazi hands – directly or indirectly – it would be logical for the party who profited from that sale to refund the proceeds before they could repossess the painting, even if it wasn't sold voluntarily. A substantial sum, given that it would have to be indexed with the general price-index figure.'

'The old repayment rule,' said Ruth. 'I thought we'd consigned that to the history books.'

'Not entirely. The rules have been relaxed, that's all. I'd like to suggest that both claimants be informed of the repayment rule. In the light of that information, they may decide to reconsider their claims.'

'If you wanted to enforce the repayment rule,' said Myles, 'you'd have to prove that the forced sale accrued to the seller's capital. There are no transactional records, so this is empty speculation. Anyway, the Ekkart Committee clearly recommends that the benefit of the doubt be given to the private person and not to the state. I reckon Lydia van der Heyden has produced sufficient prima facie evidence that the painting was her property. There's no evidence whatsoever that her brother received payment for it.'

'Quite,' said Cabrol, 'just as there's no evidence that he didn't receive payment for it. And what you *reckon* is neither here nor there. If it entertains you to predict the findings of this committee, I suggest you keep your speculations to yourself.' He looked around, as if drawing everyone in with a lasso, and clapped his hands once, clutching them together under his chin. 'What do we do with conflicting claims?'

'Regular courts or arbitration,' said the man from the Inspectorate of Cultural Heritage.

'It's not our pigeon,' said Cabrol. 'I move that the matter be referred to the Judicial Division of the Council for the Restoration of Property Rights.'

There was a show of hands in favour.

'And how long will that take?' asked Ruth.

Nobody seemed to know.

'Awarding extra time to this matter,' said Cabrol, 'is actually a privilege. We're dealing with four thousand, two hundred and seventeen objects in the NK-Collection. There's an average of thirteen hours research on the provenance of each. You can do the maths yourself. We're understaffed, but it isn't our policy to rush important matters through. It's entirely to our credit that justice comes before expediency.'

This seemed to satisfy a number of the visiting brass.

Ruth glanced at Myles and made the sound of a pistol shot under her breath.

Cabrol turned on her sharply. 'Miss Braams?'

'Both claimants are old. If a settlement decision's reached when they're in their graves, I don't really see what kind of justice that is or who benefits from it. Apart from the Dutch state, probably, since neither of them have any immediate heirs or beneficiaries as far as we know.'

Cabrol looked bored. He'd heard this a thousand times before. 'I think we're all aware that we need to speed up the restitution policy advisory process and the dispute resolution mechanism. At least for a while. As Holocaust survivors and their heirs die off, it follows that the number of claims on our collections will decline correspondingly.'

Ruth took a paper from her document case. 'May I quote something in English? Article 8, the 1998 Washington Conference on Holocaust-Era Assets. "If the pre-war owners of confiscated art – or their heirs – can be identified, steps should be taken expeditiously to achieve a just and fair solution, recognizing that this may vary according to the facts and circumstances surrounding a specific case." *Expeditiously*,' she repeated, 'not *expediently*.'

One of the unfamiliar people in the room was a short man with a bushy grey beard. He didn't look Dutch. He caught Ruth's eye, then leaned back in his chair and turned his attention to the view through the window.

He seemed detached from the proceedings.

'You said it yourself,' Cabrol replied. 'The solution may vary according to the facts. I think we're all agreed that this particular case is highly fact-sensitive. For that reason, I do think we should minute the judicial issues in detail.'

The secretary sucked the tip of her pencil and crouched over her legal pad, an athlete at the starting block.

'The first is caveat emptor, let the buyer beware. Without a written bill of sale, the buyer bears the full risk of void or voidable title. The rule of thumb is that you can't transfer to somebody else what you don't possess. But sometimes we have to deal with exceptions to this rule. If, for example, a chattel is transferred for purposes other than sale to a person who then makes an unauthorized sale to a bona fide purchaser, valid title's passed on because the vendor has voidable title. It's valid until voided, until the fatal vice in the transaction has been judicially declared. The vice may then be cured by an act of confirmation, such as retroactive purchase. I think we're agreed that Scheele's acquisition of the painting does not amount to larceny.'

There was general assent.

Ruth and Myles exchanged a look.

'Nevertheless, in the absence of a bill of sale,' Cabrol continued, 'that title's defective. There are other questions too. One is the exercise of due diligence to locate one's property. We have no evidence that any member of the van der Heyden clan made pro-active efforts to track down their lost painting. There are those who'd argue that, by default, they gave up their rights to it and that a statute of limitations should be applied. Why didn't Sander file a theft report with a computerized cultural objects registry?'

'That would've been tricky,' said Ruth. 'He died in 1955. He'd have probably had to invent the computer as well.'

A smatter of laughter.

Cabrol forced a grin.

'A non-computerized registry, then. And another question. Why didn't the van der Heyden family take out a replevin action against Scheele? We don't know. For his part, Scheele could legitimately raise the defence of Laches, the defence of adverse possession, the principle of entrustment, and his status as a good-faith purchaser for value. I suspect that deadlock will be the outcome here. This would be the case if the moral strength of the van der Heyden claim were recognized, but also if Scheele were cleared of suspicion of moral wrongdoing.'

'And deadlock,' said Ruth pointedly, 'means the painting stays put.'

'Of course,' said Cabrol. 'Consider the position of the art museums and the NK-Collection administration. Art museums and their trustees have fiduciary and legal obligations and responsibilities to the general public. The works of art in their collections are held in trust for that public, not for any one particular individual. May I also quote something, Miss Braams?' He flourished a document in the air. 'The 1998 Association of Art Museum Directors guidelines. "In the event that a legitimate claimant comes forward, the museum should offer to resolve the manner in an equitable, appropriate, and mutually agreeable manner." But, "In the event that no legitimate claimant comes forward, the museum should acknowledge the history of the work of art on labels and publications referring to such a work." I'd like to remind you that sometimes we have to deal with objects that are more than just private possessions. They have cultural and social importance. They're part of the whole community's heritage. Cultural property law may occasionally overlap with what appear to be private civil actions.'

'Would you say that's the case here?' asked Myles, an air of innocence about him.

Cabrol looked over at the little painting on the easel and other eyes followed.

There they were: the man at the window, the beautiful girl on the chaise longue, the sunburst of mimosa.

'As you may know,' said Cabrol, 'I wrote the entry on this work for the Netherlands Collection database. I had no reason then to believe that it had any special artistic or cultural value, and I've no reason to believe so now. It's a technically competent piece. But, frankly, no amount of praise is going to turn Johannes van der Heyden into another Van Gogh or Vermeer.'

'So, in your opinion,' Myles continued, 'a thousand florins was a fair price?'

'Sure. It isn't a fire-sale price. Our scales would indicate that a thousand florins was a fair valuation for this particular work – generous, even.'

'Does everyone have the labelling details in front of them?' asked Myles. '"Johannes van der Heyden. Amsterdam, Miedl. K41. RG. 937." We know who Miedl is, Bernard?'

'Alois Miedl,' said Cabrol offhandedly. 'A well-known middleman.'

'A middleman who worked with Andreas Hofer, Goering's agent.'

Ruth kicked Myles's shins, but there was no stopping him.

'Miedl freelanced,' said Cabrol. 'The art market got very lively when the Germans moved in. He was essentially his own man.'

'He freelanced, but he also worked for Hofer, as I said. And Hofer was Goering's agent. "RG. 937." RG for Reichsmarschall Goering.'

'Could be. We'd have to check on that. Initials have been misinterpreted before. Anyway, what are you getting at?'

'I think this picture was part of the Hofer collection, Bernard. As we know, Goering transferred around a hundred and fifty paintings to Miedl via his agent Andreas Hofer in 1944 in return for *Christ in the House of Martha and Mary*, painted by the forger Hans van Meegeren and wrongly attributed to Vermeer. Of course, Goering didn't know it was a forgery. I believe the van der Heyden was originally bundled in with that job lot, but Goering tried to hold it back. I also believe that at some point Dr Hans Posse got to hear about, or see, this painting, and he pre-empted it for Linz – in other words, for Hitler. Hence the Reich eagle and the Linz classmark.'

All eyes were on Myles now.

Cabrol was unmoved. He made a little church of his fingers and stared Myles out.

'We know it ended up in the Linz collection,' he allowed, 'but that in itself doesn't mean a lot. Thousands of pictures went to Alt Aussee, good, bad and indifferent. The weeding-out process never happened, thank God, because Linz never came about. We'd be living in a very different world if it had, and we certainly wouldn't be sitting here now holding this discussion.'

Ruth scribbled on the back of her agenda and pushed the sheet over to Myles: a six-pointed star with two concentric circles, a big cross slashed through the whole.

Cabrol massaged the back of his neck. His eyes glazed over momentarily, but a smile of forbearance appeared on his lips.

'You're relatively new to provenance research, Myles, if you don't mind me saying so. And I don't mean to put down your excellent track record with Sotheby's. I just want you to know that I think I understand what you're going through. We've all had that moment when we think we've come across a lost masterpiece, or a school-of painting that we're convinced is straight from the master's hand. Jan,' he said, addressing the man from The Hague, 'remember the drawing in the Koenigs collection that we thought was a Rembrandt?'

'I do indeed,' said Jan, laughing.

'And every now and then it does happen, the great find. But more often than not it doesn't. We have to learn to be historians, human beings, scientists and detectives, all rolled into one. And we have to learn not to be over hasty in our judgements. With modern international electronic databases, there are actually very few famous old masters that slip through the net.'

'I never said that the painting is a famous old master,' said Myles.

'Then what's your point?'

'I think it's a cover-up.'

'Of what?'

'Literally a cover-up. There's something underneath the painting. Another painting, maybe, by someone else. The top painting's a deliberate camouflage.'

'An eighteenth-century cover-up then, if you accept that this top painting's by Johannes van der Heyden,' said the goatee.

'I'm not even sure of that. It could be someone else using the identity of a genuine, known but unimportant artist to camouflage the artefact's true value. If I knew, I'd tell you, believe me.'

'A big if,' said Cabrol. 'Where's your evidence?'

'It's circumstantial. A possible ownership rivalry between Goering and Hitler, not to mention the rivalry between our two present-day claimants, one of whom is a man of considerable means.'

'Are you against referring this matter to the council?' asked Anne Gelder.

'No, I'm not,' said Myles, after due reflection. 'I think Ruth's comments ought to be taken into account. The council should be encouraged to process the matter expeditiously, as she says. But a slight delay will buy us time.'

'Time for what?' asked Cabrol.

'I'd like the committee's permission to have the painting put through a few tests. We can get these done at the Central Research Laboratory for Objects of Art and Science here in Amsterdam. It strikes me that everyone's been airing a lot of theories and narratives this morning, and I'm no exception. OK, maybe it's hot air. If my hare-brained theory's disproved, I shall humbly resume my seat on the panel, an older and wiser man. I'm just asking for a little papal indulgence.'

'Why not?' said Jan with a shrug of magnanimity. 'Your old men shall dream dreams, your young men shall see visions.' He looked around genially, as if he were slightly drunk.

There were smiles, an informal show of hands.

Cabrol went quiet.

He'd been upstaged.

Twenty

'You could've told me, Myles,' said Ruth, as they left the meeting. They were halfway down the corridor and out of earshot. She elbowed him in the ribs.

He elbowed her back. 'You could've arrived on time.'

'Now you've focused their minds on this thing. We were better off when it was just a regular minor claim, chugging along happily, like the choo-choo train to Morningtown.'

'I'm not so sure. Depends if Cabrol's on the level.'

'And is he?'

'That's the question, poppet. He's certainly become very public-spirited of late.'

'Champion of the nation's cultural property. Does he have a thingy about this painting?'

'A what?'

I'm sorry. Does he have a *thing* about this painting?'

'Do dogs have fleas?'

'I don't get it.'

'Think about it. Make sure the piccy stays wrapped up in stores. That way, nobody gets a look at the thing – sorry, I mean *thingy*. Now why would he want to do that? As for why I opened my big mouth, I had to put my five bob's worth in, didn't I? Had to get the fucking committee to OK the tests.'

'What d'you hope to find?'

'I haven't a clue.'

'Well, good luck.'

'Yeah. Keep your legs crossed for me.'

They walked through a service door and into the main foyer of the Stedelijk Museum. People were milling about. A chilly draught of outdoor air from the entrance.

Ruth wasn't happy with this little exchange.

'You're full of bullshit, Myles. Are you going to tell me what you're up to or not?'

'Allow me to wear my aura of mystery a little longer. I think it rather suits me.'

She looked at him askance. 'If you weren't a poof, I'd probably marry you.'

'You'd have to gun down Rex in cold blood first. How d'you rate Cabrol's performance?'

'Eight point six on the Wankometer.'

'His best score yet. It was the void and voidable titles that did for me, not to mention the defence of Laches and the defence of adverse possession. What the fuck was all that about?'

'Myles, weren't you going to introduce me to someone?'

'Oh yeah, Bob Fischer. He was in the meeting.'

'What, Rumpelstiltskin?'

'That's him. American. He was an officer with the Monuments, Fine Arts and Archives Section in the war. The MFAA, remember? He was there when they opened up Alt Aussee, he worked at the Munich Collecting Point and he's familiar with the Nazi records found at Schloss Banz. An expert on art theft. Retired now, but he still keeps his hand in. He's passing through on his way to the General State Archives at The Hague. When I heard, I got Cabrol to rope him in and win a few courtesy points.'

'He looked bored out of his skull. Are you sure he understands Dutch?'

'That's a point. Fuck ... maybe he doesn't. I didn't ask him. He didn't say anything, did he?'

'There go your courtesy points.'

Myles glanced at his watch. Twelve-fifteen.

Adrian Mathews

They both looked round.

Fischer appeared on cue from behind the main staircase.

A wiry, gnome-like figure in an Aran sweater and a bulky anorak bristling with pockets, zips, press studs and drawstrings. His handshake sailed towards them with a bright ring of confidence. Ruth instinctively liked him. He was nice in the wise and cheery way that old Americans are good at, unshackled by Old World cynicism and irony.

'Sorry! I got lost,' he said. 'Bernard had to go, I said I'd find my own way out and then I paid the price for my over-confidence. This place is a labyrinth.'

'Can we show you around?' asked Myles.

'Sure.' Fischer looked reluctant of a sudden.

'Unless you've got other plans?' said Ruth.

'To tell you the truth, I didn't understand jack shit in that meeting.'

'Oh.'

Ruth gave Myles her told-you-so look.

'It doesn't matter,' Fischer said. 'It was my fault. You get so used to everyone speaking perfect English in Holland that you kind of assume they speak English between themselves too. I'm now a chastened linguistic imperialist. Having said that, it was fun just listening, picking up the body language and looking out the window at those skaters.'

'They put the rink there every winter,' said Ruth.

'Hey, let's forget the paintings, shall we, and go for a spin? Do you mind? In Buffalo I used to take the kids ice-skating when they were young, but I'm damned if I'm telling you how long ago that was! Save culture for the vultures. I'm just your all-American philistine today.'

They left the museum and walked round to the open space of the Museumplein at the rear.

Myles was not a skater. He leaned on the low plywood wall beside the rink. Ruth and Fischer hired skates – racing skates for him, figure skates for her – and mounted the steps. They did a couple of circuits, then stopped to catch their breath.

'Myles tells me you're an expert on art theft,' said Ruth.

'Art trade and art theft. They're both big business. After oil and arms, the art and antique trade has the biggest turnover. And after drug smuggling and illegal arms trading, art theft's the most profitable international crime. Nice symmetry, eh?'

'I must borrow a little Vermeer from stores. Do you think they'd mind?'

'Course not. You go right ahead . . .'

'How much of the stolen stuff's recovered?'

'Ten to fifteen per cent, they reckon. Know when I last came here? When twenty paintings by Van Gogh were stolen from the Rijksmuseum, that's when. Art's like diamonds. Nice and portable. No matter how sophisticated your security, the determined thief always finds a way round. Shall we?'

Ruth held his proffered arm and they took off again.

Fischer was in his eighties, but he had the va-va-voom of a much younger man. Health was on his side. He broke away from her on the rink and did a couple of slick figure-of-eights and even a little turning jump.

Ruth stopped skating and watched in admiration.

'I don't know what you're on, but can I get it on prescription?' she asked when he'd finished his antics.

Her cheeks were apple-pie red with her exertions.

'Zinc picolinate and magnesium. A hundred mill' a day. A young girl like you doesn't need that shit. As for me, look at it this way – the candle flares brighter just before it goes out.'

'Nonsense!'

'Don't nonsense me, young lady. I'm old and venerable. I should know what I'm talking about.'

Myles came round on the outside and joined them. 'It's

bloody freezing,' he complained, blowing on his hands and stamping his feet.

'Five minutes,' said Fischer. 'Then we're all yours.'

Later they walked round the small park on to which the Stedelijk Museum, the Van Gogh Museum and the Concert-gebouw bordered.

'I remember that little painting from Alt Aussee,' Fischer said. 'It wasn't with the rest of the art works. It was in another section, in one of the deepest tunnels.'

'AR 6927,' said Myles. 'That's the Linz classmark.'

'AR for Arcana. The other stuff was a real jumble, mostly books. Works on alchemy, the occult, chemistry, natural history. Stones with runes carved on them. A lot of freemasonry artefacts too, if I recall. Old robes, chalices. Shit! A real Aladdin's cave. It was kind of spooky coming across all of that junk deep inside a mountain. Mystical symbols all over the place.'

'Like the one on the back of our picture,' said Ruth.

'Myles showed me before the meeting. I don't remember us picking up on it at the Munich Collecting Point, but it doesn't surprise me. The AR repository was full of stuff like that.'

'There's a back board,' said Myles. 'If you don't remove it, you don't know there's anything behind.'

'There you go then. We just had too much gear to process in Munich. We didn't have time to hang around.'

'So the Nazis were interested in the occult,' said Ruth.

Fischer laughed. 'Give me your hand. No – without the glove.'

Ruth bared her hand.

He took a ballpoint pen from his pocket and drew something on her palm.

'What's that?' he asked.

She looked at the diagram.

'A swastika. Well, a back-to-front swastika. Wasn't that a good-luck symbol for the Romans?'

'Sure, or even earlier. The swastika was suggested to Hitler by Friedrich Krohn, a Steinberg dentist and occultist. Hitler, as we know, reversed the symbol.'

'Tempting fate,' said Myles.

'Tempting fate was Adolf's favourite party game. He was crazy about the occult. He had a special interest in Landulph II of Capua, a student of the black arts, and in map dowsing. Come to think of it, redrawing maps was also one of his little hobbies. The other budding black magician was Himmler. His specialties were the Rosicrucian movement and bells.'

'Bells?'

'He thought the bells of Oxford had put a charm on the city so the Nazis couldn't attack it.'

'You're kidding?' said Myles.

'I kid you not. They even set up an occult bureau. They stamped out other people's occult writings and practices, mind you. As far as they were concerned, there was only one magus, no guesses who ... now, Hitler's big mystical obsession was with the holy lance, the one that was supposed to have pierced the side of Christ on the cross. The lance, or the *supposed* lance I should say, was part of the Habsburg Treasure. When Hitler made it to Vienna and declared the Anschluss, one of the first things he did was order the removal of the Treasure to Germany. Like Charlemagne, he thought that fate would never turn against the man who possessed the lance.'

'History proved him wrong,' said Ruth.

'The funny thing is that the day the Allies took possession of the Treasure was the day that Hitler shot himself. Pure coincidence, of course.'

'What about alchemy?' asked Ruth. 'What was his specific interest in alchemy? I've got someone working on the number code on the back of the van der Heyden painting, but we know that the big symbol represents the philosopher's stone.'

'We're assuming now that it was the mumbo-jumbo on the back that got the Nazis all steamed up, and not the painting itself,' said Fischer.

Myles nodded. 'That's what we're assuming. It's a kind of chicken-and-egg situation. Listen – would anyone fancy a coffee? We could nip into the cafeteria at the Stedelijk.'

'He's a big softie,' Ruth said to Fischer. 'Come on, let's get him back in the warm.'

They headed for the museum.

'For most people,' said Fischer, 'the philosopher's stone means gold, right? And alchemy's all about transforming one element into another.'

'It can't be done,' said Ruth.

'Ever hear of Franz Tausend? A Munich chemical worker in the twenties. He had this theory that every atom vibrates at its own special frequency. He thought that by adding the right substance to an element you could change its frequency and produce a different element. A rumour got out that Tausend had turned base metals into gold. Hitler was in prison at the time, for the abortive Munich uprising, but he had a cohort – a certain General Erich von Ludendorff.'

'Germany's chief strategist in the First World War,' said Myles.

'That's right. One crazy mother. Violently anti-Freemason.'

'He ran for president, didn't he?'

'He did, but Hindenburg defeated him. When that happened, Ludendorff started raising money for the new Nazi Party. He set up a group of industrialists to look into Tausend's gold-making process. Tausend melted up some iron oxide and quartz in a crucible, then the next day he added some white powder and when it cooled – hey presto! – they found a gold nugget inside.'

'Fraud?' said Ruth.

'Maybe he believed in what he was doing, maybe he didn't. Don't ask me. Quartz sometimes contains gold, but only minute amounts. The important thing here was that our old friend General Erich von Ludendorff was very impressed. He set up a body called Company 164 to promote the Tausend cause. Investment poured in. Hundreds of thousands of marks for Nazi Party funds. Later, share certificates were issued. In the end Tausend was imprisoned for fraud, but the investment money had been raised. It helped get National Socialism on its feet in Germany.'

'A shrewd businessman, Ludendorff,' said Myles.

'The story doesn't stop there. Tausend had a successor. A Pole in Paris called Dunikovski. This guy announced he could turn quartz into gold using radiation. He spread the mineral on copper plates, melted it with an electrical charge and then irradiated it with something he called Z-rays.'

Ruth and Myles looked at each other.

'Did I say something?' asked Fischer.

'The van der Heyden picture's painted onto a copper plate,' said Ruth.

'I'm just giving you the low-down. Make of it what you will.'

'Go on,' said Myles.

'Dunikovski also managed to attract big investment. He acknowledged that the quartz he used contained small amounts of gold, but he made out that the radiation technique accelerated the growth of the gold. An Anglo-French syndicate was set up to transport sand from Africa to a laboratory in England. Then the war broke out and Dunikovski vanished. The rumour was that the Germans had coopted him to make gold to prop up their economy. There was no proof. He was never heard of again.'

Back in the museum, they bought coffee, rolls and crisps in the cafeteria, then sat down and took their coats off.

'What made Dunikovski different from Tausend,' Fischer went on, 'was the radiation factor. Whether or not he was a fraud, that was an imaginative leap in the right direction.'

'How come?' said Ruth.

'Think about it. Alchemy's about transmutation. For donkey's years mainstream chemists thought it was impossible to turn one element into another, then along comes radioactivity. When radioactive elements like uranium decay, they give off daughter elements – right? I guess the first truly successful alchemist was Otto Hahn in 1939. Hahn was a German chemist. Basically, he discovered nuclear fission. By bombarding uranium with neutrons, you can get a nuclear chain reaction. It follows that the Nazis were interested in radioactive elements for reasons quite apart from gold-making scams.'

'Reasons that go bang in the night,' said Myles.

'Exactly. Mushroom-shaped reasons.' Fischer blew up his crisp packet and popped it, making Ruth jump. 'That, of course, was a little more than mumbo-jumbo. That was reality. They had to beat the Allies to it, and a lot of smart Hun brains were working on the problem. Werner Heisenberg ran the Nazi atomic bomb programme, but when the Allies marched on Germany the Alsos Mission discovered that the Germans hadn't made much progress in the right direction. One reason was that they'd got the science wrong. They were bombarding uranium with fast neutrons and you need slow ones. There's also some evidence that the Nazis weren't really focusing their hopes on a bomb. What they had in mind was a uranium engine, a kind of super-weapon reactor that would produce high-energy rays. This was the National Redoubt they went on about. When Germany was on its knees, just when everyone thought it was beaten, it would strike back with a uranium super-weapon from a secret mountain base in the south.'

'The champ coming round on the count of nine,' said Myles.

'Right! First, they had to crack nuclear fission before the Manhattan Project did. There were those in the party who thought that one route to nuclear fission might be through the old esoteric works, hermetic symbols and alchemical texts. That's what the AR repository was all about. They thought the old black magicians had been on the same track.'

'How deep did this go?' asked Ruth.

'I'm no expert, but I'll leave you with one last name to conjure with. Fulcanelli. The most famous twentieth-century alchemist. He's a real mystery. There's some weird evidence that his name goes back to the early fifteenth century, so either it was one guy who was amazingly old – even older than me, guys – or it was a name that was passed on, from adept to adept, over the generations. Whoever he was, Fulcanelli wrote a book called *The Mystery of the Cathedrals*. He was around in Paris in the twenties, and the book came out in 1926. His big theory was that the architecture and carvings on the Gothic cathedrals of Europe encoded instructions concerning alchemical secrets. A guy called Jacques Bergier claimed that Fulcanelli visited him at the Paris Gas Board laboratory in June 1937. Fulcanelli asked him to pass a message on to the physicist André Helbronner, which was basically a warning about the dangers of nuclear energy. He also said that the old alchemists had been there before and that previous civilizations had split the atom and destroyed themselves.'

'I can believe that some alchemists blew themselves up,' said Myles. 'Not so sure about civilizations.'

'Did anyone take this stuff seriously?' asked Ruth.

'The American Office for Strategic Services did, for one. That's the forerunner of the CIA. They went hunting for Fulcanelli after the war. He was on their list of people who had inside knowledge of nuclear physics. Basically, they wanted to round those people up to stop them defecting to the East.'

'So was he an alchemist or just a writer on the subject?' asked Myles.

'There are witness accounts of him transforming silver into uranium, also in 1937. Think about it. A nice steady source of uranium might've come in useful to a lot of people right then. There was actually a secret conference in Berlin in 1939 that set up the nuclear research programme and put a ban on uranium exports from Germany. If Hitler's physicists had got wind of Fulcanelli's alleged production of uranium from silver, they'd have wanted to talk to him, right? After the war he just vanished.'

Fischer finished the last of his roll and looked at his watch.

'I've got my train to The Hague in under an hour. Will that be OK?'

'Where's your luggage?' asked Myles.

'Back in the cloakroom.'

'We've just got time. I'll give you a hand.'

They put on their coats and walked back through the cold to the Stadhouderskade to hail a cab.

'So all of this,' said Ruth, 'tells us why Miedl, Hofer – maybe Posse too – got interested when they saw the engravings on the back of our picture. Arcana, right? They knew Hitler was into this stuff.'

'That makes sense to me,' said Fischer.

'But it doesn't tell us if anyone ever worked out what the engravings were about. They were like librarians. They just popped the work on the appropriate shelf with the appropriate classmark. They didn't actually read the book.'

'Conjecture, but plausible,' said Fischer. 'There was some Posse correspondence about the Arcana collection. I'll see if I can dig it up.'

'Back to square one, eh Myles?'

Myles looked down at her and put his arm round her shoulder. He gave her an affectionate hug. 'Back to Lydia, Ruth.'

In the *achterhuis*, Ruth switched on her computer. She had work to be getting on with for the ICB Intranet. Principessa slept peacefully on an armchair. Her father's words were turning in her mind. They'd been chatting about the philosopher's stone. 'It's all things to all men,' Joris had said. 'It's whatever you want it to be. And each historical epoch has its own forbidden fruit, its torment of Tantalus.'

He was right.

Gold to the Middle Ages. Nuclear fission to the twentieth century.

But what about Johannes van der Heyden, eighteenth-century pharmacist and wannabe painter? What was the philosopher's stone to him?

That was the question.

She went online and checked her email. A word from the Kid, asking when he could call round. A message from her parents. Advice concerning the boat insurance. A pdf file of data-entry instructions which Cabrol had promised. A fourth message, the subject line blank.

She clicked it open.

From: mystery@anonymous.com
To: rbraams@hotmail.com

We live in a world of misfortune, Chickenshit, where people will do anything to avoid facing their own souls. Can you face yours? I have warned you, but you have not listened. Now there will be no more warnings. You are in great danger. You are approaching the matrimonium alchymicum. But remember this. Man and woman are irreconcilable opposites. When united and activated, they degenerate into deadly hostility. He who fights with monsters might take care lest he thereby become a monster.

47 107.8682

'Oh, man', she whispered.

She hit the Print button.

The message chugged out, black on white.

She read it through again and slid it into the desk drawer along with the other two. Then she found Smits's email address and forwarded it to him, with a 'For info' heading. Smits was a *dummkopf*, as far as she was concerned, and congenitally predisposed to suspecting crime victims of having brought their woes upon themselves. But he was still, officially, a cop. There was no way of telling how all this would end up. She had to make a show of cooperation to keep the record straight.

She stared dead ahead and ran her hands down her cheeks.

Whoever this emailer was, he had an axe to grind. Whoever he was, *The Joy of Sex* was probably not one of his top ten books. And what the fuck was the 'matrimonium alchymicum'? The alchemical wedding, she assumed. Lucas was the obvious person to help, but she was damned if she could stomach another of his dreary homilies right now.

Nor could she work.

One poisonous little email, and the whole day felt sabotaged . . .

She wandered out, and down the corridor into Lydia's house.

Twenty-one

Lydia was sitting in bed watching TV. As ever, the eider-down was scattered with old tissues and multifarious bits and bobs. She was rubbing one of her arms. She looked anxious and uncomfortable.

'Has it gone to sleep?' asked Ruth.

'It's the arthritis. I take the painkillers, but they don't do a scrap of good. The pain just gets inside you, all down the arms and legs, especially the joints.'

'Want me to call Dr Luijten?'

'What earthly good would that do? He'd just write out another prescription. He'd tell me it's part of the ageing process – don't you hate that expression, the *ageing process*? No, I don't need him to tell me that.'

'Then what can you do?'

'Die.'

Lydia's voice trailed away pathetically on the vowel. She sounded like a languishing nineteenth-century aesthete.

Ruth sat on the edge of the bed.

'I suppose that's the next step in the process,' Lydia went on. 'You get older and older, all the time, and then one day it all stops.'

'You're not getting older, Lyd. It's just the rest of us are getting younger. I'll tell you what you are getting, though. You're getting sorry for yourself.'

'You young people don't understand physical pain. Health is

ignorance and ignorance is bliss. It's just as well, I imagine. I wouldn't wish this on you. But without understanding there's no sympathy. It's just like in the war, my dear.'

'Is there nothing that can be done?'

'My old physician, Dr Mastenbroek, used to give me a massage. That helped. I asked Dr Luijten once, but he didn't have the time. Everyone's so busy these days. He said there are places I could go, but they cost money, that's the trouble.'

Ruth bit her thumbnail. 'Would you like me to give you a massage?'

Lydia glanced at her shyly, then averted her eyes. 'Oh, I couldn't! Could I? No, I couldn't, my dear!'

'It's no big deal. I might be looking for a new career soon. Masseuse could well fit the bill. It's something to add to the CV, anyway. Versatility's what it's all about nowadays. In the brave new world of massage, you can branch out in a multitude of interesting directions.'

'You really wouldn't mind?'

'Roll up your sleeves and show me where the pain is precisely.'

Lydia pointed out the spots and Ruth began massaging with both hands, rubbing and rolling the slack flesh and muscle.

Her offer had been casual, but it hadn't been made lightly. Much as she liked Lydia, something about her was still vaguely repugnant. She'd got used to the smell of cat piss and old dinners, but she hadn't got used to the decrepitude of old age. It was a gut feeling, a muscular recoil. From time to time, Lydia simply became Bags again. Ruth couldn't intellectualize it, but that was the way it was with people. Like magnetic poles, they attracted or repelled. It was a bodily thing, quite apart from elective affinities and all that jazz. This time her upbringing and education had got the better of her. Perhaps that's what being civilized was all about. And now that she was actually kneading Lydia – soft, warm, pliable handfuls of her – the experience was not so bad. Her flesh was as smooth as a baby's, with a tendency to sag like perished rubber and wrinkle like cling film when the tautness went out of it.

Lydia closed her eyes and lay back on the pillow.

'There's a tin of Tiger Balm somewhere on the bed,' she murmured.

The balm was at once slippery and sticky. It created a hot, clammy traction between them that smelled of menthol and eucalyptus.

'This is a great comfort to me,' said Lydia. 'The pain simply eases away.'

'If there's anything else I can do for you, just ask. Don't think twice about it.'

'On the whole I'm all right, Ruth. I can get in and out of the bath. I do have difficulty washing my hair, though. To tell you the truth, it's been some time. And when it's too dirty I daren't go to the hairdresser's to get it done. It's a worry to me.'

'We'll see about that later, then.'

'In the meantime, dear, thank you so much for this massage. You can't begin to appreciate what it means to me.'

A thought occurred to Ruth. 'You've known Thomas Springer a long time. Doesn't he ever give you a massage?'

'I'd never ask that of a man.'

'What do you ask of him then?'

Lydia opened her eyes. 'Thomas comes here when he pleases. We chat. We play Scrabble. I don't ask any favours of him. I want to keep my independence and I don't want to be in anyone's debt. He says he likes it here, which I find hard to believe.'

'Oh?'

'Well, why can't he keep company with people his own age?'

'Lydia, you're an ageist!'

'A what?'

'You discriminate against people on grounds of age.'

'Do I? All I'm saying is that if I were Thomas I'd have better things to do than seek out the company of old boilers like me. There must be something wrong with him.'

'There's gratitude for you. I can only conclude that the same must apply to me,' said Ruth.

'Fiddlesticks! Thomas sought me out. You didn't. I sought you out.'

'We met by chance.'

'True, but I chose to develop our friendship. Who, may I ask, invited you to live here?'

'I'd prefer to think that the impetus for our acquaintanceship came from both directions. Do you want me to do your legs?'

Lydia put on her bashful face again.

'My old drumsticks! I used to have nice legs when I was young, like the girls in the fashionable magazines. My mother Rachel was proud of me. She thought I'd go places with legs like that.'

'I expect you did.'

'Yes – Westerbork, the transit camp. That's the furthest I've ever been from home. Not that I'm afraid of walking. I couldn't begin to count the number of times I've been to church or the shops.'

'Pittsburgh's going to be quite an adventure, then,' said Ruth, not without irony.

'I feel ready for a little adventure now. I didn't before. I've been learning English with the cassettes. I'm up to lesson four – perhaps you could test me one day. I haven't worked so hard for ages.'

'What exactly was your job? You told me on one of our outings that you used to work, but we didn't go into details.'

'I helped Sander with whatever he was up to, then after he died I worked for the big margarine company that used to be round the corner. Twenty-five years of secretarial. I was a despatch clerk in the warehouse. Had to earn my bread and butter, didn't I?'

'Butter?'

'Oh, goodness – *margarine*, I should say!'

'Lydia, enough of this playful banter. Do you want that leg massage – yes or no?'

'Just the feet, my dear. The pain's all down in the ankles today.'

Lydia pulled up the bedclothes to expose her limbs.

'So tell me more about Thomas,' Ruth said as she got to work. 'He seems an odd fish, but considerate.'

'He may be an odd fish, but there are a lot of fish in the sea.'

'What on earth do you mean by that?'

'He's a nice boy, but he has no prospects. His life isn't going anywhere. And nobody should hitch their wagon to a dead donkey.'

'I thought he was a fish.'

'You know what I mean.'

'You talk about him in a strange way,' said Ruth.

'I'm just wary for you. Women are so unsuspecting in these matters, and I know you've been hurt before, by that poor boy Maarten. You told me all about him – remember? – in one of our little chats. That's why you bite your nails.'

'I may bite my nails, Lyd, but I'm not sole proprietor of the exclusive rights to dirty habits. Your gin guzzling, for example. Ever asked yourself why you do that?'

Lydia looked mildly affronted.

'At my age one ceases to care what the world and its dog may happen to think of one.'

'Oh, one does, does one? Actually, I wasn't referring to your public image. If anything, I prefer solitary drinking to social drinking. Why pretend that we don't drink to get drunk? I mean, of course, that it's OK from time to time. What I'm referring to, Lydia, is the sorry state I find you in virtually every evening. Arseholed, in a word. You're gargling your way to oblivion. I don't know how you do it. I gave up on binges when I was eighteen. You wake up with a mouth like a Turkish wrestler's jockstrap and a brickbat arcade game sounding off in your head. It just isn't worth it. You can't be doing yourself any good.'

'I get nicer when I get drunk.'

'You get drunker when you get drunk.'

'I suppose this advice is the penalty one pays for tendering friendship,' Lydia declared aloofly, 'but it works both ways. I, for one, deplore smoking, and especially the use of marijuana.'

'How did you know?' asked Ruth.

'My dear girl, you reek of the stuff. Your clothes, your hair . . .'

Ruth shut up.

Touché.

It was no small surprise to find that niffy old Bags thought that *she* – Ruth Braams – stank. This was going to take some digesting.

'Perhaps we should declare a temporary ceasefire,' she said moodily.

'If you'd been listening to me, you'd have realized I wasn't sniping at you in the first place, young lady. I was making the point that you're someone after my own heart.'

'In what way?'

'You're independent. You don't need a man.'

Ruth stopped massaging, a perplexed smile on her lips.

'Don't I?'

'No, you don't. If you're honest with yourself, you'll see that I'm right. We're modern women in our different ways. I may drink. You may smoke. We have our peccadilloes, but we're not slaves to social taboos. And, most importantly, you have no need of a man. Neither, as I said, do I.'

'You needed Sander.'

'He was my brother.'

'Well, what about the other fellow I saw leaving your house a few days ago? You're damn cagey, Lydia. You told me you had no idea who I was talking about, but I saw him with my own eyes.'

'What did he look like?'

'Rather distinguished, actually. Curly white hair and a high forehead. Well dressed. A fur-collared coat and a smart leather briefcase.'

'Oh, why didn't you say so before? That must have been Blommendaal. He dropped by on business. He was here to help me with my affairs.'

Ruth stared at Lydia.

Lydia stared straight back.

'I don't have to tell you everything!' the old woman blustered without breaking eye-contact.

'You don't have to tell me *anything*. I just had a quaint, old-fashioned notion that friends confided in each other.'

'This quibbling is putting a strain on our friendship,' said Lydia. 'I think we should put an end to it.'

'The quibbling or the friendship?'

Lydia frowned. 'I do confide in you, my dear, whatever you may think. I have just confided in you that Blommendaal is not my boyfriend.' She fumbled for a Kleenex to wipe the corner of her mouth with a quick, fastidious gesture. 'Isn't that enough? I'm not the kind of woman who goes in for boyfriends anyway. Never have been. I've always been a go-as-you-please person, and no mere man is going to change that, thank you very much.'

'Are you trying to tell me you don't *like* men, Lydia?' Ruth asked gently.

The old woman looked offended and drew back her feet. She raised her knees and hugged them.

'I am not a lady lover, if that's what you mean.'

'I didn't think so. I can't say I ever had you down as a dyke.'

'I'm relieved to hear it. Nevertheless, since you put me on the spot, and since we're in a confiding mood today, I confess that men are not particularly my cup of tea. They can be cruel and bossy and unfeeling. It may be my advanced age speaking, my dear. It may be the war. It may be the ageing process. But as you make your bed, so must you lie on it. I've always been a bit of a rogue elephant. I do things my way. Men are wilful creatures who like to control. I've no doubt Thomas, for all his quietness, is just the same.'

'Well, thanks for the warning.'

Ruth stood up and walked to the window.

She crossed her arms and looked out across the canal. The Scheele house had a black facade and curved bell gable with new white paint on the window frames. A light burned in the front ground-floor room, just visible through the daylight reflections on the pane. If someone was in the room, she couldn't see them.

'I don't mean to be critical,' she said, still with her back to Lydia, 'but don't you think this is all to do with your anger towards Scheele? He's your pet hate, the thorn in your flesh, and somehow that hate has spread outwards towards all men almost indiscriminately.'

'Rubbish!' said Lydia adamantly.

Ruth glanced round.

The old woman had crossed her arms too and was looking sulky.

'When was the last time you actually spoke to him?'

'In 1955, I believe.'

'The year your brother died.'

'Precisely. He had the nerve to attend Sander's funeral, even though I hadn't invited him. I asked them to leave, politely but firmly.'

'Them?'

'He was with some boy.'

'Nearly half a century of silence. That's pretty impressive,' said Ruth. 'Isn't there the remotest chance that, by speaking to him after all this time, you might be able to clear the air?'

'Over my dead body.'

A silence intervened.

'Then perhaps I should take the bull by the horns and speak to him myself,' said Ruth.

'Don't you *dare* interfere in my affairs, you brazen hussy!'

Lydia almost choked on her words.

Her face was red and apoplectic.

She hawked for nearly a minute into a tissue, then let her head flop back against the pillow, the jaw dropping open.

Ruth sensed she'd gone too far.

No point in killing the old coot.

Ultimately, it was all parish-pump politics, a petty spat that five decades had transformed into a silent feud to rival the most enduring of Mafia vendettas.

'You'd better get some sleep,' said Ruth wearily. 'I've got work to be getting on with. I'll nip out later if you want anything from the shops.'

Ruth returned to the *achterhuis* and tweaked up the texts she'd written to update the ICB database.

Principessa sauntered in and – realizing that neither food nor play were on the cards – sauntered out again.

The light dimmed as the afternoon wore on. Ruth tapped quickly on the keys, adjusted the brightness of the screen.

She dunked a biscuit into her coffee and counted the seconds till the lower half broke off. She dunked another. The trick was to pull it out and eat it just before it disintegrated. She got through the best part of the packet.

Her mobile rang and displayed the caller's number. The Kid. She didn't answer.

She changed into black cords and a fine black polo neck, then worked some more. The work came in fits and starts.

She lapsed in and out of a dreamlike state.

She looked around the parlour.

The previous evening, she'd rummaged through Sander's old

desk, the one she was sitting at now. She was looking – as ever – for the letters, or anything even remotely connected to the painting. Likewise, she had already been through three of the upstairs rooms from top to bottom. If she was going to be methodical about things, the next step would be Sander's books. You never knew. She had a vague notion that past generations liked to hide stuff between the pages: money, greetings cards – and, yes, letters. There was an impressive number of volumes for her to flip through. The parlour done, she'd turn her attention to Lydia's quarters, working up or down, floor by floor, room by room. If there was anything to be found, she'd find it. After all, hadn't she come on the old family photo just like that, as if it had been waiting for her?

She stood up, stretched and went over to the wall mirror. She grimaced, scuffing the top of her hair with one hand. It needed a wash. One thing she had in common with Lydia, at least. What's more, she was tired of her natural colour. OK, gentlemen prefer blondes, but – as the saying went – they marry brunettes.

Not that she was on the make, rest assured, darling Lyd . . .

There was plenty of time for balls and chains, trips to Ikea and package holidays to Djerba, complete with kids and the canary.

Back down the corridor, back through Lydia's house, there was a ring at the front door. Had she been hammering at the keys, she wouldn't have heard it. Lydia was probably asleep. If the first ring hadn't woken her, the second might. She trotted to the door, hoping to beat the ringer's patience threshold.

It was a teenage girl in an old army jacket. Freckles, bird's-nest hair and eyes that wandered but rarely perched.

'Hi, I'm with the programme.'

She took the lapel of her jacket and pushed it forward. A badge advertising a drug rehabilitation clinic. Had Lydia phoned a hotline in the *Yellow Pages*, pursuant to their little chat about dirty habits?

But no, the girl looked more like a hophead than a counsellor. The programme had to be detox.

'That's nice,' said Ruth.

'I'm an artist.'

'Nicer still . . .'

The girl lit a cigarette, cupping the flame from the lighter, and sucked the smoke in greedily with her head thrown back.

'I like – you know – sell my stuff from door to door? That's part of the programme.'

She bent down and untied the ribbon attaching an art student's portfolio, which stood upright between her legs. The portfolio was covered in doodles, scribblings and strips of holographic rainbow tape. She pulled out the first sheet of A2 that came to hand and held it up for Ruth to see.

'The owl here is, like, wisdom. He sits up in the tree and looks down at all the crazy shit that's going on down on earth.'

'What are those guys in turbans doing there, behind the rock?'

'They're terrorists. They're kind of planning the final destruction? Probably a chemical attack.'

'And these ones?'

'They're just shooting up.'

She pulled out another one.

'Wow,' said Ruth.

'Yeah, all of these people have got like shells on their backs.'

'So I see.'

'And the shells without people, well there *are* people there, except they're inside the shells. They don't want to come out. Some have windows and holes they look through, but most of them don't have any windows or holes at all. They're the ones who've turned in. They can't communicate. The breakdown has happened.'

'And the naked person in the middle, with no shell and the feelers on her head?'

The girl grinned. 'That's me.'

Ruth smiled back. 'I thought it might be.'

The girl bent down and began riffling through for another good one.

Ruth scratched her head and watched two women pushing a pram down the Keizersgracht. A child's plastic windmill had been tucked behind one of the struts of the hood. It spun with a high trilling sound as they went along. Both women had bandaged noses.

'Listen,' said Ruth, 'this is great, but the lady of the house isn't around right now.'

'Aren't you the lady of the house?'

'No. As I said, she isn't around. And, frankly, I don't think this is really her kind of thing.'

'Yeah, yeah.' The girl looked away glumly. 'Still lifes. Landscapes. Portraits of kids. That's what they all say.'

Ruth felt sorry for her.

'How much are you asking, anyway?'

'Fifteen euros.' She watched for Ruth's reaction. 'Ten?'

'Sold any today?'

She shook her head. 'If I lied and said I had, would that make you want one?'

'Too late for that. Though it probably wouldn't do any harm to brush up your marketing strategies and presentation skills.'

'So, do you want it or not?' the girl was getting peevish.

'I'll take it. It'll give me something to think about. Can you wait there a sec?'

Ruth headed back to the *achterhuis* to fetch her wallet. In the parlour, she checked through her cash and stopped dead.

She'd had a brainwave.

She walked round her brainwave to see what it looked like from different angles. It looked good. A smile spread across her face.

She returned to the front door with a new spring in her step.

'How many pictures have you got there?' she asked.

The girl shrugged. 'About ten, I guess.'

'I'll give you a hundred euros for the whole lot, plus the portfolio.'

She looked at Ruth as if she were mad.

'A hundred and twenty,' Ruth upped, in an access of good humour.

'You're weird. One moment you're cold, the next you're hot. You haven't even looked at the other ones.'

'I don't have to. It just came to me in a flash. I can see this is quality stuff. My resistance kind of melted away. And somehow ... if you explain them too much, it takes the mystery out of them. Know what I mean? I want to find my own meanings in them, rather than be stuck with yours, even though you are the artist. Does that make any sense?'

'Yeah,' said the girl thoughtfully, sizing Ruth up. She stubbed out the cigarette, took the money and counted it. Judging by her face, a lot of things were going on in her head. 'Do you think I could, you know, go professional?' she asked, hesitating.

'You just have, honey. I'm giving you a start. Oh, and can I have the badge?'

'The badge?'

'As a souvenir, to remember this moment by. Anyway, the clinic, the programme – all that's in the past. You don't need rehab. You don't need any silly old programme. What you need is studio space and a good agent. The best.'

Twenty-Two

*R*uth shut the front door and checked in on Lydia.

Fast asleep, a scribbled shopping list on the bedside table. Ruth pocketed the list and went back to the *achterhuis*.

She sat down and weighed up the potential consequences of her plan, this time with a little more circumspection. Whatever happened, she'd play the part. She wouldn't initiate a direct discussion, either about the claim on the picture or her harassment. In the impostor business, that was called 'asking for trouble'.

A flow-chart would've done the job, but her little grey cells weren't up to it. All the same, the stakes were clear. If Scheele was her bogeyman, he was a hazard, period. Her ruse could hardly make things worse.

On aggregate, the game plan looked pretty sound. There was more to gain than to lose.

She worked on the anarcho-nihilist student look in the mirror, roughing up her clothes and hair. Some blue lipstick she'd bought for a Hallowe'en party, heavy eyeshadow to touch in hints of cold-turkey insomnia, the old leather zip-up she wore when mucking out the barge – oh, and don't forget the badge . . .

Clutching the portfolio under her arm, she closed the front door gently behind her. A slight breeze caught the portfolio so she had to turn it sideways on.

Across the canal, the light in Scheele's house was still burning.

Her heart began thumping, telling her to beware. The blood beat in her ears.

She drew a steadying breath.

There was no going back. Her mind was made up and so were her feet.

She strode across the little humpback bridge

There was a brass plate beside the door: *Emmerick SCHEELE.*

She rang the bell.

'Yes?'

She was being spoken to by a suit.

It was a smart, bespoke suit with a shirt and a tie. But the head poking out of the collar was all wrong. It wasn't old enough to be Scheele's. It was a neutral, impassive head – a head in its sixties – that made her think of equerries, commissionaires and stewards. There was an aloof control about it that went with the job. It had one raised eyebrow that was trying to sit up and beg like a question mark. There was something wrong with the left eyelid. It was stuck in the one-third-closed position.

'Hi, I'm with the programme.' She held the badge forward. 'I'm an artist.'

The man sighed with thinly disguised boredom and held the door as if about to shut it. He said nothing. He seemed to be weighing her up.

'Art?' she said, pointing to her portfolio.

'I take it you're selling something?'

She was now in little doubt. This was Scheele's PA, butler, retainer – call him what you will.

'As I said, I'm an artist.' She held up the portfolio like the wing flap of a pantomime chicken and smiled. 'I sell my stuff from door to door.'

'I really don't think . . .'

'No obligations,' said Ruth cheerily. 'Would you like to take a look?'

There was a whirring noise like a food mixer from the rear. 'What is it?' came a reedy male voice.

The man turned his head, shutting the door slightly as he did so. Grey hair, clippered to a fuzz at the base of the skull. A dull, military orderliness about him.

'A young lady,' he answered back.

'I said *what* is it, not *who!*'

He turned back to Ruth with a testy, forgetful look. Her presence seemed to irritate him exceedingly. 'What exactly are you selling again?'

'I told you – I'm an artist. I sell my own paintings.'

'Something to do with paintings, apparently,' he drawled into the interior.

The whirring got louder.

A shrivelled old man, late eighties or early nineties, rumbled up to the door in an electric wheelchair. He too wore a smart suit and tie, but they did little to beautify him. Her first thought was of a centuries-old corpse dug up out of a peat bog or a glacier on which some joker in the forensics lab had placed a pair of horn-rimmed spectacles for a laugh. The face was so heavily lined that the wrinkles looked like scars. It had a ghastly bluish tinge and the grey eyes and pale lashes were abnormally large behind the fat lenses of the spectacles. The last down of hair on the wrinkled pate resembled the green fungus that grows on rancid butter or yogurt. Similar growths sprouted from his droopy ears and nostrils.

His voice had a shrill, nervous vigour that stopped you in your tracks.

'Go and see how it's doing,' he instructed to the other man. 'I hope you set it on four. I'm warning you – if it's black again, I'll know your little game!' He turned to Ruth. 'This way,' he snapped.

The wheelchair spun round and buzzed down the corridor.

She followed it into the front living room.

A high, square room with a modest chandelier hanging from a ceiling rose, almost the mirror-image of Lydia's HQ in its proportions. The main difference was a square hole cut into the rear wall. The old man manoeuvred the wheelchair under a large table, on which stood a radio, a jeweller's microscope, a pill dispenser and the morning papers, open at the comic pages.

He leaned forward as far as he could and cleared a space.

'Give it here,' he said.

Ruth put down the portfolio. Scheele shooed her away and fumbled ineptly with the black ribbon.

On the wall above his head was a framed aerial photograph of Amsterdam's eastern docklands redevelopment, marked up with white lines, arrows and text boxes. Beside this were an old snapshot of a diamond workshop, with men sitting hunched over their labours in white coats, and a mediocre Dutch cowscape, probably nineteenth-century.

The curtains were wide open.

Ruth glanced out of the window, back at Lydia's house.

Was Scheele as strung out about her as she was about him? Did they stare at each other in impotent fury across the canal, a speechless game of *Hate Thy Neighbour* that had been going on for half a century?

It was mind-boggling.

Someone had to put a stop to this madness.

Scheele put on a piece of black headgear that looked like a child's version of a welder's mask. It had a hinged visor with a pair of high-powered magnifying lenses set into it. He pulled down the visor, threw the portfolio open and pored over one of the pictures. His eyesight was obviously atrocious. His nose hovered just centimetres above the picture surface. His head moved up, down, sideways, like a vacuum cleaner, scanning the crude watercolour in every direction, without ever getting the global view.

Not much chance of him keeping Lydia under surveillance, thought Ruth, unless he only had problems close up.

The old buzzard was falling apart at the seams.

A vague smell of burning permeated the room.

He pushed up the visor and raised his head. His hands and jowls were trembling. 'What is the meaning of this?' he said.

Ruth peered over his shoulder.

It was not the painting the girl had explained.

'Well.' She hesitated. 'The train is kind of our journey through life. There are – you know – sidings and stations. Yes, stations – where people get on and get off. Then the line splits. Some trains go to this oasis over here, and others go to the big black volcano with the vultures on the rocks and all the fire and lava. You don't, like, know which way you're going till you get there.'

Scheele stared at her in mute incomprehension.

'That's the meaning,' Ruth faltered. 'Well, sort of. There may be other meanings that I haven't thought of, but basically that's it.'

'*Basically – that's – it,*' the old man repeated flatly, trying to infer some hidden truth from her words. His myopic frown darkened.

He turned back to the painting with an expression of profound disgust.

'Destiny,' said Ruth, wishing she could be spirited away, anywhere but here. 'The tracks. Heaven. Hell. It's like a modern allegory.'

Standing on top of the volcano, Ruth noticed, was a German stormtrooper. Scheele had noticed the figure too.

'Of course, the soldier takes us back to the war,' said Ruth, amazed at this opportunity and at her own opportunism. 'I guess you know about that. You must have been there.'

'*There?* I was *here – here*, young lady! I've never moved from this place.'

'Shit . . . it must have been bad. With all those Nazis crawling around.'

'It was very bad,' said Scheele, lost for a moment in thought. 'They brought out the best in people – and the worst.'

'Did you ever meet any of them?' asked Ruth. 'The Nazis, I mean.'

The old man stared at her then, without warning, sneezed violently. Spittle flecked across the watercolour. Where it landed, the colours started to bleed. He mopped his nose and face with a huge silk handkerchief. A tendril of snot trailed across his upper lip. He took off his spectacles and gave the lenses a wipe.

'Who are you and what is this about? I have no idea why you're in my house,' he said emphatically.

'I'm just telling you about my picture, like you asked me to.'

'I thought you were here to tell me about *my* picture. Aren't you from the museum?'

'Er, no.' Ruth bit her nail, watching for his reaction.

'Then who the blazes are you?'

'I told the other guy. Maybe you didn't hear. I paint. I sell my stuff from door to door.'

A loud rattling emanated from the square hole in the wall and a platform appeared in the hatch.

So that was it, a dumb waiter . . .

A plate with two pieces of steaming buttered toast had been sent up from the kitchen. That, at least, explained the smell.

'Bring it here, will you?' said Scheele, snapping his fingers.

She put the plate in front of him and moved the portfolio out of his way. He brought down the visor again and glared through the thick lenses at the toast. His gnarled old body was rigid and quivering with concentration.

'What colour is this toast?' he asked.

'Brown and black.'

'Ha!' He raised the visor and sniffed suspiciously at the charred squares of bread. 'More brown than black, or more black than brown?'

'More black than brown, I'm afraid.'

'Black,' he repeated in disgust. His voice switched to a high, raucous register. 'This is the last straw. This is deliberate provocation! He knows full well that burnt toast is on the list of carcinogens. I would be *dead* by now, I'm telling you, if I didn't have my wits about me. That's what he wants. He wants me *dead*!'

He picked up one of the pieces of toast and snapped it in two. He did the same to the other. Then he brought his fist down on the plate and pounded the toast into black dust cloyed with melted butter. When he'd finished, he grabbed the plate and threw it towards the dumb waiter. It fell short of the mark, smashing onto the floor.

He hit the controls on the wheelchair. It spun round and whizzed forward rapidly.

Ruth stepped back in surprise, as if giving a bulldozer a wide berth.

The wheelchair stopped. Scheele leaned forward without leaving the chair. His arms were disproportionately long. The veiny hands and wrists extended far beyond the cuffs of his shirt and jacket and his whole torso was crooked, as if one day it had jackknifed at the pelvis and decided it might as well stay that way. He picked up some of the pieces of broken plate and greasy toast and flung them into the service hatch, then buzzed forward again and hit a button on the wall.

That was Scheele.

He was a wizened ape, bad-tempered and ludicrously excitable.

The platform rumbled out of view.

The wheelchair twirled round to face her.

Ruth closed the portfolio and tied the strings.

'What are you doing?' said Scheele.

'I'm going. I think I came at a bad moment.'

'I suppose you have other pictures in there, but I won't look at them,' he said, gesturing feebly at the portfolio with a hand covered in black ash and butter grease. 'One was enough. You have no talent whatsoever.'

'Thanks.'

'You can see yourself to the door.'

Outside, Ruth let out a long, low whistle.

They were quite a pair, Scheele and Lydia, with their rival claims.

Who was winning?

Neither.

It was a race run backwards. One side was just losing faster than the other. No one could tell which one it was, and no one could give a tinker's fuck because ultimately the whole damn farce wasn't worth a light.

Scheele and Lydia, Lydia and Scheele . . .

Quite a pair, indeed.

Neither was exactly an advertisement for a serene and venerable old age. It made you wonder, really it did. Was this what happened when folk got long in the tooth? Rickety tyrants, wizened monsters of egoism, doddering through life with nothing but high-octane bile for fuel? Lydia, to be fair, had her sweet moments, but – like Scheele – she had more or less broken off diplomatic relations with the rest of Planet Earth.

A garbage truck drew up at the pavement. The dustmen jumped off to fetch the bins. Ruth tossed the portfolio into the rear of the vehicle.

She fished Lydia's shopping list out of her pocket and set off up the Keizersgracht.

In the supermarket, she picked food off the shelves in a daze.

Her little social call had got her precisely nowhere. She'd had the satisfaction – if that was the word – of clapping eyes on Lydia's mortal enemy, and one thing at least seemed certain: Scheele wasn't her man in the mask. There was no way that crooked little wheelchair-bound monkey could stalk her, daub graffiti, sabotage the boat and all the rest of it.

So if not Scheele, *who*?

She dropped a packet of crackers into her wire basket.

The evening was drawing in.

She went through the checkout and walked slowly along the canal, beneath the leafless elms, trying to figure things out.

At a junction a taxi nearly collided with a bike. Ruth crossed onto a bridge to avoid the incident. The cyclist thumped his fist on the roof of the cab and pedalled off.

On the bridge there was a flower vendor and a stall selling hot chocolate and split-pea soup. She stopped for some soup, cupping the Styrofoam beaker in her hands. She leaned on the railing and gazed down the canal. A light fog hung over the water. Amsterdam was a looking-glass city, redoubled everywhere in its murky waterways. The solemn facades stretched away as far as the eye could see. From where she was standing, the watery reflection caught the top of the frontages, each with its own distinctive gable and hoist beam. There were step gables, bell gables, cornice gables, neck gables, spout gables. The long roofline looked as if it had been snipped out with scissors like a paper doily. Diversity in uniformity, with everywhere slight variations from the norm: the colour of the brick, the size of the windows, the style of the wrought-iron railing leading up the *stoep*. Each was as distinctive as a human face. In the end, it was hard to say what that norm might have been.

She finished the soup, picked up her bags and went on walking.

Every now and then one of the buildings sported a cartouche or gablestone plaque. Her father had told her once about this unusual feature. In the seventeenth and eighteenth centuries, before the days of street numbers, Amsterdam houses were identified by these stone plaques. They were pictures, let into the brickwork halfway up the house or over the door, and they represented the profession of the householder. There were sailors, spinners, butchers, fishermen, writers. Some were allegorical.

From time to time Ruth stopped to look up at a plaque and try to work it out. She'd completely forgotten about Lydia and Scheele. She was absorbed in her little game. Here was one that represented Adam and Eve in the Garden of Eden. A preacher? No, that didn't make sense. No mere cleric would have a swanky place like this.

Then she got it . . . an apple-dealer!

Pleased with herself, she strolled on.

But as she drew closer to Lydia's house, her pace quickened, she couldn't say why.

Something was eating her. Something was lying in wait, hoping to be discovered, just under the everyday surface of things.

She felt hot and bothered.

She couldn't quite put her finger on why. This thing, whatever it was, had been staring her in the face for God knows how long . . .

She stopped outside Lydia's house and looked up.

There, over the door, was the plaque she'd seen dozens of times before. The head of a gaping or yawning man, his tongue poking out with something stuck on it.

She felt a tingling sensation in the roots of her hair.

Now who on earth was this?

A Moorish face, not looking too happy, and the object on the tongue was round, perhaps a pill.

And there she had it . . .

The poor chap was obviously ill. He'd nipped round for a quick diagnosis, sticking out his tongue to be examined. The cure was the little pill. But this was not a surgeon's house, or even a doctor's. The clue was in the man's Moorish appearance, to remind customers of the remote origins of the remedies.

This was the sign of an apothecary or pharmacist.

With a jolt, Ruth remembered Cabrol's entry on the Netherlands Collection Network:

> His father, Arnoldus, moved to Amsterdam to become a
> relatively well-to-do pharmacist and supplier of artists' pig-
> ments and binding media. Johannes was expected to take
> over the family business and did so reluctantly.

Yes, there it was, biding its time, waiting for eyes that see.
Johannes van der Heyden lived here . . .

What was more, his family had gone on living here, century
after century, right down to Lydia – dear old childless Lydia,
the last withered fruit of the line.

It was incredible but true.

Why hadn't Lydia said anything?

Did she even know?

And suddenly another thought flared up in Ruth's mind and
flamed there with a strong clear light. But of course! It wasn't
just the gaping blackamoor who'd been staring her in the face.
It was much much more.

Think of the fish swimming in the sea, her father always said.
The one thing they don't see is the goddamn thing they're
swimming in. They don't see the sea! And what are *we* swimming in, Ruth? What's the sea we don't see?

The street lamps flickered on.

She glanced across the canal at the Scheele residence.

Darkness.

Lydia's room was also unlit. She was probably still asleep.

She opened the door quietly and pushed it shut behind her.

She caught her breath and looked up at the hallway ceiling,
her X-ray vision taking her up and up . . .

'Johannes,' she whispered, 'you can come out now. Johannes,
baby . . . I've got you, you whoreson dog. Yeah! I know you're
here . . .'

Twenty-three

ydia was asleep, as Ruth had supposed, but she'd been up at least once to answer the door.

A florist had called.

There were two dozen pink roses wrapped in cellophane in the hallway. Ruth opened the card that accompanied the bouquet. It was signed 'Thomas Springer'.

She bit her lower lip and winced.

Under normal circumstances, it was kind of nice for ladies to get flowers. Ruth didn't feel kind of nice. OK, she and Springer had chatted at the party. OK, he'd helped her move in with Lydia. OK, he'd set up her computer in the parlour. But that, Buster, was where it stopped. The Jojo episode and Smits's insinuations had bopped this one on the head.

Furthermore, Thomas Springer – aka the Cisco Kid – was going about things in ways that were indefinably wrong. The eel had been bad enough, just sick making. And how come he now had the right to shower her with flowers?

Whoa!

She didn't feel comfortable about this misfired courtship ritual, this bestowal of gifts. She didn't like it one bit. Morever, it didn't follow on from his attitude when last they had met, though something he'd said had, it was true, made her wonder about him.

Lover boy could stick his roses – maybe not where the monkey stuck the nuts. That would be going too far. But at least in a nice vase in his own private place.

No offence and all that . . .

For the moment, she had other things on her mind.

She dumped the shopping in the kitchen and tripped down the corridor to the rear annex. She pulled a foolscap envelope from the top drawer of the desk, returned to the main house, grabbed the torch and climbed the stairs two at a time.

In the front attic room, the old newspaper was still on the rickety chair where she'd left it.

She sat down.

It might have been the climb, but her heart was beating wildly. She shut her eyes and let her body go limp from the shoulders down.

A couple of minutes passed.

A deep calm invaded her.

Every now and then the sound of a car reached her ears, but mostly there was silence.

She opened her eyes and took her photograph of the van der Heyden painting out of the brown envelope. She held it at arm's length in the beam from the torch.

Then she looked up.

The sloping beams, the little window, the hearth and mantel-piece – it was all as it had been two and a half centuries before when the dark-haired beauty fell asleep on the chaise longue, the scent of mimosa in the air, and the sad man stood at the window, looking out over the canal. And through the window, if there was any last shred of doubt in her mind, was the top storey of Scheele's house, with its fine bell gable and white hoist beam, identical in every detail to the painting.

This was it.

This was where the gaping man had brought her.

Why hadn't she noticed before?

Because Amsterdam was full of these attic rooms overlooking the canals. It could have been any of them, then or now, but it wasn't. This was the little room where it had happened, in another dimension of time, as distant from the present moment as an alien star.

But *what* had happened?

The painting hadn't given up all of its secrets.

And yet she could feel their presence, their atoms and molecules, the dark beauty and the sad man. They were in here with her.

She stood up and moved over to the hearth, checking again with the painting. Right here, the beauty's sleeping head.

Right here, the carriage clock, ticking quietly on the mantelpiece. And here, by the window, the sad man, resting his head and shoulder against the frame, dreaming his melancholy dreams. They hadn't moved. She could hear their breathing. She could hear the clip-clop of horses' hooves from outside on the street and the cries of long-dead gulls. She could sense the perfumed warmth of the woman's body and the dull pressure on the young man's shoulder where he leaned.

If they wanted to, they would speak to her. Give them time. They knew she had found them. They knew they were not alone. Let her wake, let him gather his thoughts . . .

Whoever they were, they had tales to tell.

She lit her mobile and called Myles.

'Guess where I am.'

'I give up.'

'I'm sitting in the painting.'

There was a pause. 'I thought you were weaning yourself off that stuff.'

Ruth told him about Scheele, the gaping man and her flash of realization. She told him about the room.

'Weird,' he murmured when she'd finished.

'I know. Give me a shot of reality, Myles. Say something real.'

'Will we be seeing you at the bureau tomorrow?'

*

Back in the parlour, she put some Chet Baker on the Dansette Popular to get her head together, then carted armfuls of Sander's books down from the top shelves.

She was going to make a start.

Principessa slept on the armchair as Ruth flipped through the pages of each book in turn, first forward, then back. In some there were bookmarks, pressed flowers, even old newspaper clippings. In others there were underlinings and marginalia. These held her up. She stopped to read them, getting a feel for Sander's mind, his spontaneous reactions to words on a page. There was little in the way of fiction. It was largely works on physics, optics, travel and natural history that drew him. In the technical works, he would scribble mathematical equations or the odd diagram. Elsewhere, there would be one-word comments – 'Quite', 'Debatable', 'So true!' He couldn't resist talking back to the invisible author.

She stopped after she'd got through a couple of hundred.

The bindings of one series of books weren't colour-fast. Her hands were light red. She scrubbed them in the bathroom, came back down and went online.

No mail, apart from an office auto-reply from Smits. A thought occurred to her. She could check on Blommendaal. KPN Telecom listed two. One in van Woustraat seemed unlikely. Another fitted the bill: S. Blommendaal, Legal Services. He was just down the road from Lydia, on the Keizersgracht. Ruth leaned back in the chair and crossed her arms.

Now what could Lydia be wanting with a lawyer?

He dropped by on business. He was here to help me with my affairs . . .

On Tuesday lunchtime Ruth chose a style from the Look Book and watched her transformation.

'Don't it make your blonde hair black,' sang the hairdresser after the wash and cut.

First he spread the dye on with a spatula, then massaged it in, his hands in see-through plastic gloves. Where it touched the skin or an ear he wiped the colour away with a flannel to stop it tinting.

'We have this gel,' he said, holding up a green pot. 'It's for the just-out-of-bed look, but I don't think you'll be needing that. You're a natural spike-ball.'

When it was dry, Ruth took a good long look in the mirror. She scarcely recognized herself. She didn't know what to think.

Why had she done this?

Perhaps it had been the Goths at Jade Beach. Perhaps she just needed a change. She was bored with the old Ruth, the one who went nowhere on her going-nowhere boat. She was bored with bored. So today was a day for taking care of the detail. She was making a date with herself. And there was something about looking snazzy and well dressed that scored high in her spiritual feel-good ratings, beating the pants off anything most established religions could offer.

She treated herself to a double frappuccino and cake in a coffee shop.

She began making notes, a list of ideas for the barge once it had been overhauled. When spring came she wanted flowers and plants everywhere – an explosion of colour and greenery. She was going to turn one part of the deck into a proper garden with a creaky rattan deckchair, where she could sit and read and soak up the sun. She was going to get her act together too – take up sketching, even painting. Why not? In the past she'd dabbled in watercolours. This time she'd think big – easel, canvas, acrylics. Like the detox girl, she'd explore her inner self, or the outer world, or one via the other. And, while she was at it, maybe she'd get herself more of a social life, even a man. He didn't go down on the list, but it was a near thing.

She paused, her pencil in mid-air, and thought of the Kid.

She thought of the Kid and his roses.

Was she being hard on him?

She'd sort of fancied the guy at first sight, then so much shit had happened that he got repainted with the same old loo brush. It wasn't exactly his fault. Nor, let's face it, was she the sweetest chick on the block. 'I've noticed something about you,' Lydia had said, almost when they first met. 'The way you walk. The way you talk. You don't give anything away. There's something wrong, isn't there? I can sense these things.'

If only she could relax, chill out and get back into the swim of things, life would come more easily. At the moment some deep channel was dammed up. She couldn't think how or why. There were moments like that in life. They were a bitch. You just had to wait. Whatever was going to unblock you had to come from outside, forked lightning streaking down from the sky.

She did some window-shopping, chatted to the girl at the florist's, whose sister used to go to school with her, bought a magazine and looked at curtain fabrics, thinking of the barge.

The day was cold. The sky was beaten gold.

She bumped into Timmermans in a book store. They talked shop and she helped him find the volume of tajine recipes he was after. When he left, she checked her mobile. One text message.

Now what?

She sat in an alcove, surrounded by self-help books, and read it through.

**O magnum mysterium. Nigra sum sed formosa.
Non aurum sed lapis infernalis, petra genitrix, matrix mundi.**

Her heart felt heavy. A black mood invaded her intravenously.

Oh, man, more damn Latin . . .

It was really something when you needed a degree in classics to be able to read your hate-mail. This time there was no chickenshit and no digital signature.

Who *was* this guy?

Was it this that was eating at her day in and day out?

She'd been sure it was Scheele, but now – since meeting him – nothing seemed more improbable. So could it be someone she knew? Cabrol, Jojo, the Kid, Lucas Aalders, even Myles . . .

OK, Jojo had it in for her, but the emails predated their falling out, and anyway the girl was a social worker, not a brain-damaged cabbalist uttering dire curses in long-dead tongues.

The Kid had his weird moments, but on the whole he seemed favourably disposed. He was also a recent acquaintance.

Cabrol?

The man was a mystery. She thought of him as a droid. If it were possible to see the world through Cabrol's eyes, you'd get a New Age fighter pilot's viewfinder, with all kinds of meters and counters and gauges and trigonometric vectors displayed on the inside of the eyeball. He was Mission Control. She'd never exactly merited his quality kitemark, but she couldn't imagine a motive for the guy. Her gut feeling ruled him out. The emails were emotional. There was a demonic energy behind them. Emotion had been factored out of Cabrol's Cartesian world view. Was it his French blood that did it? He was as cold as a month-old bucket of penguin shit.

So who did that leave?

Myles – dear old Myles?

She felt bad even entertaining the thought.

She looked down at her trainers. They had a pattern of little ventilation holes on the sides in the shape of the letter S.

Was there something about Myles she'd been missing? Surely not. Myles was just Myles, a big lolloping Yogi Bear of a man – sweet, catty, a bit of a softie, a rotten old fruit and camp as a row of tents. He had a soft spot for her, true, but everyone knows that gays, like hairdressers, are a girl's best friend. He wasn't a loner either. He had Rex and Sweekieboude.

No – it was unthinkable.

Maybe Maarten was messaging her from beyond the tomb,

or there was always Smits's perverse suggestion – Andries Smits, detective *extraordinaire* – that she was simply messaging herself. Schizoid Ruth, cruising with the lights down dim, never alone with her split personality!

She went over the Latin again, tonguing the words on the roof of her mouth. Then, as she scrolled to the end, her throat tightened.

She felt a ghoulish delight.

This time he'd bungled. This time he'd slipped up.

The message hadn't been sent through a relay server. It had been sent from a mobile. And the number was there at the end of the text, plain as day, appended to the message automatically by the service operator.

She pulled out her pen and jotted it down on the palm of her hand.

Her hand shook with excitement.

What did they call it – the thing that she needed now?

A reverse phonebook! A directory that would take her from the number to the name. They did exist, but perhaps it wouldn't be necessary. Perhaps this really was someone she knew only too well.

She flipped open her address book, looking for the number, and immediately she found it. It was on the first page, right next to the 'A' thumbnail. 'A' for 'Aalders', Lucas Aalders – big old bumbling Lucas, the formless body, the bald pate and juddering milk cow's udder of a double chin. But a clever chap and no mistaking, in his dry, methodical, gloomily academic way. He thought in joined-up writing. The words came out of his mouth like sausages out of a sausage machine, factory perfect and strung together in accurate syntactic garlands. In another time warp he might have been her father-in-law, but she'd never really known the man. He was just Maarten's dad, part of the scenery, an abstract genetic projection of the ball of flab that Maarten one day might have been. But he'd changed somewhat since the good old 'Dad' days.

Now he was embittered and worn down by grief. Now he was looking for a peg to hang his sorrows.

Something was wrong . . .

She looked at the message again.

You dumb fuck, Ruth! You wouldn't piss if your pants were on fire! What are you using for brains, girl?

404: File Not Found.

There was nothing sinister about Lucas. Lucas was straight as a die. He had simply done what she'd asked him to do. The spiral and pyramid of numbers on the back of the painting. She'd been right, it was Latin. And Lucas had found the cipher . . .

A different kind of shiver ran through her now.

She tapped out his number quickly.

'It's me – Ruth,' she said, breathless. 'Thanks! You did it.'

'I had a little help.'

'Are you at work?'

'Yes.'

'Can we meet?'

'I'm about to give a class.'

'Afterwards then?'

There was a pause. 'You know the department of chemical engineering.'

'The Roeterseiland complex, isn't it?'

'Yes – Building B, on the Nieuwe Achtergracht. Where are you now?'

'Near home. The Jordaan.'

'The seven or ten tram will get you here. Building B, remember – fourth-floor, room four-o-two.'

'Got that.'

'An hour and a half, let's say.'

Lucas was leaving the seminar room when she arrived.

She spotted him from down the corridor. He was wearing a

baggy brown woollen suit, had a document case under one arm and was on his mobile. A pretty girl student with glasses was waiting to talk to him. He finished his call, gave Ruth a quick glance to put her on hold, and lowered his head to listen to the student.

Ruth pretended to read the notices on the wall, but she watched Lucas out of the corner of her eye.

He was smiling playfully, listening, answering the girl's questions in a low, gentle voice. It made Ruth like him. She'd never seen him in his work context before. It added a new, personable dimension to him. The girl laughed, shook her hair and took off down the corridor when their chat was over.

'Let's go in here,' said Lucas, as Ruth approached.

He ran a magnetic swipe card through a vertical slit. Yesteryear's technology: the great-grandaddy of the proximity access biometrics at the Rijksmuseum, with its twenty-first-century bells and whistles.

Ruth watched his finger dance on the keypad, tapping out his code.

The number was Maarten's birthday – no doubt about it – day, month and year.

'Here' was a lab, though not the kind she remembered from school with Bunsen burners, test tubes, flasks and the like, set up on Meccano scaffolding. This was high-tech: big nondescript machines in cream-coloured metal casings, diodes, computer screens and an electrical hum that suggested mechanical activity, though nothing was visibly in motion.

A girl and two lads sat hunched up at screens. They barely looked up when Ruth and Lucas entered.

By the door was an eyepiece that reminded her of an old-fashioned microscope.

'May I?' asked Ruth.

'Be my guest.'

She peered into the contraption. There was something that looked like the pattern on a 1970s T-shirt inside.

'Polymers,' said Lucas helpfully. 'These guys are plastics fetishists. They haven't even graduated, but they've already been snapped up by the industry.' The students raised their heads, smiled self-consciously and got back to work. 'Basically, they're inventing new materials. Otherwise known as a licence to print money.'

Lucas ushered Ruth to a far corner of the lab and they sat on wheely chairs. There was a smell of saltpetre about his clothes, the same smell as in his apartment.

'You cracked the code,' Ruth said. 'Thanks.'

'It was you and your dad, really,' he said, crossing his arms. 'He was right in thinking it was a number-for-letter substitution. You were right in guessing it was Latin. It wasn't so easy to find the word rules, though. I'm a chemical engineer, not a secret services' cryptographer. But we got there in the end. That's what universities are for, eh? The numbers in a pyramid shape told us how the letters split up into words.'

Ruth glanced at the Latin on her mobile again. 'So what's it mean?'

Lucas laughed dryly. 'I knew you were going to ask me that! Fortunately, every good staffroom has a resident Latin scholar. Ours is no exception. One of my colleagues helped me out with this.'

He reached into his pocket and handed her a slip of paper:

O magnum mysterium. Nigra sum sed formosa.
Non aurum sed lapis infernalis, petra genitrix, matrix mundi. –
O great mystery. I am black but comely,
not gold but the infernal stone,
the fertile rock, the womb of the earth.

'Whoever wrote that packed in a lot of allusions,' said Lucas. 'Turn the paper over. I've jotted down two of the references. The first bit, O great mystery, comes from the Christmas matins. Look.'

Ruth read the text on the verso.

How great a mystery and how wonderful a sacrament,
that beasts should see the new-born Lord
lying in their manger.
We have seen the baby and the chorus of angels
praising the Lord. Alleluia.

'The next bit's from the Bible, the Song of Songs.'

I am black, but comely. O ye daughters of Jerusalem,
as the tents of Kedar, as the curtains of Solomon.

'Our Latinist assures me that "matrix" for "womb" is on the rare side. It may come via Arabic from the Cabbala,' he added.

Ruth stared at the words. They didn't make any sense to her. 'Did I tell you where we found this?' she said. 'If I didn't, Dad must have. It was on the back of an eighteenth-century painting.'

'So I gather.'

'In the middle of all the numbers was the symbol for the philosopher's stone. Do you reckon there's an alchemical message here?'

Lucas took the sheet of paper from her and read the words again, rubbing his chin. 'OK, let's suppose there's an alchemical context. As in a child's riddle, the speaker uses the first person. He's putting himself in the place of a particular element or compound. He's black. He's born out of a particular mystical process, like Christ – hence the responses from the Christmas matins. And just in case you thought the philosopher's stone was gold, he's telling you quite clearly that it isn't. It's the infernal stone, the fertile rock, the womb of the earth.'

Ruth stared at him, waiting for more.

'Your father and I have been on the blower about this. He's been doing the alchemical homework for us. In alchemy, the black stage, nigredo, is a chaotic, death-like state where substances are destroyed beyond recognition before something new can be created. Death and rebirth. To them, the alchemist's melting furnace was a kind of womb. But here the womb is the earth itself, and that takes us back to the old animistic belief that stones and metals are alive and grow in the earth. Like corn, they come out of the earth, so – like corn – they must grow there too. There's a kind of goofy logic about it.'

'Remember pet rocks?' said Ruth suddenly. 'I guess the old days is just pre-Tamagotchi.'

Lucas smiled.

'This is a crazy thought, but do you think there could possibly be a connection with uranium?'

'Uranium?' He raised his eyebrows.

'Yeah – bombs, reactors – the big end-of-the-world stuff.'

'When did you say this picture was painted?'

'It's dated 1758.'

'Then it has nothing to do with uranium, take it from me. Uranium's been known about since 1789. A German chap called Klaproth extracted some from a sample of pitchblende and gave it a name.'

'If it's not uranium, then what?'

Lucas spun round on his swivel chair and stood up. On the wall was a periodic table of elements. He pointed to 'Ag' on the table.

'Silver,' he said. 'Or a silver salt. That's what lapis infernalis was to the old alchemists. Also known as lunar caustic. Not gold but the wife of gold. Not the sun, but the crescent moon.'

'You sound like you believe in that stuff!'

He laughed. 'Do I? Well I don't, Ruth, let me assure you. It's like religion. It's dreams. It's madness. It's myth. It's a huge projection of man's hopes onto the world around him. There's nothing objectively scientific about it.'

'But weren't alchemists the forerunners of people like you?'

'Sure, if you want to see it like that,' he shrugged, 'in a hit-and-miss kind of way. But we've made more progress in two centuries than they did in two millennia. There's no method to them, no rigour. They talk in metaphors, then they go and believe more in the metaphors than they do in the evidence of their own eyes. Things didn't get sorted out till the real scientific boffins appeared on the scene – the enlightened ones.'

Ruth stood up and gazed at the periodic table.

Silver: Ag 47 107.8682.

She stood there for thirty seconds.

'Are you all right?' asked Lucas, concerned.

She turned round.

'A verbal answer, perhaps?' he said. 'Instead of that look, I mean.'

'I'm sorry,' she shook herself. 'Yes, I'm fine. Forgive me, Lucas. I was just thinking.'

She tore herself away from the wall chart, trying to behave as if nothing had happened.

47 107. 8682.

She knew where she'd seen that number before. It was the digital mask behind which her hate-mailer hid.

Her suspicions bristled.

Had Lucas drawn her attention to the table on purpose? If so, he'd know he'd hit the nail on the head.

Lucas glanced at his watch. 'Another class,' he explained, making a grin-and-bear-it expression with his mouth. There was nothing untoward in his manner.

He led her to the door and – for a moment – put his arm around her shoulders in a fatherly way. 'I've been thinking what you told me on the phone the other day – about not loving Maarten.'

'I was in a mood. I didn't mean it to come out like that.'

'It was honest, no matter how it came out. I've said nothing to Clara, naturally, but I want you to know I appreciate your honesty. As a scientist. As a rationalist. As a firm believer in the unvarnished truth.'

'You know that Maarten and I were genuinely fond of each other?'

'Of course I do. There's no need to explain.'

She stalled. She looked down, then up again. 'There's something I've never told you. The night before Maarten went off for the skating tour, the night before the accident, I had a dream. It was crazy. I dreamt he had a motorbike accident. I dreamt he died. And then he did.'

Lucas's head was lowered, but he was looking at her from under his brows, waiting for more.

'I never dared tell anyone, but I felt awful. I felt I'd made it happen. I felt I'd willed him to die, unconsciously. Do you think dreams can make things happen?'

He half-closed his eyes and thought it over. 'It depends what you mean by "dreams". If you mean our plans, our projects, then yes – that's what they're there for, to make things happen. But if you mean our subconscious night dreams, then that's a different kettle of fish. I'd say your dream wasn't even prophetic. We dream of people's deaths when we *don't* want them to die. The dream enacts the fear. You also knew that motorbikes are dangerous, but what's new?'

'I should've warned him. I should've said something.'

'Even if you had, he wouldn't have listened to you. Maarten was pig-headed, like me.'

Ruth was relieved. 'That dream has made me steer away from people. I felt like some kind of witch, or doom-monger. The evil eye – you know.'

'You shouldn't. Our dreams are there to help us. Listen to them, but don't let them take over from life. And, Ruth – don't let this Springer business damage your friendship with Jojo. Go and see her. She's still in hospital. If not, try phoning her again. I think she'll speak to you now.'

Twenty-four

That night Ruth woke up abruptly in the little upstairs bedroom. She looked at the alarm.

Three o'clock on the dot.

She felt hot and uneasy. She flipped the pillow over to get the coolness of the other side. She got out of bed and turned down the radiator.

She had seen Lydia when she came home, but not for long. The old woman was behaving pettishly. The honeymoon period of cohabitation was wearing a little thin. Ruth didn't mind. She could keep herself to herself for the evening, feeling under no moral obligation to socialize. She had flicked through another hundred or so of Sander's books before turning in.

Now she tried to work out what had jolted her awake, what had snapped open her eyes and prised up the lid of slumber.

One of Sander's books on mirror silvering and framing had caught her imagination, but that wasn't it. She'd been turning over Lucas's behaviour in her head, not to mention the Kid's, but that wasn't it either.

Had she been dreaming?

Yes, she felt she had. She focused on the inward blackness of a few seconds before, but none of her efforts could bring back her dream. Whatever it was, it belonged to a different order of memory, a parallel zone beneath the gunwales and galley hatches of consciousness.

Then she realized what had troubled her.

Her bedroom looked onto the back of the main house and a light was on at one of the second-storey windows.

She sat up on the edge of the bed and put on her slippers.

She edged to one side of the window and looked up.

There were no signs of life. Just one naked light bulb, blazing in an empty lumber room.

Why?

It was idiotic, but Lydia's senile refrain came back to mind. 'Sometimes he comes when I'm out. Other times he comes at night when I'm asleep. He goes through my things. I can hear him. He likes to rummage when he thinks I'm not around.'

He, of course, being Sander . . .

Ruth thought of the snapshot of the teenage brother – the sporty grin, the prow-like angle of chin and nose, the flat corduroy driving cap and the odd jacket, buttoned up the wrong way round. The dapper man about town. As far as Bags was concerned, his heart attack in 1955 hadn't been the end of it. The brother was a perpetual-motion machine. He just went on and on and on. Entire world mythologies had been built on lesser foundations, and Lydia's enduring obsession with her sibling was growing into a private Olympus, a House of Thebes or Atreus, as real to her as any religion or sect is to its most faithful adepts.

The Sander effect was even beginning to rub off on Ruth. She would sit in the parlour going through Sander's books, reading Sander's jottings, thinking Sander's thoughts. There were echoes of him everywhere. If she dug down into the crack at the back of the armchair, she would no doubt find one of his hairs or a clipping of fingernail – a few atoms of the ghost she had thoughtlessly disturbed.

So did the brother really drop by at unsocial hours on his dark, otherworldly business? What had he lost? What was he rummaging for?

It was a moot point as to whether ectoplasm could rummage, but the existence of ectoplasm was something of a moot point as well.

Ruth padded downstairs and through the corridor into Lydia's side of the house. There was no need to look in on the old girl. She was snoring like a pneumatic drill in the front room.

Ruth waited at the foot of the stairs, holding the torch but not switching it on.

Silence.

She waited a little longer.

If Sander, or whoever else it might be, had heard her, this would be the game: *out-waiting.* Don't move till you're sure you can hear nothing. But the other person may know you're there, waiting to hear nothing and making no move, so you get the nothing you were waiting for.

What then?

You move and betray yourself, or you don't move and spend the whole night doing a passable impression of a tailor's dummy. That was the choice. Given the layout of the house, the person at the foot of the stairs had the tactical advantage. The way out was down, unless – like Chet Baker – you had a penchant for falling out of windows.

Ruth cursed.

Either there was someone up there or there wasn't. She hated this in movies. Why should she like it now?

She put on the torch and walked upstairs, not caring now how much noise she made. She felt surprisingly unscared. The lit second-floor rear room was empty. She switched off the light and shut the door. Then, just to be on the safe side, she checked further upstairs, front and rear.

Not a dicky bird.

Not even a telltale drop in temperature as the phantom Sander glided past, rattling his ball and chain.

She sighed.

If she *had* met Sander, it would have been the last straw. This place was not exactly short of ghosts already, as she'd established earlier in the day. Two were quite enough, unless the almighty had elected to stuff the whole of purgatory into one canalside house in Amsterdam for reasons best known to himself.

The simple explanation was that Lydia had been up there earlier, despite her complaints of infirmity. It was her house, after all. Or simpler still – she, Ruth, had put the light on that morning in her haste to get upstairs to compare the painting with the attic room. Simpler, but implausible. The light switch was inside the room, not on the landing, and what possible reason would she have had for going into that particular room first? None. She certainly couldn't recall doing anything of the sort.

She made her way down.

At the top of the last flight of stairs she took off one slipper. A bit of grit had been irritating her foot. She came downstairs, one shoe on, one shoe off, but stopped midway.

The stair carpet was wet.

She pointed the torch beam down, touched the carpet with her hand and shuddered. Rising damp from the canal. At some earlier stage in human history – the amphibious stage, for example – Amsterdam might have been quite a congenial habitat. Now it definitely felt like a step in the wrong evolutionary direction. Perhaps Pittsburgh wasn't such a bad idea after all.

Ruth put her slipper on again and went back to bed.

'You're different,' said Myles.

'The hair.'

'Maybe not just the hair.'

'OK, I admit it. I had a frontal lobotomy. The black hair was to hide the scars.'

'How d'you feel?'

'Curiously at peace with the world.'

'You have a touching fondness for major surgery. Watch your step with those doctors. It starts with a little body piercing, then nip and tuck – nip and tuck ... They're after the body parts, I tell you.'

'Look who's talking – Mr Earring. Anyway, I was only joking.'

'The sense of humour is a strange thing. I used to have a friend who drove a hearse. He'd kerb-crawl alongside pedestrians just to scare the shit out of them. It was one way of touting for custom, I suppose.' Myles held his hands to his breast and faked a heart attack. 'When he saw the expressions on their faces, it really brightened his day. He once wrote a letter to a toy-car manufacturer asking why there was no hearse in the range of children's vehicles. I wonder if he ever got a reply.'

They'd come straight back to the house from the bureau.

Principessa roused herself and padded over to greet them, her tail erect.

'I wish she'd put her tail down,' said Myles. 'I keep feeling someone's trying to take my photograph.'

He flopped down in Sander's chair and picked up the length of string with the scrunched-up ball of paper tied to the end. It was Principessa's makeshift toy. He dangled it in a nonchalant *roi s'amuse* manner, peering over the armrest. The kitten socked the crumpled paper and sent it swinging. Myles made it spin round her head till she nearly collapsed with giddiness.

'Not nice,' said Ruth, glowering as she boiled up some water for the tea.

'Niceness is neither here nor there.'

'That's so English.'

'No it isn't. *Niceness* is English.'

He made a slip knot in the string, bent down and looped it quickly over the kitten's tail. Principessa cavorted in circles, chasing herself, wopping her paws at the ever-elusive paper mouse.

'You rotten sod!'

Myles wore an air of scientific detachment. 'This kitty has the brain of an amoeba, and I bet the amoeba was glad to get shot of it.'

'I'm never talking to you again. You wait till I get my hands on Sweekieboude!'

She made a grab for the cat and untied the string. She tossed the ball of paper petulantly at Myles, aiming for his head.

'Howzat!' He caught it in cupped hands.

Principessa sat down and licked her paws. Then she yawned and stretched as if nothing had happened – arching her back and raising one rear paw off the floor – and strode regally out of the room.

'I should pour this over your fat head, you English dipshit,' said Ruth as she handed him his mug. 'You wait and see. How you treat cats in this life decides how you get treated in the next.'

'Just as well I've always liked a good flogging then, isn't it?' Myles slurped his tea. He sighed with quiet satisfaction and picked at the knot of string on the ball of paper.

She moved to the desk and booted up the computer. It was early yet, but they were planning on taking in a movie in the evening. She went online and scrolled through the cinema listings. 'They're showing *Total Recall* again,' she said without turning round. 'Or there's a Godard retrospective at the Kriterion, if you fancy French intellectual fare.'

'Me no Leica.'

'I guess not. Might as well watch bananas going black. Mind you, you could always get some shuteye. No fear of losing the plot.' She scrolled down further. 'It's that or some Chinese flick about industrial relations in a provincial sporting goods factory. Sounds like a laugh a minute.'

Myles didn't react.

'Alternatively, we could stay in. If you want the full fireworks, Lydia's fond of a game of Scrabble. Ten to one the old cow wins.'

The silence was unlike Myles. She glanced over her shoulder.

He was hunched over the ball of paper which he'd smoothed out on his knee.

'Myles?'

His head stayed down but his eyes looked up. There was a sparkle in them that she'd never seen before. Something new. Something special. A certain *je ne sais quoi*. His forehead was flushed and a single vein stood out like a winching cable in the middle.

He didn't move.

Ruth got up and walked over. She snatched the battered piece of paper out of his hand and went back to the desk. She eyed him cautiously as she did so, suspecting more monkey business. The paper was yellowed and old with a soft, raggy quality about it that had preserved it from growing brittle, though the edges were mouldy and had flaked away. It was covered with a large flourishing script in sepia ink. It was the top half of a letter.

Her heart was in her mouth.

My dearest and most honoured friend,

Nothing could have prepared me for the exquisite joy I felt this forenoon on opening your packet. When your valet appeared, not even the size and form of the thing suggested its contents to me. I was quite perplexed. How dare you, Sir! Did I not tell you of my oath never to have dealings with Breukhoven again? And yet you . . .

The words broke off at the foot of the page. She read it through once more, then stared at the paper till it sank in.

Myles watched her fixedly.

Their eyes met.

'Come back, Principessa,' he said, holding up his hands in earnest entreaty. 'All is forgiven.'

'This is it, isn't it?' said Ruth, holding the letter up as if she still couldn't believe it was there. 'Tell me this is it, Myles.'

'It's it.'

'It's Johannes.'

'It's a little bit of Johannes. Where's the rest?'

'Don't look at me. I didn't make the ball-and-string thingy.'

'If it wasn't you, who was it?'

Ruth tried to remember. 'Lydia, I guess.'

He eased himself importantly out of the chair and offered her his arm. 'Shall we?'

Lydia had her coat on in the living room. She was sorting coloured pills into her pill dispenser, which had a see-through plastic shutter for each day of the week. She jumped when they knocked and came in without waiting. A handful of pills scattered on the floor. Ruth gathered them up and shovelled them into a little pile on the table with the side of her hand. Lydia noticed Myles's mountainous bulk.

'Who's that?' she whispered.

'It's Myles, Lydia – my English colleague. You met him the other day.'

'Did I?'

'You know you did. Now, what's up with you? Are you cold?'

'Cold? Oh, the coat, you mean. No – I'm not cold. I was about to go to the shops. I need a new inhaler, I have to pick up my pension and there was something else . . . I can't remember now.'

'A crate of Bols Damrak, perhaps?'

'Mints, actually,' said Lydia, mildly affronted. 'I saw an advertisement for mints on the television and I thought that would be rather nice. The ones that you're supposed to eat after eight o'clock.'

Adrian Mathews

'So long as it's not mother's ruin.'

'I've warned you about lecturing me, young lady. If I drink jenever, it's for medicinal purposes. It helps me forget my aches and pains.'

'It helps you forget your own name.'

'What was that?' Lydia cupped her hand to her ear peevishly.

Ruth sighed. 'Nothing, Lydia, nothing.' She sat down beside her. 'Myles and I have a question to ask you. You remember you made a plaything for Principessa, a little ball of paper on a string?'

'I don't know where it is. I can't think when I saw it last.'

'I have it here.' Ruth showed her. 'The thing is, we were wondering where you *found* this scrap of paper.'

'In the house, my dear. The house is full of scraps of paper in case you hadn't noticed. Help yourself, if you want one. One of these days I must sort them out, but my sight isn't what it used to be.'

Ruth glanced at Myles and rolled her eyes to the ceiling. 'Yes, well, we thought you probably *did* find it in the house. Can you be more specific, though? Which room did you find it in?'

'Here, I think,' said Lydia. She pushed her glasses up the bridge of her nose. 'I believe I found it in here lying around on the floor. It was either here or the kitchen. As you know, I don't go anywhere else.'

Myles and Ruth gazed around. There were plenty of magazines and cuttings. There were postcards and old bills. Bags had a habit of keeping ads for free pizzas, plumbing companies, weight-watchers' associations, window-cleaning services, singles clubs and any old junk mail that came her way, 'in case it might be important'. Reading the stuff often took several hours. Ruth knew she read every word – even the smallest of small print – before deciding what priority rating to attribute to it. Nothing resembling the little scrap of eighteenth-century history was in sight.

'May I ask what this is all about?' said Lydia aloofly.

'It's about Johannes, your illustrious forebear,' said Ruth. 'Principessa's punchball was a scrap of one of his letters.'

'Oh!' Lydia's eyelashes fluttered and she clasped her hands together and held them to her breast. She looked at the paper in Ruth's hand as if it were about to bite her. It was hard to judge the quality of her surprise. It was not entirely pleasure. Other, more complex emotions seemed to have jumped into the frame. She was breathing heavily. Eventually she took the letter and pored over it with her magnifying glass.

'Sander told me there were letters. Papa had hidden them in a little box.'

'Behind a wall brick, wasn't it?'

'Yes. But Sander found them and rehid them. He said they were our treasure. I was too young and flighty to give the matter much thought. I never really asked him about them, or, if I did, he didn't go into details. He didn't always trust me, you see. He may have thought I'd sell them. We were so poor in those days.' Tears of self-pity brimmed up in her eyes.

'God knows, I've asked you this before, Lydia. Didn't he tell you where he rehid them?'

Lydia narrowed her gaze as if focusing on something distant. 'No.' There was a pause, then she broke the silence with a chuckle of surprise. 'Goodness, I've just remembered something! Silly old Sander! I remember him saying he'd left them with the queen. I didn't see what it had to do with Queen Wilhelmina, but then I never knew whether to take Sander seriously or not. He was a bit of a wag.'

'You know that Ruth's been looking for them elsewhere in the house,' said Myles, stepping forward. 'Do you mind if we look for them here?'

'Well, I really don't know,' said Lydia, looking around and referring the question to an invisible advisory panel. 'This room is rather special to me. It's where I live.'

'We won't disturb anything,' said Ruth. 'And, with your permission, we could get rid of some of the old papers and introduce the carpet to the Hoover. I don't think they've met for some time.'

'If ever,' Myles added in an undertone.

'Then I shall stay and help you,' Lydia declared.

'I thought you were going shopping.'

'The shopping can wait.'

Ruth and Myles exchanged a look.

'On second thoughts,' said Ruth, 'maybe a little Damrak gin wouldn't be such a bad idea. For when we finish cleaning up, I mean. It would be like a house-warming. Welcome to Spruce-ville . . .'

Lydia's face lit up then darkened again almost immediately. Suspicions swarmed in.

'For God's sake, Lydia, go shopping! Hop it!' Ruth blurted. 'What d'you take us for, thieves? There's nothing worth knocking off here, anyway. Even the TV's early Palaeolithic.'

When Lydia had gone, they set about searching methodically, Ruth at the window side of the room, Myles at the rear. They brought bin liners from the kitchen for the rubbish, took the bed apart, reassembled it, and rolled up the carpet, tapping for loose floorboards. There were none. Myles peered up the chimney and felt around in the sooty blackness for loose bricks – anything. Then he tapped the walls with two fingers, like a doctor doing a chest examination.

Once Ruth glanced across at the Scheele residence. She thought she saw someone at the first-floor window. She looked again and decided it was only a trick of the light against a fold in the curtain through the old uneven glass.

She pointed out the Pittsburgh poster to Myles and regaled him with Lydia's relocation plans. Then, by the fireplace, she found something. It was the other half of Principessa's toy, the other half of the torn letter. They put the two pieces together and shook hands.

'Now, what about the rest?' said Myles.

An hour and a half passed.

'Jesus,' said Myles, getting to his feet and wiping his brow. 'My granny's the same – hoard, hoard, hoard.'

'It's the war generation.'

'They must have squirrel genes which were switched off in their kids and grandchildren. I mean, nowadays it's all Zen, Ikea, Terence Conran and minimalism, isn't it? Less is more.'

'Time for another war, I guess.'

'Yeah. At least we'd appreciate the true value of old yogurt cartons, last Christmas's wrapping paper, dead batteries and empty disposable lighters. What's left here?'

Ruth was on all-fours sorting through Lydia's bookcase. She sat back on her calves and ran her fingers through her hair. 'The sofa's falling to bits. You could stick your hand into the foam rubber and have a rummage around.'

'No thanks. There might be something lurking there.'

'What, mice?' asked Ruth.

'I was thinking more in terms of a family of asylum seekers. And anyway, while we're stocktaking, what the hell's the Virgin Mary doing there?'

'Lydia's mother was Jewish. Her father was Dutch and RC. She goes in for a spot of Mariolatry in her spare time.'

'Holy Mary, mother of God,' Myles intoned in a pious Irish accent.

Ruth scratched her head. 'Funny. She must have moved it. It used to be the other side of the fireplace.'

'How could she move it? It's bigger than her.'

'It's plaster of Paris, I guess. You could sort of hug it to you and rock it or roll it along on the base. At least, I suppose so.'

There was a pregnant silence. Ruth smiled. 'Mary, the Queen of Heaven,' she said.

'Huh?'

'He'd left the letters with the queen. That's what Sander told Lydia, wasn't it?'

Myles snapped his fingers. 'It certainly was, Stanley. Quick – come here! Help me.'

He grabbed the statue to his chest and lowered it. 'Have a look at the base,' he said.

Ruth got on her knees again and peered under the tilting Virgin. 'It's hollow. They always are, I suppose.'

'Can you see anything?'

'No.'

'Can you get your hand up there?'

'Are you sure that's decent?'

'Stop faffing around, Ruth! I can't hold this damn thing all day!'

She put her hand into the narrow hole in the statue's pedestal, then jumped back as Myles groaned. A twinge in his leg had distracted him.

He let the statue fall.

It burst open with a loud crack, splitting like an elongated easter egg along one vertical fold in the Virgin's blue and white vestments. There was a separate break at the neck. The head rolled to one side and came to a halt against the brass coal bucket. A fine plaster dust floated in the air.

'Whoops,' said Myles. 'Butter fingers.'

'Fuck. Now look what you've done. She's going to kill us. If we chuck this out, how long d'you think it'd take before she noticed?'

'A near life-size effigy of the Mother of God towering slap bang in the middle of your sitting room is not something one easily misses, to be frank, particularly if she makes her devotions to it every day.'

'I could nick an angel from a cemetery.'

Myles tutted. 'Wouldn't work. She'd notice the wings.'

'You're in for it now. Iconoclasm's a mortal sin.'

Ruth recalled the task in hand. She turned over one large chunk of plaster. 'Oh, wow, Myles – bingo!' she whispered, 'Bingo – bingo – bingo!'

Nestling in the white hollow was a little bundle of letters. Some were whole, many mere fragments, victims of damp or insect life. The bundle had been tied with an old ribbon, but the ribbon had come loose and now, after the fall, they were all in a jumble. One of the letters must have slipped out through the base when Lydia was moving the statue. She'd torn it in half without thinking or looking – it amounted to the same thing.

Ruth was beaming. 'Myles! We did it! We found the things! Halle-fucking-lujah!'

They hadn't heard Lydia coming in.

She stood in the doorway and dropped her shopping to the floor, rooted to the spot.

Part Two

Twenty-five

*A*n hour later, Ruth and Myles were sprawled on the floor in Sander's study.

They hadn't told Lydia about their find. The shock of the shattered statue had left her confused. There was no point overloading her circuitry. They would break the good news to her later, they agreed – later . . .

Ruth had skimmed through the pile while Myles had gone out to buy fresh coffee. She had laid them out like tiles in a large rectangle on the carpet.

'Is this the first one, chronologically?' he asked.

'Dunno. It must be early. It's obviously the beginning of their friendship. This guy he's writing to is Cornelis Ploos van Amstel. Name ring a bell?'

'Wealthy timber merchant, prolific collector of artworks and scientific instruments, and amateur artist. There's a George van der Mijn portrait of him at The Hague – leaning back in a chair, studying a sketch, quite informal – take five, stuff.'

'So humble Johannes is pulling the right strings. I'm presuming Sander reconstructed the chronology of the relationship. What else can I do? This one's dated, but a lot of the others aren't. Some are complete, some are fragments. And when the statue broke, some came loose from the pack. We'll have to rely on what he says, on the internal evidence. Let's just read, OK, then we can sort out the overall pattern.'

'Yes, Sarge.'

'Here.'

She passed him a handful of pages . . .

19 September 1758

My dear van Amstel,

Thank you for your esteemed letter and your continued encouragements. I do not know what hope there is for my present schemes. Try as I may, the 'science' of drawing, if I may express myself thus, eludes me.

By 'science', I hasten to add, I do not mean materials and equipment. I am twenty-eight (we are nearly of an age), and these past ten years and more, as you know, I have worked in my father's apothecary on the Keizersgracht. In addition to the conventional remedies and lettings of blood, we are purveyors of pigments, binding media and suchlike and, if I may be so bold, they hold few secrets of a chemical nature from me.

What is the price, my dear van Amstel? What must a man do to achieve a fair felicity in drawing, to paint with spirited touches and fire? Must one sell one's soul to the devil? Then so be it! I will work my vitals into my shoes to get this done. The habitual slovenliness in my execution is a curse I feel all too keenly.

You told me that I must be a pupil, as you were from the age of twelve to Norbert Bloemen. Would that I were apprenticed to an engraver, or took a privatissimum! My father, for his part, will have none of it, for he will not suffer me to relinquish the apothecary, and there is no brother or cousin on whom I may discharge this unenviable task, this unwanted life. I have argued that anatomical studies would make me a better apothecary, for I would familiarize myself with the divers parts of the body, but my father did not relish this scheme, seeing it for the thinnest of pretexts, which I readily confess it was. This very morning I did put my case again, in the most reasonable and accommodating manner I could muster, and in his passion he did lock me in my

room until, in his words, I thought proper to come to my senses.
He claims that he wishes to set me fairly a-going as a man of
business. From the top of the house I heard him swearing all
along the street like a little Fury, making a most public spectacle
of himself. Yet no torture of the rack, Sir, will alter my resolution
and each fresh resistance hardens my resolve. I am an artist, not a
paltry pharmacist. I will dare anything to accomplish my
purpose, and I do not wish to put these feelings off until death
interrupts the possibility of accomplishment.

Sir, I am not worthy to be of your acquaintance. Yet my visits
to your household, thanks to the good offices of Mr Hope and his
heavenly daughter Esther, have filled me with renewed faith that I
may and shall follow the promptings of my soul. It is the soul of
an artist, coupled, regretfully, to a dullard's hand and brain, but
cannot a dullard dream? And dream I did when I was in your
delightful home. Your cabinet d'art is ravishing and, as you well
know, a collection unrivalled in the Seven Provinces. I see your
own work and my rapture is unbounded.

Let us meet again, God willing. What say you? If it is not an
imposition, I shall be much obliged for your prudent counsel.

Your friend and servant.

Johannes van der Heyden

*

I own that your unusual proposition has quite taken me by
surprise. When did you first frame the idea? (I am curious to
know.) It is a most judicious exchange of skills, though God
forbid that my father gets wind of it, or all manner of demons
will break loose. Believe me, he is beyond reasoning with. We
shall alternate, as you suggest: on Sunday, you shall teach me
drawing and, when the next occasion presents itself, I shall hold
forth on the secret lore of pigments, with you as my willing
auditor. Come, if you wish, to my lumberplace. It is but a garret,
and meanly proportioned, but there I have my fire and mixing
vessels to hand.

Mr Hope's Esther is indeed a vivacious soul and, as you say, *a spark from the sun in heaven. She has a beautiful neck, which I would fain draw, her hair is lustrous dark and unpowdered, her hands as white as snow and her eyes uncommonly large and black. Is this vision his daughter, a niece or an angel from paradise? I am much tormented with her, as you have had occasion to observe. Her grace and beauty drive me insane. Mr Hope – how apt and fateful the name! – is a genial fellow who receives me tenderly and has twice invited me to sup at his house en famille, when I sat beside Esther. I am excessively fond of her.*

But what am I saying, my dear van Amstel? Again I must dash these yearnings from my head. Esther is a young woman of quality and fashion. Hers is a world of bonnets, shawls, ribbons and satins, though she has a masculine understanding and is withal well read. Mr Hope is a banker and a man of the first rank and mighty good character. His is a world of ships, colonies and commerce. What am I to her? What am I to him? I cannot claim to live on so splendid a footing and my prospects are indeed very dim. Alas, it has come to this. Unless I flourish as a painter, the humble calling which has been foisted upon me will be my private doom. What folly! You see now why my giddy brain is so struck with your novel scheme. It is my only hope of solace and success.

I must stop. I am very scarce of paper.

I ever remain, my dear Sir, your most affectionate friend.

Johannes van der Heyden

*

Dear Cornelis, my honoured friend,

Since the inauguration of our little scheme, I pass the hours in the most brilliant gaiety. You have opened my eyes! Thank you heartily for the loan of the several octavo volumes. I have devoured them by sunlight and candlelight, till I had chronic inflammation of the eyes, and I have absorbed their lessons tolerably, being now quite a fop in learning. I am illuminated,

Sir, as if crystal circulated freely through my veins. I wish you to tell me more about the art of engraving upon wood and metal. I know something of the process whereby an image in wax or bitumen may be drawn on the plate and removed by the action of acids, but have yet to experiment it. But – you are right – above all, I must draw.

As you instructed, I have studied the effects of perspective and proportion and ventured to measure them with my eye, holding my pencil at arm's length. I have drawn a regular grid of squares upon the shop window with a ruler, to my father's consternation, and the same grid upon my paper, such that my drawing respects the disposition of objects and planes in the field of vision. My imagination takes flight. How transporting to imagine painting direct in oils upon the glass pane for, Sir, no under-drawing would be required! (Know you whether the masters have considered this before?) I have turned over the plates in Albinus, copying the anatomical drawings and learning the origin and insertion of the muscles, and it is a lamentable truth that a great number of your modern artists paint skin but they know not what lies beneath it. Accordingly, I have vowed to keep the Greeks and the great Italians in view. I have learned also to walk away, to study the effect of my touches.

I shall show you the fruits of these varied labours in due course. In faith, I find them greatly wanting, yet my spirits are not low for this is assuredly the right way for success. But how long, Cornelis, how long? At the height of my exaltation, this dread impatience undermines me. It is Esther, Sir, who pains me. On my honour, I doubt she will wait upon the slow march of years for my efforts to yield glory and prosperity, even were she apprised of my affections, though I dare hope, as you are aware, that she has a good opinion of me. So how long will my education last? I know, I know! It has scarce begun!

Pray write to me soon and very particularly.

*

Cold weather these two or three days bypast. The barges bringing the fresh water to Groot's brewery can no longer get through the ice. He is trying to arrange for fresh-water ice to be brought overland by sledge from Weesp, where it is sawed, since the ice from the IJ and the Amstel is reputed to cause disease. If you have need of firewood, let me know. His sledges will be bringing some in, along with the ice. As for me, at night, I would shiver like an Italian greyhound were I not all in combustion within!

At your kind suggestion, I called upon Breukhoven, the maker of optical instruments, and a most unusual and cadaverous fellow he turns out to be!

I was thunderstruck to learn that Canaletto and our own Vermeer are rumoured to have employed the camera obscura. Can one give credence to these tales? If so, my fear of ridicule will vanish like the morning dew! Breukhoven has illustrations of a variety of contrivances. To my delight, from behind a fustian curtain he produced one such which we did assemble and experiment. I know not how it came into his possession. It was designed by Abbé Nollet and has a most ingenious pyramid frame that can be collapsed and carried easily outdoors. The artist sits inside his dark tent – a veritable desert nomad, taking shelter from the scorching sun – and a telescopic lens-arm reflects the landscape into the top of the structure and down upon his paper. All that remains is to trace one's line! My dear Cornelis, think you my foolish dreams have been answered?

Breukhoven is adamant the design can be ameliorated. He has a new lens, he says, produced by Dolland in England, which would greatly clarify the projection. I tried to prevail upon him to sell the thing and told him what I would pay, whereupon I was abused like a common felon. I was galled, but will not despair. I count myself of a practical bent and the discovery of this instrument has given a spring to my ambition. I shall build one, Cornelis, and Breukhoven may stew in the kitchens of hell! I venture to think myself adequate to the task.

Whence this diabolical energy? Well, Sir, you know my

motives. I think of Esther, and my blood rises like a fountain.
I am infatuated with fatality.

Ever yours sincerely,

Johannes van der Heyden

*

30 November 1758

Dag, Mynheer!

Your letter came safe to my hands. I trust you are by this time
returned from your expedition.

I have made all possible enquiry with respect to the pigment
Paris blue. It is excellent when used sparingly in shadows with
madder lake. It dries passing well but takes up much oil. Poppy or
nut oil is to be preferred, as linseed oil is too granular. I believe
your friend George van der Mijn will bear me out on these points.

I have had the pleasure of calling again upon the divine
Esther Hope though – as I shall relate – it was not an unmixed
blessing.

She lives, as you know, on the Keizersgracht, not far from my
own abode. Her father and she occupy the ground floor of the
house. Mr Hope spared us an hour together and we talked of the
present war and public executions, which she deplores, and her
peacock, which is ailing, what with the cold. She is a keen
horticulturist and has a pineapple plant and a coffee bush, of all
things, growing in her conservatory. She hopes to cultivate the
Semper Augustus tulip which, they say, will fetch 5,000 guilders,
but this is a rare prize which only a few attain. She mentioned an
Italian gentleman who had visited their household, but, with a
little smile, did not seem inclined to pursue his description
further. It was a visit I shall treasure and my mind is stored with
its fruits, which feed the continuance of my passion, as you may
well imagine. However, in her father's presence, I fear I did make
much of my immature artistic efforts, pretending to a competence
I have not. I curse myself, now, for this pathetic endeavour to

*impress – particularly given the meagre skill that lies behind. But
too late! To my complete surprise, Mr Hope asked me to paint his
daughter's portrait, in return for a handsome fee. I immediately
tried to climb down from the mountain peak on which I had
stranded myself, but he would have none of it, attributing my
dismay to modesty rather than the frantic retractions of a
worthless braggart. He is a decisive fellow, Cornelis. In short, his
commission stands, and a storm of despair quite overshadows my
mind. Hope, moreover, is a man accustomed to swift results. He
gives me a month to deliver the likeness. I am at my wits' end.*

*

My dearest and most honoured friend,

*Nothing could have prepared me for the exquisite joy I felt this
forenoon on opening your packet. When your valet appeared, not
even the size and form of the thing suggested its contents to me.
I was quite perplexed. How dare you, Sir! Did I not tell you of
my oath never to have dealings with Breukhoven again? And yet
you bought the device, doubtless paying the scoundrel an
exorbitant sum. I observe that you also prevailed upon him to
install the English lens of which he spoke. Upon my soul, you are
a true friend. The dark hours of my life are over.*

    *My mother appeared through the back door of the pharmacy as
I had got the packet open and I would fain have hidden it, but it
was too late. She was most intrigued by the unusual aspect of my
new plaything. I explained its operation and, witnessing my high
spirits, she offered to take my place at the shop this afternoon. I
assure you, Cornelis, her offer did not fall on deaf ears! I gathered
up paper, a board and sketching implements, wrapped your gift in
a length of black cloth and saddled our old mare. Within half an
hour I was in the country, away from the inquisitive onlookers that
swarm like beetles in town. I made for a tranquil spot which I am
in the habit of frequenting during the summer months, where three
windmills stand across a polder and before a dyke.*

I entered my Bedouin tent and adjusted the telescopic lens arm to reflect the scenic view upon my paper. The image was perfect. Within half an hour it was traced. Outside the tent I added shading and other true effects to render the solidity and depth of the view. In the past I would have rubbed the whole picture out four or five times and sworn roundly, even abandoned the whole enterprise. Today I was ablaze with happiness and triumph. My sketch was passing fine and I was much pleased with my three windmills, both for the exactitude of their architecture and the accuracy of the perspective.

The camera obscura has this to be said for it: it sets a mirror up to nature which frees the artist from the distortions and disappointments incumbent upon a weak eye, a clumsy hand and an over-heated imagination. It is nature's art of painting, and it is with ease observed, how infinitely superior it is to the finest performance of the pencil.

Cornelis, I hardly dare detain you further. I have still many unruly passions, to which I must now add a sense of guilt or moral quandary. For what? For harnessing science to art, or for denying – on the spur of the moment, I should add – the means by which I have achieved a perfect effect of unmediated nature? Surely no craftsman on earth is obliged to divulge his methods, many of which would seem of great obscurity, artificiality and strangeness to the uninitiated? Each guild has its trade secrets and arcana, and is this not equally true, if not more so, of the painter? What matters is the end and not the means. Do we think less of our dear Vermeer, do we scorn his memory, when we learn that he too used the camera obscura? I durst hope not!

Thank you, my dear friend! I do at last believe that you have freed me from the prison of ineptitude! Pray God to enable me to be steady in my good resolutions.

Most cordially yours,
    Johannes van der Heyden

*

Adrian Mathews

17 December 1758

Cornelis,

I take up my pen this day with mixed emotions and no little
apprehension. When, late yesterday evening, as I was walking
alone down the Keizersgracht, I approached Mr Hope's house, my
pace slackened, as it is wont to do. I lingered a moment, hoping to
catch a glimpse of Esther through the window, for this alone
would be as a gentle puff of the bellows to the embers of my
passion. You may imagine my surprise, however, when – as I
passed the house – the door swung open with a great and hearty
commotion of exclamations, professions of friendship and loud
farewells. Mr Hope and Esther, the latter in a transparent black
fichu that covered her small bosom, were bidding goodnight to
their dinner guest for the evening. On perceiving me in the
shadows, they introduced me to the fellow, one Giacomo Paralis.
There was much gaiety and badinage at this, which I was hard
put to follow. The guest is Italian by birth and around thirty-four
years of age. He is a tall and striking figure of a man, despite
three pock marks on his face. He was dressed in a most
extraordinary southern fashion that would have immediately
provoked ridicule and whistles on the street were it not for the
clemency of darkness: a jacket in scarlet and gold under a fur
manteau, a batiste shirt with laced ruffles of point d'Alençon,
Swiss white silk stockings and highly polished pumps, for all the
world like some popinjay out of the Commedia dell'Arte. The
nails of his little fingers are left to grow long and pointed such
that, as Esther had informed me, they could serve as earpicks and
he smelled most pungently of jasmine pomade. Mr Hope and
Esther offered fulsome praise of Signor Paralis as an occultist
and alchemist whose unique gifts would change their fortunes.
I scarcely knew whether to take this in truth or in jest.

The final adieu came and the door closed upon us. Paralis and
I exchanged a few words in French, then he bade me a courteous

goodnight and mounted into his barouche with the aid of a
postilion. Esther had mentioned this outlandish character to me
before. She said that, at times, his speech has almost the same
obscurity as the manuscripts which have been found among the
ruins of Herculaneum. He is the descendant of a Spanish hidalgo
and, though undoubtedly eccentric, is steeped in learning and
was once a clergyman and doctor of law. He can play violin, has
written plays, knows Latin, Greek and German, the principles of
medicine and I know not what besides. Once, in morbid jest, he is
said to have dug up a

'Have you got the rest of this one?' asked Myles, frowning.

Ruth shook her head.

'Damn, I'm partial to a morbid jest from time to time.'

She stood up, stretched and rubbed a knot of pain in the small of her back. 'Esther,' she said, 'is the girl in Lydia's painting, right?'

'We don't know that yet, but things are leading that way.'

'And he used the camera obscura to paint her.'

'I don't see how. I mean it's great for landscapes. Landscapes stay put. People fidget, pick their noses and go to the loo.'

Ruth sat down again and crossed her legs tailor-fashion. 'But he was taking drawing lessons from van Amstel. Don't forget that. Maybe, just maybe, they worked out and he made fast progress.'

Myles looked sceptical. 'Hope was a man in a hurry. Johannes said so himself. What with this commission, he's on too short a fuse. And you and I know just how *bad* he was at drawing. Ruth – are you listening to me?'

'Sorry, I was lost in thought.'

'Unfamiliar territory . . .'

'Thanks a bunch.'

'What I meant was, this is *all* unfamiliar territory. We're diagonally parked in a parallel universe.'

'On the other hand,' Ruth began.

Adrian Mathews

'On the other hand you have different fingers.'

'Myles, shut up! I was just thinking – on the other hand, life is a mixture of accident and design, and sometimes accidents take the shortest route.'

'Like lightning.'

'Sort of. There's all the blood, sweat and tears – the build-up to the thing – then bang! – the big flash of inspiration. You try hard and things don't work out. Then you slacken off a bit and they do.'

'You mean like it takes only one careless match to start a forest fire, but you need a whole box to light a barbecue?'

'Something similar. Johannes is a clever chap, but his cleverness only goes so far. We know where he wants to go, and we know where he got – Lydia's painting. That's a quantum jump. I don't believe he could have made it on his own. I've got a feeling about this Italian.'

'Next,' said Myles, snapping his fingers and holding out his hand for another batch of letters.

'What you said about people fidgeting, he says it too. Now, where was that scrap of a letter? – oh, here, here, Myles, read this!'

Now, my friend, I ask you to consider my little top-floor lumberplace where I grind and heat my pigments. Is it not ideal? For the rear room is its mirror image, identical in shape and proportion. Let the front room be flooded with light (a skylight will do the job); let the back room be plunged into inky darkness. It suffices to bore a discreet hole in the wall between the two chambers, suitably camouflaged, and insert a lens into the hole. You now have a camera obscura on an impressive scale! One may sketch any object placed in the luminous room, and the size of the sketch may be adjusted at will by moving the paper closer to, or further from, the aperture in the darkened room. A human subject would either be willing and cognisant, therefore, of the method, or lured there upon some fictitious errand and encouraged to sit still

or read a book. Meanwhile the ardent sketcher labours next door
on the pith and energy of the figure. Ah, but I hear the distant
thunder of your objections! I grant that there are still
imperfections in the operation of the scheme. Nonetheless, it has
about it the mad plausibility of genius, does it not? Applaud me,
Cornelis, confound you! If my friendship means anything to you,
Sir, come round post-haste to view my designs.

*

When you left this morning, I did roke a pipe of sweet tobacco
and admire our handiwork. Much as I regretted dismantling my
tent, I am sensible that the Dolland lens is without price. The
adjustable 45° mirror on the wall bracket is undoubtedly an
inspiration too, and I take back whatever thoughtless calumnies I
have uttered in the past against our friend and collaborator
Breukhoven: he has manufactured this little component to the
most exacting standards of craftsmanship. By placing my table
beneath the mirror, I can now project the view from the next
room down upon my paper, pull up a chair and sketch in comfort,
though I must draw from one side to avoid casting an obstructive
shadow across the image with my hand, an inconvenience I am
prepared to live with.

Just after one o'clock the sun deigned to show himself through
my skylight in all his glory and I was able to put the invention to
the test. I placed my horse skull on a chair in the front room and
retired to the back. The image on my paper was of breathtaking
sharpness and clarity. Upon my honour, I am no Raffaele or
Michel Angelo and yet within the hour I had produced the sketch
I send you herewith. What think you of it? I dare say that,
presented in a handsome frame, a good many of our discerning
fellow citizens would be content to have a drawing of such
quality upon their wall, and even to pay for the privilege. Is this
vanity? I would, Cornelis, that I were a man of cooler fancy, but
to the devil with it – I am not! I shall order a quire of paper, nay
two, nay three! And why stop at sketching, I ask you? My
youthful spirits rove abroad into an extravagant imaginary

future. Could not a painting in oils be executed after the same manner? The image would needs be projected upon wood or metal, a smooth support rather than canvas, and the under-drawing executed directly upon the support. The pigment would then be applied outside the camera obscura, with the object itself – rather than its image – before one. How did Vermeer proceed, or Canaletto? I know not and doubt whether this intelligence is to be had.

My father is suspicious again. He hears me creeping around my lumberplace at the dead of night and tries the door, which I have locked. Last night he drank himself to perdition with Groot, and there is a great jarring of temper between us.

*

Upon taking the evening air, a barouche stopped beside me, and the Italian Paralis hailed me from within. He suggested repairing to his inn, the Second Byble in the Nes, and I accepted his offer with alacrity, being curious to know what brought such a flamboyant personage to our humble shores.

Wine is a great oiler of tongues, Cornelis, and at the inn I opened my heart to Giacomo (for we were soon on first-name terms) as I have to no one else save yourself, may God forgive me. Without naming her, I confessed that my soul was set upon a woman of great beauty but who was so far above my own station in life that only through success as a painter could I hope to gain her hand. 'Ah!' says he, 'if she were half as beautiful as Mr Hope's daughter, she would be a great beauty indeed!' My friend, it was as if he had read the innermost secret of my heart! 'Why,' says I, on my guard now, 'what think you of Esther Hope?' 'She is like an angel by Raffaele,' says he, 'or a statue by Praxiteles. There are no words to describe such a woman as this. Only a genius could shadow forth her charms.' Thereupon I could hold my peace no longer. 'Well, Sir,' says I, 'it is she! It is she that I burn for and I care not who knows it now! My love is in vain unless I can better myself. I wonder that I should unburden myself thus – and to you, a friend of the Hopes – but I am close

to despair and, in such straits, caution, as they say, is oft flung to
the winds.' Giacomo listened to me in earnest, then laughed so
savagely that he instantly drew the attention of all the revellers.
There were musicians present and he borrowed a fiddle from one
and leaped upon a table to play a frenzied Neapolitan air with
such brio that, before long, everyone but myself was on their feet
and dancing. Truly, my friend, I knew not what to make of this
boisterous foreigner who seems at ease with princes and paupers.

*

1 February 1759

Dear friend,

I have this moment received yours and reply in great haste. The
apothecary is closed, for my father and the carpenters are busy
constructing a new counter, and I, like a condemned man, must
crowd a lifetime into the precious hours that are vouchsafed me.

  This morning my mother sat for me in my lumberplace, while
I laboured in the adjoining room, my Plato's Cave. It was as I
had suspected. The light was good, the Dolland lens furnished an
image of exemplary clarity, and my mother is a calm soul and no
fidgeter, and yet I had the devil's own job drawing her, for truly
we are mortals of the common fabric who draw breath and who
know not stillness, until such time as the good Lord sees fit to
curtail our earthly trials. In short, my sketch was a confounded
mess. To my shame, I rebuked my mother, then rebuked myself
for doing so and begged her forgiveness most abjectly. It was not
a scene in which I could take manly pride.

  Oh, fie!

*

After ice-skating on the Singelgracht, Giacomo and I retired to a
Musico – a low establishment, the Huis van Mirakelen on the
Willemsstraat, where a juffrouw may be had for the asking (and a
handful of ducats). So little is this trade dissimulated that each
girl has a small oil painting of herself hung outside her room to

facilitate customers in their choice. The paintings are crude in execution, but we amused ourselves observing how reality departed from these ideal representations. There Giacomo confided that, the previous evening, he had taken Esther to a concert. Alone together in the carriage, he asked to kiss her hand. 'Why my hand?' Esther replied, and allowed him to kiss her on the lips. I admit that I blanched, Cornelis, at this astounding anecdote, but knowing of my passion for her, Giacomo assured me that the kiss had been Platonic, a frivolous courtesy that should be construed as nothing more.

By the by, I recalled that Esther and her father had described Giacomo as an occultist, whose special gift would make their fortune. I made so bold as to ask him for an explanation, and it is this. In Venice he was inducted into the forbidden sciences of cabbalism and alchemy and knows a secret calculus, which he terms the Key of Solomon and which was given him by a monk on a mountain when he was with the Spanish army. He had the honesty (or bare-faced cheek) to confess that he has not stopped short of bamboozling an innocent gull or two. He increased a quantity of mercury by adding bismuth and lead and sold this 'secret' to a Greek merchant for £1,000 sterling. On another occasion, he used cabbalism – fraudulently or not, I cannot venture to say – to cure the acne of the King of France's cousin, the Duchess of Chartres, and the evil humours of the Comte de la Tour. I suspect him to be a Freemason and a Rosicrucian. His friend Mme d'Urfé has a substantial cabbalistic library in Paris and a laboratory with alembics, chemicals and retorts in which he has honed his secret arts to perfection. I quizzed him on his knowledge of divers substances and their interactions, and he is indeed in possession of a sound knowledge, both chemical and medical. And yet, in my heart of hearts, I fear that Esther and Mr Hope, in their good-natured innocence, have been befooled by him, so I questioned him further concerning his secret calculus.

Esther, it seemed, had asked the oracle what her destiny would be and, by constructing pyramids with numbers drawn from

words, Giacomo extracted a numerical answer and translated it
into the French alphabet, an answer to the effect that she had not
yet taken the first step on the road to her destiny. Her second
wish was to know who loved her most, to which 'your father'
came as an appropriate Christian response.

Seeing that he had aroused both my interest and my
suspicions, Giacomo drew a paper from his pocket and invited me
to submit a formula to the oracle too. After due reflection, I wrote
the following words: 'I have contracted a disease whereof I know
not the cure.' My dear Cornelis, I was thinking of Esther,
naturally enough, for love, as you know, is a perfect fever of the
mind. I question if any man has been more tormented with it
than myself and, even as I write, my heart is torn once again by
vexing thoughts. Be that as it may, Giacomo – by what means I
know not – translated my words into a pyramid of letters,
performed a hasty but elaborate numerical calculation, and
returned the answer 'Lapis infernalis'. What, my dear fellow, was
I to make of that? As an apothecary, I am, of course, familiar with
this substance, for it is but another name for lunar caustic or
lapis lunearis, a crystal salt of silver known in French as pierre
infernale, and it is of great use to cauterize wounds, remove
warts and disinfect the eyes of newborn babes, saving many a one
from a life of blindness, as it is in the making of mirrors or the
process of silver plating. Yet the allusion bore no earthly
correspondence to my enquiry. My Italian soothsayer, however,
seemed in no doubt as to the aptness of the oracle's response, so I
begged him to enlighten me. 'You have catched a memorandum of
vice!' he intoned, gazing at me with a severe brow. His turn of
phrase left me none the wiser. 'What in the world are you talking
about, my dear chap?' I implored. 'Why, the venereal disorder, of
course,' he came back petulantly, 'for is not this the disease you
have contracted? Come, man, be not timorous with me! Thou
hast discovered some infection and it is this which repels thee
from these comely whores. Dear God, I know how you feel! My
own life has been plagued with this abominable curse, but a good

solution of lapis infernalis is as fine a remedy as you'll find! The best Italian apothecaries swear to it as a cure. I use the liquid, moreover, as ink for writing secret letters to my loves, for this horn silver has the wondrous property of altering colour and becoming dark in daylight. Letters composed by dim light, therefore, remain invisible until exposed to sunlight for a few hours.'

Cornelis, a memorandum of vice! What was I to do or say? Well, I gasped and then I laughed out loud! I had never imagined my words could be so misconstrued! I immediately apprised Giacomo of his error – for I am a man with many foibles, but whoring and debauchery have never numbered amongst them – and reminded him of my pure spiritual passion for Esther. The poor soul was quite crestfallen. He put away his paper with some despatch and groused that, though the oracle could itself be ambiguous, the questions or quandaries submitted to it should always be of a crystal clarity that is beyond reproach.

Our conversation returned to Esther, and I told Giacomo once again of my faltering hopes of becoming a painter. I did not, I confess, inform him of my experiments with the camera obscura, out of shallow pride, for I wished him to keep a high opinion of me and, if the truth be known, my projector and his oracle are peradventure of a piece, for in both cases it is the results that justify the means, and the honesty or dishonesty of those means must remain veiled in a perpetual moral darkness.

He listened, subdued, to my tale of frustrated life and love and I was curious to know what way out of this maze of uncertainty his capacious mind would find for me, for he seemed to concern himself sincerely on my behalf. 'To hell with your art,' says he after due deliberation. His reply was as unexpected as it was hurtful, but I chose to overlook Giacomo's petulance. A sallow fellow nearby, with a scar the length of his throat, had just finished a game of chess and was packing the pieces into their box. To make the peace, I offered Giacomo a game. 'Je ne joue pas aux échecs, Monsieur,' says he haughtily. 'Je joue aux dames.'

But on my way home, Cornelis, I felt suddenly elated, for something had come alive in my imagination! It was Giacomo's words – a chance remark, indeed – that gave me pause and fanned the dying embers of my hopes. I cannot tell you more now, lest the hint I have received be no more substantial than the lights produced by marsh gas. There are trials and experiments to be performed, and my exertions shall not be wanting. But fear not, Cornelis, when the time comes I shall breathe no word of this to anyone but you. Trust me.

I am, Sir, your steady friend,
Johannes

Twenty-six

'The Italian,' said Miles. 'What do you make of him?'

'A bit of a queer fish,' Ruth replied. 'Do you think he's on the make?'

'Dunno. That oracle of his may be a gimmick, an innocent party trick. If it isn't, he's limbering up for some kind of swindle.'

'It's certainly got Johannes all excited.'

'Myles scratched his cheek and frowned. 'It's not the oracle that's got him excited.'

Ruth skimmed the last page again. 'No, you're right. It's something the Italian said.'

'And tell me – what's an eighteenth-century con man going to get out of a humble apothecary? It doesn't add up.'

They crouched down over the next letter, their heads almost touching.

Lapis infernalis, lunar caustic . . .

This, if you recall, was the pronouncement of Giacomo's oracle, a most absurd misunderstanding of my plight. And yet the clouds begin to clear. Could it be that there is indeed a divine intelligence behind this oracle, over and beyond anything that I, in my world-weary scepticism, was led to expect? Allow me to explain. Giacomo had mentioned in passing that he used a solution of this salt of silver as ink for writing letters, since – though invisible to begin with – upon exposure to the sun the

liquid darkens. This remark set me musing and reminded me of
a phenomenon I had myself observed. In the pharmacy we have a
jar of these self-same lunar crystals by the window, which we
keep for medicinal purposes. Since childhood my father has
warned me to be cautious with this substance, for it is poisonous,
stains the skin brown and may be used for the manufacture of
explosives. I wonder if it is not akin to saltpetre, which is also a
stone of salt. At any rate, it should not, for this reason, be sold to
persons of uncertain character. The jar is on a shelf beside the
window, and it had often struck me that the crystals facing the
window were darker than those on the other side. Indeed, where
the corner of a lace curtain happened to drape across part of the
jar, the pattern of the lace appeared to be imprinted on the
crystals in a crude fashion. I know not whether it be the light or
heat of the sun that is to account for this effect, though I guess it
to be the light. The result, however, is there for all the world to
see. I had observed this phenomenon, as I say, on many occasions,
but thought no more of it: since the oracle spoke I can think of
nothing else.

*

Throughout my experiments with the camera obscura, the
constant obstacle to portraiture has been the movement of the
subject, however infinitesimal. People, dear sir, do not sit still,
confound them! In my Plato's Cave, the mirror on the wall
bracket projects an image down upon my paper, but no sooner do
I start tracing than the outline of my subject has shifted place.
You know too well of my frustrations on this score. If only,
thought I, my paper or board could be coated with a subtle
matter, whose first effect would be as a mirror. Yet whereas the
mirror represents images faithfully, but retains none, this
substance, by means of its nature, would preserve a facsimile of
the image that is projected upon it. The artist could then paint
upon this image at his leisure, which would be superior in
accuracy to what a man can draw. If this were possible, here
indeed would be a fine art, whose truthfulness no one could

challenge! Here indeed would be the makings of a portraitist of high renown, most eligible in every way!

And so, my dear Cornelis, it came to me in a flash that the subtle matter of which I had dreamt in vain had been staring me in the face all along – there in a jar, on a dusty shelf, in the very pharmacy I have reviled and yearned to escape.

*

If we have anything in common, my friend, it is that we are both practical men. You, of all people, then, can well imagine that I wasted no time in proceeding with my experiments. The crystals of lapis infernalis are formed by the dissolution of silver in nitreum or phlogisticated acid of nitre. To coat a canvas, it is necessary to make them into a solution or emulsion once again, which I did. I found that the solution was too liquid to grip the texture of my support, but by mixing it with albumen – that is, the white of a hen's egg – a binder was formed and this hurdle was easily overcome. For several hours I placed the coated canvas within my camera obscura, using the horse's skull once again as subject-matter, and, to my delight, this first experiment was successful in producing a faint image that I could view in dim light, for I had not foreseen that if the canvas or board is sensitive to light, the image produced will remain sensitive to light, unless some means be found to halt the process. Nor had I foreseen the peculiar aspect of this image, for that which is light in reality is dark on my image, and that which is dark is light, as, on a summer's day, one might glance at the sun, or some brightly illuminated object, and on closing the eyes an after-image is perceived where effects of light and shadow are reversed. This curiosity, however, does not affect the justice of the contour.

I have proceeded in an effectual manner this past week, constantly varying my methods, and the results are now much improved. Instead of canvas, I have used wooden or copper supports, for the surface is smoother and therefore easier to paint upon with great precision once the image is retained. I immerse the support in a solution of sal marinus and allow it to dry before

coating with the albumen solution of lapis infernalis. Exposure to
the projector is still too long for my liking, but I have succeeded
in reducing it to about one hour and hope to reduce this time
even further. It produces a latent image which I make visible by
treatment with certain vapours – I shall tell you more of this
revealing stage when we meet. Forgive me if my account is
confused and piecemeal, but I feel like an apprentice juggler at a
fair, this realm of chemistry is so original to me. Once the image
is produced, I attempt to stabilize it with various substances. A
salt of Tartarus I keep in a Hessian crucible is proving most
efficacious, and I have yet to experiment with ammonium and
hydrargyrum. The resulting heliograph, as I call it, is delightfully
detailed, and I now find that a second treatment with sal marinus
or sal gemme – in common parlance, table salt – serves to fix it
fairly well, presumably by dissolving the unexposed lunar caustic,
though for how long I know not. The image is then washed and
dried. I suspect it is easily damaged. However, if my copper plate
is slightly silvered to begin with, it reflects light like a mirror. As
such, though the image is reversed in the way I have described to
you, by holding the plate at an angle the darks become light and
the lights dark, thereby restoring the tones of the original.

    My friend, I must say no more, for fear that this letter gets
into unscrupulous hands, though I dare say I have revealed too
much already. Was ever a man more lucky than I am at this
time? Truly my mind is ablaze. I turn to the books you lent me,
and I find that Giacomo and I are not alone in our knowledge of
this property of lapis infernalis. The Dutch scientist Angelo Sala
had noted it, as did Johan Heinrich Schulze and, earlier still,
Geber, or Pliny in his Historiae Naturalis. Yet none but I, it
seems to me, has thought to combine this phenomenon with the
camera obscura. The art of painting, Cornelis, is about to be
transformed, for with the invention of my under-picture, the
artist need never again live in fear of clumsy draughtsmanship or
paucity of skill. And yet – like Giacomo's oracle and my camera
obscura – this discovery must perforce remain secret, initially for

my own exploitation, thereafter for those adepts we choose to nominate and induct into our great mystery. For is this not a magical mirror we have discovered? You have only to fix your glance upon it to leave your features there.

I do wonder if there be a secret priesthood that already possesses and guards the knowledge I have chanced upon, for did not Christ himself leave the image of his face upon St Veronica's napkin, and upon his shroud? Could this *lapis infernalis* be the philosopher's stone, the great Arcanum of the alchemists, who may thereby enrich themselves, both with earthly and spiritual wealth? If that be so, you shall be my accomplice and co-sharer in this lucrative art, for such things are not fit for milk-and-water minds, and truly no man has been so generous and open-hearted to me as yourself. Though Giacomo was at the birth of these notions, I hesitate to make him privy to my discoveries. What think you? You do not know the man, of course, but from my report, think you he is to be trusted?

For my part, I have yet to experiment upon a human subject, but am intent on doing so. And Esther it shall be. I shall have her portrait, Cornelis, by hook or by crook, as I shall later have her for my wife. And in this I need Giacomo's help, for he is so much in her favour. I am uncertain, as I say, how deep I should take this exquisite into my confidence, although the thought is in itself unworthy, since, though cunning, and despite the fact that he considers the Dutch language to be a tongue fit for horses, he has been my unwitting guide and my beacon in all this. Nevertheless, I am upon my guard.

I shall detain you no longer. My brain is giddy, for the fumes of chemicals quite unhinge my mind. But I am convinced that this is a matter of great moment.

Ever most affly, yours,
Johannes

Ruth felt a shiver travel down her spine.
'Want to take a break?'

'A matter of great moment,' Myles repeated. He replaced the letter carefully on the carpet.

She shook her head and made a grab for the Thermos. She poured another coffee and swallowed a mouthful. 'This under-picture,' she began.

'The under-picture,' he repeated in a grave tone.

He waited till she finished reading the next batch, watching her face. Her expression darkened. In silence she passed the pages to him.

Cornelis, I will have my portrait of Esther at long last, albeit by innocent wiles. The happy union of the camera obscura and the lunar caustic will, I dare hope, bring about another, happier union in the fullness of time. Whether this be trickery or not, I no longer know. All I know is that fate has chosen me for this strange destiny and I have no choice but to yield. I am in thrall to the infernal stone. Let it do with me what it will.

> *Your friend,*
> *Johannes*

*

25 February 1758

Cornelis,

I take your admonition in good part, and shall profit by it one way or other. Methinks indeed I have been shamefully used, and my certainty grows with each minute and hour that passes. I look at my painting, which is now complete, and consider it a most ingenious and cold fabrication, yet is it conceivable that I have fallen victim to a fabrication even more ingenious and cold, a wanton and dastardly trick on the Italian's part that, as God is my witness, would be tragically ill-timed to one in my situation – not least from one who professed at least a passing masculine friendship?

I feel an irreparable loss. I am in wretched spirits, ashamed and sunken on account of the disappointment of hopes which led me to endure such grievances. I curse the Italian – a conversable man, yet what a brutal and unworthy fellow, despite the magnitude and lustre of his character. I curse Esther – yes, Blest Esther! – for if my fears be grounded, then truly, frailty, as the poet says, thy name is woman. She is as lewd a minx, as ill-bred and rompish, as any at the Musico – and I, a sad dupe, am well rid of her. I curse, moreover, the roaring, bantering society of men, whose palaces are built on spiritual quicksands and whose words are bankrupt promises. And, lastly, I curse myself – for my towering hopes that were nothing but blown eggs – for my wretched credulity – for my trust in 'love', which is but a worn euphemism, daubed on the brow of the human beast.

Fie! I have the taste of ashes in my mouth.

I loved Esther, but she loved not me. From this moment I resolve to think no more of her. Wish me joy, Cornelis, of having discovered the snake before it was too late.

But truly there is no comfort left to me.

When I look upon my latest 'painting' my heart fills with dire warnings. This mirror-like representation is the devil's own work, for I have dabbled in alchemy, Cornelis, and must pay the price for this wickedness. Ah yes! It is a fine little picture, pretty, well executed, well drawn and rich in colour, a fitting testimony to Esther's physical beauty and, assuredly, were anyone to see it, they would praise its justness, its colours and the odd naturalness of its composition, and pay a handsome price – and yet I curse it with every venomous breath in my body, for I know it for what it is. It is no less, my friend, than the faithful image and agent of my own damnation. I am in it, Sir – or that phantom I must needs call myself, for he is both me and Death in person, real and unreal, breathing and extinct. This is no quaint invention of the painter's fancy. It is the demon magic of the infernal stone. My God, I cannot tell you how dead this picture is to me, how utterly devoid of joy and pleasure. I want none of it. Using the numerical code which that fine villain Paralis confided to me, I have

inscribed its secret upon the back, together with the symbols for
the philosopher's stone, the moon which is the sign for silver and
the apothecary's emblem for salt. Let he who wishes to sign a pact
with Satan discover it and do with it what he will. I, for my part,
will have none of it. I shall keep it, sure, as a reminder of my
shame, but no one shall see it, for I shall hide it away.

  Forgive me. I am not yet in a frame to write as I could wish to
you. I am thrown upon the wild world again. Every prospect that
I turn my mind's eye upon is dreary, and I know not what will
become of me. But hear this, Cornelis: our lives and fortunes are
but a throw of the dice. Let this be the moral of Johannes' life.

  Forgive this acid epistle. Now I must find my proper station
until my life comes right.

  Johannes van der Heyden

'Oh, wow,' said Myles, 'what happened?'

'I don't know.'

'There's something missing, right?' On all-fours, they scanned
the mosaic of pages laid out on the carpet.

'Is this everything?' asked Myles.

'It's everything we've got.'

'Get back there. Check the statue. Look on the floor – anywhere.'

'I can't. Lydia's there. I'll go later, when she's out.'

'You'll go now,' said Myles firmly.

She stood up, frowned, hesitated an instant, then made for
the door.

As luck would have it, Lydia was in the kitchen. The chink
of crockery and the sound of running water came from the end
of the corridor.

Ruth opened the door to the front room and went in.

The broken statue still lay where it had fallen.

There was no sign of any further letters. Nevertheless, she
got down on her knees and peered up into the darkness of the
plaster of Paris husk. She slid her arm in and felt around inside.

Then her fingers touched them – those last few stray pages that had thought they'd got away . . .

When my parents were out, the Italian brought Esther to my lumberplace, as we had conspired. She wore a large overcoat of coney fur which she removed, for I had a good blaze going in the hearth. Beneath, she was dressed in a pale blue dress of satin and a diamond necklace. The silvery light of day flooded through the skylight, and I own I was spellbound, for I had never seen her more beautiful. I was also ill prepared, Cornelis. For all my fine plans, I had not – in the interim – succeeded in reducing the exposure time for my heliographs to less than forty minutes, and how was I to get her to sit immobile for so long? The only solution was for her to pose as I sketched, and to insist that she take her example from some statue for the required duration. Furthermore, how was I to propose? When the Italian was gone, certainly, but – as I say – Esther's beauty was unsurpassed, and it had the effect of dampening my ambition and conviction, for she was so far superior to such a one as I in every way that I felt like a maggot in her presence. Be that as it may, events took a turn which I had not anticipated, as you shall hear, and my memory of the occasion – which is not a whit bedimmed – continues to perplex me unduly . . .

I set up my easel to one side of the 'eye' in the wall, which was the aperture of my camera obscura in the next room, for I did not want to form part of the composition. Above the eye I had placed a hook, and on that hook, a cocked hat, which completely covered the eye. It was enough to remove the hat for the projection and exposure of the prepared copper plate in the darkened room to begin. Such were my preparations, and I was confident that the eye or orifice was so small and unobtrusive that no one would notice it and, even if they did, would take it for a defect in the plasterwork along with many others. In the centre of the room I had placed a handsome chaise longue, upon which Esther sat at once to test it for comfort.

I told her that, throughout the sketching, she must remain as
still as the Sphinx of Cheops, and that I would draw her from
head to toe. She stood up and walked to my easel and board. Then
she looked back at the chaise longue, the room and everything.
'What think you, Giacomo?' said she. 'Should I stand or recline?
Are the elements of harmony in place? I do not mean to be vain,
but in the interests of art and posterity it were best to judge these
things before the deed were done.'

He came round, placed himself at her side and rubbed his chin
thoughtfully, then scratched the pock marks on his face with that
ghoulish elongated fingernail of his. 'It occurs to me,' says he,
'that the pale blue of your dress may be somewhat icy in isolation.
Were it to be offset, however, by – say – a sunny yellow, the effect
would be altogether superior.' He stalked pensively around the
room, still rubbing his chin, and chanced on a large earthenware
pitcher which I keep there for drinking water. He placed it behind
the chaise longue and returned to the easel. 'There!' says he. 'That
is what we need. This handsome pot and a radiant bouquet of
flowers – yellow, as I said, would be just the thing. Esther – what
would you suggest?'

'Why daffodils, surely, or mimosa. Yes, mimosa I adore!'

I reminded them that this was February and, moreover, Sunday,
with no flower market in town. 'My dear Johannes,' said Esther in
a condescending tone, 'have you not heard of a glasshouse? While I
have no mimosa in papa's conservatory, I know a fine lady who
does, and I have no doubt that, with a note from me, she would be
more than happy to contribute a bouquet for this auspicious
occasion.' She took pen and paper, wrote down the address of her
horticultural friend and handed it to me. It was a house at some
distance, out towards De Plantage. I looked pleadingly to the
Italian, but he shrugged with a certain languor and informed me
that his valet de louage had taken the afternoon off that and that he
himself had no sense of direction whatsoever in this daedalian city.
I was somewhat put out by this procrastination, but took heart and
promised to return within the hour . . .

Ruth glanced at Myles. Their eyes met.

'It's true enough,' said Myles. 'It's easy to get lost in Amsterdam, if you're a stranger to the place.' Then he grinned and shook his head in disbelief.

'Thank Christ for Interflora,' said Ruth. 'That's progress, of a sort.'

'Now where were we, my dear?' Myles ran his finger down to the line of text where she'd broken off.

Thus far, Cornelis, my mind was as a clear pool on a summer's day – but what comes after hangs upon my spirits, I cannot fathom why.

It was slow-going to Esther's friend, with the pavements being so icy, but I was rewarded with so abundant a mass of mimosa from her glasshouse that I could scarce see ahead of me on my return. It was some time after two when I got home. I climbed to my lumberplace, my spirits still vigorous and elastic, but to my surprise Esther was fast asleep on the chaise longue, looking rumpled, as one does after turning in one's sleep, and her shoes had fallen casually on the floor beside her. Of the Italian, there was neither hide nor hair.

Had he left to give me a free hand?

I knew not what to make of this situation, but proceeded as we had planned. I arranged the mimosa quietly in the pitcher and was about to wake Esther to begin either the drawing or my proposal – I knew not which – when I stopped myself, having perceived that some advantage might accrue from this tableau vivant. Doubtless, a sleeping person may move in their slumber in response to the promptings of dreams, as a reed will quiver in a breeze, but with luck Esther would hold her position for the time required to expose my copper plate. Awake, she would never have been so motionless. It was a chance worth taking. I removed the cocked hat from the aperture and went to stand by the window, keeping one eye on my carriage clock and the other on the street, vaguely expecting to catch a glimpse of the Italian.

Thus I stood for some five minutes, when I realized that I too would be in the picture. I was about to move, when indolence or curiosity persuaded me to stay. And why not? Given that I intended to paint over the heliographic plate, my background presence was neither here nor there. A little coloured oil would suffice to erase my image from history. And yet, as I stood there – as I watched the clouds pass, as I listened to the gentle sound of Esther's breathing – a sense of infinite melancholy came over me, I scarce know why.

When forty minutes had elapsed, I replaced the cocked hat and retired to my projection room. By the light of a small candle, I treated the plate with the vapours of which we spoke to elicit the image, then fixed and stabilized it. As I was doing so, I heard Esther stirring and returned to the other chamber. She had awoken and was slipping on her shoes when I entered. She was in such a frame as I have never seen her, seeming both flustered and uneasy, as if emerging from a stupor. I wavered as to my planned proposal. I asked her where Giacomo was, but either she did not hear or she did not care to reply. Then, draping her fur coat around her shoulders, she stood up and prepared to leave. 'I have had an unusual and disturbing dream, Johannes,' says she. 'At least, I would to God it were a dream, and shall treat it as such. My father must not know that you left me alone with Giacomo, or that Giacomo left me alone with you, is that understood?' Her tone and manner brooked no contradiction, and so I assented. She glanced at my paper and – seeing it blank – stared at me as if I were mad, then blushed and ran from the room, still in this strange equivocal state of which I have spoken.

You must take this for a very curious narrative, and that it is indeed. On her departure, my brooding mind began to form peculiar and doubtless groundless apprehensions. Yet I cast them aside and returned to my projection room.

The image was quite the clearest and most detailed I had ever produced. Moreover, the stabilization had worked to good effect, such that it was possible for me to remove the copper plate to the

*lit room once it was dry. Using an eyeglass, a fine brush and
superior pigments, I began to paint over it. I shall show you this
unusual artefact in due course, on reaching the end of my
labours. When every last detail is rendered in paint, no one will
ever know that the composition and just proportions owe their
being to projection and chemistry, and perhaps, Cornelis –
perhaps my ambition to obtain wealth and eminence is at last
close to fulfilment. And yet I am in the grip of a strange
mortification. Where is the Italian? What was the cause of
Esther's disarray? Will she return to me, a kinder light in her
eyes, when I present her with my picture? I fear that whatever
occurred during my brief absence, if anything, will remain as
secret as the author of Junius.*

When they'd finished reading, their eyes met. Myles shunted
the previous letter forward and placed the new one before it.

'Jesus,' Ruth whispered.

'Quite.'

'He's done it, hasn't he?'

'He certainly has.'

'I mean, he's *way* ahead of his time . . .'

'*Way, way* ahead,' Myles agreed.

'Do we show this to Lydia?'

'We must, sometime soon – after a couple of gins and a
handful of beta blockers.'

She sank back into her thoughts. 'In other respects, of course,
he's fucked it all up. With Esther, I mean. Not that it's his fault,
exactly.'

'The Italian scumbug,' said Myles indignantly.

'And *her*, Myles. And *her* . . . It takes two, doesn't it? For an
eighteenth-century virgin, she takes some beating.'

Twenty-seven

'What's the time?' asked Myles.

Ruth glanced at the clock tower of the Metz & Co. furniture store. 'Two-thirty.'

'Chinese dentist time.'

'Huh?'

'Forget it. I'm wasted on you.'

'Dammit, Myles – where are we going?'

She dodged between the warmly clad folk on the street, trying to keep up with the big Englishman in his red tartan lumberjack coat, elephant cords and forage cap. The cold snap had come. The canals were frozen thick. Sunlight dazzled down from a lavender sky and there was a special Friday buzz in the air. Skaters thronged onto the ice. A bearded concertina player closed his eyes to his own wheezy melodies. A human pharaoh statue, gold spray-painted from top to toe, risked hypothermia for the odd coin. People clutched Styrofoam beakers beside a stall selling fried sausages and hot chocolate. The smell of sizzling meat and onions trailed past on the air, hitching a lift on the lively strains of the squeeze box.

'Why do you always need to know where we're going?' asked Myles, puffing into his red cupped hands as he walked.

'It reassures me. Right now, I'm not reassured. I've got that feeling we're not in Kansas any more.'

They crossed the Prinsengracht. A horse-drawn float bearing giant papier-mâché monsters trundled past in preparation for the city's carnival. Ruth looked behind her. She was dreaming again. There was Johannes, in frock coat, breeches, tricorn hat and periwig. He was running; he was trying to catch up with her; he wanted to talk. She stopped in her tracks. Myles tugged her on. Johannes slipped past, caught up with the moving float and clambered up onto the back.

He was nothing, a bit part, a nobody – just part of the forth-coming show.

'Ruth, will you kindly get a move on?'

She jogged a few paces ahead, turned and bobbed madly on the spot as if she was about to tackle him. She clapped her gloved hands for warmth. 'So this is life in the fast lane! Do we make a pit stop for lunch?'

'No time.'

'Aw! I fancied a couple of packs of Chesterfield and a Holsten pils.'

'Advice. Give your mouth a rest. You'll get chapped lips in this cold.'

They crossed the Singelgracht, where a lone swan advanced gingerly across the ice. At first she thought they were heading for work, heading for the Rijksmuseum, but they strode straight past the Gothic behemoth – past the Van Gogh Museum – past the Stedelijk Museum – and into a sleepy backwater by the name of Gabriël Metsustraat. Then it clicked. The Central Research Laboratory for Objects of Art and Science. Myles had mentioned his plans at the plenary session.

'We come in peace,' said Ruth as they flashed ID at the guard.

In the lift, Myles glared disapproval at her.

'Stop it,' she hissed. 'You're flaring your nostrils. Didn't you know? Flared nostrils went out in 1975.'

'Bob Stijn,' said Myles as they breezed into a room. She shook hands, almost curtsied. A little guy with tortoiseshell glasses and a nose-hair problem, pottering around on the great alluvial plain of middle age in his white lab coat and fawn moccasins.

He had three V-Balls in his breast pocket, each a different colour, and a sticking plaster covering the impressive bump of a boil on his neck.

'So what happens here?' Ruth asked, trying to sound perky.

'A bit of this, a bit of that,' said Bob. 'Infrared reflectography, molecular pigment analysis, microscopic analysis of thread density on canvases. You guys look at the paintings, period. We get in underneath, like forensic scientists at the murder scene – picking through the blood and guts.'

'Nice,' said Ruth.

Myles was nearly two heads clear of the little man. He put his arm round Bob's bony shoulders and spoke in a 'That's mah boy!' tone. 'Take a painting on wood. This fella can give you a precise date by dendrochronological examination. He looks for tiny variations in the width of annual growth rings.'

Bob grinned. 'Every picture tells a story.'

'Ours too?' asked Ruth.

'Sure. It's written in a foreign language. We can't read it. But there's some kind of tale there too, if you can get at it.'

He led them to a light box on the far wall of the lab and slipped an X-ray under the metal flip-down clip along the upper rim. 'Radiography,' said Bob. 'That's the oldest way of getting at the meat. Now mercury and lead show up really well. Especially lead. It has a high atomic weight and it's opaque to X-rays – and that's what the old painters used to mix up their white. Ergo, if there are lots of nice white passages in the initial lay-in of the underpainting, they shine up like a Dutch brothel.'

'I don't see anything on this X-ray,' said Ruth, peering at the transparency. 'I mean, nothing you don't see on the painting anyway.'

'There's something there, but we're not tuning in to it. At least, it doesn't look any different from what we can see with the naked eye.' He ushered them to a table and took some photographs out of an envelope. 'Next step, infrared reflectography. We warm up the painting using a low-wattage light

Adrian Mathews

bulb – high tech, huh? – then take digital snapshots on the infrared spectrum. When the painting's toasted, we can pick up carbon traces, which absorb the light's energy, and calcium, which reflects it. That works pretty well with a lot of eighteenth-century paintings because the underdrawings were often done with charcoal or burnt animal bones. Carbon, in other words.'

Ruth and Myles peered at the eerie pictures with their foggy tones. 'And here?' said Ruth.

'Another blank. Sure, there's carbon in some of the pigment, but we're not getting through to any substantial underdrawing.'

'Could be because there isn't one,' said Ruth.

'Could be,' said Bob, looking at her quizzically. He shook his head and jostled the infrared snaps back into their envelope. 'That leaves polarized light microscopy, for pigment analysis. We did that and it's authentic period stuff.'

'None of your modern jiggery-pokery,' said Myles.

'Nope. Eighteenth century, that's for sure. The weirdness comes from the scrapings.'

'Scrapings?' said Ruth.

'The ones Mr Palmer gave me and the ones we took ourselves.'

Myles folded his arms and bit his lower lip. 'I kind of neglected to tell you, Ruth. Last time we looked at the picture in stores, I scratched some stuff off the back.'

'Confidence reigns supreme,' sniped Ruth.

'It wasn't pigment. There was a deposit on the rear of the copper plate.'

'A silver salt,' said Bob. 'Christ knows what silver was doing there, but that's why we weren't getting any sure-fire readings. For a quantitative analysis of silver, and to get right down to the deepest layers of the painting, there's nothing like neutron activation autoradiography.'

'Tell me more,' Ruth said. 'My mind's a thirsty little sponge.'

'Basically, it's like this.' Bob grinned. 'You irradiate and activate the painting with white-beam cold neutrons, then the different rates of isotope decay are used to blacken films or imaging plates. You do gamma-spectroscopy with a Ge detector at different times over several weeks to get a data fix on those deep layers – the dark stuff, the dead-coloured forms in the monochrome underpainting. In short, what you guys want here is an autoradiograph. It's a cinch. The painting loses its acquired radioactivity after three months, then it's safe to stick back on the wall.'

'Not to be tried at home, kids,' said Ruth.

'Um, not exactly. You need a nuclear reactor.'

She sighed. 'Well, I guess a handicap is what you make of it.'

Myles looked left behind. 'Bob, when you called me, you said you were going ahead with the autoradiograph.'

'We are. Sorry. I should have said you *used* to need a nuclear reactor. Now they have industrial instruments that use Californium-252 as a neutron source.'

'Sounds like a new Dylan album,' said Ruth.

'Huh? Oh yeah. I never thought of that before. No, Californium-252's a synthetic radioactive element that's produced in nuclear reactors. You get trace quantities in helium isotope bombardment of curium. They've got one of these new irradiation facilities at the university, and they've helped us out before. You stick the painting on a support in front of a neutron guide end and shift it around to get uniform activation. The facility's inside a secure closed container, and then you need a shielded room for the film exposure and gamma-spectroscopy.'

'Shit,' said Ruth. 'Where is this facility?'

'The department of chemical engineering.'

'The Roeterseiland complex?'

'That's it.'

'Funny – I knew you were going to say that. Except you didn't, did you? – I did.'

Bob's phone warbled. He answered and excused himself. Ruth and Myles ambled over to the transparency on the light box.

'An X-ray of a painting of a photo,' said Myles. 'No wonder Johannes's little picture's holding back.'

'Maybe it isn't. Maybe what you see is what you get. I mean, as far as Johannes was concerned, it was painting by numbers. You're not going to get any startling discrepancies between what's underneath and what's on top. All he did was colour it in.'

'Look at the carriage clock,' said Myles with a burst of genuine enthusiasm. 'Remember – when we first saw this picture, you said there was only one hand?'

Ruth thought about it, then snapped her fingers. 'A forty-minute exposure. That's what he said in the letter. The hour hand hardly moves, but the minute hand goes through 240 degrees.'

'So?'

'So you don't see it. It blurs on the plate, and – when Johannes does his overpainting, he doesn't paint it in.'

'Bingo,' said Myles. 'Which either shows a colossal lack of imagination on his part or a conscious decision to plant a little clue.'

'Riddle-me-ree . . . Like the symbols and code on the back. Does he know?' said Ruth, gesturing back to the absent Bob with her head.

'No, but he's getting there. The silver salt's got him all excited.'

'And who authorized the auto-wotsit?'

Myles cocked his head and read the paperwork in the plastic sleeve on the table. 'Cabrol,' he said. 'He signed yesterday.'

'That figures.' Ruth sat down and rested her head against her knuckles. 'We've got time to play with. Three months, he said. Too much damn time, if you ask me.'

'Too much for what?'

'I was thinking of Lydia.'

'Three months on top of two and a half centuries doesn't seem so far-fetched.'

'She isn't that old.'

'You know what I mean,' said Myles.

'Cabrol knows what you mean too. Time's what he keeps buying, on the instalment plan. He knows that paintings tend to outlive people.'

'I guess he does.'

She bit her nail. 'I'm not exactly working on all thrusters, Myles. Not since we read those letters, I can't get him out of my mind – Johannes, I mean. What do you think happened to him?'

'I don't know. His world fell apart. He lost it, girl and all. Remember what Cabrol's entry on the Netherlands Collection Network said: "Nothing is known of his later career." Precious little was known of his earlier career, come to that, until we found Sander's little hoard.'

'Do you think he died?'

'I'd imagine that's a distinct possibility.'

'Let me rephrase that. Do you think he did himself in?'

'Could be. Or went mad. He was so stuck in the groove of his life and times that he didn't see the impact of what he'd stumbled on. He was ashamed of himself. He wasn't getting on with the painting. He was a cheat with wounded pride. Or else he saw the impact and simply bottled out. We don't really know.'

'Black magic, alchemy and devilry.'

Myles went back to the light box and walked his gaze over the X-ray. 'And all the poor corn cob did was take a snap.'

'Click, clack – Kodak,' Ruth murmured.

'For the first time in history, admittedly,' Myles added, 'though nobody knows that yet. The world's encyclopaedias say it was Joseph Nicéphore Niépce, a Frenchman from Burgundy, in the eighteen-twenties. A dull little picture of the view from his window. Then along came Daguerre, master of illusions, produced the Daguerrotype and commercialized the discovery. But we know that our old mate Johannes had been there before – over half a century earlier. And why not? It's an easy enough equation. Silver salts plus camera obscura equals photography. Both had been known about for ages. History was just drumming its fingers, waiting for some poop to bung 'em together, like bangers 'n' mash or fish 'n' chips.'

'Which is why everyone's wetting themselves over Lydia's little picture,' said Ruth.

'That's debatable. OK, it's the penny black of the art world. But we don't know who knows or knew what. What did the Nazis know – Miedl, Hofer, Goering, Hitler, Posse? Chances are, it was the occult data on the back that got them in a twitter. Fischer filled us in on their dabblings and the payback they were after. Nazis aside, what does Scheele know – or Cabrol, or Bags? Other people may have read those letters in the past and spilled the beans.'

'Through wind and darkness, I summon thee,' Ruth intoned. 'Want to know a secret? Promise not to tell?' Her voice normalized abruptly. 'Are we round the twist, Myles?'

'We've been round the twist. Now we're coming back the other way.'

'Could we possibly take a little reality check, then?'

'Shoot.'

She stood up and joined him again in front of the X-ray. 'What is our primary objective? Do we tell Lydia about those letters? She has a right – it's her ancestor, after all. Do we even leak and go public? If we do, isn't that going to undermine Lydia's case? Remember what Cabrol said about objects that are more than just private possessions. If it gets out that *Recumbent Woman with Mimosa* is the first photograph ever taken, cultural property law muscles in on the private civil action. Then, even in the unlikely event that Lydia won the action, she'd never be able to afford the fucking insurance. And in the meantime, the van der Heyden's down at chemical engineering, waiting to get nuked.'

'Yeah,' breathed Myles, staring at the beautiful Esther, asleep on the chaise longue. 'That'll put the glow back in her cheeks.'

On the light box the painting was etched in milky mono-chromes. The X-ray shifted the scene into another adjacent dimension, where tonal values slipped and slithered and clinical diagnosis, rather than aesthetic pleasure, seemed the order of the day. Ruth half-expected to see Johannes's ribcage or a pale femur and pelvis beneath Esther's dress, the skulls and bones behind the skins – perhaps even the dark malignant shadow of the cancer that lurked here, love unrequited, social prejudice, slack morals, the Italian Mephisto, blame who or what you will.

The artist's life . . .

'Houston, we have a problem,' said Myles.

She joined him at the window. Down below, in the street, Bob Stijn was talking to someone. They were obscured for a moment by a number sixteen tram rattling towards the little square at the end of the road which took its name from Vermeer. Everything had painterly connections in this part of town. When the tram moved away, even the two men in the street made an interesting composition, which an artist like Gustave Caillebotte would have relished in the last century but one. Cabrol wore his pretentious black winter cape with the gold clasp at the neck, a peculiar hybrid of Dracula and an anaemic, whittled-down version of Aristide Bruant. He was talking with quick, fussy Gallic gestures and shifting from one foot to the other like a hen on a hot griddle.

'What d'you think?' said Ruth.

'I'd say he had the cream of garlic soup again for lunch.'

'Well, we did warn him, didn't we?'

Myles put his tongue out and blew a slow, flatulent rasp-berry.

'What is it with Cabrol and our picture?' said Ruth search-ingly.

'Think about it, poppet. He's a museum man, a caretaker of history. He's also French.'

'So?'

'So the French are a proud nation, a nation of artists. They more or less invented modern painting. They invented the cinema, with the Lumière brothers. And, as we said before, they invented photography – Niépce and Daguerre. Now, just supposing he knows what we know, how do you think Cabrol feels about the possibility that photography was in fact invented by a common Dutch pharmacist?'

'So what did God want?' said Ruth when Bob Stijn came back to the lab.

'He and FedEx just chaperoned your painting. The usual compliance and verification protocol to rubberstamp and clear.'

Something in the technician's attitude had changed. He was hesitant and circumspect. He failed to meet Ruth's gaze.

'That all?' she delved.

'Well, he kinda wanted to know what you were doing here.'

'I hope you told him,' said Myles. 'She's only here for the beer.'

Bob frowned down at his moccasins and scratched the boil on his neck. 'Am I allowed to say?' he murmured in an awkward aside to Ruth.

'Say *what*?'

'About – you know – this morning? Cabrol just told me.'

'What did he tell you about this morning?' Ruth asked. 'That the rising sun was like a Daubigny skyscape? That the baker ran out of pure butter croissants?'

'No. That you quit.'

Ruth stared at Bob. Bob stared at Ruth. Ruth stared at Myles, then back at Bob again.

'You mean I just got slung out?' she flashed.

'Er, no. He said you like tendered your resignation. By email. And he – well, he accepted. *Noblesse oblige.* I'm sorry, Miss Braams, but you've no right to be here. You hung up your tools. Your clearance is terminated.'

Ruth felt tears well up in her eyes. 'I knew I was too happy,' she said in a pettish, little-girl-lost voice. 'And now this.' She forced a smile, but her lower lip quivered.

She folded her arms and turned to face the wall, the light box, then the door.

Myles put an arm round her shoulder. She fended it off. 'Let's get this straight, Ruth. I take it you didn't resign?'

She shook her head glumly.

'Do you want me to speak to him?'

'No. Fuck him. I'll speak to him myself. I'll set my lawyers on him. I haven't got any, but I'll set them on him all the same.'

'I'm going to, um, nip off and do something useful,' murmured Bob Stijn, 'like get my head sharpened.' He slipped out the door, holding five fingers up to Myles as he did so – one for each minute he'd be away.

Myles sat Ruth down and squatted on the floor beside her. 'Slow breaths, Ruth. We'll just wait for your blood pressure to drop below critical.'

They stayed like that, in silence, for a minute or two.

'I didn't know the job meant so much to you,' he said in due course.

'Neither did I. Frankly, it didn't – not until Bags. Up until Bags, it was all admin. It was one long world-consuming yawn. But meeting Bags changed all that. Meeting Bags made it all worthwhile.' She wiped her eyes on the back of her cardigan sleeve.

'You once told me you couldn't care less about Bags.'

'I was lying. I could care less.'

'You could care more.'

'Maybe,' she confessed, 'but I could care less too. Let's leave it at that. I suppose this resignation thing's a hoax – my phantom emailer again.'

'Sure. It's a glitch. If you didn't resign, there's nothing more to be said – never mind how eager Cabrol was to pounce on the opportunity. You go home. I'll see the old rat shagger and set the record straight.'

Adrian Mathews

'Someone's going to pay dearly for this,' said Ruth, 'and I wouldn't mind betting that someone is me.'

'Don't talk like that. You're not exactly out on your arse. Not yet, anyway.'

'You don't think it's him – Cabrol himself – do you? You don't think it's him who's trying to drag me down?'

'No, I don't. But I reckon you're right about Bags. I think it's high time she got her picture and high time we did a little stonewalling – having got this far.'

'How can we do that?' said Ruth. 'It's out of our hands now, certainly out of mine. You can't stop progress. Nobody can.'

He smiled his fat-cat smile. 'To the victor, the spoils,' he said.

She sniffed and looked at him with more than passing curiosity. 'You speak treason, Myles.'

Twenty-eight

When Ruth got back to Lydia's place, there was an ambulance parked outside. Her throat tightened. 'Oh, man,' she sighed, 'not again.'

The front door was open.

She ran up the steps and into the house, throwing her duffel coat off in the hallway. The old woman was in bed and one of the two ambulancemen was checking her pulse. The facetious brat who'd rolled up after Lydia's evening of binge drinking was not there, thank God.

'Lydia?' said Ruth sharply. She sat down heavily on the side of the bed and grabbed hold of the old woman's free hand.

Lydia looked at her in wan half-recognition. She was confused and not her usual self. The skin on her face was tight and smooth, a textural cross between ancient Assyrian parchment and kitchen cling film.

'I live here with her,' Ruth explained to the nearest paramedic. 'What's up? Are you taking her to hospital?'

'We've just brought her *from* the hospital, lady. She was at a cable TV outlet when she felt a bit out of sorts. They gave her a check over at outpatient's, and her own doctor's due any moment. Nothing to worry about. You're feeling all right now, aren't you, dear?' he said in megaphone tones, making himself heard across several generation gaps. 'Firing on all eight cylinders, eh?'

Lydia didn't answer. A blue vein that straggled across her right temple stood out alarmingly as if it was going to pop.

At the door, out of Lydia's earshot, the paramedic adopted a different tone. 'She's had a little stroke. What we call a transient ischaemic event. She went numb down one side for a while and got a bit bewildered. She's all right now, but she'll have to take it easy. Don't let her get worked up. The doc will give her something to take for it.'

'What the hell were you doing at a cable TV shop?' Ruth blurted as the ambulance pulled away outside.

'What d'you think I was doing?' grumbled Lydia faintly. 'Signing up for cable TV, of course. You don't get the BBC and CNN on the ordinary TV. I need it for my English.'

'So you're serious, then – about Pittsburgh?'

'At no point was I *not* serious.'

The doctor was a long-jawed man with kind eyes and a stoop that made him look taller than he was – or rooms smaller than they were – as if doors and ceilings created a perpetual Max. Headroom problem for him.

'This is not the first time, is it?' he asked.

Lydia looked away prissily. A tiny bubble formed in the saliva at the corner of her mouth.

'Tell me if you've had spells like this before.'

'Once or twice,' she admitted.

'They're sending me the results of the blood test from the hospital,' he said. 'We may need to take you back for a scan later on. In the meantime, I'm giving you some Lipitor. This'll cut down the chances of a repeat performance. Make sure she takes it, will you?' he added to Ruth, then turned back to the old woman. 'Have you got your medical card?'

'I don't know, Dr Luijten. It's somewhere around.'

'Would you mind looking for it later?' he asked Ruth. 'I need the name of her health insurance company and the membership number. Give me a ring with the details, if and when you find it. And keep an eye on her, will you?' he added with a confidential wink.

As he left, Lydia fell asleep.

Ruth moved over to Sander's final agony chair and sat there for an hour, watching the old lady's chest rise and fall, observing the little bubbles of saliva form and burst at the corner of the mouth where the lips didn't quite meet. The old girl was not just Lydia. She was Lydia van der Heyden, descendant of Johannes van der Heyden – apothecary, letter writer, furtive and unsung inventor, artist *manqué*. Her distinctive profile – the flat forehead, the sharp nose, the obstinate mouth – might well have been his too, on the other side of the turned head in the picture, as indeed it was Sander's, or so the snapshots suggested. What did they all have in common, these doughty van der Heydens? Rigour, drive, independence, aspirations – and blighted, loveless lives. Nothing worked out for the poor beggars in the long term. They were losers and also-rans, a bankrupt breed of thwarted, moaning misfits. In other words, they were all too human, trying to build golden castles out of common rubble and dirt. Ruth admired their backbone. A daft lot, but for sheer pluck they were hard to beat. The modern tribes were all wimps and baa lambs in comparison.

And now a stroke . . .

A fuse had been lit. There was no telling if it was long or short. But this was the beginning of an end.

An hour or so later Lydia woke up. She put out her tongue for the pill in unconscious imitation of the cartouche on the facade of the house. Ruth gave her a glass of water to wash it down.

'So what about you?' asked Lydia vaguely, as if she'd been stealing the limelight and wanted to make amends.

'Me?' said Ruth, massaging Lydia's arm gently on the side where the numbness had struck. 'Oh, nothing much. Somebody resigned me from my job, that's all.'

'You'll be spending more time with me, then?'

'No doubt. I'll have to redirect myself. I'll need a new skill. Something useful, like switching light bulbs on and off just by looking at them. Or a career in music – I could be a gong tuner.'

'There's no hurry,' the old woman murmured, her eyes half shut. 'You can stay here as long as you like.'

'Thanks, Lydia. What would I do without you?'

One eyelid tweaked open, wary of irony. There was none.

'Have you been having a difficult time, my dear?' Lydia asked.

'Story of my life. I was a breech birth – that's when my troubles started.'

'Right from the beginning, then.'

'Not exactly. I had nine clear months of relative peace before that.'

'Oh, I forgot to tell you. There were some phone calls for you this morning when you were out. People calling about the boat. They wanted to see it and they all wanted to know why it was so cheap.'

'So cheap?'

'Two thousand euros, they said you were asking.'

'My boat isn't for sale.'

'Well, they seemed to think it was. They said there was an ad in one of the papers.'

Ruth thumped a fist against her forehead and shut her eyes. More aggro. When was this persecution ever going to stop?

A thought occurred to her.

'Which paper was it in?'

'*Het Parool*, I think.'

Whoever placed the ad would have had to pay. It was a long shot, but you never knew. This time, they might have slipped up. She phoned through to the small-ads section and posed the question.

'You paid for it, Miss Braams,' said the surprised secretary. 'One of our operators must have taken your call and it's paid for on your credit card.'

Ruth reeled off the numbers of her card to check. Sure enough, she'd paid for it herself. So who the hell had access to her credit details? That was the question – or *another* question to add to the now formidable stockpile.

She cancelled the ad, then rang the bank to stop her card.

'Actually,' said the bank manager, 'we were going to ring you – sooner or later, anyway. Let's face it, you've been over the limit for the last few months. If you'd like to apply for a new card, Miss Braams, may I suggest you drop by at my office for a little chat?'

Around six o'clock, Ruth brought in a cup of tepid tea. 'I have something to tell you,' she whispered when Lydia had taken a first sip. 'We found the letters. Johannes van der Heyden's letters. They were in the statue of the Virgin Mary. It turns out that's where Sander hid them. That's what he meant when he told you the queen was looking after them.'

Lydia smiled. 'He always did have a peculiar sense of humour.'

'Do you want me to read them to you?'

'Later. I think I'd find it difficult to concentrate right now. I'm not in pain, but I feel awfully tired.'

Again Lydia fell asleep.

The doctor had asked for her medical card.

Ruth started searching the room.

Since the last search, she had learned something of Lydia's order-in-chaos, the idiosyncratic filing system that determined what went where, with what else, and why. Anything connected with officialdom was either up on the magnetic noticeboard in the kitchen if it required urgent attention, or stuffed into an old shoebox on the rickety wooden bookshelf beside the bed. But which old shoebox? There were about ten there right now, all of which they'd riffled through quickly on the previous occasion. She got them down, one by one, and sifted through their contents more carefully.

The contents were all much of a muchness: bills, vaccination certificates for the cats, books of savings stamps dating back to the 1960s, hire-purchase agreements, a receipt for Lydia's fridge, and so on. In one box there was a backlog of prescriptions and other vaguely health-oriented paperwork, but nothing resembling the medical card.

A thick rubber band had been strapped round the seventh box Ruth opened, suggesting privileged status, and this indeed was the case: the deeds of the house were here, along with Lydia's identity papers and other vital documents. She was about to close it again when she noticed a vellum envelope with a red-wax seal and a recent date stamp: Friday, 1 February. The wax seal was evidently for decorative purposes only. The envelope flap had simply been tucked in.

She shot a glance at Lydia.

Still fast asleep.

She slipped the document out and began to read:

LAST WILL AND TESTAMENT

THIS IS THE LAST WILL AND TESTAMENT of Lydia VAN DER HEYDEN.

1. I HEREBY REVOKE all wills and testamentary dispositions of every nature and kind whatsoever by me heretofore made.

2. I NOMINATE, CONSTITUTE, AND APPOINT, my

solicitor, Hans BLOMMENDAAL, to be the sole
Executor and Trustee of this my Will.

3. I bequeath my moneys, wearing apparel,
articles of personal use or ornament, household
furniture, books, pictures, plate, linen,
china, glass and household and consumable
stores, of which I shall die possessed, to Miss
Ruth BRAAMS.

4. I devise and bequeath the real estate and the
residue of the personal estate of which I shall
die possessed (hereinafter called my 'Residuary
Estate') unto the same Miss Ruth BRAAMS, for her
personal use and occupation or to dispose of as
she sees fit.

Ruth's eye jumped to the end:

I declare this to be my last will and testament,
in witness whereof I have hereunto set my hand
this 1st day of February . . .

The document was witnessed by Blommendaal and another
lawyer: evidently the solicitor hadn't bothered with a second
witness in situ, simply taking the will back to the office for a
colleague's countersignature and posting it on the same day.
Not exactly pro forma practice, but time-saving and expedient
no doubt.

Ruth slid the document back into the envelope and put the
envelope back into the box.

So this had been the 'business' that Lydia had reluctantly
admitted to: 'He dropped by to help me with my affairs.'

She was about to close the box when she noticed another
envelope, folded in two, with a broken wax seal. Inside was

another will. It was identical to the one she'd just read in every
detail but two: it had been drafted four years previously and
another name took the place of hers. Her eyes alighted on
paragraph 3:

**3. I bequeath my moneys, wearing apparel,
articles of personal use or ornament, household
furniture, books, pictures, plate, linen,
china, glass and household and consumable
stores, of which I shall die possessed, to Mr
Thomas SPRINGER.**

The words 'Null & Void' had been scrawled across the
document with a pink highlighter in what looked like the
lawyer's hand.

She put the second envelope back into the box, the broad
rubber band onto the box, and the box onto the shelf.

A flutter in Lydia's breathing, then a gentle snore resumed.

Ruth left the room and went back in a daze to the *achterhuis*,
nearly slipping on the damp carpet.

She sat at Sander's desk. Principessa hopped onto her knees
and rubbed her ear against the rough fibres of Ruth's pullover.

So now she knew what Lydia felt about her, if ever she'd
been in the slightest doubt. She'd ousted the Kid in Lydia's
affections.

It was love, true love.

Everything was hers: the house, the miraculous painting,
Lyd's niffy 'wearing apparel', even, one assumed, her epony-
mous bags.

It simply beggared belief. The cost of the house alone would
set her up for life, if she opted to sell. And the painting, once
the truth got out, would be worth a king's ransom. Yes, now
she could join the cream of Dutch society: thick and very, very
rich. From rags to riches, from Queer Street to Easy Street in one
scratch of the pen.

Thanks, Lyd, and thanks Johannes – thanks for the Philosopher's Stone.

This was definitely going to take some getting used to . . .

But the more she thought about it, the more her mind shuddered and flinched away from nasty complications. They leered out of the inner darkness like luminous, howling cut-outs in a fairground ghost train ride. The painting wasn't hers. It wasn't even Lydia's – yet. And what had been pure fellow feeling on her part now took on a different colouring altogether.

Look at her – look at her mean little eyes. She was in it for the money, preying on the weak and elderly, you know! She sank her own boat, just so she could move in, then she got the old biddy to write that will. That's how they do it, these wicked sharks. They find some lonely old bird, rub her up the right way – all nice and friendly like – then in they plunge for the kill. Emotional con-merchants! Prison's too good for them. They should be put up against a wall and shot! And to think what the poor thing went through during the war. She deserved a little peace and quiet, especially in her sunset years.

At best, Ruth was a freeloader and parasite who knew which side her bread was buttered. At worst, it was a clear-cut case of naked greed and cold-blooded thievery. Even her own name on Blommendaal's document rose up out of the ink to mock her.

This wasn't Lydia van der Heyden's last will and testament. This was Ruth Braams's death warrant. This was prima facie proof of guilt. This was the writing on the wall.

Who, dear Ruth, will believe you now?

She was potentially compromised with everyone – even Myles, even her parents. As for Jojo, Lucas and Smits, they would simply have their worst suspicions confirmed. She could tear the will up, she could put a match to it, but Blommendaal would have a copy in safe keeping. Of course, she could always face Bags for a friendly showdown at the OK Corral, get her to write the will off. She could even pretend she'd never even seen the damn thing. But, deep down, why in the name of hell should she? Bags wanted her to have it all and what was wrong with that?

It was hers to do with as she pleased.

Where else would it go, if not to her: a cattery, a gin-drinkers' detox clinic, a home for battered budgies?

So did Ruth want it, or didn't she? It really came down to that.

Now it was up to her. She had to grab this beast by the tail.

Bags had acted out of loving kindness, but she'd hardly thought through the consequences. Ruth felt like hugging her, then wringing her scrawny little neck.

And other questions continued to pop like fireworks . . .

What if there'd been no will – what would have happened to the house and painting then? But there *was* a will: the previous one that this one revoked. Did the Kid know he'd been her sole beneficiary? Like Ruth, he'd had ample opportunity to rummage through her affairs. And did he know he'd been deposed, dispossessed of a remarkable inheritance that a whim had bestowed on him and a whim had taken away? In a momentary flash, Springer's pale, boyish face lit up in Ruth's mental midnight sky. He'd come to the house only seconds after Blommendaal left on that now fateful day, 1 February. Had Thomas Springer, aka the Kid, seen that will, and, if so, what had he thought? The eel – the flowers – the misfired Mantovani overtures. It all seemed to add up to one thing. Maybe the hate-mail added up to the same thing too, but simultaneously? Come to think of it, the mail and messages pre-dated the second will.

She picked up Sander's African paper knife, carved from a single piece of ebony, and balanced it on the tip of her forefinger.

No – not the Kid.

It didn't feel right. Odds were, he knew nothing about either will.

But this much was certain: if Lydia won her claim on Johannes's painting, then the painting was, or would be, Ruth's – in the slow burgeoning of time. For the moment nothing would change that, and that's what could find against her. Which was what you got for helping old ladies across the street, for just trying to be neighbourly.

It was a right old shithouse, every way you turned.

There was no crawling out from under it.

Her mobile buzzed on the desk top. It made her jump. The paper knife fell with a clatter onto the desk and Principessa pounced down from her knees and pattered away. The phone's vibration function was on and, with each buzz, it moved along a few centimetres, like a fat black clockwork cockroach. She snatched it up.

A text message:

> **Chickenshit: You have not heeded my warnings. Like all women, you are foolish and vain. Soon the devil will want to be paid. Perhaps your soul is still alive.**

She put the phone down, but after a while it buzzed again. The message continued.

> **Perhaps you know who your real enemy is: after all, it is staring you in the face. I have something you need.**

She clutched the phone in a daze. A couple of minutes passed. It buzzed again.

> **Meet me tonight at 10 by the Magere Bridge, the Kerkstraat side. Just you. Remember: nothing escapes my wise little eye. 47 107.8682**

Oh, wow, thought Ruth. *A date! Now, who'd have believed it? And just when I thought my courting days were done.*

She held her breath and shivered involuntarily. She stood up, caught a glimpse of herself in the mirror. What she saw surprised her.

She saw the fear in her eyes.

Twenty-nine

'isten, Smits, how should I know who it is?' she yelled at the phone. 'You think I'm making it up? OK, if that's how you want it, I'm making it up. I get there, to the bridge, and there's this one-eyed toffee-apple seller with wild grey hair, a beard down to his shins and a Bolivian chinchilla on his shoulder. I say, "The toffee looks less than crunchy today." Then he winks twice – the chinchilla, that is – and lets me enter his magical chinchilla kingdom. Is that the sort of thing you had in mind?'

Ruth listened intently as the cop shifted into reverse and some kind of backtracking rumbled into motion.

'All right, all right,' she said. 'Forget it. I'm sorry I lost my temper. But it's like in the movies, Smits. You're supposed to keep out of sight. Then, as he takes aim and empties the pump-action shotgun into my chest, you leap out of your hidey-hole and catch the bullets with your bare hands before I go down with lead poisoning. Get it? That's your job.'

She holstered the phone and checked in on Lydia. The old woman was still dozing. She turned over and broke wind in her sleep. The fart smelled like formaldehyde.

Ruth left the house, grabbing her skates on the way out.

Across the canal the ground-floor lights were blazing at Scheele's place, the curtains open. As she stood there, swaddling her scarf round her mouth and raw nose, tucking it into her coat, Scheele appeared at the window – or rather the top of his head slid supernaturally into view, for he would be sitting in his wheelchair.

She froze for a moment and narrowed her eyes.

He remained there, motionless and at peace, the small silhouette of his primate head tilted up at a sharp angle. He was not spying on her. She followed the direction of his gaze. He was not even looking at Lydia's house. To all appearances, he was simply admiring the evening sky.

She lingered herself, lost for a second or two in the airy subtleties – heather, foxglove, gentian and the slow seep of indigo, as night brimmed over the dark parapet of Amsterdam's gable ends.

She crossed the street and followed the Keizersgracht till she came to some worn stone steps that descended steeply to the frozen canal. She sat on the top step, pulled on her skates and laced them up tightly.

This was how she had planned it.

Mr Periodic Table, Mr Long John Silver, would be expecting her to approach at street level, not down below on the ice. What's more, he'd be expecting her to come from the north, where the Keizersgracht met the river Amstel, which was the shortest route to the bridge. Instead, she'd circle round via the Leidsegracht and the Singelgracht, just out of bolshiness, just for the cheap thrill of nonconformity. A tactical advantage, perhaps: to see her persecutor before he saw her – even for a second, just time to compose herself, time to marshal her thoughts.

She had no illusions.

It would make no more difference than that.

Skating on the canal, you had to be careful. It wasn't like a rink. Flotsam and jetsam locked into the structure of the ice, potential hazards for dreamy skaters. Then there were chains and cables from the houseboats, arks and barges, not to mention natural irregularities where the water had hardened with a finish like roughly hewn quartz. On top of that, kids threw stuff onto the ice to watch it skid and, when it finished skidding, it just stayed where it ended up – stones, branches, Coke cans, even bicycle wheels – adding interesting features to the obstacle course. Luckily, the street lamps cast a lateral glow that grazed the surface, defining a clear, skateable channel down the middle and picking out the debris between the dense shadows of boats, trees, cars and the canal banks themselves.

She took it easy, skating with long, leisurely strides, her gloved hands clasped behind her back in the time-honoured tradition.

From down below, you had a different perspective on the city. Ruth was a purblind, burrowing creature that had scrabbled its way up through the frosty crust of darkness to find a big bold world of alien activity above.

Then the snatched glimpses through houseboat portholes – a man reading a map, a child brushing down a dog – and the strange, hollow resonance of her skate blades, knives drawn in long clean movements across a whetstone.

With a slick thrust of the right skate, she turned into the Singelgracht and swept under the facade of the de la Mar theatre, beneath the shadow of the bridge and past the Leidse-plein, where the chandeliers sparkled like diamond fountains in the casino, then alongside the dour, stolid frontage of the Rijksmuseum. She pulled a long face when she came upon it, as if she'd done her best to make it laugh, but there was nothing doing.

My ex place of work . . .

But, as she passed the old Heineken brewery and, further on, the Nederlandse Bank, her insouciance gave way to a growing sense of pleasurable tension and focus. It was a tingly sensation, rousing her, like the blue electric sprites you get touching a door handle, shaking someone's hand, after scuffling along a nylon carpet.

She felt fit, reckless and invincible.

Was it the adrenalin that did that? Part of her – the wise Ruth, the god in the machine – advised caution, but the strange wellbeing that blew through her like a spring breeze didn't listen.

Life was good. Life was strong.

How could anything spoil this sweet rush of vitality?

Then all of a sudden the broad expanse of the Amstel opened up ahead of her under a starry gasp of sky.

Here it was perilous to skate mid-river. There was no telling what flaws and infirmities lay hidden beneath the seamless, brittle expanse of ice. To underscore the warning, there were no other skaters in sight.

She stuck close to the bank, skirting the moored boats, occasionally grabbing at rusty bolts and projections from their hulls when she fancied she heard a creak or sensed a tilting motion beneath her feet. Her knees and ankles began to ache with the effort. And suddenly she was a little girl again, wobbling on the first pair of chalk-white skates her father had bought her when she was seven. The flashback was picture-perfect, neatly puncturing the hermetic cell of the memory so that it flooded her brain with its details.

By the time she reached the Magere Brug, she was edging forward on her skates at slower than walking pace. The white struts of the wooden drawbridge were as bright as old bleached bones in the darkness. People walked briskly across overhead. A couple leaned on the white barrier, above the red stop light for shipping, taking in the view, their warm talk vaporizing around them.

Now she melted back into the shadows.

In the dim light she tried to pinpoint the solitary individuals, on the bank or on the bridge, who looked as if they had assignations.

No one fitted the bill.

She slipped under the bridge and pawed her way along the dark, damp brickwork.

She came out on the other side and looked up again. There

were one or two potential candidates, but the angle was too steep. She could make out nothing more than vague silhouettes. In all probability, they were getting a better view of her.

She skated to the nearest steps, put her skates into her shoulder bag and changed back into her boots. She climbed up to street level. Her feet felt heavy and the drop in stature had an equivalent diminishing effect on her spirits. The little drummer boy of her heart beat hard and fast, alarming her with his stridency.

All at once, she felt sick.

Little anxieties gnawed at her confidence.

On one side of the bridge, at the juncture of Sarphatikade and the Kerkstraat, a white Fiat Panda was parked sloppily, halfway up on the pavement. At least Smits was as good as his word. The windows were misted over on the inside – all but a small peephole rubbed in the condensation on the driver's side window. Ruth felt like going over for a chat, but that would never do.

Somewhere, a clock struck ten.

Her watch was five minutes fast. She adjusted it and stood prominently on the bridge, pacing, pausing, scanning the faces of passers-by, the way people do when they have a date with a stranger, seeking the same interrogative stare in return.

On every lamp post and taped onto the main arched supports of the bridge were posters for a circus at the Theater Carré, which was lit up on the opposite bank of the Amstel. Evidently the show had finished, for, around quarter past, families with children starting crossing the bridge. The children carried bright helium balloons on strings. Some had been made up like clowns. Others waved plastic torches with coloured fibre optics sprouting like fluorescent grass from the top.

Ruth caught snatches of conversation: a little girl enthused about a clown with three legs; a father mimicked a blindfolded juggler; another kid wanted to be the baby princess on a white stallion.

The groups of circus-goers reduced to a trickle and then they were gone.

Half past ten.

Had she been stood up?

All this waiting around was making her cold. It was also pissing her off.

She was in a quandary.

She could give up and go home, but then the great black question mark that fumed over her life would never go away.

She could stay on and on – till eleven, midnight even – catch her death and, at the very least, feel satisfied she'd fulfilled her part of the bargain.

And how long was Smits's patience going to hold? In a sense, he was duty-bound to stake out as long as she did, but he wouldn't like it one little bit. She could hear him already, muttering his misogynies to himself in the car: *damn female fantasizing . . . wasting police time . . . nothing better to do with herself than swan around, inventing mystery bogeymen . . . get a life, lady . . .*

Her mobile buzzed.

> **Ruth: Change of plan.**
> **Meet me at Jade Beach now.**
> **It's been a long time.**
> **M**

Her head swam.

She steadied herself on the guard rail of the bridge and took a deep breath.

This was not happening . . .

'M' could only mean one thing, but that one thing was beyond belief.

'M' was how Maarten had always signed himself off.

She stared and stared at the phone display, willing the LCD message to float apart in some surreally kaleidoscopic, Busby

Berkeley style, and reconfigure into something more meaningful – anything: Just Kidding, Joke Over, Got You There!

It was not to be.

Her forehead prickled with sweat.

If this is funny, how come I'm not laughing?

But now the tacit question posed itself in words: was she seriously being asked to entertain the possibility that Maarten had engineered a spectacular comeback from the grave?

Tacked on the loo door in her boat was a poster for 'Carter the Great', an old magic show. A dapper magician in evening dress was opening a box, from which all manner of horrors took wing – horned, red demons, slavering skeletons, cackling witches and stout comical hobgoblins. The caption read: *Do the dead materialize? The absorbing question of all time.* More or less, that put it in a nutshell.

Did she really believe that people could come swaggering back from the dead?

Surely not.

Then again, was there any doubt that he'd actually died? The glossies were always full of 'Strange Tales', 'Amazing Facts' and 'Believe It or Not' stories. Every now and then some desperate oddballs really did contrive to split their lives in two for tax purposes, leaving their nearest and dearest none the wiser. And it was true that she'd never seen his body after the accident.

She'd seen nothing but a sealed wooden box.

Was she now being asked to think that it had all been a stunt, that Maarten had been standing at the back of the crematorium chapel, lurking behind a pillar, vicariously freeloading off all that grief?

No, Maarten. Please.

This was definitely not in the brochure.

A change of plan . . .

She couldn't tell Smits. She might be under surveillance. She could ring him, but that would be just as dumb. If Smits hadn't crapped out in the car, he'd have seen her take the call. He'd have done the mental arithmetic. There was no telling, of course, with that lunkhead, but nonetheless hope springs eternal.

Sometimes you just have to put your trust in trust.

She set off smartly down the Kerkstraat.

She passed Smits's car on the pavement opposite but avoided looking at it, even out of the corner of her eye.

Music spilled out from the fan vents of a brown bar. A man in a snap-brim hat, sitting at the window, dipped a finger into the froth of his beer and sucked it thoughtfully. A bearded tramp approached her with a stampless envelope in his hand, preparing a routine sob story. No such luck. She was way too fast. Before he could utter a word she was halfway down the street. She couldn't turn her head, but, please God, a white Fiat Panda would be following her at a respectful distance.

A hundred metres down her step faltered.

Where the blazes was Jade Beach?

She'd forgotten the address and the young Asian chick in the satin sausage-skin hadn't given her a card. She'd made some numinous comment about finding the place when you needed it. The one sure thing was that it was within spitting distance of the Prinsengracht Ziekenhuis, the hospital where Jojo had bad-mouthed her, wishing her dead. Ruth had fled out into the night and found her way to the dive.

She cut through to the Prinsengracht, then into the broad fantail of side streets that radiated from the city centre as far as the Singelgracht, where the old town stopped and the rectilinear grids of the outlying districts began.

At one dark intersection, she at last dared look behind.

No white car. No back-up. Nothing.

Fuck you, Smits – you incompetent spunkless shitkicker. Always there when you didn't need him, never there when you did. Some detective! He couldn't detect the cheese in a cheese sandwich except by appointment, and he'd probably be late for that.

Now she was well and truly on her own.

She pulled off a glove and bit hard at her thumbnail with her incisor, glaring to left and right.

A sash window banged down at a first-floor window on the other side of the street. The curtains drew shut.

A cat appeared by some railings – two coins of yellow phosphorescence pointing at her – then shot out of sight down some basement steps.

Ruth crossed the road.

There was no one else about.

She took a few paces in one direction, then changed her mind, turned and walked back as far as an alleyway where some building work had been abandoned for the day. The corner house had scaffolding up the front and a stack of roof slates in heat-sealed polythene stood on the pavement with a traffic cone on either side.

The alley was a passage into an inner courtyard.

She followed it, then turned on her heels and studied the rows of glowing windows on all sides. A fat club sandwich writhing with humanity, people getting on with their niche existences, oblivious to the other goings on above, below and to either side.

This wasn't it.

She came out again into the street and took a flying kick at one of the traffic cones, knocking it over.

A curtain twitched.

She could continue wandering like this all night, for all the good it would do her. Logic suggested she should go back to the hospital and retrace her steps from there. It had started with three nuns. She'd asked them for a cigarette. She cringed. How dumb could you get? Then some kind of panic attack had seized her and she'd scuttled off into the maze. Actually, the panic had struck earlier, if 'panic' was the word: 'jitters', perhaps, or a 'flap' – a fight-or-flight synapse that suddenly engaged, a peripheral overflow switch to protect the delicate arabesques of her internal circuitry.

But in which direction was the hospital?

She had no idea.

There was nobody to ask.

A band of tension stretched across her chest and the flibber-tigibbets were gleefully tightening the wing nuts between her shoulder blades.

She wished they would go away.

At the end of the street a traffic light turned from green to amber to red, signalling to invisible vehicles. She waited, count-ing the seconds by snapping her fingers. At length, the light turned green again. The coloured lights redoubled in the pearly glaze of frost upon the road.

She walked as far as the junction and looked round.

A late-night corner shop was familiar. Her spirits rose. She'd seen it last time round. The club was only a stone's throw from here, but in which direction?

The noise of an electric drill came from an upper window, where a late-night DIY session was under way. It put her teeth on edge. In another house, a man on a sofa, watching TV, frowned slightly as she passed by outside, a grey shape on the dim street.

Footsteps approached the junction from which she'd just come, then turned and moved away.

The street was unusually narrow, even for Amsterdam, and after a while she came to another intersection. Now only a gurgle of water from a down pipe could be heard – that and a low intermittent buzz, like the wasp she'd trapped under an old tin in her parents' garden one summer when she was no more than five or six. The buzz seemed to come from very close by, but, for the life of her, she couldn't see where.

Then she raised her eyes.

Above a narrow door, with a grilled shutter set at nose level, a tiny white and green light flickered angrily at one end of a neon tube. The neon wasn't on. The firing mechanism was faulty. But in the half-light she could read the looping cursive of the extinct sign:

Jade Beach

She caught her breath, pushed the door and went inside.

Thirty

And down she went like a diver – deeper and deeper into that warm, cavernous sweatiness – a thick soup of tobacco smoke, the atmosphere of an exclusive little planet of boozy clubbiness.

A trilling riff on the guitar sped up madly and suddenly rang shut on an exuberant final chord, followed by a couple of grace notes that made light of it all. There was a resonant lull and a smatter of applause.

A murmur of voices slipped into the vacuum left by the guitar.

At the foot of the spiral staircase she came out under the giant papier-mâché dragonfly that hung from the ceiling beside the bar.

It was all as before, barring the clientele.

Cheetah looked up as she entered but didn't recognize her. The woman's gaze bounced back off an invisible force-field a few centimetres from the end of her flat nose.

There were one or two drinkers at the bar and a scattering of people at the tables.

Ruth took a deep breath, shut her eyes and opened them again.

An old waiter helped her off with her coat and took it away. She managed a smile and a 'thank you'.

Mr Shine sat on the podium and pulled on a cigarette, pinching it between thumb and forefinger, while he chatted to one of his cronies. His blue guitar leaned against a wall.

Someone turned up the stereo. A big-band number, 'Blue on Blue'.

Ruth controlled her breathing, willed her body into a deep hiatus of relaxation.

Slowly she took in the scene.

And there he was – she caught sight of him immediately in one of the crescent love-seats – running one finger thoughtfully up the side of a tall cylindrical glass. The back of his head, the side of his face, one shoulder and the shadow of a thigh.

That was enough.

She'd have known him anywhere.

Maarten – her Maarten – back from the Underworld, back from the Great Divide. The poor guy had aged, that much was clear. He'd put on weight too – a diet of pure ambrosia ... But it was him, the way he turned away, thinking his thoughts, holding out in that small solitary dimension of intense inwardness where she couldn't get at him, which she couldn't share because that tight folded-in nucleus, that ball of masculine concentration, was way off limits, a threshold she could never cross, a window she could never break, a word she could never speak.

It was a living death.

The formula that would make his head turn, the alchemy that would snap him out of it, simply hadn't been invented, or was light years away from her grasp – it came to much the same thing.

People had noticed her.

She stood in the middle of the club, her arms hanging at her sides.

A man pulled his chair in, making way for her, then shrugged his shoulders when she didn't go past.

Furtive glances, furtive smiles.

They were wondering what she was going to do next. Obviously, they'd be thinking she was the worse for drink. She wasn't – she would show them. But in parts of the cellar, instead of thinning, the blue smoke curdled into turbid puddles of fog, drifting across faces and bodies and all but concealing them from view.

She was not going to lose him. Not now.

It had been a long time.

She put one foot forward, then another.

Someone was playing tricks on her.

Everything was slowing down.

The waiter sailed by like the *Mary Celeste*. The music ground down to a low bass growl. A blubbery walrus of a woman with a jet cigarette holder turned to watch Ruth and froze: cheeks dusted with violet talc, mean crimson lips, Fabergé eyes, a streamer of smoke hissing like kettle steam from the pearly teeth.

Maarten was restless.

The drift of attention was tugging at him too, drawing him out of his reverie. He started to turn. He saw her. He stood up. A big hand came out, caught her by the waist, urged her down, out of the limelight and onto the crescent love-seat. That smell of saltpetre again – gunpowder on his sleeve! The hand rested, concerned, on her arm.

It was not Maarten's hand – the computation was slow in bearing fruit.

It was not Maarten's hand, nor was it Maarten, nor was it Maarten's ghost.

But it was his dead spit, his alter ego, inflated with a bicycle pump. It was his dad, it was Lucas – podgy old Lucas, the son in the father and the father in the son. Which came first, the chicken or the egg? Myles had an answer to that one, as Myles – dear old Myles – had a goddamn answer to everything. 'Chickens,' he'd say, 'are things that eggs create to make more eggs. Remember that, Ruth, and you won't go far wrong. And don't eat chicken and egg sandwiches. It's unethical.'

'I think a drink would help,' she said feebly.

Playing for time . . .

She wanted to get there quickly, but the heavy subterranean

air was hobbling her brain. She had ruled Lucas out of the equation. There hadn't been a shadow of a doubt. So what was he doing here? Lucas had nothing against her. At the university they had made their peace. True, she hadn't made up with Jojo as promised. True, she'd been steering clear of Clara. But she'd successfully allayed his fears of any rivalry over Thomas Springer, hadn't she? She'd been honest about herself and Maarten, hadn't she? He said he'd appreciated that.

Now everything was up for grabs.

Her skin felt cold.

There was a nasty squirming sensation in her gut.

The hate-mailer's signature came back to her: the atomic number for silver. Lucas had discreetly pointed her nose at this himself. He was a chemistry teacher. It was right up his street. Had he been dropping a heavy hint? It was the sort of thing killers did – deliberately drawing attention to themselves – a grown-up version of hide-and-seek, of catch-me-if-you-can.

A neat Scotch touched down in front of her. She knocked it back in one. The squirming turned into a burning, as if she'd swallowed paint stripper.

Her head was spinning with questions.

Is it me? she thought. *Am I going mad? Is poor old Ruthy three sausages short of a barbecue? Or does this guy sitting next to me – Maarten's illustrious progenitor, my father's bosom pal – have it in for me? Is this my personal nemesis, sweating slightly at the temples, frowning into his G and T like he'd seen a penguin peeping out between the icebergs?*

'So,' said Lucas, after a while. He nodded his head with a 'Well, here we are!' smile.

'So!' Ruth said, echoing the gesture without sarcasm.

She couldn't fathom him.

Was this vengeance incarnate? Was this naked hatred assuming a human form? What had she failed to see? It occurred to her that they were sitting where the necking Goths had been on her previous visit.

'Ruth – is everything all right?' He had dropped into a low confidential tone. There was an edge of genuine concern.

'I think I forgot my boarding pass.'

He grinned and patted her reassuringly on the arm. 'You look rather down in the mouth.'

'I'm a melancholic, I admit. Actually, I'm a site-specific melancholic. This place is one of my sites.'

'So you've been here before?'

'Not you?'

'No – never. It's a new one on me. But then Clara and I don't get out much these days.'

'Then how—?'

She was about to ask how he knew about the place when something caught her eye.

On the far side of the cellar, sitting alone, was a dark-haired goddess, pretending to read a book. She was not in uniform today. She wore black jeans and a tight Aran rollneck that hugged her surprising breasts. Ruth had a fleeting mental image of a pair of dolphins leaping for sheer joy from the crest of an ocean wave. Her own were neat little cupcakes by comparison.

Bianca Velthuizen.

The cop looked a million bucks.

She glanced up and their eyes met for an instant, then darted away. Suddenly, everything was OK. A warm wellbeing spread through Ruth's bloodstream. Somehow, God knows how, Smits had discharged his functions. Somehow he'd come up to scratch. Except that, contrary to Ruth's expectations, he'd kept himself out of the picture, delegating to Bianca instead.

'How what?' asked Lucas.

'Uh? Oh, nothing.' She sighed and raised her shoulders, then let them slump. 'I'm afraid I'm tired, Lucas. Forgive me. I can't remember what I was going to say.'

At last he removed the unwelcome weight of his hand from her arm. He was in shirtsleeves and a tie with golf balls embroidered on it. His brown woollen jacket, with its silk lining, was draped on the seat between them. There was an air of carefully concealed impatience about him.

'So who speaks first?' he said. 'You? Me? Nobody? You'll have to help me. What's the routine?'

'Routine?'

'We're here to talk, right? Isn't that what this is all about?'

'If you say so.'

'Well, isn't it?'

They sat there, staring at each other.

Ruth's eyes hardened by degrees.

'You summoned me, Lucas. First to the bridge, and then down here. Don't tell me you didn't summon me.'

He didn't blink. He looked weary all of a sudden.

He handed her his mobile.

There was a text message from Ruth, making the date at Jade Beach. It said it was urgent. It said they had to meet.

Tit for tat, she showed him hers, with the last message she'd received.

'Who's M?' said Lucas.

Ruth brought her hands to her face. Tears jerked into her eyes. 'I thought it was Maarten. I thought it was Maarten, come back to tell me what's what.'

'I see. An inspired substitute for the ouija board, if I may say so. My son always did have an original cast of mind.'

She rubbed the tears angrily from her cheeks. 'Oh, hell – of course I knew it wasn't Maarten, Lucas, but that's how he signed himself. You know that. Someone's fucking with my emotions. Someone's screwing up my life.'

'Who's the joker?'

'How should I know? This is rapidly turning into a crash course in advanced reality, and I'm an opsimath. Know what an opsimath is, Lucas?'

He shook his head indifferently.

'It's someone who learns late in life.'

'In that case, you have a lot to learn. I hope for your sake you never learn it.'

'It's to do with the painting, I know that much,' she said, ignoring his snide remark. 'The painting and the old lady. Somebody wants me out of the way.' She rubbed thumb and forefinger together in the international money gesture. 'That's the smallest violin in the world. Just about everybody's queuing up to play it.'

Lucas observed her closely.

'So this incognito somebody set up a cosy chat between you and me,' he said. 'Now what could anyone possibly gain from that? Are they here, watching us, do you think – enjoying the spectacle of our confusion?'

Reflexively, they both looked round.

Bianca was buried in her book. Cheetah was doing her lips. Mr Shine was at the bar.

Otherwise, there was no one she knew.

When Lucas had his head turned, she caught Bianca's attention and signalled to the loos with a sideways flash of the eyes. Bianca dutifully put down the book and left the room. Ruth gave it a moment, then excused herself.

The cop was waiting by the washbasins. When Ruth came in, she wagged her over to a far corner by the hand dryers. 'Is he the guy?' she said intensely. Her breath smelled sweet, like snowdrops.

'Depends what you mean by "the guy". That's Lucas, my ex's father.'

'I know.'

'You've met him?'

'He was in a snapshot you had on the boat. A picture of you, the boy and the parents.'

'He's not the bogey-man. We both got the fast shuffle and

a blind date. I went to the bridge as planned, then I got redirected.' She showed the message and explained the initial. 'Can you pull anything out of this? Smits fed me some line about server rerouting. Said you couldn't really trace anything back.'

Bianca looked apologetic. 'Andries doesn't know as much as he thinks he knows. He's good, but he's still struggling through the course.'

'He's pre-geek. That's what I figured. Wrong generation.'

'Give me the phone. We may get a lead from the chip.'

Reluctantly, she surrendered her mobile. 'Take care of it, please. It has twenty-five polyphonic ring tones.'

Bianca slid it into her back pocket.

'You're a good cop, you know,' said Ruth. 'You got here without me even noticing. You pick up clues.'

'People are flaky. They leave trails. They drop bits and pieces all the time. Like this.' She held up a small fluffy feather by the shaft. 'I knew you weren't lying. You were with your mum and dad. You went to a pheasant farm near Utrecht.'

'Smits found that.'

'He found it and gave it to me. He knew it would speak to me.'

'I could've planted it on myself. I could've picked it up anywhere.'

'You didn't.'

Ruth stared at her. 'Pinch me and tell me I'm dreaming. You DNA-ed the pheasants?'

'It's not the pheasants I'm interested in,' said Bianca, a quick flag of red in the cheeks.

'Oh, sure – me neither. Some people hang them till they're wormy, and then – those mouthfuls of grapeshot, yuk!'

'Your hair's different,' said Bianca. 'It's black.'

'I dyed it. I wanted to change my look. I guess I was tired of being unpopular.'

'It suits you. Perhaps, you know – ' Bianca reached out and ruffled her fingers shyly through Ruth's hair ' – some gel . . .'

'Thanks for the style tip.'

The conversation was off on an odd scenic detour.

Ruth couldn't resist: she looked the cop up and down admiringly. She was like something out of a magazine, untouched by graphics software. Colour balance, contrast, texture, pixellization – all naturally optimized. She should have been modelling beachwear, not tracking delinquents and dishing out parking tickets. She radiated health and beauty.

'How old are you, Bianca?'

'Twenty-five.'

'Wow. I was twenty-five once too.'

'You were?'

'Yeah. For a whole year.' Ruth scratched the back of her neck, wondering what to say or do next. 'Listen – you might as well go home. I can deal with Lucas. And thanks – thanks for being my guardian angel.'

Bianca left first.

When Ruth came out the glamorous cop had gone.

She returned to her place.

Mr Shine was plucking idly away at his guitar again and Lucas was absorbed, turned sideways, his legs crossed and facing the little green podium. He'd ordered another drink for them both. He glanced at Ruth, then back at the iridized guitar. It seemed to hypnotize him. His jacket was still draped between them, the wallet poking out of the inside pocket.

Instinctively Ruth knew what she had to do.

The idea had been there from the beginning, preformed but unvoiced. She hadn't subjected it to the slightest moral questioning.

It was the reason why he was there.

It was the reason why she was there too. She slipped two fingers into the wallet, keeping her gaze fixed on Lucas, wary of the tiniest fissure in his concentration. There was none. She parted her fingers and glanced into the wallet. His cards were ranged in little slits down one side. At the top was the one she wanted. She teased it out and slipped it into her trouser pocket. Then, cool as a cucumber, she walked her gaze round the room.

No one had noticed a thing.

Shine's lazy improvisation stopped and Lucas resurfaced from his reverie. 'People should listen to music like that more often,' he said. 'It's good for the soul. It puts you in the mood. In fact, I suddenly feel like a small cigar.'

'Perhaps you can get one at the bar.'

'I shouldn't. I stopped two years ago. It was bad for my tubes.'

The thought of pungent cigars got Ruth thinking.

'Lucas, can I ask you a personal question?'

'Fire ahead.'

'Why do you smell of explosives?'

'I'm a chemist. Chemistry wouldn't be chemistry without the odd explosion. Trial and error. It keeps us on our toes.'

'I'm serious. Maarten had the same smell about him. It was in his clothes.'

'Didn't he ever tell you, Ruth? Our flat is in a converted warehouse, as you know. They used to stock fireworks there. The walls are impregnated with that smell. It gets everywhere. We've got used to it over the years. We're even rather fond of it. It's the odour of home.'

The last word was a foothold of sorts.

'I promised I'd come round, didn't I?' she said. 'And I didn't.'

'That's right, Ruth,' he nodded, emphasizing his words. 'You promised, but you didn't.'

'Perhaps I could come round tomorrow. To see Clara. To see both of you.'

'That's a nice idea. Very kind and thoughtful. Why don't you give Clara a ring now? Just to check that it's all right.'

She reached into her pocket for the phone.

Then she remembered it was gone.

A little lateral thinking came to her rescue. 'We're in a cellar, Lucas. It wouldn't work. Could you ask her for me? I'll call to check that it's OK.'

'Very well.' He stretched back, yawned extravagantly without covering his mouth and shut his eyes. When he opened them again, he looked at Ruth as if he'd forgotten, in the interim, that she'd been there. 'Do you believe in God?' he said after a pause.

'Could you be more specific?'

'God, Ruth, God. Do you believe in him?'

'It kind of depends on definitions. I believe in the mystical force that hides my socks behind the radiator and switches on the rain every time I go out without an umbrella.'

'I wish I could believe in God. God, the personal God. I expect that must surprise you.'

She nodded in confirmation.

'Old Lucas, the empiricist, the die-hard scientific rationalist, wishes he could believe in God. It's a wish that's been growing in me lately and I can't do anything to control it. I wish I could believe God was watching us right now. And I wish I could believe in his spirit world. Imagine, for a moment, that all that blind superstition, all that old hocus-pocus, was true. Now you came here to meet Maarten, in a manner of speaking. Suppose that Maarten was here right now, with us, sharing this moment, sitting between us.' He patted his hand on the fat lump of the wallet in the silk pocket of his jacket. 'I'd like to think that was so. I miss my boy, you see. When you're young, life is full of gains. Then the losses begin – your dog dies, you split up with a girlfriend or boyfriend, you mess up an exam, that sort of thing. And the older you get the more the losses outnumber the gains. It's inside and outside. Your stamina goes, your eyesight goes, your legs get rickety. People you know die. You look at your partner, you look at your friends, and they're all going through the same rotten process. Loss, loss, loss. Growing up, Ruth, is about accepting that loss, getting along with it and putting your faith in life. But there is no loss like the loss of a child. How can anyone accept the loss of a child? It's against nature. It's a foul perversion of the cycles of life. Of course, wars come along and epidemics and accidents – and it *does* happen, we all know that, and I don't contest it. But how can the parent *accept* this loss? That's what I'm asking, Ruth. If you have the answer, I would dearly like to know. The answer to that question would be our salvation. You see, Clara and I are standing in the smoking ruins, wondering how we survived. But the truth is we didn't survive. The truth is we are bereft of life. We are the dead, we carry our death around with us like a sign, branded upon our foreheads.' He smiled wanly. 'It doesn't exactly make us the best of company.'

'I'll come tomorrow – tomorrow afternoon,' Ruth murmured.

'Please do. I know it's no fun. I know it must seem like a dreary duty, but please do. For Clara, if nothing else. For Clara and perhaps for yourself. Because the more you fathom our death, the more you will understand what it is to be alive. It's all luck, Ruth – all luck. Some have it, others don't. The trick is to know it when you have it because, as the good book rightly says, tomorrow we shall die.'

He put on his jacket and took out the wallet. He began counting notes.

'Don't worry, Lucas. These are on me.'

He turned in mild confusion. 'That's very kind of you, Ruth. I'm sorry if I've bored you.'

'You haven't bored me.'

'And if you're in trouble – I'm referring to the individual who arranged our impromptu meeting – perhaps we could discuss things at our place. I'm fond of your parents, as you know, and there's nothing I wouldn't do for you, or them for that matter, that I wouldn't have done for my own son.'

'Thanks.' She lowered her eyes.

He got unsteadily to his feet and crossed the floor.

He climbed the spiral staircase, almost hoisting his ungainly bulk up by the banister, and when he neared the top he stopped for a moment and looked down, smiling sadly. He was smiling at her, Ruth thought, though his mind must have been wandering, for his gaze fluttered indecisively over the room below and failed to alight on her. Then the smile switched off as abruptly as a light.

Ruth stood up and went to the bar.

She asked for the bill.

Cheetah totted up the four drinks on a scrap of notepaper, sucking the point of the pencil between lines. She pushed the note over. 'You come here before,' she said, eyeing Ruth suspiciously. 'I doan forget a pretty face.' The black hair blocked the memory, but soon it came through. 'Yeah, I got it. You come with some udder guy.' She leaned forward, her breath smelling of stale menthol. 'You like 'em older, huh, sweetheart?'

Ruth looked in her purse, ignoring the question.

No cash.

She handed over her credit card.

Cheetah pouted and pushed it in the reader. She tapped out the numbers.

The Christmas photos were still taped up under the pelmet of the bar. Ruth squinted at the faces, picking out Cameron's big beaming mug whenever it put in an appearance. He looked like the caretaker honcho of a rogue African state. In one he was off to the side, chatting to another man. You could only see the back of the other guy's head, slightly out of focus. It looked familiar. The Kid? No – too chunky. But blurs always looked familiar. A little creative vagueness and folk tend to slap their own interpretations on things. They see what they want to see. With snapshots, as with paintings, the real mystery was the one face you didn't see: the guy who paints the picture, the gal who snaps the shot. That was the real absence, yet those were the eyes you were looking through. It was a quantum leap into somebody else's subjectivity, a kind of virtual body-snatching. In some nutty metaphysical dimension, you were sitting inside their head.

And the face you never see is the one you're looking out of.

'Problem, honey,' said Cheetah flatly. She was tapping a long painted nail on the top of the card reader with a bored stare like a whorehouse bimbo in a spaghetti Western.

The LCD on the machine read: 'payment refused'.

'Shit,' said Ruth. 'I didn't think. I stopped the card myself earlier today.'

'Oh yeah? People stop cards when they lose them.'

'Someone got hold of the number, if you must know. They stole the number, not the card.'

'Nice friends you got.'

'Who said it was a friend?'

'How you gonna pay?' Cheetah had one hand on her hip now, ready to bitch. The pock-marked skin around the high cheekbones looked red and inflamed.

'Give me the address. I'll send you a cheque.'

'No way, José!' She puffed her cheeks and blew the air out contemptuously.

'Then what do you suggest?'

The girl leaned over the bar and grabbed Ruth by the wrist. Her little hand was like a bird's claw. She raised Ruth's arm till it was under one of the tiny halogen spotlights.

'Cool watch,' she said. 'Rolex?'

Ruth pulled her arm free. 'Forget it. It isn't a Rolex, and I'm not giving it to you anyway. I *need* my watch. It's worth ten times those drinks!'

'An' I need that money, sweetheart. Two gin. Two Scotch. You pay. I'm runnin' a business. Wha' you think this is, a soup kitchen? That good liquor. People come a long way for that. They come in on crutches. They walk out on their own two feet. Call it security. You come back wiv money, I give back the watch. Deal?'

Ruth sighed, slipped off the metal wristband and tossed the watch in the air. The girl caught it adroitly.

'Fuck you,' said Ruth as she made for the stairs.

'Yeah – fuck you too, sister!' called Cheetah, high and reedy, laughing and flouncing her shoulders.

They flashed smiles at each other and that was that.

Up on street level, Ruth bent her credit card in two and flipped it into a bin.

If time was money and money was time, she'd just managed to lose both of them in a matter of hours – not to mention that basic necessity of modern wheeler-dealing, the mobile phone. And it certainly was tough being common white trash without a cent to your name.

Right now she could do with one of those hotshot corporate T&E purchasing cards you saw on television: American Express, Diners Club – the ones that made the world grovel, the ones that bought respect. She still had one card up her sleeve, come to think of it – Lucas's. And Lucas's card had one big thing in common with all those glitzy charge cards, apart from being a wallet-sized plastic rectangle.

It opened all the right doors . . .

But thoughts troubled her on the way home.

Frankly, it couldn't have been more convenient, bumping into Lucas like that.

She'd been thinking of stealing that blasted painting for some time now, or at least toying with the idea. All she needed was the wherewithal. Then, suddenly, it was handed to her on a plate.

What if the whole thing was a set-up?

If it was, she'd swallowed it like a prize puppet-head. And if it was, who was doing the setting up? Lucas himself – 'Take a card, any card'? She couldn't believe his stifling moroseness was part of some cheap little plan.

Then, if not Lucas, who?

Perhaps nobody, after all.

Sometimes providence simply provides. It looks down, from whatever fur-lined nook of the empyrean it happens to hang out in, and picks out someone in need of a break. Or maybe it just helps those who help themselves. Either way Ruth didn't feel like a sap. She felt like someone calling the shots.

That's how she felt . . .

There was only one way forward and that was forward.

Life was like that.

You go through a door, it shuts fast behind you, and that's it – you've got to go on.

Thirty-one

Lydia was on the way out.

This knowledge, and the intuition that brought it home, was haunting Ruth. It was not the minor strokes – the ones she knew about, for there might have been others. It was not the last will and testament, recently made or revised. It was something more direct, more conclusive and yet less tangible. It was an aura of gentle loosening and extenuation. It was as if nearly a century of human history was gradually pulling down the shutters, yawning and calling it a day.

Previously, Lydia had been decrepit – for decades, or so it seemed. But her decrepitude was a dirty strength, the wiry, unwashed vigour of the old trooper. She gasped and drank and ached and cursed. Now the fight was going out of her. She was softer, sweeter, more pliant – a piece of fruit decaying in a bowl. A heavy odour of futility hung about her. She was gradually losing ground.

Then again, who could say how close the end was?

Gods have laps and nobody can see what's in them.

But Ruth didn't like the odds.

Back in the *achterhuis* an email was waiting from Myles. There was more info in the pipeline from Fischer concerning the Nazi connection. He'd unearthed a letter from Dr Hans Posse which appeared to refer to the van der Heyden. She fired off a one-line riposte:

✉

Dear Corn Cob, I'm relieving you of managerial duties as of today. Ruth.

The email had the desired effect. Within ten minutes, he was on the phone.

'Can I come round?' he said.

'Now is not the moment, Myles. I'm on my way out.'

'Then at least tell me what it's all about – this relieving me of managerial duties.'

'Later, pal.'

'You're getting your own back, aren't you? For me not telling you about the scrapings. Tit for tat, an eye for an eye. You women are all the same, constantly balancing the emotional ledgers.'

'You tell me about Posse first and that letter you mentioned.'

'I haven't read the letter, but Fischer says Miedl dealt with Scheele and didn't like him one bit. He felt Scheele was nervous and had something to hide. When they discovered the runes on the back of the piccy, they got to work and decoded the Latin. The Latin got Posse all in a lather. In the letter he used expressions like "revolutionary process" and "great historical importance". I didn't tell Fischer, but it's clear to me that the Nazis had worked out that it was a photograph. That's what led to the pre-emption for Alt Aussee. There – now you tell me what the hell you're up to.'

'I'm going out to do some shopping.'

'Please don't get slippery with me.'

'Myles, as ever, we're in perfect symbiosis. But experience shows that the left hand doesn't always need to know what the right hand is doing.'

'Is that so.'

'Yes.'

There was a peeved silence. 'Anyway, poppet,' he relented, 'I've got some good news for you. Or *news*, if you prefer – take it or leave it.'

'And what's that?'

'Both Smits and I reported to Cabrol that you'd been under-going harassment and that your resignation was a spoof. Cabrol had to rescind his acceptance. He's so happy to have you back in the fold. It was all he could do to control his joy.'

'Oh, thanks, Myles.'

'Don't mention it.'

'To be totally honest, I'm not sure that I *can* come back right now.'

'The sweet taste of freedom?'

'That – and I'm keeping my options open. Be a darling, and play him for time. Tell him his acceptance undermined my confidence. I need a couple of days to crank up my ailing morale.'

'OK,' said Myles, 'but remember: *here be dragons*. Keep me in the loop. There's bad weather coming, and you're not going to manage out there on your own.'

She grimaced, put down the phone and glanced at her watch. There was no watch to glance at. It was morning, that was all: one hair past a freckle.

A sharp-edged sun threw a medley of geometrical shadows down into the dank courtyard.

Today was the day she was going to pull a heist.

She was doing it for Lydia, first and foremost.

To hell with Cabrol. To hell with the law. To hell with the slow march of bureaucracy.

Lydia would have her picture, she'd see to that. She couldn't let the old girl perish without it.

She was doing it for herself, second and aftmost.

By stealing the picture, she'd pre-emptively clear her name. That was the crackpot logic of it. Suppose Lyd died and Blom-mendaal popped out of the woodwork, brandishing the will. Ruth took all: house, painting, pussycat, bags. Ergo, she was in it for the pickings. Ergo, she was a leech – lower than whale shit, lower than the spots on a grass snake's arse.

By lifting the painting first, she'd silence her future critics. She did it for the old woman, that's clear enough. Why should she steal from herself? She didn't know about the will – she couldn't have!

And that was assuming she got caught.

Strangely enough, the thought of capture, the thought of a trial, the thought of prison, never crossed her mind. It was nothing a loaf of bread with a file in it wouldn't fix. The moral cat's cradle was what really mattered, the greater justification.

If she didn't get caught, all the better. The grousers would grouse, the bleaters would bleat, but she'd still feel good with herself.

In the end, it came down to that: Ruth making her peace with Ruth.

She wished to Christ she'd never seen that will . . .

She took in Sander's room, then peered out of the window into the small frosty garden, and up at the old ceiling painting of the sugar-pink angels frolicking in the clouds.

Not so long ago she'd felt like a thief in here. It was precognition. Now she was about to become one. The crucial difference was that Sander's spirit was not her victim but her beneficiary. She was settling his old debts. She imagined him, for a moment, as one of the rosy-cheeked angels, gazing sweetly down on her and giving her the celestial thumbs-up. The only problem was her c.v. There was little in the previous work experience to shortlist her for grand larceny.

She realized, with a start, that she was scared.

She clenched her fists and held them up till the knuckles went white, willing away the fear and trembling.

There was nothing to it, she told herself. She'd told Myles she was going shopping and that was close to the mark. Stealing was just like shopping. The only difference was that you bypass the checkout.

But there were always cameras – god-like eyes in ceilings and walls. It was a damn police state, wherever you went, keeping everyone under surveillance. How was an honest thief supposed to make a living? The minute you set foot in the humblest snack bar you were biometrically taped and tabbed.

What she needed was a disguise.

She rummaged through her bag of clothes. Nothing suitable. They were all Ruthy things that made her look like her.

Beside the bookcase was an old mahogany wardrobe that she'd checked out once before. It was full of Sander's effects. She opened it and shunted the clothes hangers, one by one, along the rail.

Suits, shirts and a couple of long winter coats.

She sniffed them warily. They smelled OK. In fact, they'd survived half a century remarkably well in the private Brother Museum. Not even the camphor or naphthalene whiff of a mothball. The moths had probably done a bunk to Lydia's end of the house where the pickings were infinitely richer.

She stripped to her underwear and tried on a shirt with a stiff fifties collar, an American tweed suit and a long Ulster topcoat.

A good fit, if a little loose at the waist.

She found a belt for the trousers and pulled it tight. She stopped short of putting on the dead man's shoes, but a flat corduroy driving cap from the top shelf of the wardrobe was her size, more or less.

The look was complete.

She admired herself in the mirror. With her black hair, she was remarkably like him. You just had to half-close your eyes.

She decanted her keys and personal objects to the pockets of the Ulster and called Lucas from Lydia's phone in the hall – overtly to confirm her visit, covertly to check he was not going into the department.

Only one thing missing now – a bag. Her own were too small. This was no cause to be down-hearted. Of all the houses in old Amsterdam, Lydia's would surely come up with the goods.

She made for the pantry. This was the *sanctum sanctorum*, the Aladdin's cave.

She was spoilt for choice.

She picked a sturdy commonplace Dutch one with the Hema store logo, not to draw attention to herself. It was just the right size.

But, as she headed out, she passed by the open door of Lydia's room. The old lady looked up from her quiet conversation with the cat. Her hand stopped stroking. Ruth stalled and caught her eye.

'I'm, er, just on my way out,' she managed.

'So I see,' said Lydia. Her gaze was misty. She didn't seem all there.

'I'll be back later.'

She started off, but Lydia called after her sternly. 'Sander. You're a very naughty boy, you know.'

'Am I?' Ruth stepped back into sight.

'Yes. Mama asked you to put a tie on when you go out. We have to keep up appearances. We don't want the neighbours to think we're uncouth.'

'Well, next time maybe, Lydia.' She pulled the lapels of the Ulster closed to hide the absent tie. 'I'm in a hurry now.'

'Next time, next time, always next time.' Lydia shook her head. She sighed and returned to stroking the cat. 'Boys will be boys, Principessa. Unfortunately, boys will be boys . . .'

The Roeterseiland complex was all glass planes and cantilevered beams, a myriad windows ablaze with the morning sun.

She chained her bike in the students' bike park and made for Building B. Getting in would be no problem. No one had challenged her last time. It was the weekend, but the department was open and lectures or seminars seemed to be under way. Students to-ed and fro-ed down the concrete gangways. Despite her thirty-two summers, she could still pass for one of them: some of the real students were actually older than her. At the door, however, a ponytailed woman in uniform was checking people through. Ruth took her place in the short queue, wondering how to bluff it. She fingered her Rijksmuseum ID in the coat pocket. She rehearsed a couple of imaginary scenarios. But when she got to the head of the queue, the woman said 'Meeting?' – Ruth nodded – and she was in, no questions asked. A programme of some kind had even been put into her hand to make up for the missing credentials.

She took off her cap.

People were massing in the lobby and waiters served coffee from an urn. There were free-standing signposts with group designations – 'A2', 'F3', 'D7' – and arrows pointing left, right, up and down.

She felt a hand on her back.

A cheerful man with jungly eyebrows. He looked as if his job was to make people feel at ease. 'Here for the meeting?' he asked.

'Yes.'

'We'll be starting in half an hour. Just time to wet your whistle. Did you come last year?'

'Oh, definitely.'

'Then you'll know the ropes.'

He breezed off, but a woman in a red wasp-waist jacket homed in like a fighter, tailgating the exchange.

'This way,' she said, another hand planted firmly in the small of Ruth's back. 'I live for these meetings, don't you?'

'Oh yes. It's a pity they're not held more often.'

'That's exactly what I said to my husband this morning! Here.' She passed Ruth a stiff black coffee. 'The meeting is only once a year, but it re-echoes, as it were, for months on end. The feedback is intense. Do you mind me asking, which branch are you?'

Ruth sipped her coffee, spilling some of it into the saucer. 'I'm afraid I'm not at liberty to disclose that.'

'I see.' The woman was taken aback. She stared at Ruth with renewed curiosity. 'I'm sorry. I didn't mean to pry.'

Ruth shrugged in apology. 'I feel so stupid saying that, like some kind of incompetent secret agent. But the powers that be have asked me to keep a low profile. I hope you understand. There are significant private interests at stake. I'm sure I don't need to tell you that.'

'No, quite,' the woman concurred, her head bobbing uncertainly.

Ruth handed back the empty coffee cup and shook her free hand. 'Perhaps we shall meet later.'

Away from the crowd, she opened the programme.

She was none the wiser.

It was a conference on something called the Coriolis Effect.

A corridor stretched ahead and two workmen carrying a long metal pole advanced towards her. She strode past them decisively, then slowed down when she came to the end.

Fire stairs up, fire stairs down, and three new corridors departing in new directions.

She took one at random, a pale green empty tunnel to nowhere.

The sun was warm on her face through the long strip of spotless windows. Her footsteps were clean and crisp on the smooth vinyl flooring. There was a faint smell of lemons in the air.

It was all a dream. Nothing about her surroundings felt real.

'Get in, get it and get out,' she said to herself. But 'get in' where? Stijn could have aimed her in the right direction. There was an irradiation device holed up in this complex, but Christ alone knew how to get there.

First floor: haberdashery; second floor: ladies' evening wear; third floor: household appliances . . .

A man in a Nehru jacket came round a corner and made straight for her. 'Lost?' he said, with a cut-glass accent.

'Astray. Nearly six months, and I still can't get the hang of this place.'

'It's the female brain. No offence and all that. Men have abstract maps in their heads. Women orient by fixed landmarks – trees, statues, letterboxes. Look around you.' Following his lead, she gazed up and down the corridor. 'Nothing. Everywhere looks like everywhere else. No wonder your compass won't function. Now what exactly were you looking for?'

'Neutron Autoradiography,' said Ruth.

'Basement D. You can't miss it.'

'Thanks. And *Vive la différence*, I guess.'

'*C'est le cas de le dire*,' he replied in perfect French.

She retraced her steps to the intersection and took the stairs one storey down.

The swing doors were heavier in the basement. The atmosphere was stale. She breathed fast, as if double the effort was needed to get the required oxygen.

The facility was easy to find.

She checked left, checked right, then swiped the card through the access terminal and punched in the numbers: Maarten's birthday – day, month, year. She'd always remembered it, but had never imagined it coming in quite so handy. The six digits each had a different tone, like the buttons on a telephone: Happy birthday, dear Maarten, happy birthday to you . . .

The door buzzed open and in she went.

She wasn't doing Lucas any favours. The terminal probably logged all entrants. It was the first thing they'd check if a theft came to light. In this respect, time was of the essence – not less, but more. The longer it took to discover the theft, the more candidates there'd be. The footprint of Lucas's ID card would be one among many. Lucas himself was safe as houses. He'd always have an alibi. But the minute the questions were asked, he'd have her number, as she now had his, and he'd know it was her. Whether he'd whistle was anyone's guess. The one sure thing was that Ruth's little caper had a countdown on it. At least her fears about security cameras appeared to be unfounded.

Right now, she had to be fast. The trick was to pull out in time – as Snow White said to the seven dwarves. That's what Myles would have said in similar circumstances. Myles was a wag, with a special gift for the not-so-subtle crack. She was almost his understudy, she could second-guess him so well.

A quick once-over suggested a monitoring room of sorts.

A window and glass-fronted door giving on to an inner vestibule. Two work stations. A neat black anodized aluminium instrumentation panel beneath the window.

The VDUs had identical screensavers: a gorgeous geometrical shape that rotated and mutated like an alien life form which existed purely to be beautiful, advancing and receding through fathomless virtual space.

In the further room was a secure closed container, some three by five metres, width and height. Cables passed through the wall from one unit to the other. Red words on the door – 'Keep Clear' – and a black trefoil on a yellow background, the international symbol for radiation.

Ruth's operational resolve began to fail her. She tried to recall what Stijn had said. The painting would have to be irradiated. The imaging came from isotope decay. Three months, he'd said – she remembered that. After which you could stick it on the wall.

Outside, voices – male voices and footsteps, advancing down the corridor.

She held her breath.

The walking stopped but the talking continued. With a bit of luck they were taking a pause. With a bit of luck they'd move on. But a six-note harmonic said otherwise.

A rush of adrenalin went to her head.

In a second the lock would buzz.

In a second the door would open.

There was nowhere to hide.

If she didn't move, in a second it would be too late.

She slipped through the glass-fronted door and into the rear vestibule. In an instant she'd mapped the room.

There was one blind corner.

No more than a gap between some functional japanned shelving and the near wall. She forced herself in, squeezing her ribcage to fit, and crammed her bag down between her knees.

Her heart was pounding in her chest, but she was just out of sight.

'Is this going to upset me?' said one of the voices.

'I don't know,' said the other. 'It's white-beam cold spectrum, but the typical flux readings are wrong.'

Ruth leaned forward. She could see an acute triangular segment of the control room, no more. A finger tapped on a keyboard. The beautiful alien vanished and one of the VDUs woke up.

'Here's the last session.'

A raft of data cascaded down the screen.

'It doesn't make sense. Why *do* machines keep breaking down?'

'They wouldn't be human if they didn't, poor darlings.'

A hand rattled away at the keys, then pointed a pen at the screen. 'There's your gremlin. What's the open area of your neutron guide end?'

'Three point five by twelve point five.'

'You're scanning a twelve point five centimetre strip. So your typical flux should be one point ten to the power of nine, with uniform activation. Trouble is, your data log's set for a different transmission speed. It's purely downstream. The process isn't affected, but your counter's ballsed up by the wrong setting. A piece of cake – look, you just have to change the value.'

'Think we should check the container?'

Their faces appeared at the window, two featureless planets.

Ruth flattened herself even further into her corner.

And there, on the shelf, was the van der Heyden painting, leaning against the wall. She noticed it with a jolt for the first time. The frame had been removed and it stood next to a crate of fossilized shellfish and another small canvas that lay face down.

Suddenly, she felt sick.

She closed her eyes and wished herself elsewhere. A beach, palm trees, the sun. A man playing bongos. A cocktail would be nice. She raised one virtual arm and waved lazily to the bar.

'I think we should measure the guide axis, just to be sure.'

The handle turned.

The door began to open.

'Second thoughts, let's wait for Max. He went through the specs on the Berlin facility. I saw him at ten. Just off to get a bike for his kid. He'll be back after lunch.'

A moment's hesitation, and the door clicked shut.

More muffled talk – 'How did Maya get on with that visiting-card rep?' – then the outer door opened and it shut too. Four feet padded away.

She opened her eyes.

She let her jaw drop and exhaled.

Safe . . .

'Safe', however, was not quite the word.

She stayed in her gap as if jammed there, staring at Johannes and Esther – the egg-blue dress, the tousled hair – her mind bathed in the yellow radiance of the mimosa.

The feeling of sickness was yellow too, and it wasn't planning on going away.

There was a little something she needed to know. There was a little something she'd neglected to consider.

Had the painting been irradiated yet or not?

Staring at it wasn't going to answer that question. *Nothing* was going to answer that question, at least not in the next few minutes. The picture had arrived recently. There was a chance that it was waiting here, on the shelf, that it hadn't been bombarded with neutrons. There was another chance that it had. It was fifty–fifty, even Stevens, heads or tails. And if it had, was it safe? Not if Stijn's spiel was anything to go by.

This was something of a dilemma . . .

Californium-252.

Pinned against the wall, Ruth took stock of the situation.

Where she was now, that was the present, though tomorrow it would be history. Whichever present you inhabited, everything was relative to that. At any given second, the conjuncture of compelling circumstances was unique, and your thoughts and actions were minutely calibrated to them there and then, only to readjust the next – hence hindsight and foresight were both useless dipsticks.

Right now, Lydia was one of her compelling circumstances.

She thought of her contorted face when she heard about Scheele's rival claim. She remembered the hollow dismay.

Whichever way you turned, there was no getting the picture out of the picture. To Lydia van der Heyden, it was the be-all and the end-all. It was her lifeline with the past. It was the fulcrum of all her hopes and fears. To repossess it was her last and deepest wish.

Ruth pulled the bag out from between her legs and caught her breath.

Thirty-Two

'What have I been up to?' Jojo echoed flatly. Her face was set like stone. 'I've been trying to figure out precisely what kind of person you are.'

At midday Ruth had taken the painting back and found Lydia asleep. She propped it up on a chair beside her bed with a note: 'For you. Still some red tape to snip. Best not mention it to anyone.' She prepared a light meal for Lydia and left it on a tray by her bed.

She changed back into her own clothes. Smits rang to check that she was OK. He said he'd drop by one day soon. Spread-eagled on cushions on the parlour floor, she tried to catch some sleep. Her mind had other plans. It was a raucous merry-go-round that never stopped. Part of her was elated by what she'd dared to do. And Sander's cherub levitated over her with those inscrutable lips. She wanted to scribble a toothbrush moustache over them and run.

The dark repose would not come.

At two, she kept her appointment with Lucas and Clara at their home in the Entrepotdok.

The Aalders had their hidden agenda and this was it – Jojo, Ruth and Jojo, sisters again, hallelujah, the great reconciliation ... She couldn't refuse, how could she? It was what she wanted too. But she would have preferred to be the instigator. Instead everything had been arranged. She felt passive, as if the Aalders were pushing her along on little wheels. And the whole charade had the joyless contrivance of a surprise birth-day party.

In silence, Lucas drove her out to the bland concrete estates and urban wildernesses of the Bijlmer. In silence, Jojo's mother saw her in. Now here she was, while Lucas waited in a kebab joint, reading a paperback. It had been sprung on her and she didn't know what to say. All she could ascertain was Jojo's emotional temperature. It was hovering around zero – warm, for a polar bear.

'So how are you?' asked Ruth. She was in self-censorship mode, tamping down her natural impulse to ride high.

'As you see.'

What she saw was Jojo slumped in bed at an angle, the plaster-cast leg swung out and resting on a low table that had been cut out of a single slice of tree-trunk. On the wall, a poster of white-water rapids, the flayed skin of a big lizard – possibly a cayman – and, hanging from the ceiling, a huge white tin bell cage with a plastic macaw on the perch.

The room was cold.

The wintry light did little justice to this vignette of exotica, the black girl sunk in the shadows of the corner, her thick braided hair, her dark, wary eyes.

Ruth moved over to the seventh-storey window, her back to the room. Below three kids were mucking around on the big grey esplanade, kick-fighting and playing catch with a cigarette packet. One of them had flashing diodes in the plastic soles of his sneakers. Snow clung in patches to the tufts of weeds that pushed up through the uneven paving stones.

'This wasn't really my idea,' said Ruth. 'Lucas and Clara wanted me to come.'

'Still making sacrifices.'

'That's not what I meant. I tried to phone you at the hospital, but you were never available. What I meant was, I wanted us to get together of our own accord. I wanted us to make peace.' She glanced back into the room. 'Do you actually remember what you said to me when we last met?'

There was a long, laden silence.

'Maybe you were concussed, maybe you weren't,' said Ruth, 'but, either way, we've got to clear up this mess. Unless you'd rather not. Just tell me, if that's the case. If you want me to go, I'll go.'

The black girl was still silent, but with a small movement she shook her head.

A provisional truce.

Ruth turned back to the window again.

The kids had gone. A plastic bag frolicked across the empty space.

'For the record, I didn't try to flood my own boat with you in it,' she said matter-of-factly. 'In case you thought otherwise.'

'No, I know. I flooded it.'

'You flooded it?'

'I had some dirty jeans and T-shirts. It was me who put on the washing machine, so I guess I did it to myself. Then again, I wasn't to know about your dicky out pipe.'

'So who told you?'

'The cop. Never trust a woman who does her own plumbing, he said.'

Smits and his gloomy chauvinism. The thought alone was a leaden limpet mine strapped to her heart.

She let the comment pass.

'Funny that your out pipe should pick on me and not you, though,' Jojo added. 'Sod's law, I guess.'

'Someone tampered with the pipe. He must have overlooked that bit.'

Jojo examined her nails, aloofly refraining from comment.

'He said you saw something in the boat, something that disturbed you. What exactly was it?'

'It was a photo, of me, you and Maarten. One that wasn't in your albums.'

Ruth racked her brains. 'What photo?'

'You know very well which one, it was in your drawer. The three of us were on a day trip to the sea. You blacked me out, Ruth. You blacked me out in the photo.'

'I blacked you out?' Ruth couldn't believe her ears.

'With ink. You wanted to get me out of that photo, out of your memory. But you couldn't cut me out. I was in between you and Maarten. So you blacked me out with ink.'

'Oh, my God, Jojo – *that* picture! Listen – you've got to believe me – a ballpoint pen *leaked* onto it. I didn't black you out, I swear. Didn't you look at the picture? It was a leak stain. If I'd blacked you out, you'd have seen where the pen scored the surface.'

Jojo was undecided.

'If you're in any doubt, I'll find the damn thing again and show you, if it survived,' Ruth added. 'When did you see it – before the flood?'

Jojo nodded. 'I couldn't stop crying, I wanted to go home, but I was too shaken up. In the end I stayed. I cried myself to sleep. Then, when I woke up, there was water everywhere. I was so scared.'

'We have to talk about this, Jojo. Not the flood. But about you, me and Maarten. Too much has gone unsaid.'

'You were jealous of me,' Jojo blurted. 'You were jealous because I made him happy. I never felt comfortable when you were around.'

Ruth sat on the edge of the bed and hugged herself, leaning earnestly towards the other woman. 'You should have said something. You shouldn't have bottled it all up. Look where it's got us now. As for me, I've had a lot of time to think about this, and you may be right. I *knew* you made Maarten happy, and I couldn't work out why I had failed. It was a mystery I couldn't solve. When I think of him, that's what I feel. It's a kind of guilt, hovering over me.'

'You were always hanging round us. You never left us alone.'

'Is that how it felt? Oh, Jojo, I'm sorry, I'm so sorry. Maybe it's true. Maybe I was feeding off your happiness, or just watching it, trying to work out where it came from, trying to work out the secret.'

'Perhaps it cuts both ways. Perhaps I was jealous of you too,' Jojo confessed.

'Do you know why? Can you put it into words?'

Jojo grimaced and spoke falteringly. 'I guess you'd had so much more time together, so much more history. When I turned up, I was the outsider, the interloper. I wanted to do some blacking out too – blacking out Maarten's past to make his present more important to him. Something like that. Then one day there was no more present, no more future – only the past.'

They sat in silence for a moment, their minds enlivened by these confidences.

'This jealousy thing,' said Ruth, talking out of her thoughts. 'We did it again, didn't we, with Thomas Springer?'

'*We?*' flashed Jojo, with sudden pointedness.

Ruth bristled with her own resistance, her own sense of offended justice. 'You're right, Jojo, it wasn't *we*. What am I saying? It was *you*. This time it was you, all on your own. Because – listen to me carefully – I wasn't after him. I never snaked you. I never made a play for Thomas Springer.'

Jojo teased out the strands of a tassel on a pink cushion on her bed and started plaiting them tightly, manically, pointing all her attention at the task, a hard set to her small angular jaw.

'On the contrary, in fact,' Ruth added, nailing the point home.

'I don't believe that,' Jojo came back with low intensity, still squinting closely at the tassel.

'I have to ask you this. Before the party at your offices, did you and Thomas ever talk about me? Did he even *ask* you to invite me to that party?'

'What *is* this?' blurted Jojo, giving up on her plaiting and punching the cushion into the air. It clipped the side of the macaw's cage and sent it rocking.

There was movement outside. The mother – loitering within earshot.

'Well, did he?' she pressed neutrally.

'No!'

'And did you talk about me?'

'Yes, no, maybe – I really don't know! Why don't you ask him yourself?'

'I don't trust him.'

'And you trust *me*?' Jojo glared at her now in disbelief.

'I trust you to tell your particular truth, yes. I don't think you have or had ulterior motives.'

'Ulterior motives for what?'

'For anything.'

'And Thomas does, is that it? Let me try to get a handle on this thing. Thomas Springer is so smitten, so desperate to make your acquaintance – on what basis I can't imagine, unless your reputation precedes you like a . . .' – her hand fluttered impatiently – 'a glittering tsunami through the beau monde of Amsterdam – that he deliberately cosies up to me to get you invited to the party. He couldn't just cross paths with you at the old lady's. That would be too easy. Then he makes sure I'm out of the way, looking after someone who was taken ill at his meeting.'

'*His* meeting?'

'Yes, *his* meeting. Thomas called that meeting. Like me, he's a humble social worker, in case you hadn't noticed. So – where was I? Yes, Jojo's out the way. Now he's got his dream girl all to himself, he can move in for the kill. Except it doesn't quite add up, does it? I mean it was *you*, not Thomas Springer, who started talking to him on the balcony. It was *you*, not Thomas Springer, who suggested a ride back to town. And it was *you*, not Thomas Springer, who asked for a hand with your removal.'

Ruth raised a hand and stopped the rocking bird cage. 'I was on the balcony before he was, Jojo, and, in answer to those last two points, he's a man with a van. He happened to be around. I needed his help. How do you know all this stuff, anyway?'

'How d'you think? Thomas told me. He's a nice guy. He's gentle. He's generous. He's not very well – you see – and he's just a little bit shy with women. And he got confused by your attentions.'

'*My* attentions?' gasped Ruth. 'He gave me a fish. He bought me flowers.'

'He gives those stupid eels to everyone. As for the flowers, he bought them for the old lady and left them in the hall. I should know. He took me out in a wheelchair and I helped choose them. The poor guy's a bit of a loner. He's so unsure of himself he doesn't even know how to choose flowers.' Jojo pushed the low table over and shunted herself into a semi-standing position, propped awkwardly against the edge of the bed. 'Come on, Ruth – be honest with yourself for once in your life. You were after him from the start. The moment I mentioned him to you, the moment you knew I was interested in him, you couldn't help yourself. That always was the trouble with you. You think your bum's vanilla ice cream and the whole damn world wants a bite.'

Ruth's anger had gone. The territory was so strange that nothing but extra-planetary serenity could help her over it. She levelled her tone. 'When I met him, I never even knew he was the guy you were going on about. You didn't give me much of a spec sheet, remember? I only cottoned on when he saw me off at the boat. That's God's honest truth. And, OK, I quite liked him to begin with, but – no disrespect to your rave party, or Thomas Springer – I wasn't exactly spoilt for choice.'

Jojo pulled a face.

'Let me make myself very clear, once again for emphasis,' Ruth said firmly. 'I never had designs on Thomas Springer. I'll tell you that for nothing.'

'That's probably what it's worth.'

'Nor do I think Thomas was ever smitten. Not with me, at any rate. To be frank, I've got one of those subtle feminine intuitions he hates my guts.'

'Why should he?' A flicker of improvement in Jojo's attention.

'I took over from him with the old lady. He's jealous. As he sees things, I snatched his sceptre, I seized his crown.'

Jojo snorted mirthlessly, then wiped her mouth on the back of her hand. She glared at Ruth, trying to get to the bottom of things. 'You're quite a one for the theories, aren't you? What's so special about the old lady? Does she come with gift vouchers?'

'You tell me something. Who exactly is this guy Cameron?'

'What do you know about Cameron?'

'He was at the party. Thomas couldn't shake him off.'

Her words struck home. Jojo's face clouded, her tone changed.

'Cameron's a fat mouth. He ploughed his every last cent into some disbanded grain silo on Java Island. The city's hottest night spot – that was the big idea. Just waiting for them to build that bridge out to the eastern docks. Trouble is, bridge building's slow and Cameron's strapped for cash. He's a man in a hurry.'

'I knew that, or most of it. Where does Thomas fit in?'

'He wants Thomas as his partner. Time and energy now. Cash later.'

'Thomas is a humble social worker. You said so yourself.'

'I know. Thomas knows. But Cameron can't seem to get that into his dumb head. He says Thomas has potential. He says Thomas is his hope chest.'

'Oh well.' Ruth shrugged. 'Money isn't everything, as I keep proving to myself. We may be talking natural human resources here. Plus, Thomas has a great address book. A clientele of octogenarians, but let's be positive. It's an untapped niche market. What kind of club did he have in mind anyway, a slipped disco?'

Jojo baulked at the sarcasm. 'This is all to do with that painting, isn't it?' There was a fretful softening in her eyes. 'Are you going to tell me what's going on?'

'I doubt it.'

Ruth offered her hands. Jojo took them and held them for a minute in silence. An air of nostalgia, of blocked compassion, settled between them.

'A cup of tea, perhaps?'

Ruth shook her head.

Jojo squeezed her hands, half-smiled, half-frowned, as if it were all a bit of a conundrum. Her voice grounded to a confidential undertone. 'You've changed. Your hair. *You*. I don't know you any more.'

'Last time we met, the general conclusion seemed to be that I *never* changed. That was the problem.'

'So you've made new friends?'

'Oh yeah, my brand new A-list social life. And you? Are you and Thomas seeing each other?'

Jojo nodded. 'Off and on. You're barking up the wrong tree. If Thomas held a grudge, I'd have heard about it soon enough.'

'I'm barking up a forest of trees. There's bound to be a grouchy pussycat stuck up one of them. All the better if it isn't him.'

She freed her hands and let them drop lifelessly on her knees. They tingled. It was either pins and needles or radiation sickness. She tried to picture Lydia's face when she woke up to find the painting next to her.

At least she'd got that right.

System override. Bring a little cheer into an elderly person's life, though the whole world and its dog see things otherwise.

'You're scared,' said Jojo. 'What kind of trouble have you got yourself into now?'

Ruth didn't answer.

A freak fanfare of sunlight broke cover and lit up the brass heads of the drawing pins in the wall. The bright points hurt her eyes. For a minute or two there was nothing but the sound of their breathing and the hum of a lift somewhere in the building. In the end she raised her shoulders a fraction and let them drop.

'I didn't go looking for this,' she said. 'It found me. A guy called Johannes van der Heyden did something a little unusual about a quarter of a millennium ago, and now it's all coming to a head. You know why I became an art historian, Jojo? Because I wanted to be bored shitless. There's nothing I like more than nothing. And the past seemed to be a safe place because it's not going to happen again. But life wouldn't let me get away with it. The past does go on happening whether you like it or not. Now I feel like a plate-glass window is going to walk into me any minute.'

'Or you into it.'

'Thanks. You should go into business. *Hairs split, while you wait.*' Her gaze fell on the symbol for the philosopher's stone on Jojo's plaster cast. '*That's* what this is all about,' she said. 'Someone spray-painted it onto my boat. Thomas copied it onto your leg – innocently, or so he says. And it's scratched onto the back of the little painting. It's an eye, following me around.'

Half an hour passed.

The mother brought tea and cakes.

Ruth told Jojo everything. She hadn't intended to, but she did. The truth was reckless. It wouldn't go on hiding behind silences and evasions. It wanted to be out in the open. It wanted to be laid on the line. If Jojo reported back to the Kid, so be it. She wasn't some Deep Thought supercomputer. She couldn't think all of the consequences through.

What she could do was relax, open up, let the strange river follow its course and take her with it, wherever it might lead.

Outside, the light began to fail.

They switched on a bedside lamp and talked in its aura, holding their mugs even when they were empty.

Ruth remembered Lucas. He'd still be waiting in the take-away kebab grill. She made her excuses. Jojo caught her by the arm. 'I can't believe you stole that picture.'

'Neither can I.' She roused herself and smiled.

Outside night was falling, and a light snow with it.

A wind chime tinkled as she entered the neon brightness of the kebab grill.

Lucas looked up. 'Well?' he said.

'Peace and love, sort of.' She made the appropriate gesture.

He slapped his paperback book shut and grinned broadly.

A great relief washed over him as they walked back to the car. She felt it too. One bridge mended. One friendship pulled back from the brink. Not much on the global balance sheet of profit and loss, but it was vital all the same. It mattered deeply, more deeply than she would have thought.

And Jojo's complicity – if that's what it was – magically redeemed her own self-esteem.

Lucas aimed his key ring. The central locking clunked open. She got in first.

She dropped his ID card discreetly onto the floor by the clutch pedal.

He spotted it on opening the driver's door, tutted reproach at himself for his carelessness and put it back into his wallet.

They drove in silence once again, but not the silence of deadlocked resistance. It was a new silence that flowed freely between them. It was a silence that cradled and soothed.

He put on the heating.

She adjusted the vents.

The snow swarmed down madly in the cones of light from the headlamps as the car picked up speed and the wipers batted faster.

She closed her eyes and yielded to the sure forward motion.

She was a passenger. She was letting life take her places. Maybe it was foolish, maybe it was smart. She couldn't tell. But it was easy, this surrender, as easy as falling asleep. Because to flow you had to let go of things. You had to release your anxious grip on false reassurances.

You had to cast yourself adrift, with no regrets, on the swift black torrent of the night.

Thirty-three

Ruth let herself in and padded halfway down the hall.

Lydia's door was ajar.

She was not in bed. The TV was on a dead channel where the static sparked and fizzled like monsoon rain. The tray of food she'd left was untouched apart from one slice of bread which had been reduced to a crust.

Lydia was sitting asleep on the sofa in her nightgown, the remote control wedged under one thigh. Her head hung limp. Her breathing was uneven and throaty.

There was no point carrying her back to bed. It would only wake her.

Ruth switched off the television and pivoted Lydia round into a lying position. She tucked a cushion under her head, wiped the corner of her mouth with a tissue and covered her with a blanket.

The fire in the hearth was out, but she switched on the mobile convection heater.

And the painting?

It was still on the chair where she'd stood it earlier, now turned to face the wall. An old cardigan was draped over the back rest, one sleeve flopping across the rear of the copper support with its arcane symbols and numerical codes.

Nearby was the big chocolate box that Ruth had used to store Johannes's letters. It was open and Lydia's reading glasses lay in the upturned top. Evidently she'd been poring over the family archives.

Ruth closed the box and gazed thoughtfully at the slumbering woman.

Whatever had been going through Lydia's mind, Ruth would have to find out tomorrow.

The next morning the city awoke to a freezing fog. It hunkered down in a smothering mass, the bluish tint of cigar smoke. It erased the sky and the upper storeys of the taller buildings in town.

Ruth went out for some bread and milk.

In the street people bustled along with shoulders hunched and scarves coiled round their noses and mouths.

The lamps stayed on. Their light was mushy. The air had curdled and trapped the yellow radiance in a clammy, gelatinous mass.

Sounds – the warning bell of a tram, the bark of a dog – loomed up like ghosts with a life of their own and veered away or snuffed out just as abruptly.

The familiar signals were not linking up in the usual ways.

Time itself had been tamped down into a thicker, viscous medium. Seconds faltered, minutes slackened, hours groped blindly along.

The doctor called just as Ruth had made Lydia's breakfast tray. He took it from her and shut the living-room door behind him.

Back in the *achterhuis* Ruth drank her coffee, then plunged her hands into her pockets and looked out of the window.

The fog clung to the ivy on the wall of the little garden. It snaked round the tangled tendrils, licking the dark, wet leaves. The whine of a vacuum cleaner reached her ears from next door. She twiddled the dial on the radio. A voice sang 'In questa tomba oscura'. Another twiddle, and a programme about dwindling owl populations. She left it on, listening to the talk of endangered species.

When it was over, she mentally checked off the things she should do: catch up on email; see Myles so he didn't feel left out; maybe contact the Kid; reclaim her watch and her mobile; get the low-down from Driest on her boat; sort out pending insurance matters; get a job (or get back her old one); get a life . . .

Instead, she took a shower, clipped and filed her toe-nails, lit a patchouli joss stick and made another pot of coffee.

Then she sat at Sander's desk and blew into her conched hands, trying to reproduce the owl calls she'd heard on the radio: the tawny owl, the barn owl, the screech owl . . .

The day was losing its edge.

Stacked beside her were the books she'd borrowed from Mr Moon. In the chaos of her life, she'd forgotten to return them. She opened one and casually turned the pages. Alchemical horoscopes, old diagrams – distillation, evaporation, calcination – the gold chain of the elements, bizarre and lustrous illuminations from bygone times and tomes, the oracular utterances of the old occultists: *All are united into one, which is divided into two parts; the Rebis, or Hermaphrodite; Smoke loves smoke; The wind carries it in its belly; The boy becomes leprous and unclean, because of the womb's corruption; Conjunge fratrem cum sorore & propina illis poculum amoris; I beget the light, but darkness too is of my nature.*

She closed the book and ran the tip of her finger down the ridge of its spine.

That last phrase was familiar.

Her mystery penpal had used it in one of his messages. We must read the same books, she thought. Soulmates and other selves – two minds with but a single thought.

Her alter ego had gone surprisingly quiet of late. She almost missed his sinister attentions . . .

The doctor must have left.

She strolled back to the living room.

Lydia had not got up.

On seeing Ruth, she smiled faintly but said nothing. Ruth returned the low-wattage acknowledgement. She took the cardigan off the chair and turned the painting round to face them, then sat on the edge of the bed. Principessa rose to greet her, arching her back and stretching her legs. She tickled the kitten under the chin.

'All right?'

Lydia nodded.

'Mission accomplished.' Ruth indicated the picture. 'The frame's gone missing. I'll get a new one, then we'll pop it up over the fireplace, just like in the good old days.'

Lydia put on her heavy Bakelite glasses and scrutinized the compartmentalized pillbox. 'Be a dear and tell me. Have I taken the red ones?'

'Yes – all gone. Just two green sweeties left for after dinner.'

'Sweeties? You're making fun of me! When I see all these pills, I feel a terrible old hypochondriac.'

'Even hypochondriacs get ill.'

'It's peculiar, but I don't think of myself as being ill. I'm just old and heading for the bone yard.'

Ruth patted her on the knee. 'Could we have a close-up on the glistening tear that's tumbling down my cheek, please, Mr Selznick?'

'You're making fun again, my dear. It's no joke, I'm telling you. Everyone wants to live a long time, but no one wants to get old. That's the long and the short of it.'

'You should be glad.'

'Why?'

'You're not young and vulnerable any more.'

Ruth lost interest in this much-travelled avenue of conversation. She coiled a lock of her hair around her finger, then gave up on it and bit her thumbnail.

She stared blankly at the painting.

'Why *do* you do that?' said Lydia.

Ruth pondered her gnawed thumbnail. 'God knows. I don't pretend to understand the brain pathways of addiction. Maybe I haven't got enough to do. Maybe I'm just soul-searching.'

'About what?'

Ruth bit her lip, then overcame her reluctance to speak. 'Ever since I met you the weirdest things have been happening.'

'Oh?'

'I've always believed in judging things by their appearances. Now I'm beginning to wonder. I'm beginning to think that some key issues are clouded with facts.'

'What on earth are you talking about?'

Ruth frowned, picked up an old lottery coupon and tore it carefully into strips. 'I'm talking about you. I'm talking about me. And I'm talking about that painting. I no longer understand what's going on. Anyone would have thought your life depended on it. I bust a gut to get it. Then, once you've got it – not a peep.'

'You mustn't think I'm ungrateful . . .'

'Then what *must* I think, exactly?'

'It's the letters, my dear, the letters. I read them all. That poor man and all he went through. He was disappointed in love. I wonder what became of him.'

'Given that you're his descendant, I imagine he finally succeeded in getting some tail.'

'Some *tail*?' said Lydia, frowning. 'Sometimes I despair of ever understanding you. What has tail got to do with it?'

'Playing mummies and daddies, Lydia. Johannes was quite an inventor, but I presume he stopped short of inventing human cloning. Anyway, by the sound of things, he was a regular warm-blooded male.'

'I feel sorry for him, really I do. Nothing has ever been easy for us van der Heydens. It's a curse. We are fish in troubled waters.'

Ruth shuffled the strips of lottery coupon together and tore them off into little tabs. 'I suppose you're thinking of Sander again, that other pea in your pod.'

The old woman's face lit up. 'Oh, I didn't tell you, my dear. I saw him! I saw him yesterday. I told you he came to visit me!'

Ruth let go of her home-made confetti and it fluttered to the floor. 'What you saw was *me*. I'm sorry to disappoint you. It was a bit nippy outside so I borrowed some of your brother's winter clothing from the wardrobe. I hope you don't mind. And I'm sorry if I gave you a surprise. It was thoughtless of me. However, I fail to see how you square the known fact of his death with a cheery belief that he's pottering around this bloody house. I don't want to be pedantic, but your powers of reasoning seem somewhat flawed.'

Lydia flushed. 'There's nothing wrong with me, young lady! You have a very free and easy way of talking to me. I am beginning to regret feeling sorry for you and taking you into my home.'

'Feeling *sorry* for me?' Ruth exclaimed. 'I thought—'

'Yes? What exactly did you think?'

'Nothing. But I'll tell you what I think now. I think we deserve each other, really we do.'

'Did you feed the cat?'

'Stop changing the subject.'

'I presume you consider that you are the only one who decides what the subject should be?' said Lydia haughtily.

'Right this moment, yes – just for a change. I'm tired of beating around the bush. I'd like a few straight answers, if it's not too much trouble. Like did a black gentleman by the name of Cameron ever call on you with Thomas?'

'A black gentleman?'

'Don't tell me – you've forgotten. Or you never get any visitors. Those are the usual excuses. Which is it to be?'

'I do remember the person in question, as it happens. I was

not favourably impressed by his manners. He drank half a bottle of my gin.'

'Was I mentioned at all in the conversation?'

Lydia snorted. 'I can hardly be expected to remember what was certainly nothing but small talk. We *may* have spoken of you or we may not.'

'Very helpful, I must say. Let's try another one. Do you remember why Mr Blommendaal called?'

The old woman shut her eyes tightly, deliberately blocking Ruth out.

'You see, I *know*,' Ruth continued, her manner softening. 'I *know* about your will.' She took hold of one of Lydia's hands, but the old lady wrenched it away. 'And I know your intentions were kind. It's just that the whole situation has got out of hand. Did you tell either Thomas or his friend that you meant to change your will?'

Lydia shook her head mournfully and opened her eyes. She spoke in a small, miserable voice. 'You rummaged in my things. You abused my hospitality.'

'I admit I rummaged. If I hadn't, we'd have never found the letters. But I also rummaged because you're far too cagey. You want me as your confidante, but you feed me a diet of half-truths, delusions and lies.'

'I have given you everything.'

'I know that too.' Ruth sighed and buried her head in her hands. She didn't know what to say.

The old lady looked worried. 'Is Scheele still bothering you? Is that it?'

'Scheele's old, decrepit and completely daft, not unlike you. Whoever's bothering me, it isn't Scheele.'

'Of course it is,' said Lydia with newfound stridency. 'I've been telling you that all along.'

'The rival claim is his, but there are other interested parties out there. I assume, if you read the letters, you know why.'

'The painting,' said Lydia flatly.

'The painting – yes. But what about it?'

'It's a new process, of sorts.'

'It's a goddamn *photograph*, Lydia,' said Ruth, losing her patience. 'Probably the first photograph in the history of human-kind. That means *mucho dinero*. In your terms, a colonial mansion in downtown Pittsburgh and neat gin a-go-go straight from the gold-plated kitchen tap.'

'I don't want the picture. It's yours.'

'Oh? May I ask why?'

'I don't like it.' The old lady was adamant. 'I thought I did, but I don't.'

They both turned to face the painting.

There was Johannes, still looking out of his window.

He wasn't gathering dust in a museum now. He wasn't even in a department of chemical engineering. He'd come home. Back to the Keizersgracht, back to the apothecary, back to his lumber-place, back to square one. Johannes the misery guts, upstaged and down with the vapours, still wondering why the whole world had let him down. No wonder Esther had done it. At least Giacomo got on with things. He didn't spend his life bitching and belly-aching. Granted, he was a lowlife – a horse's arse, if ever there was one – but there was something refreshing about his ruthless pragmatism.

Ruth had to agree with Lydia.

It was a bilious little painting – or photograph – or whatever it was. For all its expert draughtsmanship, for all the pretty mimosa, for all of Esther's beauty – frankly, she didn't like it either . . .

'Well, that makes two of us,' she conceded with a sigh.

'Then why did you steal it?' the old woman flashed back.

'I beg your pardon?'

'Don't tell me you didn't. I know you did. There was no review. There was no conclusion. And Scheele's claim still stands. You took that painting. You helped yourself to it without a word to me. And you have the gall to talk about half-truths, lies and delusions! I may have made you the beneficiary of my will – for which I *apologize*, my dear – but *you* have made me an accessory to theft. A policeman could arrest me for receiving stolen goods. Which one of us, I ask you, has been well served by the other?'

'Will you stop getting yourself so worked up?' said Ruth in desperation.

Lydia's jowls were trembling with rage.

In her state, anything could happen.

Another attack, and that would be the death of her. Not theft, but a murder rap – that's where this was leading.

'OK, I confess,' said Ruth. 'I helped myself to the painting. And do you know why? Because there comes a time when, if you want something done, you've damn well got to do it yourself. From the moment I met you, that painting – or the idea of the painting – has been centre-stage. It's what brought us together and now it's the thing that's dividing us. You wanted it desperately – for sentimental reasons, or so you led me to believe. We then discover that others want it too – for unsentimental reasons, shall we say. It's true, I pre-empted the result of the bureau's enquiry. They'd have probably found in your favour, but when? In a year – two years – five? Nobody lives forever, Lydia. Posthumous satisfaction, I think you'd agree, is no satisfaction at all. So, yes, I stole the painting. And now I find you don't want it. It's not the money – oh no! You simply don't like the picture. OK – fair enough. But, for Christ's sake, you could have told me earlier! You've been shagging around on this issue since day one . . .'

'Don't get snippy with me! If I came to dislike the painting, it was because of you.'

'Because of *me*?'

'You found the letters, didn't you? That's what did it – the letters changed the context. We had always assumed, in the family, that the young lady in the painting was our ancestor. It is now clear that not only is she not related to the van der Heydens, but that she is guilty of a gross betrayal. Despite herself, she made a misery of Johannes' life, and this peculiar art work bears witness to her ugly deed. I do not see how I can be expected to tolerate it. The blasted object is a plague upon us!'

'Look at it this way. If she hadn't snubbed Johannes, you probably wouldn't exist. And anyway, Sander had read those letters. He must have known. It didn't stop him wanting to get the painting back.'

'I am not my brother's keeper.'

'I thought that was precisely what you were.'

The words tripped off Ruth's tongue before she could stop them.

Something changed.

Lydia had turned to stone. A cold fury radiated from her eyes. 'Get out!' she hissed. 'And take that painting with you!'

For a fraction of a second, Ruth hesitated.

Was this some kind of joke? Was Lydia hamming it up? Then anger rose in her too. It was no joke. Far from it. Between them they had pushed things to the limit. And she, too, had had enough. From the outset Lydia had used her. Ruth wondered, even, if their second meeting had been set up. But to achieve what? Not the painting. Lydia didn't want it. She was a ridiculous mess of contradictions. Her wires were crossed; she was shorting on all circuits.

Part of Ruth wanted to stay. It was not compassion, it was necessity. At a certain level Lydia had become her responsibility. She was Lydia's mother, her sister, her child. But now a point of honour hung in the balance. She felt stifled, frustrated, vexed.

She stood up stiffly and took the painting under her arm.

'Is this what you really want?'

'Yes,' said the old woman firmly. 'It's what I really want. *Really*. Just take your things and go.'

Thirty-four

The fog was denser still along the Keizersgracht.

Ruth fastened the top toggle on her duffel coat and pulled up the hood.

She had spoken in haste, but she'd spoken in truth, and some vital pipeline of sympathy between her and Lydia had snapped. There was no going back – except, eventually, for her things. In the meantime, she only had one possession in the world. It was the last thing she'd ever wanted to have. The painting was in its bag. She gripped it to her side.

Her eyes watered in the cold. The blood beat in her brain.

It had all been so sudden, yet the road to the break-up had been anything but. The abscess had been growing for days. A few words had sufficed to lance it. There was still something like regret. Her thoughts were fouled by anger and annoyance. The simple fact of knowing this, and being impotent before the fact, made things infinitely worse.

The Vijzelgracht passed away behind her and she came out onto Muntplein.

She slipped on the kerb and crouched to rub her calf. The muscle had knotted and sang out in pain. She looked up from her cramped position. The old Munt tower had lost its steeple to the fog. Trams trundled out of the gloom and bicycle bells rang out at each near miss. She started walking again – briskly, to shake off the muscular torque.

Her habits led her to Dam Square. She headed up the Rokin,

but, on impulse, renounced instinct and took a bridge cutting north-east towards the Nieuwmarkt.

She was in the *wallen*, with its sex shops and erotic theatres. Despite its seediness, the place was oddly comforting – *la zona rosa* – a pink emporium to human desire. A whore in a Dolly Parton wig and frilly negligee sat cross-legged in the flamingo glow of her shop window, smiling as if she meant it at the dark shadows that peered in. A Salvation Army band struck up at a street corner, a trumpet croaking its mournful refrain. A policeman stopped to chat with a street vendor selling clockwork begging dogs with waggly tails.

The soft lamps and beer taps of the bars beckoned her, but she too was wound up like clockwork, a fidgety tension that no amount of sitting down and mellowing out could diffuse. She needed to walk it off, to burn it away. And in the back of her mind there was the *Speculant*, her boat. It seemed an eternity since she'd seen it.

She wanted it back.

It was her rusty cocoon. It was her skin, her carapace. Without it she was a tortoise without a shell.

What craziness had got her involved with Lydia, anyway? She didn't know. It was always the same. She'd leave the boat to make contact with the outside world, then the contact palled and soured, and she'd need it again.

Now she needed it more than ever.

She needed it as if her life depended on it.

The canals broadened and a chill sea air stabbed through the fog and surprised her lungs.

She was on Prins Hendrikkade, opposite Centraal Station.

She crossed the bridge to Stationsplein.

A girl backpacker bumped into her and gabbled something unsavoury in an Eastern European tongue.

A busker hopped from foot to foot and strummed madly at his guitar, more for the warmth he generated than the musical effect.

She was at a loss as to what to do.

But in the back of her mind a plan, or at least a direction, had been taking shape out of her wanderings.

A tram heading east stopped across the road. The doors banged open. She dodged through the traffic, limping slightly, and hopped on. It was not a route she was familiar with, but it was pointing the right way. She fumbled in her purse for a card and found it. The address was out of town, and she still hadn't got a plan, but it was too late to do anything about that.

One way or another, she'd find her boat.

One way or another, she'd follow her nose.

The vibration lulled her into numbness. She let her body go limp and sway with the tram's motions as it trundled alongside the Oosterdok. Then, sooner than she'd expected, it clanged to a stop and the doors opened. The driver killed the motor and announced the terminus.

They were just off Piet Henkade.

She descended with the last few passengers and continued east along the IJ Haven.

Metallic spars and structures loomed out of the air – derricks, conveyor pipes, elevated jetties, booms and marker lamps. They were made of the same dream stuff as the fog itself, standing out like embossed hieroglyphs on a grey card background. She heard the clamour of a big dog yelping and straining at a choker chain behind a warehouse door as she passed.

The rare phantom vessels that passed sounded their fog-horns, each one a sacred 'Om'.

There were residential streets to her right, a cold sweat of damp on their walls and cobbles, but nobody was about. These odd thoroughfares stopped abruptly at the water's edge, where the masts of moored sailing ships bristled at jumbled angles and made eerie clicking and whirring noises. The fog denatured them further. It was poison gas. All the inhabitants were done for, quietly expiring behind dull sash windows and dripping gutters and downpipes in a latter-day Pompeii.

The Ersthaven, then a bridge over the Amsterdam-Rijn Kanaal, and she was heading out to Zeeburg and the IJmeer.

There were busy roads nearby – she could hear the cautious growl of traffic.

She stuck, wherever possible, to the dockside.

The temperature dropped the further she strayed from the city.

This marginal place belonged to the stevedores and merchant seamen. When the weather broke, they slouched off the freighters and tankers and container ships, into the flophouses or hot little corner bars that cropped up now and then, with banknotes from around the world tacked to their ceilings and coins superglued to the floor, glowing electric clocks in the shape of beer glasses, jukeboxes, satellite TVs on wall brackets and bar football. Frankly, she felt safer on the streets. The bars were boozy little global villages of nomadic men, killing time and brain cells in the accepted matelot ways.

But what was she doing except just that?

Together, the cold and the fog had seized everything up, suspended it all in a buffer zone between day and night, wakefulness and sleep, life and death.

By degrees the waters debouched into the Markermeer, and then – somewhere out there, through all the cotton wool – into the open sea. The fog had turned to a fine frosty mizzle, wavering between rain or snow, pinpricks on her skin. She wiped her face on the back of her sleeve. Ice-cold drips collected on her nose and chin and found secret routes under the ramparts of clothing.

She was getting wetter and wetter.

And the damp aggravated the pain in her calf, which was not, as she'd hoped, showing any intention of going away. In spite of gloves, her fingers had frozen stiff, curled round the lower edge of the painting in its plastic bag. When she tried to wiggle them, they were reluctant to respond.

Another bridge.

Below, a freight train shunted through a broad tangle of rails and points. On the far side the pavement stopped and an alley between high wire fences took her out onto a broad wharf of container parks, prefab warehousing, machinery stores, maritime offices and processing plants. The wind was arctic. Occasionally it blew clearings in the fog and the orange and red lights of an oil-storage depot glimmered across the waters.

The sign above a chandler's announced its address. She checked against the card in her pocket. It was somewhere round here, though there were no numbers to go by.

Then, out of the clouds of greyness, a star appeared beyond the edge of the quay. It was ox-blood red.

A six-pointed star in the centre of which was a circle and, within that, a smaller circle.

The star was on the galley hatch.

She had found her *Speculant*.

The boat's emergency mooring was hard against the wharf. There was no gangplank, but a jetty, and she simply straddled the narrow gap.

On-board, she tried the door. Locked – and she didn't have the keys. But if the boat was here, the dry dock and repair shop couldn't be far afield.

She disembarked and continued walking.

A square of broken concrete wasteland that served as a car park and Portakabin dump, and there it was: 'Driest Topside Marine Construction, Repairs and Outfitting'. Below the main sign, another: 'We build and repair crabbers, offshore supply vessels, push-boats, factory trawlers, river-boats, passenger vessels, tugboats.'

It was a huge, shabby hangar with an apartment stuck on top like a cabin, complete with a little roof garden. From inside the hangar came the sound of music. She stopped in her tracks, thinned her breathing and concentrated.

She knew that tune.

'The Mooche' – Baby Cox, with Duke Ellington. It was pure

sleaze, but she loved it. What's more, it was her goddamn record – a little scratch ticking by exactly where she was expecting it.

Her hackles rose . . .

She hauled open the big sliding corrugated door and went in.

More gloom, with shadowy maritime clutter hulking out of it. The upturned fibreglass shell of a small sailing dinghy. Nets and flotation gear from a fishing smack. A giant propeller tilted on its side. Some chrome guard rails, fresh out of their packaging, waiting to be fitted to a ritzy motor launch or cabin cruiser.

The jazz came from the back, where a single light bulb burned under a bare-board mezzanine and some steps leading up to the rooftop living quarters. She stepped over a pile of life jackets and headed for it.

The spit and crackle of welding equipment accompanied a fountain of dazzling sparks. A man was working on a large brown rudder that lay across wooden trestles. He was wearing headgear. She couldn't see his face, but it had to be Driest. She figured that from the music.

The Ellington number issued from an old wind-up gramophone with a black-and-gold ribbed flower horn. Baby Cox did her scat singing, the brass belted out the melody, then the number shut off steam with a brisk, businesslike finale – suggesting the musicians were eager to get to the bar.

Ruth put down the picture, ran a finger along the dusty edge of the gramophone's quarter-sawed oak cabinet, then lifted the heavy pick-up off the record and placed it with care on its cradle.

Driest stopped welding and raised the face shield.

'A Victor the Third,' she said.

He removed the headgear and switched off the welder. 'Double spring motor,' he replied, wiping his hands on a rag. '1919. It's my pride and joy. Sorry about the Ellington. I couldn't resist. The rest of the collection's back on your boat.'

He drew up camping chairs and invited her to sit down.

'You look hungry,' he said. 'I haven't got much.' He disappeared for a few minutes and came back with sardines on toast. They drank hot silty coffee, followed by schnapps, and talked.

Her boat had been dry-docked, the hull double-plated in parts. One last repair and she was done. Driest had dried her out with portable oil stoves and put everything back in place. 'Home sweet home,' he said, grinning broadly.

She'd forgotten this man.

He'd been there the day she'd come back from her parents, the day the *Speculant* had nearly gone down. They'd talked, but perfunctory stuff – to do with the accident, or sabotage. He'd been a reassuring presence, making light of things. He'd helped her tamp down her emotion and get things into proportion. Now here he was again, in a grubby blue boiler suit with silver zippers, black sheepdog hair peppered with grey and straight dark eyebrows, unshaved and pointing that grin at her. He had an offhand way of waving one hand around while he was talking, as if it was a fan or a little windmill.

And, for Christ's sakes, the man was wearing clogs.

Where did he think he was – *Holland*? She felt like passing comment, but discretion was the better part of valour, or so proverbial wisdom had it. Something about him got her talking all the same, a tranquil, unhurried thing – sunny and unemphatic, with no particular axe to grind – that set her mind at rest and even, dare she say it, brought out her better side from whatever grubby little grot hole it had been hiding in.

Was it his voice, those eyes, or what?

Was it the grin or the clogs?

Some undeniable atavism in her blood seemed to warm to him.

And here she was, talking about herself again.

Me, me, me . . .

The more she talked, the more her self-editing tripped on

contradictions, the more she cornered herself into divulging the truth.

She showed Driest the painting, leaned it against one of the legs of the wooden trestle. She didn't tell him it was the world's first photograph; she didn't say she'd stolen it. The guy was a total stranger. There was no real basis for trust, other than her increasingly acute sense that the withdrawal of trust was a damn sight worse than the risks in trusting – a bleak prospect, imprisoning her in a dumb bubble of secrecy. And, as these two impulses wrestled it out within her, she grew pale and edgy. The old anxieties returned. She bit her nails.

Eventually he asked her if anything was the matter.

She looked at him, as if – then shook her head.

'Try again,' he said.

'It's that painting,' she admitted. 'You're going to think I'm crazy, but there's a possibility it's radioactive.'

He leaned forward on his knees and stared at her. She counted the seconds. He didn't blink.

'Don't ask me why or how,' she broke back in a quick nervous patter. 'It just is. Or might be. And I've been carrying it around with me, on and off, for the past twenty-four hours. I feel weird – off-colour – but I don't know if it's that. I don't know what's real and what I'm imagining. I can't tell the difference any more.'

'The difference between what and what?'

'Anything. Just anything. The mind plays tricks. Doesn't yours?'

'Irradiated in a laboratory?' he said after a while.

She nodded.

'Silly question – couldn't you ask the laboratory?'

She shook her head.

'What kind of radiation? Do you know?'

'Neutron. Californium-252.'

He stood up and went to the back of the workshop, returning with what looked like a large telephone. For a moment she thought he was going to call the cops or even the nut house, but it wasn't a phone. What she'd taken for the receiver was a heavy-duty handle on one side of the box, just below a digital readout.

'Portable radiation sniffer,' he explained. 'Internal PVT plastic scintillation detector. Picks up gamma and beta radiation, but also neutron. Actually, this is the display unit. I'll get the rest.'

He put it down and fetched some more equipment, then cabled the display up to a detector on the end of a telescopic pole and fiddled with the settings on the readout.

'Pinch me – I'm dreaming,' said Ruth. 'How the hell did you happen to have a radiation detector just lying around?'

He chuckled – more of a grunt. 'It's standard gear in the scrap-metal industry. We use it all the time to check out shipping. You wouldn't believe it, but there are radioactive materials just about everywhere – not just nuclear submarines. Take your boat.'

'My boat's radioactive?'

'No – but you've probably got a Teflon pan. They use radioactivity to get the Teflon to stick to the pan. That's just an example. Then virtually all the fruit and vegetables in your fridge have been irradiated.'

'Stop!'

He swept the surface and back of the painting carefully with the detection unit, like a witch doctor casting a spell. The machine emitted a regular audio beep. When he'd finished, he sat back, kneeling on the floor.

'All clear. No increase in frequency means no hot spots. Just as well, eh? Nice of you to bring suspected hazardous materials into my workshop, though.'

'I was looking for my boat. If I'd had the keys, I wouldn't have bothered you.'

They gathered the painting, the keys and the borrowed records, put on their coats.

On their way out another man came in. Driest introduced his brother. They ran the repairs and outfitting business together.

Driest and Ruth crossed the wharf to the *Speculant*.

Inside, she was just as Ruth had left her, pre-deluge, pre-helping little old ladies across the street. Those were the halcyon days when time obliged by standing still. The electrics worked, wired to a power point on the wharf. The place was warm and cosy and all her possessions were just where they should be. *The Jewish Bride* was back on the wall, along with the photo of her parents. There were no tide marks on the teak panelling. The old velvet curtain was dry and ironed and draped over her chair, the records were shelved and orderly, and the pink leatherette Dansette Popular four-speed with autochanger was still centre-stage.

Tickety-boo . . . a miracle . . .

Truly, this man is the son of God, she thought.

She gave him a quick hug, accompanied by a bashful smile. 'I really can't thank you enough,' she said. 'Things have been rough recently and – well, it's just very sweet of you, that's all.'

'It's my job.'

She flashed him another smile and peered into the brass housing of the porthole. A flimsy web hung down one side, strung to the suspended cut-glass pendant.

'If it's good enough for the orbatid spiders, it's good enough for me.'

A bottle of Bordeaux and a bowl of fruit stood on the table.

'Courtesy of the management.' He bowed like a 1920s' room valet.

She found a corkscrew, opened the bottle and lit a candle, switching of the electric light. Driest put a record on.

'Kick off your spurs,' she said.

He slipped out of his clogs. They sat down, clinked and drank in silence, listening to the chugging rhythms of Lil Armstrong's 'Harlem on Saturday Night'.

And so time wore on . . .

Talk, music, wine, and the dear relief of familiar surroundings in the friendly glamour of candlelight.

She wasn't destitute.

She wasn't radioactive.

She wasn't alone.

The wine, with its redolence of oak casks and bygone summers, took over where the schnapps had left off. It made itself at home in her bloodstream. It raised her spirits to a state of mild euphoria, which felt like wisdom or philosophy, a ripe, good-humoured reach of mind that budded, grew and opened its petals in the provident rays of congenial company.

It had been a damn long time since she'd felt this good.

Even the pain in her calf began to fade. And Driest was her happy partner of the hour in the perpetual cosmic dance.

The singers and jazz men they both knew, whose names they reeled off with feeling: Laurel Watson, Bessie Smith, Valaida Snow, Fats Waller, Eva Taylor, Clarence Williams' Blue Five – and on, and on, and on . . .

'I confess to a weakness for techno and trance too,' he said.

'Have you consulted a specialist?'

'It's a common syndrome in single men. You run smack into your forties, and you realize you're suddenly middle-aged. So you try to buy time by digging the new youth culture.'

'Clutching at straws.'

'Clutching at anything.'

Inwardly she ticked the 'Single' box. Had he been trying to tell her something? She thought twice about it, then screwed up the hypothetical document, unsure whether it was a questionnaire or an application form. What the heck was she doing, anyway? She was too broke to fall in love. She didn't even live in the hope of falling in love. Hope drives people crazy. What she needed was a good booster jab of melancholy and despair. The usual, in other words.

'The beauty of being an old jazz fan – I mean, a fan of *old jazz*,' said Ruth dreamily, 'is that it doesn't date you. It's pre-natal nostalgia. It comes back in cycles, but nobody can quite tell which wave of revival you're on.'

'Tell me about you,' he said after a while.

'I already have.'

'Tell me more. I'm asking out of idle curiosity.'

'Can't you wait a couple of months for the official biography to be published?'

He poured them both another glass of wine.

'I'm fond of children and animals,' she allowed. '*Some* children and *some* animals, I should say. I draw the line at most grown-ups. I can be smart when it's important. Otherwise, I'm a girl with the wonder gone out of her eyes.'

He made a sad-clown face.

'Actually,' she corrected, 'I'm a bitch and a scumbag, if I have to be honest – and probably too old to change.'

'My mother always said, "You're never too old to change." '

'Oh yeah? My mother always said, "If you don't belt up, you'll go to bed without any dinner." '

'Look no further. That's how the bitch was born.'

'I guess you're right. I'm a victim. And I've always been a bit of a rebel. I get up people's noses, then they turn against me. It's really tough. I don't suppose anyone's ever tried to sink your boats.'

Driest laughed and milled his hand again in a way that seemed to do some of the answering for him, fanning away preambles and unnecessary words. 'My brother – the guy you just met – in the bath. I'm talking three and a half decades ago. He scuttled my plastic ducks too. Otherwise I try my best to stay afloat. That's the name of the game. It's the family business.'

'Once a marine, always a marine,' Ruth smiled.

She felt tired all of a sudden.

She sat on the floor and lay back, her hands behind her head. Above her was the skylight. Outside, night was drawing in, not that it made much difference after such a sunless, Stygian day. The fog rolled and billowed overhead and the reflection of the bright little vertical eye of the candle flickered in the glass, as did the painting – with its yellow puffball of mimosa and Esther's satin dress.

A slow blues number invaded her brain like opium and she closed her eyes, but the music drifted off into another annex of consciousness.

Time stopped.

She woke up.

The eye of the candle was dancing and glittering overhead. The music had come to an end. A low electrical hum from the record player's loudspeaker.

Otherwise, silence.

She was still lying on her back.

She raised her head and propped herself up on her elbows. There was Driest. He was not asleep. He was lying on his stomach, his chin resting on his crossed arms. He was watching her in that ruminative way of his. She wondered how he did it without blinking. Movie actors learned the trick for close-up shots. Driest was a natural. But what was going on behind the silent vigil?

She rolled onto her side, resting her cheek in the palm of one hand.

'You were dreaming,' he said. 'I could tell by your eyes. They were closed, but they were jigging around under your eyelids.'

'It was strange. I saw myself, as a kid, standing alone in a playground. Then there was just the shadow of leaves in soft sunlight, moving on the ground. It was kind of beautiful and hypnotic. Dreams! It's this damn weather that brings them on. I've probably caught a chill.'

He moved closer and placed his large hand on her forehead. His fingers half-covered her eyes.

'Have I got a temperature?'

'Sure. Thirty-seven degrees.'

'Wow. With a hand like that, who needs thermometers?'

He smiled. 'I'm rather proud of it.'

He withdrew his hand and rested on his side, mirroring her position, waiting for her next move.

He was not brazen. She sensed a hesitancy in him that was to his honour.

The blood had risen to her cheeks.

She felt the breath from her nose warm in the little hollow above her upper lip. She could smell him too – the odour of his pores, the molecules that his hand had left behind on her brow. He smelled of boats and engines and diesel. The smell of oil, lost worlds, organic fossil remains from millions of years gone by.

She shied away from his gaze, amused and embarrassed at the latency of the situation. It could go either way. It was unique and cliché ridden at the same time – history repeating, another oft-told tale . . .

'You need to believe in yourself,' he said.

'Do I?'

'Yes. We only get one chance.'

'Maybe I've had mine.'

'I don't think you have.'

She flushed again.

She stretched out her arm towards him.

She heard him hold his breath.

He stroked her cheek and she shut her eyes.

He moved closer.

The timbers of the boat groaned softly. The loudspeaker, for some reason, no longer hummed. Blindly she reached out and cupped the back of his head in her hand, letting her fingers tunnel deep into his hair. She pulled him down. His breath was measured and warm. She felt his lips on the lobe of her ear, a hand on her breast.

'We don't even know each other,' she protested gently.

'We could *get* to know each other.'

'Later. Let's save the preliminaries for later.'

His cheek brushed her face. He drew his lips across hers. First the rough, then the smooth . . .

She had come back to the precise point in deep inner space she had visited only yesterday in the radiation unit, the point where everything was still, and past, present and future fused like molten ore. Then it had scared her. Now it held no fear. She could see it in her mind's eye.

X marks the spot.

You are here. Stay here, honey. It's a fine old place. There's no bus out today, but what the hell – there's nowhere else worth going any-way . . .

Two hours ago, there had been no question of this.

Two hours ago was another life.

A foghorn boomed.

Driest had stopped.

She could sense him still, poised above her – his back arched, his chest swelling and contracting. But an infinitesimal change had come to pass in the muscular frequencies of his body. His atoms had suddenly reversed polarity.

She opened her eyes.

The sight of him startled her, a jolt of high-voltage juice.

He was on all-fours, his limbs in a quivering deadlock of rigidity. For an instant, he looked like a grey wolf, head lowered, zeroing in on its prey. There was an intentness about him that had nothing to do with the person who'd been there a few minutes ago.

He was a different animal altogether.

Her heart raced.

With a fidgeting of her feet, she pushed and squirmed herself away from him, jacking her body back into a protective huddle against a shelf. He stared across at her, with the same focused alertness. He brought his finger to his lips. Then, with the same finger, he pointed down.

He was pointing at her full glass of wine.

Was he mad?

She had let things go too far with a total stranger. God alone knew who he was, or what he was capable of. His gestures didn't make sense.

What the fuck was this all about?

She was paralysed with uncertainty. She followed his sight line.

Something was amiss.

Her fear gave way to curiosity. She unlocked, eased up and moved closer.

The wine was swaying hypnotically in the glass.

She peered down at the dark, rocking liquid, then up at Driest.

She looked back at the wine.

The liquid rocked at a steeper angle and the glass tipped. She was just in time to catch it. One drop spilled and ran down the sloping timbered floor.

Again their eyes met.

Why wasn't the loudspeaker humming?

The only sounds came from the vessel itself, but its familiar creaks and groans were now not so familiar. There was a pained edge to them that was anything but comforting. The structure was coming under stress. Invisible forces were quickening all around.

They scrambled to their feet and rushed to the portholes.

Fog, fog, fog . . .

But where was the brick wall of the quayside? It should have been to port. Instead – just haze, just the dim cloud of unknowing.

He tried the switch – no go. The power had been cut . . .

He grabbed her by the hand and wrenched her through the galley and up the stairs.

The deck was wet and slippery. The barge was rolling – now gently, now at a sharper, pitching incline when it met a hollow in the water or nosed diagonally against the grain of the current.

Her foot slipped and she caught her ankle on the edge of the wheelhouse wall. She seized hold of the large hook she used for her clothes line.

The fog was patchy. When the wind parted it, they could get their bearings. The quay was some twenty metres away and the distance was increasing.

She looked round wildly.

Driest was nowhere to be seen. Her heart skipped a beat.

'Oh, my God! Where *are* you?!'

She edged round the boat, clutching at the tarpaulin that had been lashed down over a box of kit to one side of the wheel-house. The canvas was so tough it refused to buckle into hand-sized grips.

With a great groan, the boat rolled to starboard.

Her feet slithered under her. She thrust her fingers into the gaps between the rope that zigzagged tightly through the tar-paulin's eyelets, tearing a fingernail away from the flesh in the process.

She managed to hang on.

When the boat righted itself, she saw the blood but felt no pain.

The waterway was in full spate.

Like it is for a passenger peering through the porthole of a plane as it comes down to land on an overcast day, the one index of their speed was the fog, though it too was moving and she couldn't work out in which direction – with or away. *With* would mean an illusion of slowness; *away*, to the back, would create an illusion of greater speed. But why in hell was she fretting over schoolboy physics' problems?

A slide rule wouldn't save her.

'Driest!' she screamed. 'Oh, Jesus – where *are* you?'

A repeated banging, then he appeared from behind the wheel-house. 'The keys!' he shouted. 'Give me the keys!'

'I haven't got them. You have.'

'I gave you the galley key. The others weren't with it.'

'Then we'll have to fucking find them, won't we?' Suddenly she hated him. 'Did *you* moor this boat?' she shouted.

'Fore and aft. We have proper capstans. It was tied fast.'

'Not fast enough. Listen – if you kick the door in, you can steer her. At least we'll get out of this torrent.'

Another lurch, and he crouched down for a lower centre of gravity.

'No we can't,' he said, his face up against hers.

She stared in furious incomprehension at him.

'The rudder I was repairing in my workshop,' he hissed, 'it was yours.'

'*Mine?*'

He let the knowledge sink in.

'But my rudder wasn't broken.'

'*We* broke it getting to the yard. We strayed into shallows, it grounded for a few seconds, then we floated off on a swell. That was enough. The rudder was buggered.'

'So why didn't you fix it?'

'Normally, we'd have refitted in the dry dock, but we were behind schedule. There was another boat coming in. I had this tub towed to the mooring. I was going to fit the rudder tomorrow.'

She grabbed him by the sleeve. 'I don't believe this. We've got no rudder?'

He stared at her in dumb silence.

No rudder . . .

She shut her eyes and let out a low moan.

All at once, the barge got its nose right. There was a swift boost of speed. The velocity lent an artificial stability to the deck, like the flat spinning disc of a child's gyroscope.

They stood up to their full height, clinging to each other's clothing, and stared back at the land through a broad clearing that had opened up in the fog.

Lamps, at long intervals, demarcated the quayside with a low band of coppery light.

There, rushing away from them, was Driest's workshop, there was the car park, the jetty and the chandler's shop. Then the row of lamps took flight, describing a smooth arc as they followed the sweep of the bridge over the railway freight yards.

Someone was standing on the bridge.

Just a speck, really, against a glowering reverb of Amsterdam's fires bouncing off the cloud mass in the western sky.

A man, by the looks of things – a man in a hat.

She tried to focus on him, but he was too far off for any detail to resolve.

He turned and walked away with hesitant steps, disappearing over the gentle camber of the bridge.

She wanted to point him out to Driest, but something stopped her.

For a moment, there was a distinction about the way the man had turned away – maybe just the angle of his head – that gave her pause for thought. He had turned away in exactly the same way that Lydia did, when they parted in the street, or on leaving a room. It was the same body language – visible even over such a distance.

Crazy, but that's how it was.

Thirty-five

They pulled clear of the fog.

What Ruth saw was the oil storage depot.

What she saw was the silhouette of the Flevocentrale power station and – along the coast on the perimeter of the polder – rows of wind turbines, giant white three-petalled flowers with slowly rotating heads.

Car headlights dotted the distant dyke road linking Noord-Holland and Lelystad, a luminous perforation dividing the Markermeer from the IJsselmeer. Anything could happen, but at the moment they were rolling and bucking straight for it. It was only a matter of time before they ploughed into its embankments.

She hugged herself. Her teeth chattered.

A high cold wind soared across the waters.

'Got a mobile?' she shouted.

'No. You?'

She shook her head grimly. 'What the fuck's Plan B?'

'Like I told you, find the keys.'

'What good's that going to do us? You said it yourself. We haven't got a rudder.'

'We're not going to have any steerage, but we could get the engine going and put the screw into reverse. It might slow her down in this current.' He saw Ruth looking doubtful. 'Have you got a better idea?'

'No.'

'So where are they?'

'What?'

'The keys!'

Ruth fished one key from her pocket and held it up. 'The galley key. That's what you said. You were the last one to have the others. I haven't been near this tub for weeks. Think,' she said. 'When and where did you last see them? What would you have used them for?'

'Opening the wheelhouse or the engine room, I guess.'

'They can't be in the wheelhouse. It's locked. You couldn't have locked them inside.'

They clambered down to the engine room.

Locked too . . .

There was no sign of the keys.

Driest snapped his fingers. 'The workshop!'

'I've got a workshop? Since when?'

'Oh, shit – the area by the bulkhead, I mean. I fixed one of the oil stoves in there. It's just a chance.'

They ran through together, almost jamming shoulders and hips in the narrow doorway.

The keys were on the work surface.

He grabbed them, tossed them triumphantly in the air and caught them with the other hand.

They scrambled back on deck.

The wheelhouse open, he turned the key to start the engine.

A weak electrical stutter, then nothing.

He tried again.

Still no joy . . .

'Jesus,' whispered Ruth. 'Look!'

They'd been too busy searching for the key. It was some minutes since they'd taken their bearings.

Something critical had changed – a cross-current, perhaps, surreptitiously snipping in from the IJsselmeer and scotching the Markermeer's natural desire to flow cleanly and unimpeded eastwards, where they would eventually have grounded.

The barge was no longer heading for the dyke road.

It had veered to port, racing headlong, jostled by churning waters in a vast aquatic pinball game.

A foghorn boomed.

Due north, a massive freighter plied round a bend in the coast towards Hoorn.

'It's a fucking shipping lane,' she moaned. 'These are busy waterways, full of barges, coasters and cutters. Nobody can see us in this gloom. We need flares! We need light!'

'You won't get any electrics till the engine kicks in. You should think about getting an independent generator.'

'I'll put it on my to-do list.' She elbowed him out of the way. 'This is a Detroit diesel. There's a special knack to it. Goddamn . . . It's ages since I've done this.'

She jiggled the key in the slot.

More electrical throat-clearing.

Nothing.

Driest winced, a sharp intake of breath. 'You'll kill her completely. It's single-push, twenty-four volts. The pack's nearly flat.'

Another horn, sharp and peremptory this time.

They both looked up – up and out of the grubby wheelhouse window.

The barge had indeed slipped into a strong counter-current that was tugging her inland, then north-westward, as if on the perimeter of a giant whirlpool.

Now the sky was full of lights – orange, red, blue.

The petrochemical plant, with its huge storage tanks, wire-mesh compounds and aerial gangways, was a good deal closer than it had been only a couple of minutes before.

An outlet pipe projected from a long, high iron jetty into the water. At the end of the jetty, dead ahead of them, a pumping or supply unit and a flotilla of barges. There were at least a dozen of them, grouped in pairs and riding at anchor. They were big black ugly beasts, twice the size of the *Speculant*, with glimmering beacons on their prows and industrial flags. There were no signs of human activity.

The whole fleet looked deserted.

Ruth steadied herself against the wheel.

'Holy cow . . .'

Her hands were shaking.

Blood darkened behind her torn fingernail.

A queasy, punchbag sensation in her gut.

There was no doubt: the *Speculant* was bearing down fast on them.

'What's in those things?' she breathed.

'Don't ask.'

'I *am* asking, dammit. What are they?'

'They're carriers.' She didn't like the sound of his voice. His face was flushed and devilish in the glow from the depot lights. 'Liquid petroleum gas,' he added hoarsely. 'Ruth – life jackets . . . have you got life jackets?'

She stared at him in disbelief.

Then she stuck the key in the ignition and focused hard, narrowing all of her willpower to a bright, scintillating little point.

Remember, Ruth –

Remember Maarten.

Remember Deventer, and the brand-new 180hp Detroit engine. The glorious smile on Maarten's face when it fired first time round. He stood right here at your side, in this very wheel-house. He put his arm round your shoulders and hugged you to him. Happy – with that boyish, new-toy happiness that was so irresistible, so infectious. Chook-chook-chook-chook, Chook-chook-chook . . .

Ahoy there, my hearties! A life on the ocean wave . . .

Your hearts beat as one to the cheery chug of that motor as it bore you proudly across the IJsselmeer.

Just remember, Ruth, just remember –

Everything will come out right in the end . . .

'Go on,' whispered Maarten. 'Try again.'

She glanced at him, with his upturned collar and glasses. The smell of gunpowder . . . that pale, diaphanous smile.

She wiggled the key in the slot, flicked it clockwise, paused, then brought it back with a sharp, decisive action. The knowledge had been in her bones all along.

The engine spat and growled into life.

The light flickered on in the wheelhouse.

The whole vessel came alive. It trembled with a powerful low vibration – the secret bass organ note that rocks the cathedral into ruins.

Then the world started to hurtle out of control.

'Reverse!' yelled Driest, 'Reverse!'

Curious – the engine was alive, but it was full throttle forward.

And what was all this about reverse?

She was falling free, the wind screaming through her hair, the sweet certainty of doom like the thick taste of wine in her throat, on the roof of her mouth.

Her hand wanted to grab the lever, put it into reverse, but all she could do was stare at it with a dreamy fascination.

Maarten was gone, but he'd left his smile behind. There it was, next to her in the wheelhouse. A parting gift – that wizard smile without a face. It was talking to her. It was telling her what to do.

Relax, babe – let go . . .

Don't worry, little child.

Don't be sad.

Everything will be just fine, you'll see . . .

She was smiling too, but something told her it was all wrong, terribly wrong. Something told her there was another way – a way back, a way out.

A harsh klaxon again, louder now . . .

She glanced at Driest.

His mouth was open.

He was staring at her, trying to decipher.

The smile died on her lips.

Her skin went cold.

How long had these thoughts taken?

How long did they have left?

Then another energy surged in and took over. Was it hers? Was it Driest's? He was hustling her outside, shouting things she didn't understand.

The klaxon blared right beside her.

It made her jump.

It scared her to the core.

There was someone else out there. A light motor launch racing alongside them. It banged into the hull – an out-of-control toy – flinched off, then pulled in again, its engine whining, trying to match speeds.

'Jump!' he yelled, dragging her to the edge.

She looked down. At least a three-metre drop. The man at the wheel egged her on. It was Driest's brother – the guy from the hangar.

'Jump!'

'Oh, Jesus – no. I can't!' Her old dizziness came on.

A great tearing sound. The launch scraped up against them once again, losing part of its guard rail.

'Jump – jump! Jump! Jump!'

The moment had gone.

The launch faltered, lagged behind.

For an instant, Johannes's painting flashed on her inner eye. It was still down in the saloon. She wanted to fetch it, but the colossal stupidity of the very idea was inescapable.

My dear Cornelis . . . my esteemed friend . . .

Life, Ruth – not *things* . . .

There was a roaring in the air.

Driest gripped her by the arm. His fist was in the small of her back. His eyes scrambled with computations.

He was waiting for the moment.

It would come again soon. He was holding and pushing at the same time.

He was a cocked cannon, ready to launch her into some unknown yonder.

Then suddenly her resistance collapsed. Suddenly her body obeyed.

Her knees flexed, compressing like springs. A stab of pain from her aching calf, the piston in her back and it was done.

She was in the air – falling, flying, flailing . . .

But the flat rectangle of deck at the rear of the launch was so small!

She would never make it . . .

The sea would swallow her whole . . .

O God, lift up our hearts . . .

O Jesus, deliver us from evil . . .

Lighten our darkness, we beseech thee, O Lord.

The impact rang through her body.

Her legs crumpled beneath her.

Another drum thud somewhere nearby.

The launch reared up and tore away, nose high in the air. The engine ratcheted up to high whining scream. Driest was sprawled beside her. He grabbed the back of her head with the flat of his hand and pushed it down, smack on the wet timbers of the deck.

Her nose was squashed.

Her cheek was flattened.

Her limbs ached like mad.

She twisted her head sideways, one eye half-open on the world.

There was the broad stern of the *Speculant*, the water churning white behind her and the light glowing in the empty wheelhouse. And, full steam ahead, the projecting bow of one of the big petroleum carriers.

There was just a chance that it would miss, but – with each split second – that chance crumbled further away, narrowing the probability wave, leaving a tiny hollow silence before the end.

First it was the heat – a percussive shock wave of scorching chemical fire that blew across her. It came on a wind of its own making, a synthetic outrush of atoms through time and space.

Then it was the light – a great yellow rocket soaring upwards, billowing solid smoke that was blacker than the blackest sky. The smell screeched through her nostrils. The blaze filled the world.

She ringed her arms round her head like a hermetic seal and pushed herself back against the deck.

Where her skin was exposed – the shins, neck and hands – the fire swept over her like a blowtorch.

It was Maarten's smile, blazing through the cosmos.

It was an explosion of mimosa in a small dull room.

The air cooled and darkened by degrees as the launch put distance between them and the fire.

She raised her head and her eyes met Driest's.

He covered her hand with his.

'I'm so shit scared,' she said.

'There's no need. We made it.'

'It isn't over.'

'It is.'

She shook her head and closed her eyes. 'You don't know. You don't know what can happen next. There's something worse – it doesn't stop here.'

'You know who did this?'

'I feel I know the person, but he doesn't have a face. I can hear his voice in my head. I can feel his anger. He needs help. He has poison in his soul.'

'You must give him shape. Fear has to be seen. It has to be confronted.'

'I'm confronting a ghost or a demon – my own blackest shadow. He's incubating in me. I have to hatch him out. I have to crack the evil egg.'

'Do it,' he said. 'If you don't, he'll just stay there, rotting inside you. Kick him out. Push him back – out – out where you can see him.'

She rolled onto her back, stretched back her head and took a long deep breath, filling herself with the cool night air.

The peace was short-lived . . .

The beat of rotor blades overhead.

A siren out at sea.

And, on the quayside, lights, cars, people . . .

The party animals were out.

They moored at the same small jetty where her own boat had been.

A paramedic helped them into an ambulance and checked them out – pulse, temperature, blood pressure. He bandaged Ruth's finger. He rubbed cream into her aching calf. He pressed her flesh, worked her articulations.

'Does this hurt? . . . And this? . . . And this?'

Outside again, a dented white Fiat Panda nudged through the sightseers. It pulled up alongside and a door opened, and someone familiar emerged. Kremlin hat, lantern jaw, dark rings under the eyes, that dumb protruding lower lip.

'Hi, Smits,' Ruth shivered. 'Still want to live on a boat?'

'I've just changed my mind,' he replied.

He came close to her and lowered his head in a gentle, confiding way. 'Are you all right?'

She glowered at him, couldn't answer.

He turned away and gestured an instruction to someone inside. The driver's door opened. Black, fur-trimmed bomber, shirt and tie, peaked cap. Bianca Velthuizen adjusted her belt and holster against her broad hips and came round. Those lips – those kind, solicitous eyes.

'I'll catch up with you later,' said Smits. 'In the meantime, Bianca will take care of you.'

'Where can we go?' Bianca laid a gloved hand on Ruth's shoulder.

'The hangar. It's Driest's place.'

'Driest?'

'The guy who fixed my boat.'

The cop stopped in her tracks.

'I mean the good guy who repaired my boat, after the bad guy fixed it,' Ruth explained wearily.

They turned to face the distant blaze on the waters. It was just a flame now, no bigger – apparently – than the small gold flambeau on Bianca's cap.

'You're shaking. You're cold.'

'Am I?' Her eyes were dark with exhaustion.

Bianca hugged Ruth to her. 'I don't think you realize how lucky you are.'

Ruth shivered in her embrace. 'If I get any luckier, I'll be the luckiest girl in the cemetery.'

Inside the repair shop, Bianca sat Ruth next to a stove. She draped a car blanket over her. She massaged her calf.

Ruth let herself be taken care of, watching the policewoman out of the corner of her eye.

'I don't understand you,' she said after a while. 'Why are you always so *nice* to me?'

Bianca blushed.

'You're just another weirdo. A weirdo *and* a cop.'

'I believe in my job. I was put on this earth to bring order and justice and love.'

'I thought cops had to be hard as nails – like Smits.'

Bianca stopped massaging. 'Don't mistake him. Andries is a sensitive man.'

She remembered Smits at Jade Beach, blubbing to Cheetah's tacky rendering of 'Besame Mucho'.

'He wears white Reeboks,' she protested.

'They're kind to his corns.'

A thought crossed Ruth's mind. 'How did you manage to get here so quickly?'

'Your phone.' She handed the mobile back. 'He called again. More text messages. We couldn't trace them – he's still working the networks. But I knew it was trouble. He slipped the ropes, right?'

Ruth nodded.

'Did you see him?'

'I saw someone on a bridge. A guy in a hat.'

She sank into a reverie.

The row of lamps.

The bridge over the freight yards.

And the way he turned away, with that peculiar tilted motion of the head that looked as if the head was turning the body, having to coax it to point in the same direction.

Just like Lydia . . .

All at once, she didn't like this at all. She glanced at the phone and tapped on the menu button. 'There's another message?'

Bianca nodded. 'Several,' she said.

She hit the button again and, one by one, scrolled through six consecutive messages.

> **The waters have covered my face and the earth has been polluted and defiled in my works, for there was darkness over it, because I stick fast in the mire of the**

deep and my substance is not disclosed. Wherefore out of
the depths have I cried, and from the abyss of the earth.
Ecce, virgo peperit. Metals can become

diseased in earth, just as a boy in his mother's belly
contracts an infirmity from a corrupted womb because of an
accident of place and through corruption,

although the sperm was clean, yet the boy becomes leprous
and unclean, because of the woman's corruption. Now the
white swan shall turn into the black crow

or raven. The dragon and the woman shall destroy one
another and cover themselves with blood. Remember this,
little Chickenshit: if you gaze for long into

the abyss, the abyss gazes also into you.

47 107.8682

'Ruth?'

She looked up, dazed.

'Does it mean anything to you?'

'I'm not sure about the Latin. "Behold, a virgin" – or something like that. The number at the end's the atomic weight of
silver. The rest is just crazy biblical bluster. Pseudo-religious, I
should say. It's the old alchemists. They talked like that. It was
their lingo. But this stuff about the diseased metals, the corrupted womb – I know it. I've read it before.'

The cop was on her knees. She squeezed Ruth's hand and spoke in quiet entreaty. 'He's trying to tell you something. Listen to him. He's trying to tell you who he is.'

Ruth snapped the fingers of her free hand. 'Albertus Magnus,' she said, 'in an old book called *Gratarolus* from the sixteenth century. It's one of the volumes I've got back at Lydia's place. Jeez . . .' She shook her head, wonderingly.

'What is it?'

'I knew it. I felt it before. He and I read the same stuff. And none of it's exactly on the bestseller list.'

She stood up.

The blanket dropped to the floor.

'Ruth?'

'I've got to go.'

'You can't. You're not well. And Andries wants you for questioning. It's a criminal damage case, now – maybe attempted murder.'

'It was before, but Smits wasn't listening then. Then I was the culprit, now I'm the burnt offering. Some people are like that. It takes a firebomb to wake them up.'

Bianca stared at her, lost for words.

'Get Driest to tell you what happened. I'll come back to you. There's something I have to see to first.'

'Look at you. You haven't got a coat. You haven't got transport. You need help. Can't you see that?'

Some of Driest's clothes were hanging under the stairs. She grabbed a coat and scarf.

'You want to come?'

Bianca nodded.

'Then get rid of Smits – just for the time being. Put him on hold, and rustle up a car.'

Thirty-six

It was past eleven.

Hardly surprisingly, Mr Moon's occult bookshop on the Prinsengracht was closed. Ruth thumped the roll-down grille and cursed. Behind the darkened window dusty tomes, glass pendulums on gold chains, runic stones, brass Buddhas and fanned-out Tarot packs stoically bade their time. She kicked the high stone step for good measure, crossed the street, stood for a moment with her hands on her hips, then strode back again, murder in her eyes.

Bianca observed her from the car, parked up on the corner of the Bloemgracht.

Mr Moon lived above the shop, but there was no independent entrance. She took a few steps back to the middle of the narrow cobbled street beside the canal. The yellow fog rolled in sinuous strata through the air. Up above, the lights glowed behind the net curtains. She had her mobile now, but she couldn't ring him. 'Mr Moon' was her own coinage. She'd never known his real name, and there was nothing so obvious as a telephone number on the shop facade, as if this information, too, was only available by esoteric means.

She stuck her thumb and forefinger in her mouth and wolf-whistled.

No go.

She grabbed a handful of dirt from the roots of a tree and chucked it at the first-floor window.

It pattered against the pane.

This time, Moon's unmistakable silhouette appeared above – the big, bald beachball balanced atop the more generously inflated dirigible of his body. He flung up the sash window and leaned out precariously.

'Whozzat?' he yelled. 'Get lost, 'fore I call cops.'

'It's me,' said Ruth.

He turned to speak to someone in the room, then peered down closer.

'I doan know you, lady. What you want? You know what time it is?'

'It's Ruth, Ruth Braams. My barge used to be moored out here. Remember? I'm sorry, but I have to talk to you.'

Mr Moon keyed open the glass door and raised the grille just high enough for Ruth to duck underneath. The shop reeked of amber, exotic spices and stale incense.

He switched on a table lamp. The base of the lamp was a snarling cast-iron weasel, the shade a ball of multi-coloured glass. It threw kaleidoscopic slashes of crimson, sulphur yellow, sea green and cyanic blue into the dark corners of the emporium, in a flamboyant bid to outdo Moon's trademark psychedelic tie.

He leaned heavily on the counter. It was strewn with peanut husks. He awaited her explanation.

'You lent me some books,' she said, breathless. 'I'm sorry – I should have returned them, but I didn't. I will, I promise.'

'You come here to tell me that?' His face didn't look real.

She had to admit it sounded like a bad joke. She shook her head and paused for air. 'I've had troubles,' she said, 'lots of troubles.'

'Yeah,' he agreed with a bland dolphin-like smile, 'plenty trouble. That's life, Miss. No piece of cake. Nobody get it easy.'

The smile drained away through his teeth.

'The books on alchemy,' she pressed on regardless, fumbling

for a plausible excuse, 'they're full of strange words. I want to understand them, but I can't. So I think to myself: maybe, in this town, there are other people who read the same books. You know what I mean? Other people who can help me understand. I need names. I need addresses. You must have a list – a list of your regular customers?'

Moon's mouth contorted into something resembling disgust. 'That's private. I'm runnin' a business here, not some kinda frennship club.'

She nearly wept with frustration. 'Show me the list, I beg you.'

Her display of emotion scared him. He was pulling himself away from her – resisting, stubbornly failing to comprehend. He ballooned up to his full height. The mouth contorted further.

'I doan get it. You come here, middle of night. You need someone help you read some book. Whassa big hurry? How come you doan wait till tomorrow?'

He hissed his scorn through the gap between his front teeth and waved her summarily away.

She brought her fist down with a bang on the counter and spoke in a quiet, intense voice, still short of breath. 'You see that white car out there? There's a cop in it waiting for me. This is cop business, right? Now, if you want, I can go out there and haul her over, then we can make this official, with all the paperwork – warrants, signed depositions and the rest. Or, if you prefer, we can just look at that list – it won't take a minute – and that'll be the last you hear of me. I'm not looking for more trouble. I'm in it up to my eyeballs as it is. So you decide, neighbour – the high road or the low road?'

His face sagged, defeated.

He rummaged in a drawer and pushed a hardback exercise book towards her with the stubby pork sausage of his finger, strangled above the knuckle by the exotic silver ring.

She opened the book under the lamp, running her finger down the list of names and orders:

Maathuis, van der Geist, Rieder, Siekman, Vunderink, Feen-stra, Jager . . .

And there it was – on the third page, and again on the fifth page, and again on the eighth . . .

Was it possible?

Had Lydia really got it right from the very beginning?

Ruth hadn't believed her . . . the old bag was too toxic with hate.

'Of course it's him,' Lydia had said haughtily. 'I've been telling you that all along.'

Now here it was – black on white: 'E. Scheele'.

And, alongside each entry, were orders for *Bibliotheca Chemica Curiosa, The Book of Minerals, Alchemical Death and Resurrection,* a *History of Occult Sciences, Secretum Secretorum, The Emerald Tablet of Hermes Tristmegistus* – oh, and many more besides . . .

There was no denying it.

No wonder Lydia had been impatient with her.

Scheele was her persecutor – that wizened old fulminating ape in the wheelchair. But no: it was physically impossible!

Her mind raced through what she knew of the man.

Scheele, the *bewariër*, the Aryan guard, the Christian neigh-bour, a then-young diamond merchant, who had taken Johan-nes's painting into his protection over half a century before.

Lydia whispered in Ruth's ear, her breath smelling of rancid mutton, 'He undoubtedly did sell it to the Germans, but for a substantial figure – much more money than he ever admitted – for his own personal enrichment. And to think he tried to fob us off with a handful of silver! I still get angry at the thought. Naturally, I would have none of it.'

And there they'd been, all those years, facing each other across the canal in a lifelong duel, a stand-off to the crack of doom . . .

'Don't you see? That's the way things have always been. Him over there, me over here. I can read him like an open book.

I know his every thought. I'm not afraid of him. I'm not intimidated, to use your word, or weakened. On the contrary, his presence gives me strength.'

Ruth bit the corner of her thumbnail and glared into the iridescent ball of the lampshade.

So, if Lydia was to be believed, he sold the painting for big bucks, recompensed Sander with a pittance after the war, and then, to add insult to injury, chanced his claim when the painting came back into circulation, pitting it against Lydia's.

Why?

To get at Lydia, or because he knew its true value and needed cash? The latter, probably.

How did he know its true value?

Because someone had told him. Maybe Goering, maybe Hans Posse, Hitler's special emissary, if he'd had any direct contact with them. Or, more likely, Alois Miedl – the German business-man, dealer and banker. A man with a Jewish wife. Hadn't Myles said that he was one of Scheele's pals? And Miedl's name had been there, stamped for all to see, or – *correction* – for all who were in the habit of scrutinizing the backs of paintings.

But no – it didn't hold water.

The Germans had a different take on things, at least accord-ing to Fischer. They were after another alchemy. They were after a Bigger Bang. Any arcana was grist to their mill – any suitably obscure formulation of ancestral wisdom that might have con-solidated their own esoteric lore and suggested a path towards the philosopher's stone of uranium, that ultimate power to annihilate, the nuclear secret of the stars.

So did Scheele know the truth or didn't he?

He'd owned the damn painting, at least for a while.

Maybe it had spoken to him, as it had spoken to her.

Maybe Sander had spilled the beans.

Maybe Scheele had seen the letters, or at the very least heard about them.

The possibilities split into endless quantum configurations . . .

'Him,' she said firmly, turning the book and showing it to Mr Moon. 'You know him?'

Moon took out his spectacles, blew the dust off them, poised them on the broad bridge of his nose. He focused fussily on the page.

'Sure,' he said, looking up. 'Erland Scheele. He come in all the time.'

'It must be difficult for him – I mean, getting over that step.'

The Chinaman stared at her as if she was mad.

'I'm talking about the wheelchair. Do you help him over it?'

He continued staring.

Obviously she wasn't getting through. She wondered, for a moment, whether the wheelchair was just for show, a hypochondriac's prop, an expensive style accessory, the geriatric equivalent of a Porsche or a BMW. Perhaps, when out shopping, he relied on his trusty old pegs and the motorized vehicle was just for indoors.

Sheer perversity, but she wouldn't put it past him.

'Never mind,' she said and closed the book.

But something was bugging her, something that Moon had said.

In a flash, it hit her.

'His name,' she gasped, almost jumping at the shopkeeper. 'What did you say his name was?'

'Scheele – Erland Scheele. What's up wiv you, lady? You're damn weird, you know! I doan like this one lil' bit. You see it yourself in the book!'

She threw the order book open again and brought her forefinger in to land. 'I see *E*. Scheele – not *Erland* Scheele. Just an initial. Are you sure the name's Erland?'

'Sure I'm sure. He come in an out all the time! A good customer. He doan go borrowin' stuff an just disappear wiv it!'

And now Ruth had it.

Some ineffable force was pulling the disparate junk of experience into shape.

She remembered the brass plate on the house opposite Lydia's. She remembered his name being mentioned at the plenary session at the Stedelijk Museum.

It wasn't *Erland* but *Emmerick*.

That was the old guy's name.

So who was Erland?

She knew who.

She could see him now, shaping out of the shadows in her mind: standing on a bridge, smoking a cigarette, sitting behind her in a church, glimpsed in a bar, sipping a beer. He'd been there all along. She'd known him all her life or someone like him. That surrealist statue in the Vondelpark – a fellow in a dark overcoat, the collar turned up, carrying a violin case and raising his hat to passers-by.

But beneath the hat there was nothing, not even a head.

Except now the tables had been turned.

'What was all that about?'

Ruth leaned on the roof of the car and gazed down the fogbound canal. She steadied her breathing. 'I'm OK. I don't need you now.'

Bianca gripped the steering wheel, crestfallen. 'You're wrong, you know. You're making a big mistake.'

'I'll check in tomorrow, promise. Thanks for the lift. Is this going to put you in the soup with Smits?'

Bianca shrugged the question off. 'Where will you go?'

'The old girl's. I've still got the key.'

The cop reached out and touched her lightly with the tips of her gloved fingers. 'I put my number in the memory of your mobile. My personal number. If there's the slightest thing, *anything—*'

Ruth smiled. 'I'll be all right. Don't worry about me.'

'But I do. I'm sorry, but I can't help myself. This is your hour of need. We should all have someone, and you – oh, God, you're so terribly alone . . .'

Back at Lydia's, Ruth climbed the steps and tried the key.

The door opened freely.

That meant Lydia hadn't bolted up.

Had she secretly hoped Ruth would come back? A pang of regret, since their last sour exchange?

Across the canal, the lights were out at Scheele's – in all but the semi-basement. A dim glow emanated through the slats of the venetian blind.

Indoors, all was quiet.

She cupped her ear to Lydia's door.

A light intermittent snore merged with the high tremulous hum of the fridge from the kitchen.

In the gloomy entrance hall, Principessa came up to greet her, tail erect and questioning, rubbing the side of her head against Ruth's shin. Ruth crouched down to stroke the kitten and steadied herself with one hand on the floor.

The carpet was wet.

She ran the back of her hand across the pile.

Her thoughts had been overpopulating, pullulating, trying to break free of the little citadel of her skull. On the way to the house she'd been talking out loud to herself, relieving the neural pressure points within. Now the wetness silenced those quarrelsome voices. This was not the first time she'd noticed it, true. Before, she'd put it down to rising damp from the canal. Amsterdam was a wet city, undeniably. Wet on the outside, wet on the inside. But this was different. This was wet in patches.

She shrank back, wrinkling her nose.

She touched the carpet again.

Her curiosity was getting the better of her.

She grabbed the flashlight that Lydia kept at the foot of the stairs and switched it on. On all-fours, she shuffled forward, the damp penetrating her jeans at the knees.

A damp patch here . . . A damp patch there . . .

She envisaged some giant prehistoric slug or bog monster squelching through the premises in the dark hours and shuddered involuntarily.

The wetness continued, deeper into the house and down the marble-floored corridor that ran between the *voorhuis* and the *achterhuis*.

In the middle of the corridor was a door that gave onto the courtyard separating the two buildings.

Here the dampness stopped.

Ruth scrambled to her feet and went outside.

The lights were out in Sander's old den, her own private quarters until a misplaced word had terminated her tenancy agreement earlier in the day.

She turned and gazed up at the dour cliff face of the rear of the *voorhuis*.

No lights here either – nothing.

She shone the torch down on the concrete ground.

The fog left a gleaming slime on everything, but darker, more saturated patches of wetness – four-square footprints, with heavy patterned treads – were visible nonetheless. They crossed the courtyard to the low wooden door beside the outside loo which led to the underground utilities. She had passed this door dozens of times, but never given it much thought. Her imagination had settled the matter already. Behind the door would be a bucket and broom, perhaps an old deck chair with rotting canvas, a few rusty gardening implements and some kind of boiler room. But now she pulled the door open, ducked and went in.

She pointed the flashlight into the narrow, cobwebby space. It smelled of mildew and graves.

The stone walls were soft and dripping wet, with strips of

soggy moss furring their crevices. There were indeed a few bits and bobs, as she'd imagined – a mop, a coiled green garden hose hanging from a large hook, a length of discarded guttering – but beyond these the ceiling suddenly sloped down at an angle of forty-five degrees and irregular stone steps descended into a long lightless hole.

She squeezed past the hose and went down.

The steps came out into a level tunnel, bulb-shaped in cross-section, which doubled back under the house in the direction of the canal.

The roof was low, obliging her to hunch her shoulders and duck her head.

From the distance came the faint sound of trickling water and a sweet, almost flowery smell.

She was undoubtedly in the sewage system – that huge prosthetic continuation of the collective urethra and long intestine – which, in the old days, would have blithely disgorged all domestic detritus directly into the Keizersgracht canal. Her suspicions were confirmed. The tunnel came to a dead end at a bricked-up wall. This, she thought, would be under the water level. But to her right another steep flight of stone steps with a metal handrail led off further underground.

She pointed the flashlight down.

A rat squeaked and scuttled quickly towards her, rather than away, darting in a panic between her legs and back down the tunnel.

Carefully, she went down the stairs, trailing the fingers of one hand along the wall as she did so.

From time to time there were markings – an arrow, the words 'Keizersgracht Noord', followed with what appeared to be house numbers, even a crude daub of phallic graffiti. Then these stairs too met a newer, cleaner tunnel, straight as a die.

The flashlight picked out a steel wall ladder beside her.

She looked up.

A dark shaft – presumably to a manhole in the street.

And here there was a confluence of outlet gullies that chan-
nelled the combined effluvia of several households into this one
transverse tributary tunnel which – further on, well below canal-
bed level – itself fed a larger artery in the sanitation system, a
higher, broader, roomier tunnel that followed the angular
geometry of the Keizersgracht.

Both the tributary and the main tunnel had side ledges that
could just about be negotiated, with much ducking and wall-
clinging given the camber of the wall. In the centre was a
watercourse – a canal in miniature, as it were – that was
evidently one of the main voidance conduits for the city's
private excretions. The ledges were wet and slippery with
sludge. The odd turd, blood-blown tampon or bedraggled garland of toilet paper drifted past her.

Contrary to what she might have expected, there was no
nausea – no overwhelming, gut-wrenching smell. Just a fragrant
niff, like cheap deodorant or Juicy Fruit gum, and the agreeable
burbling of water. She crossed the intersection with the larger
gully, and continued to the other side of the canal. Here, there
were more stencilled wall markings – 'Nieuwe Spiegelstr.' off
in one direction, and 'Keizersgracht Zuidelijk', dead ahead, with
a neat array of numbers and arrows, each corresponding to an
individual canal house.

One was Scheele's number.

She paused a moment, taking her discovery in.

So this was it. This was how he did it . . .

The man had free access to the van der Heyden household at
any hour of the day or night.

Between the sewer exit in the courtyard and the entrance to
the corridor – and, thence, to the *voorhuis* and the *achterhuis* –
there were no locked doors.

For her own part, it had never seemed necessary, given
Lydia's siege mentality and the armoury of bolts and chains on
the main front door.

He was no doubt familiar with every detail of the old girl's private dealings and, indeed, with her own. That added up to a sizeable database: Lydia's makeshift filing system, the time capsule of Sander's quarters, and Ruth's own paperwork, computer, diary, address book and – until recently – her mobile.

Quite enough info to facilitate surveillance, stalking and electronic harassment.

But he'd evidently used this channel long before she popped up on the scene.

What was it Lydia had said? 'Sometimes he comes when I'm out. Other times he comes at night when I'm asleep. He goes through my things. I can hear him.'

He, in the dotty old lady's worldview, being Sander . . . But what had he, being *Erland*, been looking for all those years?

The letters, of course.

He'd turned the place upside down, but never found them. It hadn't occurred to him to crack open a life-size plaster of Paris statue of the Mother of God.

Some people just have no imagination . . .

From here on, the navigation was easy. It was more of the same, but in reverse.

Steps led up to canal level.

Another bricked-off wall.

A straight tunnel boring under the Scheele house and the poky dungeon steps up.

A short trip through the looking glass, but what kind of flip-over mirror world awaited her on the other side?

The dank subterranean air gave way to cool downdraught.

She cleared the last steps and came to a wooden door.

She turned the handle and pushed.

The timber was swollen with damp and stuck to the jamb.

She leaned her weight against it. Then, drawing herself back, while holding the handle open, she aimed her shoulder into it and thrust.

A dull thud and the door sighed open.

Thirty-seven

A bare courtyard, an *achterhuis*, the sheer rear wall of an Amsterdam canal house. She could have been back at Lydia's, but what had she expected?

It was almost reassuring.

She had to remind herself she was on hostile territory and – furthermore – she had no earthly right to be there. She was an intruder, an interloper, and these were no ordinary criminal circumstances.

She was jaywalking on the brink of the abyss.

A light glimmered way above. The old man in his bedroom. The other man – Erland, the equerry, the commissionaire, the steward, whoever or whatever he was – hung out in the semi-basement. That was what she'd deduced, for that was where she'd seen another light from the front.

But what was driving her, and what was she driving *at*? Did she really want to confront him?

The very thought of him – the heavy build, the fuzzy neck, the lazy eyelid, the twisted fulminations of his messages – made her skin crawl, yet she had to know. She had to throw open a window and chase out the pall of lethal gas that was slowly polluting her soul.

A rear door was unlocked.

She entered the house.

She was now at the back of the long entrance hall, which she'd looked down from the opposite end when peddling her spurious artistic wares. The main room in which old Emmerick had received her was in darkness. Stairs down – and a pale glimmer of light just as she'd anticipated.

She cocked an ear.

Somewhere up above, movement. Below all was silence. That meant nothing. He could be sitting motionless in a chair. He might be in bed, staring up and through the ceiling at her, tuned in to her approach.

She listened longer.

Not a breath.

She took one, then two, tentative steps down the stairs. The old timber creaked loudly.

She froze.

A vibe of hollowness, of absence. If Scheele Junior were down there, surely the noise would have brought him out? This was far from conclusive. She had little to go on, but her instincts told her no one was there. Maybe he, too, slept upstairs.

People emit force waves that slip off both ends of the visible spectrum. Here there were none.

She continued, more confidently, down the stairs and pushed open the door.

A kitchenette – cooker, toaster, sink – alongside a hatch in the wall. And through a further door, the long, low room, a single bed at one end and a study area at the other.

She edged forward.

He was definitely out or somewhere else in the house. A band of tautness went out of her shoulders and arms as she switched from red to orange alert. She was groggy with fatigue. But what if he were to return? She needed a way out. There was a front door and, outside, steps up to street level. A key was in the door. She turned it, opened the door a fraction, then closed it again. Now she could get out fast in both directions. She hadn't traipsed into a trap, like a cornered cat.

She sat at the man's desk, as she had at Sander's, and gazed around.

Books, computer, primly made bed, trousers neatly ironed and folded over a clothes horse. A Chesterfield coat and a snap-brim hat hung on a hatstand as if a well-dressed ghost were standing there, lost in ghostly thought. The coat and hat could have been Sander's. On the table the pens were laid out in a tidy row and the in-tray was aligned precisely with the right angle of the table corner. Women noticed little telltale details like that.

An orderly man, as grey and functional as his voice and appearance. A bit of a yawn.

She peeped into the two desk drawers.

Paperclips, a stapler, a pencil sharpener – the conventional equipment of the administratively competent mind.

Ho, hum . . .

For an instant she thought she'd got it all wrong. What was she expecting – *chaos*? There were no bubbling alembics, goblets fashioned from human skulls, racks or thumbscrews. It was all as thrilling as a dentist's filing cabinet. But as her powers of observation passed through the first level of perception, quiet confirmations emerged from the background, pressing them-selves into her brain. The alchemical texts were there, imposing tomes with Latin titles on a simple laminate shelving system. The other books were concerned with finance, system software, Dutch history and religion.

She sifted through the in-tray.

Domestic bills and, amongst them, correspondence about docklands development, with quotes from contractors and installation suppliers. They related to a certain grain silo on Java Island, eastern docks. A circular letter, showing access routes and a projected bridge, had a list of some twenty recipients, presumably investors. Scheele's name was amongst them – so was Cameron's, as it would be. The silo, she recalled, was his baby. Then a snapshot: Erland Scheele and Cameron, grinning and raising glasses at a party, a giant paper-mâché dragonfly suspended above their heads.

Jade Beach . . .

Things were beginning to click.

Had Cameron passed her the matches as a lead? Probably not: he'd have nothing to gain from pointing her to one of his nocturnal haunts, unless it was to contrive an accidentally-on-purpose rendezvous at said watering hole between himself and Miss Ruth Braams, which was not the case – she assumed – since it hadn't happened. Besides, who goes anywhere on the strength of a matchbook ad? The matchbook was, just as she'd thought, one of destiny's arbitrary little hinges, linking people and places in eerie, inscrutable ways.

But Cameron undoubtedly knew who *she* was. He was in with the Kid; he'd called on Lydia; he'd sussed the Jojo connection. And Cameron needed cash. He knew the painting was worth a fortune. He knew that little old ladies don't last forever. Through Scheele, he probably knew about the first will with Thomas as beneficiary. Through Scheele, he probably knew about the second will now as well. Was Ruth's invitation to the party a Cameron set-up? Surely not. The party was on 6 February, she saw the lawyer leaving Lydia's place on the 1st, and Jojo had invited her before that. Basically, he knew that Ruth was in with the old lady and that was enough.

That was it, that was the rusty old key in the lock of the whole conundrum . . .

Cameron was keeping an eye on things. Cameron was keeping his options open. Suppose Scheele lost his claim and Lydia got the picture. Then Scheele and Cameron would still have Thomas on a string, ready to pull in, if and when things got lucky. And – like Lydia van der Heydens – Thomas Springers don't last forever. He too, it now dawned on her, was one of the genuine victims. The Kid had been in the Bijlmer, like the others, on 4 October 1992 when the El Al jet came down. The depleted uranium was inside him too, shortening his hours and days. This was her assumption. Jojo had let slip that Thomas was not a well man. Cameron would know that too.

And how did Cameron know quite so much about the whole world and its hound?

Because Cameron knew Erland – Scheele Junior.

Cameron was nothing, really, a factotum, going places where Erland Scheele couldn't show. And Erland was what it was all about.

Oh Lydia, why didn't I listen to you?

Emmerick Scheele had moved out of diamonds and into dockland development. So had his son. Father and son – a family business of sorts. Unless they were brothers? The possibility teased her for a minute, then she dismissed it. The age difference was wide, but not impossible. No – this was Scheele & Son, she'd swear to it. The son was now branching out on his own. Together with Cameron, he'd paid major kickbacks to get that Java Island bridge. First they'd bought the island real estate because, with the bridge, prices would sky-rocket. But the bridge construction had been delayed, plans were slow to take off and the only things sky-rocketing were the bills. They'd been pumping away at a dry well. More cash was needed urgently. And that's where Johannes came in. Get your hands on the world's first-ever photograph, pull out the stops for the full media hype, flog it off for a heap of brass and you're laughing all the way to the bank.

The Midas touch . . .

It was spinning gold out of straw.

Now she was speculating freely, but what she saw here backed up her hunch.

Erland and Emmerick, as she'd had occasion to witness, were constantly at daggers drawn. Another example of destructive symbiosis, not unlike Lydia's and the old man's. Emmerick clearly controlled the purse strings. Just look around! This basement room, the humble furnishings – not exactly the trappings of a bloated plutocrat.

Erland wanted out.

He was under the old guy's thumb and sick and tired of

being there. The venture with Cameron was his big chance. It was make or break. Then who turns up to fuck with all his plans?

Sweetie-pie Ruth.

Lil' ol' Chickenshit in person . . .

Ruthy's a smart-arse art historian who's zeroed in on the painting. Ergo she's got Johannes's number. She wheedles in with Lydia and works her wicked way. The old hen makes over the whole estate to the goddamn bitch. Thomas is putty. Ruth is grit. Erland would rather she didn't exist. She's clogging up the well-oiled wheels of commerce. She's the squatter, the upstart cuckoo in their nest. Ruth understood how he felt. She wouldn't want herself around either, if she were in his oversized shoes. But there was one glaring flaw in their otherwise seamless logic. Ruthy was not some leech-like asset stripper. Ruthy was a simple honest soul, the girl in the boat next door. She never went in search of any of this, oh no. She didn't want no trouble. She just wanted to be left well alone. It was all Lydia's doing. It was all Ruthy's *un*doing. Lydia had thrust it upon her. And now she'd lost home, job, credit card, watch – you name it – everything bar her reason, which was probably upstairs packing its reinforced Samsonite suitcase for a long protracted convalescence at this very moment.

Why, Lydia?

Why?

Not even the putrid little painting existed any more. It had doubtless gone up in the petroleum fireball along with her hopes and home, then plummeted to the bottom of the sea, a buckled lump of old copper, now a refuge for barnacles and slugs.

If only Bags had never got past the Rijksmuseum guard.

If only they hadn't bumped into each other in the street.

If only she'd never been an art historian.

If, if, if . . .

And if only Ruth had a hummingbird's brains, why – she'd fly backwards . . .

That's where she was, scrambling up the learning curve.

Something was wrong.

Something was refusing to fit.

She looked up. A beach postcard from the USA was pinned to the side of a cupboard. 'The Other Pittsburg', the legend ran . . .

A sudden mechanical rumbling startled her out of her reverie.

She sprang up and flattened herself against the wall. She made for the door, then stopped and turned – questioning. The noise was getting closer. Then with a great rattling crash it stopped. She'd heard this fracas before. Where? In the upstairs room.

The dumb waiter.

Not so *dumb*, as it turned out.

In the kitchenette, a tray full of dirty cutlery and crockery had promptly appeared in the hatch. Remnants of mashed potatoes, meatballs in gravy, a carafe of sticky red wine with a fat black upside-down housefly drowned in the bottom. The whole lot perfunctorily dropped down the shaft to the chief cook and bottle-washer.

So the old boy was up and the young boy was out . . .

But the hour was late. He might well return soon.

She went back to work, renewing her efforts, riffling through boxes of papers. In one, she found old snapshots of Lydia, Sander, Asha and all the van der Heyden family – filched from the house across the way. In another: two old letters, in German, signed Alois Miedl. These she pocketed.

She wadded a handkerchief to her nose.

The smell of soggy cold meatballs was beginning to pong out the basement. She felt like doing the washing up herself, but that would be less than circumspect. The room was getting to her. She was rummaging through someone's unconscious, and nothing was coming clear.

The computer was asleep.

She brushed one key and it came alive.

The Screensaver was another beach scene, not unlike the postcard: tanned gods and goddesses rollerblading along a boardwalk under an endless line of palms. The file and folder names held no surprises: *Accounts: February>March, My Docs, Spreadsheet 2*. What she was looking for was an application: his mail browser. Whatever remailers or wormholes in the dark Satanic net he used, she'd have him here. The source messages would be in his Sent box. Unless he deleted them. But, judging from this room, judging from the perfect gridlocked hierarchies of the virtual desktop, this guy didn't chuck anything away. Like Lydia, he was a hoarder, but with a pigeonhole brain that pigeons would kill for.

She was looking for the browser but another icon pricked her curiosity.

She clicked and a webcam window zoomed open.

A monochrome, motionless picture of a room. Low light: there was little contrast between the soft, inter-melding shades of grey. Sticking her nose to the screen didn't help: the pixels floated apart as she journeyed into deep space, through the pictorial atoms of things. Sitting well back in the chair did: a wide-angle view – lumpy bed, bookcase, poster and crucifix on the wall.

A black shape pounced up onto the bed.

It was a little kitten.

The recognition sank in.

Lydia's room – under real-time surveillance.

'Oh, brother,' Ruth whispered . . .

A tiny, low-resolution camera, she imagined, high up in the street-side corner of the room. Who would have thought? She'd never spotted anything suspicious. Then again she didn't make a habit of sweeping pelmets, lintels and cornices for state-of-the-art spyware. And what other rooms had this weird individual wired up? Hers? She checked the contextual menus, but no other goodies were on offer.

His was a one-window view of the world.

A view of a lump, huddled up in a bed.

She whistled softly and bit her nail.

This was not just a matter of assets and rival claims. Of course, she'd known that all along. It was not just historical revisionism, a ruthless settling of scores, or Cold War armies marching silently down Cemetery Road – though it was all that and more as well. It was something deeply personal, a wedge that had been driven down the middle of this man, sundering him in two, so that one half of the deep core of his being was no longer communing with the other. Under these circumstances, intelligence is a whore. The heart is dead, or the gateways into it barred and guarded by the devil's own sentries. She wanted to get beyond the lurid delinquency to the source event, some tiny impairment that had triggered the slow necrosis from within. He spoke in riddles, communicating his unmentionable secret through the quotations he chose from Moon's alchemical books.

> For all things are woven together and all things are taken apart and all things are mingled and all things combined and all things mixed and all things separated and all things are moistened and all things are dried and all things bud and all things blossom in the altar shaped like a bowl.
>
> Corpus infantis ex masculo et femina procedit in actum.
>
> The waters have covered my face and the earth has been polluted and defiled in my works, for there was darkness over it, because I stick fast in the mire of the deep and my substance is not disclosed. Wherefore out of the depths have I cried, and from the abyss of the earth. Ecce, virgo peperit. Metals can become diseased in earth, just as a boy in his mother's belly contracts an infirmity from a corrupted womb

because of an accident of place and through corruption, although the sperm was clean, yet the boy becomes leprous and unclean, because of the woman's corruption. Now the white swan shall turn into the black crow or raven. The dragon and the woman shall destroy one another and cover themselves with blood.

It was staring her in the face.

He was Lydia's little boy.

She'd had him too young, most likely – outside wedlock during the Occupation. Was it social shame that made her disown him? Ruth checked herself abruptly. *Disown* was hardly the word. Lydia had erased him for all time from her scheme of things, refuting all knowledge of his existence. She'd taken a knife and cut him carefully out of her heart. If she had any vestigial memory of him, it was so thoroughly calcified that nothing could chip it open.

Only Emmerick had stood fast, assuming his parental obligations, with however ill a grace.

And yet, as with Emmerick, the boy had been right in front of her all her life – a canal between them, even a little bridge. It was as if an unconvicted murderer continued to live in the same street as his victim's family ... but this victim was still alive, alive and kicking.

Ruth was beginning to appreciate Erland's point of view. And where did she slot into this glorious historical perspective?

I know your little game, Chickenshit.

You wander in the labyrinth without Ariadne's thread. Seeing, you do not see. Hearing, you do not understand. Get out while you have the chance ...

You women live by your fucking lies. The truth has become a stranger to you. You wish to receive, but you give nothing in return ...

Like all women, you are foolish and vain. Very soon the devil will want to be paid . . .

You wouldn't like the kind of games I play . . .

With the last point, she wholeheartedly concurred.

Now one thing was as plain as daylight.

She had robbed him of his entire inheritance.

Not just the picture: everything.

Lydia, whose heart was dead to her own son, had warmed to her. Him she had spurned; her, she had taken to her withered bosom.

Yes, my dear. I was just thinking. It's soppy, I know, but I feel like a little girl again. Oh, goodness, should I tell you? I was thinking we shall be like sisters, living here together.

OK, Lydia had thrown her out too – only today, as it happened. But the deep damage had been done.

Ruth had kindled a fire, where Erland had known only ashes.

She fixed her gaze on the sleeping Lydia once again and – for a moment – hated her with a pure white hate. The baffles, the duplicity, the defections.

A thought occurred to her.

Did this go further? Did Erland have microphones too? Did he *hear* what went on between them?

The oblong mound of the old woman's body hadn't moved. She put the computer back to sleep.

She would go back.

Not to wake her, not to shake some sense into her, not to shake the terrible truth out of her in some almighty showdown. It was futile. The lie Bags had nurtured was a living, breathing lie. To expose it would leave her nowhere to stand, no place to go, nothing to call her own. Whatever words were to pass between her and the old lady had already done so. They'd had their say.

Nor was she going back for want of a place to spend the night.

She was going back for one last look; a final effort to understand. It was really Ruth she wished to put to the test. She wanted to find compassion within herself.

It was her way of bringing herself to life.

Thirty-eight

*B*ack at Lydia's place the lights were out. Ruth continued using the torch.

Down the corridor – into Lydia's room.

The pillow from the bed had fallen to the floor. Lydia's head had no support. Ruth decided against trying to slip it back under. She didn't want to wake Lydia now.

In the dark room, the luminous crucifix shone with a fierce greenish light. Principessa stood up to acknowledge Ruth's arrival, stretched, then curled up again in the crook of Lydia's knees. The only sound, the kitten's regular, hypnotic purring.

She pulled up a chair and sat next to the bed.

She felt drained, depleted.

A thousand thoughts had been thronging through her mind. Now there didn't seem to be one. They had swarmed off else-where, leaving her a gutted shell.

She was unstuck in time.

A few minutes ago she had been so sure. Now she had no idea what she was doing here. Instead of thinking, she focused her mind on Lydia, aiming for a pure act of attention. The green phosphorescence of the crucified Christ tangled in a few stray hairs and brushed the promontories of Lydia's cheekbone, the sharp bridge of her nose, the right-angle bracket of her jaw. One scrawny arm protruded from the short sleeve of her nightdress. It hung limply over the edge of the bed.

There was so little to the human frame in the end.

A machine designed to survive in order to die. Whatever did not kill it made it stronger and, paradoxically, weaker at the same time, as if weakness were strength, and strength weakness, the mind and body turning on each other in a finite dance of figures, combinations, antinomies.

Lydia was all paradox. Strength and weakness, truth and lies, courage and despair. She was the architect and wrecker of herself. Among the seeds we plant, the seeds of self-destruction.

But something was wrong.

Lydia van der Heyden wasn't there.

What, then, was this bedraggled beast lying in her bed?

For a couple of beats the kitten had stopped purring and – in the space of that narrow interval – silence.

Ruth stood up and bent slowly over the mound in the bed. She observed the bedclothes over the old lady's chest.

Not a flicker of motion.

She moved closer to the face.

The flesh on the cheeks had a smooth sheen with a fine oily iridescence in the Jesus light. It sagged down like little hammocks.

A loose hair on the mattress. She picked it up and held it under Lydia's nose.

Nothing.

Was it possible? Had Lydia upped and gone, leaving this strange simulacrum of herself behind? Surely, it couldn't be. She was made of sterner stuff. Deep down, she was strong as an ox. She was a hardy perennial. That's what everyone said. It was common knowledge.

Ruth raised Lydia's arm lightly by the wrist and released it.

It flopped back without resistance.

She sat on the edge of the bed and stroked the kitten with the back of her fingers.

So this was it, Lydia's exit.

And their last words together had been harsh.

Each leave-taking is a little death. It should be a moment of peace, vision and reconciliation. She had forgotten this simple wisdom. Anger and pride had got the better of her. Now the time for healing was past.

Nearly eight decades, and it came to this. She wanted to feel solemn and important. A person's death was an occasion. It demanded high seriousness and ceremony, but she couldn't bring herself to such a pitch. Ultimately, she couldn't help feeling, it was nothing – nothing at all.

It was blowing out a candle.

It was switching off a light.

Her remorse over their hard words had gone. A quiet relief took hold of her, easing her troubles away.

There had been no pain, judging by Lydia's expression. It was what they call a 'good' death. And, after all was said and done, it was just like sleep – the sleep of ages, from which she would never wake.

'Goodbye, Lydia,' Ruth said.

And stroked the woman's brow.

Something jarred, nudging her concentration off-centre.

She turned and looked down at the fallen pillow again. It had grip-like indentations on either side.

'I've been thinking about things, Chickenshit,' said a man's voice behind her. 'You and I have a great deal in common.'

She jumped, then willed her gaze into the shadowy far corner of the room.

It was Erland Scheele.

A shiver of terror passed through her body.

'With Lydia?' she managed to come back, her voice pinched and constrained.

'With her, with each other, it makes no odds. We are all different but the same. It is as they say in the old books. We are fire, air, water or earth. We are moisture, dryness, cold, heat. But each is potentially latent in the others. I feel that strongly with you.'

The wet on the carpet.

She hadn't thought.

He'd been here all along.

He knew exactly where she'd been.

He was nothing but an amorphous shape, a heavy, military kind of man squeezed into Sander's agony chair. Once again, she had the distinct feeling of being spoken to by a suit. An aloof control about the urbane voice, verging on boredom. A PA, a butler, a retainer. A protocol about him. Discreet duties to perform. But what duties? This was her demon, make no mistake. No tail, no horns, but this was he – a fellow creature who had done his level best to terminate her existence. The knowledge was too much for her. His simple presence paralysed her will. Nothing but words could save her now.

'Lydia was your mother.' She hadn't intended to speak. She was surprised, even, that this power remained to her, tripping in like an emergency back-up, the words escaping of their own accord.

'That might be one way of putting it.'

'I don't know another.'

He held his head back, scenting the next way forward. 'She knew very little of the gestation, birth and, above all, nutrition of a child.' He weighed the three formal nouns, not quite knowing what to do with them.

'You never spoke to her.'

'Once, when I was a boy. I phoned her and pretended to have a wrong number.'

'That was all?' She cursed the tremor that undermined her voice. She tried to compensate it out, strengthening her tone. 'You never spoke to her afterwards?'

'She wouldn't have wanted it. You must realize that by now. You had ample time to study her little ways. An obedient son does not go against his mother's will.'

A lethargy in his voice.

Had he been drinking?

A man on the slide, slithering through a morass of half-formed thoughts and stifled emotions. He seemed to detect it himself, unhappy with his slippage.

He locked his elbows back on the armrests, squared his shoulders, cleared his throat.

'Let me try to spell it out to you,' he said stiffly. 'You are familiar now with the old ways of expression. Perhaps you see where the old science was heading. *Lapis infernalis.* The infernal stone is the image stone. When we have mastered it, it throws back the truthful image of our selves. It's derived from two things and one thing, in which is concealed the third thing. And what is life itself? The same. A bringing together of two substances to make a third. There is a right and a wrong way to go about this. *Lapis, ut infans, lacte nutriendus est virginali.* The stone, like a child, must be nourished with virgin milk. That is the right way.'

'And the wrong way?'

'*Her* way.'

Outside, a van rumbled over the cobblestones.

Ruth considered the dead woman.

'In this kingdom,' he went on, 'nothing prospers, nothing is truly begotten. Fallen angels have instructed us in this art.'

She shook her head. 'Oh, man, you really believe all that stuff . . .'

'I suppose I do. I believe that, somewhere in nature, there is a pure matter which converts all imperfect bodies that it touches. The radii of this secret extend every way, but they all meet in a common centre and point only at one thing.'

'You know what it is – this *thing*?'

'No. Do you? We all try to bring the elements into balance. We all, ultimately, fail.'

The kitten was on the move.

It came sniffing at the corners of Lydia's mouth.

Ruth brushed the animal away automatically, amazed that her body was responding again.

She managed a sigh.

'I feel sorry for you both,' she said truthfully. 'I really do. In case you don't realize, I didn't get myself involved in your private affairs on purpose. It was all chance. We were thrown together, Lydia and I.' She looked down, bothered. 'In fact, it was partly your doing. I mean, she took me in, when you flooded my boat. You must have known she'd do that.'

Her words had struck a nerve. He shifted uncomfortably. 'As a matter of fact, I didn't. I thought you would have friends to stay with, presuming you survived. I never ever imagined she would break far enough out of her selfishness to actually want to *share* –' His gaze swept the walls, rising gloomily to the ceiling ' – to *share* this appalling mausoleum with anyone. When she did that, it surprised me. It was a glimmer, a ghost effect, of the mother she should have been. In reality, she was utterly extinguished inside. I am prepared to believe, however, that your coming together was perhaps not entirely fortuitous, but part of some higher design.' He got to his feet and turned to look out of the window, his hands clasped behind the rectangular expanse of his back. 'It's as I say. The bringing together of two substances. Something is generated. A life, or a death.'

His every movement, his every word, sent a chill through her.

Her fear now had substance and shape.

He was like the old wanderers in the desert, the solitary seafarers, hermits and saints. The wilderness of his life was populated from within.

She had a choice – she could try to talk his negotiable language to keep him going, the only definite strategy that had occurred to her. It was all playing for time. A spy, guessing at passwords, she could hunt for a way in. But, in her ignorance of the codes, she might just as easily arouse his suspicions or scupper a civilized exchange with a misplaced word or thought.

There was another way.

She could steer him round to the world of facts, a realm where words had a more or less fixed rate of exchange, or so people liked to imagine. Did he live in this world? Did he know it?

What did she represent to him? The emails gave her a fair idea. But now – had things subtly changed?

He glanced at her – one eyebrow raised, a begging dog – then turned his back once more.

He has killed Lydia.

He is wondering what to do about me.

The front door . . .

Could I make a run for it? Is the door bolted and chained? It wasn't last time I looked.

In all probability, Scheele had locked it himself. This certainty now possessed her. After all, he'd been waiting for her. He'd been looking forward to this moment for quite some time. Why should he let it slip away? Why spoil the fun? He was a careful man, a man who believed in covering all eventualities, in patiently shaping situations to his own inexorable ends.

A new idea pressed in on her . . .

In her pocket was her mobile phone. She couldn't take it out, even if she didn't use it, but there was another way. She was remembering what Bianca had said. The cop had said she'd put her number into the memory.

But how?

She ran her finger over the Braille of buttons and pressed tentatively, relying on tactile memory, hoping the bip function was off, as it usually was.

No bip!

Once right, to access the list.

Once left, to search.

Once left again, for the scrolling list.

The question now was: where was the cop?

Bianca Velthuizen . . .

'B' or 'V'?

If 'B', one press down, after 'Aalders'.

If 'V', one press up, to the end of the revolving list.

At least, if she was not mistaken. Was there anyone else in the first two letters of the alphabet? Was there anyone else in the final five?

She thought not.

So which was it to be: 'B' or 'V'?

'B' was her first choice. Bianca wanted to be pals, maybe more. Unless, when programming phone memories, she opted for formality, or the phone-company logic of a surname-based list. That's what a by-the-book cop would do.

She hesitated.

Pal or cop? Cop or pal?

She thought of Bianca's kindnesses, her little attentions, her hugs and friendly caresses. One press down, and she hit the call button.

The room was intensely quiet.

She could hear the phone dialling in her pocket, the tripping harmonic of bleeps.

Panic seized her.

Could he hear it too?

She couldn't say.

Talk was vital. Not only to cover the beeps, or Bianca's voice when she answered, but also to tell Bianca what was up. Maybe she had name and number presentation on her phone, maybe she didn't. Ruth couldn't gamble on it.

She had to talk, to give context, but what could she say?

'Lydia loved Sander, didn't she? Before he died, and *since* – if we come to that.'

'Hello? Hello?' A tiny, wiry voice from the phone. Ruth coughed to cover it.

A woman's voice, but was it Bianca's? She couldn't tell.

'Hello? Hello? Is anyone there?' Another clearing of the throat.

There was a pause and the line went dead.

No one would help her now.

Scheele didn't stir.

Her heart was sinking with the failed phone call, but she

couldn't let that distract her. Scheele had stopped talking and started brooding. This was not a good sign. Had she said something wrong? She fumbled quickly for a way through.

'What I mean is, Lydia was not all bad. And Sander's death really got to her.'

'Sander's death?' Now he did turn round, the eyebrow fully levitating.

'Well, I know she imagines he rummages around, but that's *you*, isn't it? Sander went in 1955.'

'Yes, he did,' said Scheele eventually, 'but not in the way you mean. He went to Pittsburg.'

'Pittsburgh in Pennsylvania?'

'No, there's another town of the same name. A small place in California. Spelt without an "h". He lives there still. In a retirement home. I understand the climate is most agreeable.'

Ruth stared at the poster over the bed.

'Then why?'

'Why *what*? Why did Mother want to go to Pennsylvania? Because she'd heard he was in Pittsburgh and got the wrong town, of course. Geography never was her forte. And *he* certainly wasn't going to put her right. He wanted nothing to do with her. He never wanted to see her ever again.'

There was silence as Ruth took this in.

'You don't understand much, do you?' he said with throwaway scorn. 'Sander wanted to get as far away from her as he could – half a planet away.'

'They were two peas in a pod. She said so herself.'

'Precisely.'

'Precisely?'

'Pods split.'

'Then what had she done?' Ruth whispered.

He ran a hand through his hair and sighed. 'I've told you before. *Ecce virgo peperit*. You really should learn Latin, you know. "Behold, a virgin shall give birth."'

'Your father is Emmerick.'

'My *foster* father is Emmerick. He was the custodian, the *bewariër*, and I was the chief object in his custody. The payment, you see, was the painting – that's how the van der Heyden family wanted things. My adoption took place in the early days of the war. Then the Nazis forced Emmerick to sell. Both he and Sander knew the picture's true value, but what could be done? Emmerick had to sell. He wanted to pass the thousand florins back to Lydia's family. For all his misanthropy, he was and is a painstakingly honest man. It is his chief failing. The van der Heydens weren't the only ones he helped in the war. He was with the Resistance, you see. Since those days he has fulfilled his contractual obligations as a foster father admirably, I must say. I have tried to serve him in return. As for you, you disappoint me. I really would have thought you'd have worked this out for yourself. Emmerick's claim to the painting is my claim. It's the price Lydia paid to rid herself of me. He's making it on my behalf. Ultimately, it's the legitimate one – not mother's. She renounced hers when she renounced me.'

'Why didn't you mention this in the documentation?'

'I wanted the painting – *we* wanted the painting. But not at the cost of Lydia's dignity, her dark secret. People are curious. I think Emmerick rather liked her, or the person she once was, though they haven't spoken to each other for over half a century.'

'The picture's gone,' she murmured. 'It was in the boat.'

'Good riddance to it.'

'That's what Lydia would have said. That's what everyone seems to say. You've read the letters?'

'I have. Thank you for finding them. At least we have now laid that particular ghost to rest.'

Outside, a car crept by slowly. The light from the headlamps scanned across the room. It brushed the yucca plant by the hearth, and the eight silver branches of the Hannukkah menorah on the mantelpiece, sending long grey fingers of shadow scampering up the wall, then scurrying down. It picked out, for an instant, the odd, back-to-front snapshot of the teenage Sander, standing proudly outside the American Hotel, his flat corduroy driving cap on his head, his leather document case under his arm.

Two women laughed as they walked past the house.

Again Ruth's gaze alighted on the discarded pillow.

He observed her closely before speaking.

'A dead thing cannot change into a living thing directly. It must first return to matter before the change into its opposite can take place.'

'*Who* was your father?'

He smiled wanly. 'A man of shame.'

Sander, thought Ruth. *His father was Sander*. Her blood ran cold. Now the whole sorry story was blindingly clear.

Suddenly he was halfway across the room.

She leapt to her feet in fear.

'I have to admit, I dislike you quite intensely,' he said. The coolness had gone from his voice. In its place was a bland viciousness. 'You are an interfering person with little regard for other people's feelings. You act, like most people, out of naked self-interest.'

The TV set was between them.

He stopped and stared at her, an unpleasant smile on his lips.

'I learned a poem once,' he went on. 'Shall I recite it to you? It goes like this. "Take a bucket and fill it with water. Put your hand in up to the wrist. Take it out and the measure of water is a measure of how you'll be missed." '

His hand was moving into his jacket pocket. She did not wait. She summoned up all her strength and kicked the TV, aiming her foot at the upper rim. It flew back against his shins with a smash of glass.

He stumbled and fell.

She ran out into the corridor.

O, holy Mary, mother of God . . .

The door, as she'd feared, was bolted and chained. She grabbed at the chain, sliding the catch out of its notch.

Her hands shook uncontrollably.

Adrian Mathews

She was hyperventilating, gasping for breath.

In the other room she could hear him getting to his feet – carefully, unhurriedly, knowing full well that time was on his side.

The bolt was stiff.

She realized, aghast, that she was pushing it the wrong way.

She reversed direction, thrust it open, slid back another and fumbled for the latch.

But Scheele was too fast. Scheele was behind her.

One hand on the latch, she turned to face him.

He was coming forward, observing her as if he'd recognized her at a social event and was trying to recall her name. The lazy eyelid made him look half-asleep. The other eye was wide awake. Each side of his face had a different expression. One was fixed on her, the other was miles away.

A big rectangle of a man, in that angular suit, that formal tie – a big man, getting bigger.

She could smell his breath. It smelled of cigarettes.

He had found what he wanted in his jacket pocket. A loop of electrical flex.

'Don't,' she whispered.

'I have to,' he said, almost regretfully. 'We have brought things thus far.'

She turned the latch, wrenched the door open.

With one hand, he seized the rim, holding it firmly, resisting – his arm rigid and taut.

There was not enough gap to get through.

She tugged desperately at the door, trying to pry it open, but his big static strength was too much for her. Then, in a flash, she knew. She knew what she could do. She stopped pulling and pushed. She shouldered her whole mass against the door, with every last ounce of energy she could muster.

He was taken by surprise.

The door slammed on his fingers with a crack, then bounced ajar again.

He threw his head back, clutching the bloodied hand to his chest, and let out a low guttural moan.

She stared at the blood and limp fingers, amazed at what she had done.

The moan died out. He was breathing heavily, a dull reproach in his eyes. His boulder head sank into his shoulders. The stubbly nape of the neck, the hair grey, the flesh red, stuck out of the white shirt collar.

The flex was still in the other hand, but something had gone out of him.

He had forgotten what he was going to do.

She watched him, mesmerized, waiting for his next move, but it never came. He was not even looking at her. His mind had disengaged, backing out of the present situation so fast that all the detail was gone.

Vehicles were pulling up outside. Voices – urgent, imperative. A slamming of doors. He frowned oddly and went back into his mother's room.

She was free.

She opened the door.

Bianca ran up the steps. Other officers brandishing pistols were behind her. From the rear, Smits lumbered forward in his big coat and fur hat. He too was carrying a handgun.

'Wait,' said Ruth urgently, signalling to them to hold back.

She returned slowly into the house, back to Lydia's room.

He was kneeling beside the old lady's body, resting his temple against her withered arm. His eyes were shut. He gripped the flex with his bleeding hand as if holding a rosary.

The cops were at the door. Smits pushed forward and restrained Bianca with a hand on her sleeve.

They held back an instant, looking to Ruth for answers.

She leaned, exhausted, against the wall.

'Give him five minutes,' she said, her voice almost extinct. 'Please, do what I say. Just give him five.'

Epilogue

Driest Topside Marine Construction, Repairs and Outfitting.
We build and repair crabbers, offshore supply vessels, push-boats,
factory trawlers, river-boats, passenger vessels, tugboats.

Myles hauled his bulk up the staircase and emerged head first –
puffing and sweating – in the little apartment that sat, like a
cabin, on top of the workshop, complete with roof garden.

It was a radiant day.

Ruth was watering a mass of geraniums and hortensias.
Beyond the balcony, the sea stretched far and wide, glittering
with sunlight. On the horizon, tall white wind turbines dotted
the perimeter of the polder like a picture-perfect flower border.

'Blonde again, huh?' he remarked.

She frowned and turned back to her geraniums.

He wandered round, admiring the masses of blooms. 'I see
the anger-management course worked out, then.'

She put down the watering can, smiled and rubbed her
hands together. '*Wilkommen, bienvenue*, welcome ... A drink,
Myles?'

'Get me a beer.'

'What kind you want?'

'Any kind with foam on it.'

She opened the fridge in the open-plan kitchen. 'No beer.
Just Pouilly fumé, 1996.'

He shrugged. 'If that's all you've got ...'

'A dry white wine.'

'I always thought wine was *wet*.'

He inspected the giant rusty rudder that hung from the wall as if he were in an art gallery, running his finger over a seam of welding.

She found the corkscrew and opened the bottle.

She poured two glasses.

'Why is it, do you think,' she asked, shoving the cork down into the neck of the bottle, 'that once you've taken a cork out of a bottle, it will only fit back in again if it's the other way round?'

'An interesting question,' he murmured. 'Interesting, but *stupid*.' Now he was out on the roof garden again, fiddling around with her bike. He squeezed the rubber bulb of the horn. 'What happened to the bell?'

'Someone nicked it,' she called back. 'How long before you say, "I told you so"?

'Consider it said.'

She sat down, tailor-style, on the floor and he came in. They clinked glasses.

'How are things at the bureau, Myles-y baby?'

'Much as ever, much as ever, you know.' He eased into a big round wicker chair from the sixties and flopped out his arms like a pontiff on his throne. 'Cabrol has mellowed out a little, now he's realized they won't be having to bring out a new edition of all those Larousse encyclopaedias for the time being, *faute de preuve*. And his cousin – the one who runs the Niépce photography museum in Burgundy – dropped by and took us all out to a very posh French restaurant, thank you very much. Cabrol's switched to garlic capsules, by the way. They're odour-free. A wise decision, if you ask me. The atmosphere at work is much improved.'

'How's Rex? Are you two still arguing?'

'We don't argue. We're in complete agreement. We can't stand one another.'

Adrian Mathews

'I don't believe that for an instant, Myles. You *complement* each other. What about Sweekieboude?'

'She's taken to using my trousers as scratching posts. The bottoms are ripped to tatters. I'll have to cut them down into shorts.'

'You could do worse, what with this nice weather.'

'And Principessa?'

'Purr-fect.'

There was an easy pause.

He continued to gaze round admiringly. '*You* seem to have got yourself sorted out, my dear.'

She followed his gaze, rediscovering her new home with him, observing with pride the little things that seemed to hold his attention. 'Yes, I don't bite my nails any more, I don't smoke and I'm happy to be here. In fact, I'm happy to be anywhere.'

'And *busy*, with it . . .'

'Today's the maid's day off.'

'You're still a very attractive woman, you know.' A suave matinee idol voice, accompanied by a lascivious wink.

'Thank you. Men still rub up against me in the buses and trams. I guess that's kind of encouraging.'

'It's certainly encouraging me.'

She freed one leg and kicked him playfully on the ankle. 'Go milk a duck! I'm answered for, Myles, in case you'd forgotten. So are you.'

He held up the glass and scrutinized her inverted image through the wine. 'I'm dying to know. How exactly did you two get it together?'

'It all started with an almighty bang.'

'Doesn't it always,' he moaned.

'In fact, it was relatively painless, if you must know. He asked me if I wanted to be his girlfriend. I said yes. I asked him if he wanted to be my boyfriend. He said yes. We just sort of took it from there. As it says in the song, there's a boy for every girl in the world. It also made sense to pool our collections of seventy-eights. It was kind of a merger.'

'I thought as much. Globalization . . .'

'It's the price we pay for a world of choices. Like "Marlboro or Marlboro Light?" And anyway, Laurens is good to me.'

'I should hope so too. As they say in the East, "Only very foolish mouse make nest in cat's ear."'

She scowled. 'I'm not the only one here with a past, you know.'

He gave up examining her through the glass and raised it a little higher. 'Well, the luck of the Irish to you, anyway. Are you two going to have kids?'

'Dunno. Maybe.'

'Careful, my dear. Remember what they print on plastic bags. "To avoid suffocation, keep away from babies."'

'I'll remember, Myles. If you say so.'

'You don't miss the boat?'

'No.' She drew the monosyllable out, thoughtfully, seriously. 'Of course, we repair them here. But *mine* – it's kind of weird to think it's just out there, under all that water. It's my past life. It's Maarten. I can't see it, but I know it's there, with the fish swimming in and out of it.'

'Do you still think about him – Maarten, I mean?' Myles asked seriously.

'Not in the old way. I see him for what he was. It's strange, but on the boat – just before the explosion – he was there, egging me on. Not to save me, but to destroy me. It was so clear. He wanted me to die, to join him on the other side. I said no then. I've been saying no ever since. Of course, it wasn't the *real* Maarten. It was what my mind had turned him into.'

'And you sold the house . . .'

'Yes. Did I tell you? We made a packet. Frankly, Laurens and I are rolling in it.'

'You can't take it with you, you know.'

She pouted. 'If I can't, then I won't go.'

'Of course, you could have *kept* the house . . .'

'I couldn't, Myles. I couldn't. It was too full of ghosts. That's what Lydia should've done – sold up and moved out. She'd probably have had a better life.'

'You spare her a thought from time to time, then?'

'Sure – don't you? Despite everything, when I think of her it's with real affection. She taught me something, a lesson of life.'

'And what lesson was that?'

'How to open up, I guess – how not to hide. Let's face it, she spent her whole life hiding from others and herself. We all do it, to a certain extent, but as you get older there are more things and people to hide from. Oh, and that's another thing I've learned – what age does to people.' She leaned down to stroke Principessa, who had quietly entered the room. 'God knows what I'll be like if I ever get to those sour old seventies. It doesn't bear thinking about.'

'Perhaps Lydia learned something from you too.'

'I can't imagine what.'

'The same – not to hide. She confided in you, didn't she?'

'Yeah, well,' Ruth began sceptically, 'she kept up the mad stream of consciousness, that's for sure. I should know. I nearly drowned in it.'

'Talk is good, however evasive it seems. You listen to what people say, then you work out what they haven't said and fill in the gaps. The real message is in the gaps.'

Ruth chewed this thought over for a while, wondering whether to give it credence. 'I wanted to see Emmerick,' she said after a while, 'to get his side of the story. But he died within a month of Lydia. It was weird, as if her presence had been keeping him alive. Wars don't just start and stop, do they? They go on and on, inside people's heads and hearts.'

Myles spotted something on the far side of the weatherboard room. He heaved himself to his feet and lumbered over.

Ruth followed.

'What's this?' he said.

There was a table with an easel beside it. Tubes of paint. A plastic palette. Brushes. Little sea sponges. And, on the easel, a cheery watercolour of a vase of flowers.

He took the painting off the easel. 'Is this *you*?'

She nodded. 'What do you think?'

'It's pretty,' he said without conviction. 'It's kind of *free*.'

'Well, I don't want realism. I want poetry. I see beauty in everything.'

He eyed her warily.

'I'd always promised myself I'd take it up,' she added in a straighter tone. 'And now I have. I know it's crap, but I don't give a damn what anyone thinks. You included.'

He stared at the painting, at her, then back at the painting again, trying to find something to say.

'It never ceases to amaze me,' he said. 'You've got your Otto Dixes and your Kokoschkas and your Edvard Munches – your tortured expressionists, you know – but all people ever really want is flowers, pussycats, children and little country cottages. It defies belief.'

'You're telling me . . .'

'At the end of the day, human nature's simple.'

'At the end of the day, the sun goes down. Life's short, Myles, in case you hadn't noticed.'

'Too short for labouring several years over one's craft, let alone a single opus.'

'Would-be mushroom stuffers, take note . . .'

'So did you drag me here to show off your newfound skills and rub my nose in my own inadequacies?' he intoned huffily.

'I didn't drag you here. You came here voluntarily by taxi. I saw it dropping you off. As for *why* you're here, it's because I've got something to show you.'

She took a large old green-backed book entitled *The Technique of Watercolour Painting* off a shelf and let it fall open in her hands. Inside were some yellowed sheets of paper, raggy in quality, covered in elegant scrawl. Myles's eyes popped. The format and script were all too familiar.

'Sit down,' she said, 'and fasten your seatbelt. It's Johannes's final letter to his pal. We came across it when we were cleaning the house up, prior to the sale.'

He sat down and read it through.

6 May 1760

My Dear Cornelis,

I cannot sufficiently thank you for your letter, and scold myself that it is some two years – nay more – since last we communicated.

Some of my doings you may recall from our last vexed meeting, in March – I believe – of 1758, when I conjured you to promise that you would not divulge our communications without my consent. I shudder, now, to think of my wretched agitation at that time.

I was, indeed, the victim of cruel usage at the hands of that brutal varlet, the Italian Giacomo 'Paralis', whose real name – I was later to discover – was a fancy word I forget, signifying 'New House' in his own singsong tongue, though it be a house I would fain not visit, even were I without a roof on a stormy night.

As for the wretched Esther, I have not seen her from that day to this, nor have I had news of her, nor desired it. She has quite passed out of my sphere, and I from hers, and I am by no means sombre on this account. For, my friend, I have entered the married state. My wife is Hanna, daughter to Groot the brewer. She is a woman of sound common sense and much gaiety, a faithful partner and friend. With her, I enjoy some of the most pleasant days I have ever passed in my life. Moreover, she has blessed us with a child, whose first birthday it is today. As I

write, the little fellow crawls round my feet, wondering how to
distract his father's attention from the scritch-scratching of his
quill.

In short, gone are the days when I walked about the earth with
inward discontent. I see now that my old projects and sanguine
expectations were utter folly, vanity and vice, so stillborn that no
advantage could come of them. I did destroy the ingenious
fabrication – my Plato's Cave, my lens, and all – without regret.
The final heliograph I kept, though it is painted over. I keep it not
for pleasure, for it is concealed behind a wall in my lumberplace,
but more as a reminder to myself that, to a speculating and very
feeling mind, all that life affords will at times appear of no effect. If
others find it, its secret, as you know, is engraved on the back, but
in such terms as would require a wise and godly brain to delve the
matter further. I dabbled in alchemy, Cornelis, and the devil awaits
those who commit the sin of pride. Is not this the true reason for
the perversion of the image? You will recall that, on exposure to
light areas, the copper plate became dark; and on exposure to dark
areas, the plate became light. This, I now perceive, is the very sign
and stamp of the hornèd one, the print of his cleft foot. The light
and dark of the Christian day reversed, exchanging places in
Satan's shadow world.

I have taken over the pharmacy in fulfilment of my father's
dearest wish, and I run the business with a good heart, and none
of the reluctance or resentment I once might have felt and
expressed. My motto? Si tu pensam tuam prestare possis. "If
you can perform your daily stint." I have done tolerably, such
that my family may enjoy a life of comfort.

You ask whether I still draw.

I certainly am utterly unsuited to the life of an artist, of this
I am now most certain. However, my error lay not in that
ambition, but in the ends it was designed to procure: wealth,
renown, society, a showy and inflated sense of my own vain
importance.

To sketch, in itself, is no sin – and sketch I do, for my own

pleasure. A year ago, when Hanna was pregnant, I did draw her
with iron oxide chalk. In addition, I have executed some
landscapes, as and when a view took my fancy. I have found a
simple pleasure in this practice that far exceeds the fretful
endeavours that preceded it, however inept they may be deemed.
Is not this the secret to a full and happy life? To do things with
energy, with a warm heart and mind, such that the work
produced is a living record of the soul and not a dull mechanical
copy that issues from a dead hand or contraption?

I am thankful for this fine weather. The daffodils you sent are
planted on the sill.

Let us not lose sight of one another.

I remain ever your most affectionate friend.

　　　Johannes van der Heyden

Myles slipped the letter back between the pages of the book
and went out to join Ruth in the garden.

She was potting seedlings.

He plunged his fists into his trouser pockets and stood beside
her, gazing out to sea. He jigged his shoulders back and forth to
work out a cramp.

She glanced at his gymnastics and knitted her brow.

'Are you trying to take off, or what?'

'If we were meant to fly, my dear, we'd have boarding
passes,' he muttered. Then, 'So we'd got it all wrong, didn't we?
– about Johannes, I mean.'

'Wrong?'

'The drawings. Not the painting. Well, the drawings *and* the
painting, actually. We thought the drawings were the early stuff,
and the painting was the mature work. In fact, it was the other
way round.'

'That's right.'

'Let's face it, he got *worse*.'

'Yes, exactly.' She lined up her pots in neat little rows and made a viewfinder frame of her fingers to inspect them. 'There's hope for us yet, then, isn't there?'

'Is there?'

'Any ideas who the Italian gent might have been?'

He pushed out his lips like a thoughtful wine-taster. 'Your guess is as good as mine.'

He played moodily with his earring, then yawned and scratched his chest.

'I'm going home,' he said after a while.

'Good idea.'

'Tired of me already?'

'No, Myles, but you have responsibilities. Sweekieboude, for one, will be missing you.'

He raised his eyebrows and sighed. 'That just about sums up my life. The human can opener, you know . . .'

'It could be worse.'

'I'm delighted to hear it.'

A bee bumbled harmlessly across the balcony, looping round his head. He hopped back, startled, flapping his hands pathetically in the air. 'Oh, God, a bee,' he grimaced. 'How awful! The natural enemy of the tightrope walker! I want to go back to town.'

The grimace stuck as he watched it putter away.

His hands were still raised in horror.

'Wait,' she said, 'don't move.' She'd been holding up her finger-frame again, capturing the event for posterity. She snapped her hands together like a clapper-board. 'Cut. Print. That was perfect.'

'What was perfect?' he asked, mildly indignant.

'That *Myles* moment. It was so *you* . . .'

'You mean I've got poetry in me too?'

'Why not? It comes in the unlikeliest shapes and sizes.'

'Very diplomatically put, I must say. And what happens *now*, may I ask?'

'You can go. The audition's over. Don't call us, and all that – we'll call you.'

He humphed and turned his back on her. With a despairing wave, he plodded out of sight down the stairs.

She went back to her geraniums.

She shifted the trolley they were standing on forward, moving them out of the shadow of the awning. They looked as if they needed a little more sun.